A Moment for Vengeance . . .

"I saw Morgan come in," Nophaie said. "Is he there—with Blucher?"

"Oh—yes," gasped Marian. "They're locked in. You mustn't . . . Oh!"

Nophaie pulled a gun from somewhere, and lunging at the locked door he shoved his foot against it with tremendous force. The lock broke. The door swung in. Nophaie bounded across the threshold.

Marian, suddenly galvanized into action, ran after him.

Miss Heron lay on the floor in a faint. Blucher sat back in his chair, mouth agape, eyes wide. Amazement had begun to give way to fear. Morgan was ghastly.

Nophaie, with his right hand, held the gun low. It was cocked and it had an almost imperceptible quiver. With his left hand Nophaie significantly touched the bloody bandage round his head.

"I am going to kill you both," said Nophaie.

Books by Zane Grey

Published by POCKET BOOKS

THE VANISHING AMERICAN

ZANE GREY

Revised Edition
Foreword by Loren Grey

PUBLISHED BY POCKET BOOKS NEW YORK

Cover art by Murray Tinkelman

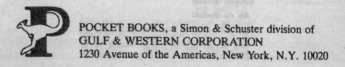

POCKET BOOKS, a Simon & Schuster division of
GULF & WESTERN CORPORATION
1230 Avenue of the Americas, New York, N.Y. 10020

Copyright 1922, 1923 by Curtis Publishing Co.
(Ladies' Home Journal), renewed 1950 by Lina Elise Grey.
Assigned to Zane Grey, Inc., in 1953.
Foreword copyright © 1982 by Loren Grey, Ph.D.

Published by arrangement with Harper & Row, Publishers, Inc., and
Zane Grey, Inc.

This is a revised edition of the book previously published by
Harper & Row, Publishers, Inc., copyright 1925 by Zane Grey,
renewed 1953 by Lina Elise Grey.

ISBN: 0-671-83587-4

First Pocket Books printing March, 1982

10 9 8 7 6 5 4 3 2 1

POCKET and colophon are trademarks of Simon & Schuster.

Printed in the U.S.A.

Foreword

I HAVE ALWAYS FELT THAT *The Vanishing American* was
one of my father's finest books, but it was only recently
that I learned about the controversy surrounding its
first publication in 1922 as a serial in the magazine,
Ladies' Home Journal. It was not published in book
form until December 1925 because the magazine release created such a furor, particularly among religious
groups who were offended by the way he depicted the
missionaries' treatment of the Indians on the reservation. Instead of converting them to Christianity, the
missionaries ended up raping their women and stealing
their possessions and land—all in the guise of Christianity.

Before and during World War I, the period in which
the story is set, those missionaries who honestly attempted to help the Indians were driven away by others
who were in league with the Federal Indian Agents
administering the reservation. The historical data behind these revelations were accurate, despite the emo-
tionalism with which they were often presented. The
background information for *The Vanishing American*
was furnished to my father by the trader, John
Weatherill, and his wife, Louisa, who had spent their
entire lives on the reservation trying to help the Indians
survive the degrading conditions they were forced to
endure. In this book they are represented by the
characters John Withers and his wife.

As might be expected, my father was subjected to a
great deal of pressure from his publishers, Harper &
Brothers, who refused to publish *The Vanishing American* unless he removed a great many of the offending
passages, however accurate they were. A portion of his
letter to William Briggs and Henry Hoyns, his editors
at the time, shows his anguish at having to, in effect,

pervert the truth of what was happening on the reservation:

Avalon,
May 25, 1925

Wm. Briggs & Henry Hoyns
Harper & Brothers

My dear friends:

I am answering your letters in this way because I do not want to repeat in separate answers.

Your letters were kindly meant, I know. I am sure you do not often write business letters with such friendly and intimate frankness. I do not misunderstand in the least. Nevertheless, I am surprised, and in one particular disgusted. So I am going to ask you to take the trouble to reread them, after reading this.

Before I forget, let me say that the jacket for *The Vanishing American* is fine. It is strikingly attractive, and very simple and beautiful.

As to the motion picture, I have eliminated entirely the missionary element. This I was forced to do by the influence brought to bear upon the Will Hays office, by missionary powers.

I just returned from Arizona, where I went to confer with Hubbard and Griffith. While there I got the proper angle on who was back of the propaganda. These missionaries would not stop at anything. My personal Arizona men warned me that it was actually not safe for me to go on the reservation. There are hirelings, and even some missionaries especially, who might shoot me from some canyon wall.

This is the first time in my life that I have been driven away from the truth, from honor and ideals, and in this case, from telling the world of the tragedy of the Indian. It is a melancholy thing. I wonder what effect it will have upon me.

I sent back to you most of *The Vanishing American* novel, cut as much as I could bring myself to do it. The remainder, which I hoped was fine, I destroyed upon receipt of Briggs' letter. I will rewrite the conclusion and strain every faculty to give the novel a tremendous climax.

It is a very good thing for my publishers that I am able to do this and not fall prey to morbidness and gloom and hopelessness, such as would affect most writers confronted by this situation.

Now as to the business side of your letters. I am very sorry indeed that conditions are bad. But I beg to call to your attention this fact: that it is the reading public and the book business that have slumped. Not I! My work grows better. I know, because I am doing it. And I shall see to it that I do not fall down.

Though, as the letter states, my father promised faithfully to destroy the material which was left out of the book, knowing him and my mother, I felt quite certain that this had not been done, and was able to locate the original holographic manuscript for both endings. The publishers had also demanded that the original conclusion be changed so that the Indian hero, Nophaie, did not marry his sweetheart, Marian. In that day it was acceptable for a white man to marry an Indian woman but not the other way around. This is why Nophaie dies under quite mysterious and really illogical circumstances at the end of the book, which was first released on December 1, 1925.

So, presented here is the complete, unexpurgated version with the portions that were even left out of the 1922 serialization in the *Ladies Home Journal*.

Of course, after the grim revelations of the tragedy in Jonestown, Guyana, and what we have learned of some missionaries' treatment of the Polynesians in Hawaii, Tahiti, New Zealand and other parts of the South Pacific—as well as the financial exposés of some of the self-styled evangelistic cultists who, even today, rob millions of innocent people in the name of Christianity

—much of this book will certainly not be as shocking to readers today as it was when it was first published sixty years ago. However, because we are still far from righting the wrongs that are being perpetrated on the Indian today, I feel that the unexpurgated edition of this book is even more important a story to be told than it was then.

This book contains some of my father's most magnificent descriptions of the desert, the mountains and the wilderness—where Nophaie finally resolves the conflicts between his Indian heritage and his white upbringing. I believe that to my father, Nature, even in its harshest manifestations, was akin to God, and perhaps the only God he could wholly relate to during his lifetime. So there is much of his own personal philosophy in the book, as well.

Some readers may interpret *The Vanishing American* as an attack on orthodox religion as a whole. However, my father was careful to distinguish between those who persecuted the Indians and other religious leaders who genuinely tried to help them. In fact, the only mention made of any specific denomination was his description of the efforts of some Roman Catholic priests who also worked on the reservation in those years. Although he felt their attempts to convert the Indians to Christianity were largely futile, he did acknowledge that they did a great deal more good than harm. Unfortunately, they were largely ignored by the Indian agents and their co-conspirators, and had little effect on the ultimate tragedy, whose aftereffects still haunt the reservation today.

My hope is that this new volume will help readers gain a new perspective about not only the still desperate state of the Indians—whose forebears were really the first Americans—but also the need to eliminate prejudice and oppression of any people or race anywhere.

Loren Grey, Ph.D.
Woodland Hills, California

Chapter 1

AT SUNRISE NOPHAIE DROVE HIS FLOCK OF sheep and goats out upon the sage slopes of the desert. The April air was cold and keen, fragrant with the dry tang of the uplands. Taddy and Tinny, his shepherd dogs, had wary eye and warning bark for the careless stragglers of the flock. Gray gaunt forms of wolf and tawny shape of wildcat moved like shadows through the sage.

Nophaie faced the east, where over a great rugged wall of stone, the sky grew from rose to gold, and a splendor of light seemed about to break upon the world. Nophaie's instinct was to stand a moment, watching and waiting without thought. The door of each hogan of his people opened to the rising sun. They worshiped the sun, the elements, all in Nature.

Motionless he stood, an Indian lad of seven years, slim and tall, with his dark face turned to the east, his dark eyes fixed solemnly upon that quarter whence the light and warmth always came. One thin brown hand held a blanket round his shoulders, and the other clasped his bow and arrows.

While he gazed, a wondrous change came over the desert. The upstanding gloomy wall of rock far to the fore suddenly burned with a line of flame; and from that height down upon the gray lowlands shone the light of the risen sun. For Nophaie sunrise was a beginning—a fulfillment of promise—an answer to prayer.

When that blazing circle of liquid gold had cleared the rampart of the desert, too fiery and intense for the gaze of man, Nophaie looked no more, and passed on down the aisles of sage behind his flock. Every day this task was his. For two years he had been the trusted shepherd of his father's sheep. At five years of age Nophaie had won his first distinction. With other children he was out in charge of the accumulated flocks of the tribe. A sandstorm suddenly swooped down upon the desert, enveloping them in thick yellow pall. Except Nophaie, all the little shepherds grew frightened and fled back to find their hogans. But Nophaie stayed with the sheep. They could not be driven in the face of the storm. They wandered on and on, and became lost. Nophaie became lost with them. Three days later Nophaie's father found him hungry and fearful, but true to his charge. He was praised. He was taught. He was trusted. Legend and lore seldom told so young a boy, were his to ponder and dream over.

Nophaie's shepherding task was lonely and leisurely. He had but to drive the flock from grassy flat to sage slope, slowly on and on, and back again by sunset to the home corral, always alert for the prowling beasts of prey.

He seemed a part of that red and purple desert land. It was home. He had been born under the shadow of the wonderful mountain wall which zigzagged from east to west across the wasteland. Its niches were canyons. Its broken segments were pinnacles and monuments, shafts of red stone lifted to the skies, bold, stark, and mighty, chiseled by wind and sand and frost. Between these walls and monuments spread the sandy floor of the desert, always gray-spotted with sage, always gray-green with patches of grass and weed, purple in the distance.

That spring the lambs had come early—too early, considering the frosty breath of the dawns. A few lambs had succumbed to the cold. Many a pink and white little lamb had been tenderly folded in Nophaie's blanket, and warmed, and cared for until the heat of the sun made safe its return to its mother. The lambs and kids were all several days old now, fleecy and woolly, grown sturdy enough to amble in the sage. A few were solid black, and many were all white, and some had beautiful markings, spots of black on white, and four black feet, and two black ears. One was pure white with a black face; another was all black except for a white tail. The dead stillness of the desert dawn was often pierced by the sweet, high-pitched bleat of these lambs and kids. Nophaie wandered on with them, finding a stone seat from time to time, always watching, listening, feeling. He loved the flock, but did not know that. His task was lonely, but he did not realize it.

The flock leisurely traveled on, a white-dotted moving mass against the background of gray, tearing at the sage, nipping at the weeds. Taddy and Tinny trotted to and fro and around, important and morose, Indian dogs that knew their work, and they seldom had to bark a warning. Nophaie leisurely plodded along behind, intent and absorbed. An eagle pitched from his lofty perch on one of the red towers, and shot like a thunderbolt down and over the flock, until he saw the Indian boy on guard, and then he swooped up and up wide-winged and free, to soar away across the skies, a dark bowed shape against the blue. A coyote wailed his desolate note of hunger. From the cliff a canyon swift trilled his strange, sweet, wild song.

The sun rose higher. The golden belt of sunlight along the tops of walls and mesas and monuments widened downward, encroaching upon the shadow and shade. Dawn with its icy edge paled and melted before the warming day. And the desert changed again. Shadow and color and freshness seemed swallowed by an intense and all-absorbing light.

Nophaie was no different from other Indian lads, except that the dominant traits of his tribe and his race seemed to be intensified in him. His was the heritage of a chieftain. His mother had died at his birth, whispering strange and mystic prophecies. The old medicine men, the sages of the tribe, had gathered round him during the one illness of his infancy, and had spread their sandpaintings on a flat rock, and had marveled at his quick recovery, predicting for him unknown and great feats. He was named Nophaie, the Warrior.

Through song and story and dance the traditions of his tribe were forever impressed upon his sensitive mind. The valor of Indian braves in war was a memory of the past, but the spirit lived. The boy was taught to understand the nature of a warrior, and to revere his father and the long line of chiefs from which he had descended. Before Nophaie could walk he had begun to learn the secrets of the life of the open. Birds, lizards, snakes, horned toads, packrats and kangaroo-rats, prairie dogs, and rabbits—these, and all the little wild creatures of the desert, were brought to him to tame, to play with, to study, and learn to love. Thus the brilliant and intense colors of desert life were early stamped upon his brain. The love of natural beauty, born in him, had early opportunity for evolution. The habits and ways of all desert creatures became a part of his childhood training. Likewise the green covering of the earth, in all its beauty and meaning, soon occupied its place of supreme importance in his understanding— the grasses, green in the spring, bearded and seeding in the late summer, bleached white in the fall; the sages with their bittersweet fragrances and everlasting gray; the cactus, venomous yet fruitful, with their colors of vermillion and magenta; the paintbrush with its car-mine; the weeds of the desert, not without their use and worthiness; the flowers of the deep canyons; the mosses on the wet stones by the cliff-shaded brook; the ferns and lichens; the purple-berried cedars and the nut-bearing piñons of the uplands; and on the mountains the great brown-barked pines, stately and noble, lords of the heights.

Next in order Nophaie learned the need and thrill and love of the hunt. By his own prowess as a hunter he must someday survive. The tracks and signs and sounds and smells of all denizens of his desert environment became as familiar to him as those of his hogan.

Nophaie wandered on with his sheep, over the sage and sand, under the silent, lofty towers of rock. He was unconsciously and unutterably happy because he was in perfect harmony with the reality and spirit of the nature that encompassed him. He wandered in an enchanted land of mystery, upon which the Great Spirit looked with love. He had no cares, no needs, no selfishness. Only vaguely had he heard of the menace of the white race encroaching upon the lands of the Indian. Only a few white men had he ever seen.

So Nophaie wandered on with his flock through the sage, content and absorbed, watching, listening, feeling, his mind full of dreams and longings, of song and legend, of the infinite beauty and poetry of his life.

How lonely the vast sweep of purple sage land that opened out from the red battlements of rock! How silent and dead the gleaming, beetling walls! How austere and solemn the day! But Nophaie was never lonely. He did not understand loneliness. The soft, sweet air he breathed was rich with the whispers of spirits. Above the red wall to the west loomed up a black and white dome—a mountain height, pure with snow, fringed by pine—and this was Nothsis Ahn, the home of Utsay, the god of the Indians. He dwelt there with Utsay Asthon, his woman, and together they had made the sun out of fire—they had made all. Utsay was the Great Spirit, and sometimes he communed with the medicine men through their sand paintings. Nophaie that morning, as he turned from the sunrise to the looming mountain, had breathed a prayer to his Great Spirit.

> High chief of the mountain, the beautiful
> mountain. To me tell your secrets that it
> may be well before me as I go.
> Behind me tell me it may be well,

Beneath me tell me it may be well,
Above me tell me it may be well,
Tell me let all that I see be well,
Tell me that the Everlasting will be
merciful toward me—
Like the Chief of the Good, tell me
that it is well with me.
That the God of the medicine will let
me talk well, tell me
Now all is well, now all is well,
Now all is well, now all is well.

And Nophaie believed all was well with him, that his prayer had been answered. The rustling of the sage was a voice; the cool touch of the breeze on his cheek was a kin of an invisible and kindly Spirit, watching over him, the rock he leaned a hand upon left a clinging response, from the soul therein. When a hawk sailed low over Nophaie's head he heard the swish of wings driven by the power he trusted in. The all-enveloping sunlight was the smile of Utsay, satisfied with his people. Nophaie stepped aside to avoid crushing the desert primroses, thriving in the shade of the sage. Through these wide white blossoms looked the eyes of departed relatives who watched him from the Happy Hunting Grounds below. Would he walk straight? Would he talk straight? When love lived on, and was eternal, there was no death of Spirit for Nophaie and his kind. There was no evil except what he thought, and to think evil of himself, of anyone, was a sin. To think evil made it true.

So Nophaie wandered on and on over the sage trails, proud and fierce as a young eagle, aloof and strange, dreaming the dreams conjured up by the wise men of his tribe. At seven years of age he had begun to realize the meaning of a chief, and that a chief must someday save his people. What he loved most was to be alone, out in the desert, listening to the real sounds of the open and to the silent whisperings to his soul. In the shadow of the hogans, among the boys and girls there, he was only Nophaie. They were jealous. They resented his importance. But out on the desert, in the cold rosy dawns and the solemn hot noontides, and the golden sunsets, when the sunlight stole down softly and white stars smiled at him from the velvet blue—then Nophaie could be himself, could listen and feel, and know the four winds of heaven whispered of his future, of how he would make the medicine to save his people.

Nophaie did not walk alone. Innumerable spirits kept pace with his light steps. The sage was a carpet of purple, fragrant and sweet, through which breathed the low soft sigh of the wind. The shallow stream of water, murmuring and meandering in the red sandy wash below, lined white along its margins, spoke to Nophaie of winter snows now melting on the heights, of water for the sheep all summer, of Utsay's goodwill. To east and west and south heaved up the red gods of rock that seemed to move with Nophaie as he moved, shadow and loom over him as he halted, watch him with vast, impassive faces. Though they were far away they seemed close. In their secret stony cells abided the souls of Indians—many as the white pebbles along the stream. The flash of a swift-winged canyon bird was a message. The gleams of melted frost, sparkling and pure, were the teardrops of his mother, who forever hovered near him, wandered with him along the sage trails, in spirit with his steps. The sun, the moon, the crag with its human face, the black raven croaking his dismal note, the basking rattlesnake, the spiders that shut his little door above him, the mockingbird, singer of all songs—those held communion with Nophaie, were his messengers. And all around him and above him, in the great silence, in the towering barriers of stone, in the vast flare of intense sunlight, there seemed to be life in harmony with him, a voiceless and eternal life that he felt but could not see.

Toward sunset Nophaie was far out on the open desert, with many of the monuments and mesas and masses of rimrock between him and the golden purple glory of the West. Homeward bound with his flock, Nophaie had intent eyes for the colorful panorama of sinking sun and transfigured clouds. A pageant somehow in affinity with his visions crowned the dome of old Nothsis Ahn and shone down behind the great shafts and pillars of rock that speared the horizon light. The sun was going down behind the broken masses of soft clouds, creamy and silver where the rays struck, golden in the center of the west, and shading to purple where the thick, mushrooming, billowy rolls reached to the blue zenith.

While Nophaie gazed in the rapture of his wandering, eager heart there came a moment of marvelous transformation. The sun dipped its lower segment from under a white-rimmed cloud, firing the whole magnificent panorama with blaze of gold and rose and opal. A light that seemed beacon of the universe burned across the heavens, clear to the east, where the violet and lilac haze took on a sheen of gold. Against the effulgence of the western sky stood up the monuments, silhouetted on that burnished brightness of sunset, black and clear-cut, weird and colossal, motionless and speaking gods of stone.

A warning bark from one of the shepherd dogs drew Nophaie's attention from the sunset. A band of white men had ridden down upon him. Several of them galloped ahead, and came round between the Indian lad and his home. The others rode up. They had extra horses, and pack mules heavily loaded. Both men and beasts were jaded.

Nophaie had seen but few white men. None had ever tendered violence. But here he instinctively recognized danger.

"We gotta hev meat," one dark-visaged man called out.

"Wal, we'd better find the squaw who owns this bunch an' buy our meat," suggested another.

"Moze, you know it all," growled another. "Why squaw?"

"Because squaws always own the sheep," replied the other.

These men of the desert were tired and hungry, perhaps not honestly so, judging from the extra saddle horses they were driving. More than one furtive glance roved across the sage to the east. Sullen heat and impatience manifested their signs in the red faces.

"We haven't time for thet," spoke up the dark-faced one.

"Wal, we don't want Indians trailin' us. I say take time an' buy meat."

"Aw! You'll say next let's eat hossmeat," returned the man called Moze. "Knock the kid on the head, grab some sheep, an' ride on. Thet's me!"

Moze's idea seemed to find favor with some of the band. The dominating spirit was to hurry on.

Nophaie could not understand their language, but he sensed peril to himself. Suddenly he darted out between the horses, and swift as a deer, flashed away through the sage.

"Ketch thet kid, somebody," called out the voice of authority.

One of the riders touched spurs to his horse and, running Nophaie down, reached a strong hand to haul him across in front of the saddle. Nophaie hung there limp.

"Bill," called the leader, "thar ain't no sense in hurtin' the kid—now you all wait."

This man was tall, gaunt, gray-haired, and lean, with the eyes of a hawk. He scanned the sage flats clear to the pillars of stone. Neither Indian nor hogan was in sight. Presently he spoke.

"Bill, hang on to the kid. An' some of you drive the sheep ahead of us. Thar's water over hyar somewheres. We'll find it an' make camp."

"Huh!" ejaculated the man Bill, in disgust. "Talkin'

about sense, what's the idee, cap, packin' this heavy kid along?"

"Wal, it ain't decent to kill him, jest fer nothin' an' it is sense to keep him from gettin' back home tonight."

"All right, you're the boss. But I'll eat sage if them Indians don't track us, jest the same."

"Bill, you're a bright fellar," returned the other. "Mebbe this kid's family will find our tracks by tomorrow, but I'm gamblin' they won't."

Nophaie hung limp over that horse for several miles before he was tumbled off like an empty sack. The band had come to a halt for the night. Nophaie's hands and feet were bound with a lasso. He heard the bleating of the sheep, and then the trampling low roar of their hooves as they were driven off into the desert. One of the men gave him food and drink; another covered him with a blanket. Nophaie's fear eased, but there was birth of a dark heritage of hate in his heart. He did not sleep.

At daylight the band was off, riding hard to the southward, and Nophaie had no choice but to go with them. Toward nightfall of that long day the spirits of the men appeared to rise. They ceased to look back over the rolling ridges of purple sage, or down the leagues of cedar aisles. They avoided the Indian hogans and sheered off well-trodden trails. Next day some of the band were in favor of letting Nophaie go free. But again the leader ruled against them.

"Reckon it's tolerable lonely along hyar. We don't want the kid to be lost an' starve."

About noontime one day later they let Nophaie go free, and pointed down a road toward an Indian encampment. Then in a cloud of dust they trotted on. Rough but kind they had used him, unconscious of their hand in his destiny. But Nophaie never reached the Indian hogans. Another party of white people, of different look and voice, happened upon him. They were travelers of leisure, seeing the West, riding across the reservation. They had wagons and saddle horses, and western men to care for them. Again Nophaie ran, only to be caught by one of the riders and hauled before the women of the party.

"What a handsome Indian lad!" exclaimed one.

"Let us take him along," said another.

An older woman of the group, with something more than curiosity in her face, studied Nophaie for a moment. She, too, was kind. She imagined she was about to do a noble thing.

"Indian boy, I will take you and put you in a school."

They took Nophaie with them by force. They took him out of the desert and far to the east.

And Nophaie lived and studied in the white man's school and college for eighteen years.

Chapter 2

AS THE TRAIN NEARED THE WESTERN TOWN which was her destination Marian Warner realized that this ride was not a dream, but the first act of the freedom she had yearned for, the first step in her one great adventure. All the excitement and audacity and emotion that had been her undoing now seemed to swell into a thrilling panic.

Long days of travel had passed since she had boarded the train at Philadelphia. The faces of friends, of her aunt—the few who loved her—had grown dim, as if every revolution of the wheels had deadened memory as well as lengthened miles. Little had she guessed how she had cut herself adrift. But to the last she had kept her secret.

Somewhere back along the way, where she had crossed the line into this desert state, she had become conscious of a quickening of her long apathetic feelings. Had her first glimpses of the bleached gray of the desert stirred her heart? What of that strange line of red and yellow cliffs—bold rock fronts almost incredible to her? Deep and vague was the emotion they roused. It was April, and the clouds were gray, the weeds tumbling over the land before the wind, the dust puffs whipping up and circling into yellow columns. Bold and raw and inhospitable indeed this desert land! Its bigness began to amaze and frighten her. Miles and miles of bareness —rocks—flats of gray—black mountains in the distance —and again those strange facades of red cliff! Few and far between were the ranches. And the occasional herd of cattle appeared lost in immensity. Marian strained her tired eyes searching for horses and riders, for the flashes of red blankets of Indians, but these were denied her.

Then, as many times during this long ride, she had recourse to the letter that had influenced her to come west.

Oljato (Moonlight on the Water.)
Feb. 10, 1916

Dear Marian:

Your letters and gifts were welcome as May flowers. I did not get them at Christmas time because I did not ride into Kaidab. The weather then was cold and I had my only living relative to look after. He was ill. He is better now.

I rode the ninety-odd miles to the post between sunrise and sunset, over a trail known only to Indians. And all the way I thought of you, of the love for you that only strengthens with distance and time. Remembering your fondness for horses and how you used to long for wild and lonely places, I wanted you to be with me.

But in spite of the joy that came with your remembrances, my ride back from the post was full of bitterness. I was again brought into contact with the growing troubles of my tribe, and with the world of white men which I have given up.

Marian, my people now are very prosperous. The war has brought false values. Wool is fifty cents a pound. Horses and sheep bring higher prices than any Indian ever dreamed of. They think this will last always. They will not save. They live from day to day, and spend their money foolishly. And when the reaction comes they will be suddenly poor, with the traders' prices for food and clothing higher than ever.

More than this, the mark of the missionaries distresses me. Whenever I come in contact with it I grow sick. I could not tell you in few words the wrong they are doing to my people. You would be

shocked. They are slowly grasping the richer pieces
of land from the Indians. Forcing them off! Someday these missionaries will possess all the really
good land of the reservation. Religion! These men
of the white people's God do not preach religion.
They sow fear, doubt, distrust, and hate in the
minds of the Indian boys and girls. The Indian's
own religion is best for him.

I have been here nearly a year now, and have yet
to find one single Indian who is a Christian. The
Catholic priests do more good than the other
missionaries. I have gone all over this part of the
reservation. The Indians tell me there have been
two good missionaries among the many sent out
here. Two white men who were kind, who studied
the Indians' need, who helped them with their
hands, who might in time have won their confidence. Both these missionaries were removed by
the powers at Mesa. Powers of evil, Marian! White
men in employ of the government, and with the
authority of missionaries, are preying upon the
Indians. Believe me, dear loved one of a race alien
to mine, I tell the truth.

Come out here to the reservation and work for a
year or two among my people. It could not hurt
you. And you might do much for them. You could
be a teacher at Mesa or one of the other schools.
None would ever know that you came for my sake.

Your letters heaped upon me terms of reproach.
Marian, I have not forgotten one moment of our
summer at Cape May. I love you more than I did
then. It seems I am old now. Wisdom came to me
here in my desert home, under the shadow of old
Nothsis Ahn. I was born under this great mountain. When a boy I was stolen from my home under
its red walls. And after eighteen years I have come
back. I burned my white man's clothes and books
—even the records of my football games—all ex-

cept your picture. I put on buckskin and corduroy
and silver. I never speak English and I am again an
Indian. No more Lo Blandy, but Nophaie!

I was young and full of fire that summer at Cape
May. I drank the white man's liquor, Marian. I was
praised, feted, sought because I had become a
famous Carlisle star—the football and baseball
player, winner of so many points against the great
colleges. I danced and played the same as white
college men. Then I met you, Marian. You were
different from most of the white girls. I loved you
at sight and respected you when I knew you. I
stopped drinking for you. And for an Indian to give
up whiskey once he knows its taste is no small
thing. I loved a white girl. I called you *Benow di
cleash*, the white girl with blue eyes. And I'm sure
your influence kept me from the fate of more than
one famous Indian athlete—Sockalexis, for instance, who ruined career and health in one short
year.

But when I returned to my people the great
change came. Not in my love for you, but in my
youth. I am a man now, old as these sage hills, and
I've learned from them. It was selfish and wrong
for me to run after you, to love you, to take your
kisses—wrong though it was the best influence of
my life. I am an Indian.

Then, once here, whatever wild dreams I may
have had were forgotten. I see the life of my tribe
as a tragedy. The injustice to them is the blackest
of white men's baseness. The compulsory school
system for the Indian boys and girls has more bad
points than good. The missionaries are the apostles
of hate and corruption. I am an educated Indian. I
see their misery. I see them vanishing.

I cannot marry an Indian girl because I love you.
I cannot have a child because I love you. I cannot
know any woman because I love you. When an

Indian loves he loves forever. It is infinitely easier
for an Indian to love a white woman than for her to
love him. I don't know why.

So, Marian, I am here, no longer Lo Blandy, but
Nophaie. My name means Warrior. The red sand I
trod is part the bones and flesh of my ancestors. I
will live my life here and mingle my bones with
theirs. I will do all I can for them. But, alas, the
eighteen years' education forced upon me by the
whites enables me only to see the pitiful state and
the doom of the Indians.

Come, Marian, to Oljato—come to help me
awhile or just to see the wilderness and beauty of
my home, so that always afterwards your memory
will be full of the color and music and grandeur and
fragrance of the Indian land.

Nophaie

Marian put the letter away, conscious only at that
moment of her emotions. Every perusal of it seemed to
glean new sensations of pain, regret, sweetness and
love, and awe.

"Nophaie, the Warrior," she soliloquized, dreamily.
"Somehow it suits him."

She recalled the first time she had ever seen him. It
was at Cape May, where a group of college men
maintained baseball games with visiting teams, profes-
sional and otherwise. Her aunt, with whom she lived,
and most of her Philadelphia friends, always spent
some weeks at the seashore. And Marian enjoyed
games and bathing and dancing as well as anyone. One
summer afternoon a friend took her to the athletic field
and pointed out the famous Carlisle Indian star. How
curious she had felt! There was a strange pain in the
recall of that first sensation. Her eyes fell upon a tall,
bare-headed athlete, slenderly yet powerfully built, his
supple form broadening wide at the shoulders. His face
was dark, his hair black as coal. Striking and handsome

as he was it was not his appearance alone which thrilled her so. She was a thoroughly modern young woman and had seen her share of college games. In action, the Indian was simply beautiful. He had earned his great fame as a football star, and had been picked by experts for the all-American team three successive years. But he did not need to be as great a baseball player to be good to look at. He played an outfield position, and the chances of the game fell so that he had little to do except run. And his running grew more and more thrilling to Marian. How easily he moved—what a stride he had! Marian found she was not alone in her admirations. This Indian athlete did not need her applause. Toward the end of the game, which was a critical time for the home team, he hit a ball far beyond reach of the opposing fielders. The crowd roared its delight. The Indian dashed down towards first base, and turning appeared to gather speed as he ran. Marian felt the pound of her heart, the sudden shock of delight and pride in the Indian's sheer physical prowess. He ran as must have the Greek runners, garlanded for their victories. How fleet! How incredibly faster and faster! Then he was making the turn for home base, and the crowd was yelling wildly. He seemed to be facing Marian as he sped on, magnificent in his action. He beat the throw and scored his home run, a feat the audience applauded with prodigious abandon. Marian then became aware that she too had been rather undignified.

That night at a dance one of Marian's girl friends had asked her, "Have you met Lo?"

"Lo! And who's he or she?"

"He's the Carlisle crack. You say him play today. The Indian—Lo Blandy."

And so it came about presently that Marian found herself facing the Indian athlete she had admired. Not just then had she realized it, but the truth was she had fallen in love with him at first sight. Something in her nature, never dreamed of before, went out to the Indian. He had a fine face, dark and strong, with eyes of piercing blackness. There was something noble in his stature, or the poise of his head, or the eagle look of him.

"Will you dance with me?" he had asked, and appeared as much at ease as any of the college men.

Marian found herself dancing with an Indian—a very strange and momentous circumstance, it seemed. Evidently he had not made dancing one of his college courses, as most young men had. But he was light and strong; he carried her on without the bold contact so prevalent among the modern dancing men; and so Marian enjoyed that dance.

They met again by accident on the beach, and because no one else came and they were interesting to each other, they talked for long. After that day Marian went to all the baseball games. And Lo Blandy became one of her numerous admirers, to the amusement of her aunt and friends.

But these meetings had been deadly earnest for Marian. She loved the Indian. She fought for long— then surrendered and fought no more. He had more principle and better habits than any white boy she knew. So that summer, in the cool, amber-lighted mornings by the seashore and on the moonlit nights when dance and music held their sway, Marian quaffed the spiced draught of love.

She wondered: Did she have as true and steadfast nature as the Indian? Would she love once and once only? Vain queries! She loved now and that was all of pain.

Marian gazed out of the train windows at the scenery flashing by. The topography of the country had changed. Dark bushy green trees, very beautiful, had appeared on the slowly rising desert land, and the spaces between them were white with bleached grass. No more cliffs of stone passed under her sight. There were wooded hills in the background. And presently these low green trees gave place to larger ones, growing wide apart, brown-trunked, with spreading branches and thin green foliage at the tops. Pines! She welcomed them. She greeted every little gain of pleasure or knowledge, somehow trying to persuade herself that there was to be education and broadening of sympathy in this wild trip to the West. Marian had not been ashamed of her love for Lo Blandy. She felt that she might reach a point where she would glory in it. But she had shrunk from making confidantes of her aunt and her friends. No one guessed the truth of that summer at Cape May. And now she was on a train, far out in the West, soon to take whatever means offered to reach the Indian reservation. The farther on she got the more untrue her situation seemed. Yet she was glad. A deep within her stirred to strange promptings. She strove to justify her action in her own eyes. Surely one flight of freedom need not be denied her. The laxity of Marian's social set in no way gave her excuse for wildness and daringness. She hated the drinking and smoking of women, the unrestrained dances, the lack of courtesy, the unbelievable letdown of morals since the beginning of the World War. She had welcomed an opportunity to escape from that atmosphere. Outside of love for Lo Blandy or an earnest desire to help his people had been a trenchant call to some subtle, innate wildness in her. The prairie, the mountains, the sea, the desert all called to her in whispering voice. Someday she would surely have listened.

"I have no close family ties," she said to herself, in sincere deference. "I am twenty-three. I am my own boss. I've always dreamed of love with honor—of marriage with children. Perhaps in vain! My aunt, my friends, would call me mad. They do not understand me. I am not throwing my life away. I can do good out here. I can help *him* . . . Nophaie—how strange, how beautiful a name! I am not rich. But I have some

money, and that I will gladly use now. Let the future
take care of itself."

So she settled the matter of perplexity and of conscience, and gave up to the singular appeal of the
prospect before her. Always Marian had yearned to do
something different, unusual, big. She had traveled a
little, taught school, tried journalistic work, and had
one short weakness for dramatics. And she knew she
had accomplished nothing. Here indeed was the bright
face of adventure, mysterious and alluring, coupled
with a work she might make up-lifting and all-
satisfying.

Flagerstown, being the first western town Marian had
ever been in, was not at all like what she had imagined
it would be. Her impressions of the West had come
from books and motion pictures, which mediums, she
was to learn, did not always ring true to life.

It was quite a thriving little city, bustling with
motorcars, and active over its lumber, railroad, and
cattle interests. It bore no signs of the typical frontier
town. What surprised Marian a little was the fact that
neither hotel proprietor nor banker, post-office official,
nor clerk in the store, nor a cattleman she chanced to
address showed any curiosity in her. When she made
inquiry about the Indian reservation she simply stated
that she was interested in Indians and might do some
journalistic work out there. Marian was compelled to
confess that these western men did not seem to be
impressed with her. They were courteous, and kindly,
yet somehow aloof. It was a novelty to her. In the East
she had been endlessly confronted with the fact of her
femininity and youth and attractiveness. Here she
seemed to catch a breath of life not thick and heavy
with the atmosphere of sex. The West was young,
virile, open. Already she began to feel free of fetters
that had weighed upon her. Back home the ideals of
most people were the pursuit of wealth, pleasure,
excitement. The cities were congested. Young people

left the wholesome countryside to flock to the centers of population, there to mix and strive in crowded places. Marian felt the futility and falseness of such life—that the threshold of decadence had been crossed.

She ascertained that a mail carrier left Flagerstown twice a week for the places on the reservation—Mesa, Red Sandy, and Kiadab. And the post-office man was kind enough to arrange passage for her. Next morning the hotel porter called to take her luggage. Marian saw the most dilapidated Ford car she had ever seen in her life. What there was of it appeared to be wired and roped together. And it was loaded heavily with mailbags, boxes, and sacks. There was a coop containing some chickens going parcel post. Next to the driver's seat had been left a small space, evidently for Marian.

"Goodness!" ejaculated Marian, as she surveyed this doubtful contraption. "Will it hold together? Is it safe to ride in?"

"Why, miss, sho thet injun will get you thar," replied the porter.

"Indian! Is the driver an—Indian?"

"Yes—sum. An' sho blowin' snow er sand makes no difference to him."

Marian could have laughed, in spite of her uneasiness. But all she could do was to gaze helplessly at that machine. Then appeared a young man in ragged dark suit. His small feet were encased in brown buckskin moccasins with silver buttons. His dark face appeared to be half hidden by a black sombrero. She could see that he was young. She noted his hands as they slipped over the wheel—dark, thin, nervous, sinewy hands, well formed and mobile. Then he got into the driver's seat and looked up at her. He was only a youth. His face was keen, smooth as silk, without a line, dark as bronze. He had a level brow and eyes black as night. Suddenly they gleamed with intelligence and humor. This Indian sensed her consternation.

"You ready go?" he queried, in good English. The

tone of it gave Marian a little shock. Something about it, the low pitch or timbre, recalled the voice of Lo Blandy.

"Y-Yes, I guess so," faltered Marian. Dare she trust this frightful junk-heap of a car and its Indian driver on a long desert journey? Marian's eastern compunctions did not die easily.

"You go Kaidab?" asked the driver.

"Yes," replied Marian.

"I get you there—four o'clock," he returned with a smile. It seemed a flash of understanding. He read her mind, and wished to reassure her. Marian's new spirit revived her with a rush. She had burned her bridges behind her.

"Will it be cold?" she asked, as she was about to climb into the car.

"You need blanket for while," he said.

Marian had no blanket, but she had brought a heavy coat which would serve as well. This she got out and put on. Then she squeezed into the small space beside the driver. The grinning porter called: "Good night," which dubious farewell in no way diminished Marian's concern.

The Indian driver moved something that made the rickety car crack like a pistol and lurch forward.

Marian could not stifle a gasp. The square-fronted buildings with their queer high board signs began to speed back out of her sight. Ahead the white asphalt road merged into one of dark earth, and there appeared a long slope of pine trees. Cold, keen, biting wind fanned Marian's cheeks. It nipped with its frosty breath. And it brought a strange dry fragrance. The car passed the line of buildings, and to the left loomed a mighty green and white mountain mass that hid its summit in gloomy rolling clouds.

"Storm," said the Indian. "We hurry so get way from snow."

If anything more were needed to complete Marian's

demoralization she had it in the gathering speed of that car. It belied its appearance.

"Oh! If they could see me now!" she murmured, as she snuggled down into the warm coat and peeped out at the wonderful green slope of forest. She thought of those at home who would have looked aghast at her boldness. Perhaps this was the moment of severance. Whatever it was, above all Marian's misgivings and defiance there pealed a subtle voice of joy.

Chapter 3

THE ROAD UPON WHICH THE INDIAN WAS driving Marian led out into a pine forest, between the stately trees of which she caught glimpses of cloud-enshrouded mountains.

The cold, the raw wind, the increasing gloominess of the day, with its ominous threat of storm, in no way checked Marian's momentary enthusiasm and awakening joy for the open country. She must see all, experience all with every sense acute. For as long as she could remember she had been cooped up in a town. And in her heart love of nature had been stultified. At last! She breathed deeply of the keen air. And the strong, pitchy smell of pine began to stimulate her.

"What mountains?" she asked.

"Spanish Peaks," replied the driver.

She asked him other questions, to which he gave brief and unsatisfactory reply. Perhaps it took all his attention to keep the car on the road. Besides, it made such a rattle and clank that conversation was really not easy. Marian ceased asking questions.

The road led through such a forest of pines as Marian had never seen, wonderfully fragrant and exhilarating after the cities and railroads. The grass was dead, bleached white, but the green of the pines gave relief to her eyes. Ten miles of forest the car traversed, then an open valley, fine ranch country, Marian judged, from which view of the mountain range was magnificent, and then it entered the forest again with the difference that the ground appeared to be all cinders. The car chugged uphill, losing much of its velocity.

From a ridge top Marian's eyes were greeted by a

strange and desolate spectacle—a wide, black valley, a
slope of black cinders, and a stream of red lava crusted
and jagged, and beyond these foothills of black cinders
smooth and steep, all waved and ridged like sand dunes
carved by wind. A line of pines crested the first hill, and
under this green stretch was a long bank of snow, its
pure white contrasting so markedly with the ebony
cinders. A range of those foothills rose off toward the
south, growing higher and smoother, weird and sinister
monuments to the havoc of volcanic action in the ages
past. Beyond and above this range towered a mountain
of cinders, strangely barren, marvelously colored in
purple, black, and red.

Marian saw so much in this scored and devastated
region that she regretted passing on so rapidly. Soon
her Indian guide reached a downgrade in the forest, ran
out of the cinder zone upon hard road again, and here
Marian feared every flying mile would be her last.

Eventually the pines began to decrease in size and
grow farther apart, so that glimpses of open country
came to Marian. Then from round a rocky ridge quite
abruptly the car sped out into thin forest from which
stretched a vast waste of gray. The desert! Marian did
not try to repress an exclamation of delight and awe.

She was looking down over many leagues of desert.
The pines failed, the cedars began, and beyond them
rolled and waved away the white billowy miles of
wasteland. Only two colors prevailed, black and white.
How soft and velvety! Only the west appeared barren
from limitless gaze; and there a succession of rounded
hills, bare except for grass, led away down into the
desert. These and the cedars, and the winding road
lured Marian's sight to the farthest reaches, to what
seemed a dim and mounting succession of colossal
steps, vaguely colorful, unattainable, and incredible.
Where did the horizon line separate that purple remote
land from the sky? But the sky was obscured and
horizon-wide clouds of dull leaden hue and trailing veils
of storm filled the vastness above. For Marian the

moment was one of realization. The ocean was indeed vast, but only a few leagues of it could be seen. The desert sloped many leagues after leagues and rolled upward majestically doubling leagues, all open to the eye. Marian's realization was that she had never until now known what it was that she wanted.

Marian feasted her eyes, trying to grasp what it was that she saw; and as moments and miles passed a gray squall of rain and snow swooped down from behind, enveloping the car. It brought a piercing cold. What rain there was soon changed to sleet. It pelted Marian, many hailstones bouncing off the glass windshield to sting her face. Gloves and pockets appeared little protection against such cold. Marian suffered. Her cheeks, her eyes, her ears seemed to congeal to ice. The world around that car was white, swept by a blizzard, with snow fleeting across the ground. The sky was obscured. When Marian opened her eyes—at intervals —she could not see far in front of the car. This obscurity did not deter the Indian from driving fast. So that between her pangs and fears, Marian had to make heroic enjoyment out of this hour.

At length the gray cloud lightened, the snow thinned out, and the blue of sky shone through a thin haze of white. That too faded or melted away, and then the storm veered away, leaving clear a great open space above. Marian grew aware that she was now far down in the desert, with open, bare ridges all around her, and the distant prospects out of sight. The snow failed. The earth changed its white and black hue to a dull red. Once again the car sped out upon a height from which Marian had a second look at the leagues. Here the immense reach and slope struck her more forcibly, and especially the great volume of light.

The sun came out from behind the cloud bank over the east, and the desert magnified lines and colors, and suddenly unmasked an appalling beauty.

Once the Indian stopped the car to examine some of its mechanisms. Thus Marian was enabled to get out and stretch her cramped, cold limbs. After that, when the journey had been resumed, she soon grew comfortable under a warming sun, and at length forgot both pangs and fears in absorption of this desert land. Her driver traveled downhill for no less than three hours. This brought them to what seemed an incongruity—an iron bridge spanning a rock-walled gorge, through which ran a muddy stream. Here in this valley the sun was hot. Marian had to remove the heavy coat.

Beyond the river stretched a gravelly plain, hard packed by wind, and its slow ascent at last gained another height, from which Marian confirmed her wondering expectations. Three level benches of colored desert, as high as mountains, lifted their wondrous reds and purples and grays and golds toward the blue sky. It was a land of painted steps. It was beyond her power to grasp. She could but revel in a mosaic of color and a strange expanse of earth and rock. This was but the portal to Lo Blandy's country. What then would Oljato be like? Marian felt confounded in her own impressions. Once she glanced behind her, as if to make sure of distance she had traversed, of land she knew to be solid and not a substance of dreams. The spectacle to the rear was vastly different, a gray desert slope, a red desert slope, league on league, shelving back to rise and lift to a great dark plateau from which the Spanish Peaks showed white, pure snow against the sky.

The ensuing hour, during which the Indian driver crossed the bare plains of sand and gravel, and climbed the successive steps of colored rock, passed by all too quickly for Marian. The sun beat down hot. Her watch told the hour to be eleven o'clock. To the north, in the direction the car was heading, more storm clouds were gathering. Above the last desert step the earth appeared a place of ruin and decay, a zone of sinister red and strange drab, where rocks and clay had been weathered into fantastic shapes. Marian likened the region to an inferno. Soon it lay behind, and Marian found herself confronted with a wide valley between glowing walls of rock. Dark rich green fields of alfalfa formed the floor of this valley, making the hot walls of stone naked and stark by contrast. Marian saw clusters of trees beginning to show green, and the roofs of two flat houses.

"What's this place?" she inquired.

"Copenwashie," replied the Indian.

"Are those green fields Indian farms?"

"Some are. Missionaries got most land now."

"But isn't this a reservation for the use of Indians?" went on Marian, curiously.

All the reply she received was a grunt of disgust. The Indian drove fast up this level valley, making the dust fly from under his car. When he came to the first house he stopped and carried packages in. Marian saw no one. In the fields, however, were picturesque laborers she took to be Indians. Upon resuming the journey her guide pointed out some low stone houses, standing back under shelving cliffs, surrounded by greening trees. These were the houses of the missionaries. From that point the road ascended the side of a steep gorge. Up on top of this elevation the land was level, covered with rough low brushes, dull green in color. Gray and red buildings showed in the distance, and long lines of bare trees. In a few moments the car had reached them. Marian was consumed with interest and curiosity.

"Mesa. We stop little while," said the driver, coming to a halt before one of the stone structures. It was large, with few windows, and appeared rather inhospitable looking. Little ragged wild ponies wearing crude, square-topped saddles stood nearby with bridles down.

"Are they Indian horses?" she asked.

"Yes. Not much good. You wait," he replied, with his reassuring smile. "This trading post. People friendly. You go in. I take mail."

Marian got out, glad to stretch her limbs again, and

strolled to and fro. She saw a wide, tree-lined avenue, with well-built gray stone houses on one side, and large, red stone buildings on the other. These latter she took to be the government school quarters. How out of place they seemed! The great tableland of desert seemed to encompass them, accentuating their incongruity. That avenue was quite lengthy, so that Marian could not see what lay at the upper end. Then her attention was attracted toward the trading post. Three men, Indians, had just come out. They wore white man's garb, even to shoes and hats, and did not rouse Marian's admiration. What swarthy faces, secretive and impassive—what sloe-black eyes, beady and sharp! These Indians watched her. Marian suffered something of disillusion and disappointment at sight of them. Then a white man appeared, tall, sandy-haired, and open-faced.

"Come in. I'm Paxton, the trader," he said. "My wife is always glad to meet visitors. You must be tired and hungry. And it's a good ways to Kaidab."

"Thank you. I am hungry, but not tired," replied Marian, as she followed him in, wondering how he had learned where she was going. He led her through a huge, ball-like storeroom, in which counters and shelves were loaded with merchandise, to another part of the house, into a living room, most comfortable and pleasant. There Marian met the trader's wife, a young and comely woman who was most kindly and agreeable. Neither by word nor look did she show anything inquisitive. She was merely glad to meet a strange visitor and to give her a little rest and refreshment. Marian liked her.

"I'm on my way to Kaidab," she felt it needful to say. "I want to see something of the Indians—perhaps write a little about them, or work with them."

"You're not a missionary?" quickly queried the woman.

"Oh, no, indeed."

"Well, I'm glad of that. It's fine of you to be interested. God knows the Indians need friends. We traders believe we are about the only friends they have."

Marian asked casual questions about the Indians, being careful not to go beyond ordinary interest. And altogether she spent a pleasant half hour with Mrs. Paxton.

"I hope you come to Mesa again," said her hostess, as they passed out through the store. From the door Marian saw a white man standing beside the car, in conversation with the Indian driver.

"There's Friel," went on Mrs. Paxton, and evidently the recognition of this man changed her train of thought.

"Who's Friel?" queried Marian.

"He's a missionary," she replied.

"I'm interested in missionaries, too," said Marian, with a smile. "Thank you for your kindness. I'm sure we'll meet again. Good-bye."

Marian walked out to the car. At her step the man designated by Mrs. Paxton turned to see her. Marian was used to meeting strangers and classifying them after the manner of women. But she had not any recollection of a type like this man.

"I'm Mr. Friel," he said, touching his sombrero. "Can I do anything for you?"

"No, thank you," replied Marian.

His face had the brown of the open, but it was not one that inspired Marian to interest or liking. Quick was she to see the gleam of curiosity in his eyes, and then as he took a good look at her, the leaf of admiration. He was not young enough for that to be quite a quick and natural reaction.

"You're traveling alone," he said. "May I know your errand?"

Marian told him what she had told the trader's wife. Then she felt rather than saw an increased interest in her, with something of antagonism.

"Have you permission to go on the reservation?" he inquired.

"No. Is it—compulsory?"

"I—well—no, hardly that. But it is always best for visitors to see Mr. Blucher."

"Who is he?"

"The agent in charge of the reservation."

"Very well. Where can I find him?"

"Unfortunately, Mr. Blucher is away attending an investigation. But I can take it upon myself to—to make everything all right. Wouldn't you like to see the school?"

Marian felt that perhaps she had been prejudiced against missionaries in the first place. This one was well-spoken enough. But apart from that Mr. Friel had the look in his eyes which she hated. And she never met that look twice. Nevertheless she must accept people out here on the desert as she found them, and if possible without suffering indignity, she must learn from them.

"It would be interesting to see the Indian children. I may return here and find some kind of work with them. But I've no time now."

"I can get you a position here," he said, eagerly. He was too eager.

"What authority have you?" asked Marian, bluntly. She omitted thanking him.

"Well, no outright authority to hire government employees," he returned, suavely. "But I hire people to work for me occasionally. And I'm hand in glove with Morgan. He's the power here."

"Morgan?"

"He's been here over twenty years, and runs things."

"What is he?"

"Missionary, of course."

"So—and if I return here to find work—whom should I see first?"

"Come to me on the quiet. Then we'll see Morgan. If you got a job before seeing him you'd soon lose it."

"Indeed. Well, I'll think it over," returned Marian, as she stepped to the car.

Friel took hold of her arm, not to assist her, but to keep her from entering.

"Let me drive you to Kaidab. I have my car here. There's no room in this filthy junk box. Besides, a handsome girl like you oughtn't to be riding alone with one of these Indians."

"Why not? He's the mail carrier. I'm paying him for driving me."

"They're all alike, these Indian louts. You're not safe with any one of them."

"If that's true, Mr. Friel, it doesn't speak well for you missionaries. I'll take a chance on this Indian. Good day."

With that Marian resumed her seat in the car and signaled the driver to start. He did so after a fashion that presupposed he was glad to leave the vicinity of the missionary. Marian sat back, just as glad as she imagined he was. The breeze was pleasant. The wide, colored spaces beckoned. She was a little amazed to realize the heat running along and cooling out of her veins. How disgusting and irritating! A preacher, a so-called missionary among Indians, a man animal, vain and wooden-headed and utterly lacking! Upon sober reflection Marian discerned that she resented most the insult to the Indian. She turned to him.

"Did you understand what that missionary said?"

"I savvy him. His head big stick with skin stretched over."

Marian was forced to admit that this Indian had discernment and originality. Then straightaway she dismissed the irritations from her mind. The ride over the desert was all important. How far was she from Kaidab—from Oljato? Every speeding mile brought her closer to the home of Lo Blandy. She whispered his Indian name over and over again, trying to accept it and make it familiar. She could not succeed. And every thought of him augmented a mounting consciousness of an ordeal to come, baffling and tremendous in its significance. Yet, what sweetness of thrill—of strange fire and magic!

The gray clouds soon obscured the sun, and Marian again felt the chill of the wind. She bundled up once more. Her driver had turned off to the north from the Mesa road, and was following a depression of land, only which Marian could not see far. There was a stretch of sandy going, then a climb up a long slope that led to a level plateau, sparsely green with plants, and monotonously gray with distance. Here the Indian put the car to its limit of speed, too fast and too noisy for Marian's pleasure. Yet she gazed from one side to another, eager to see. Eastward were long ragged lines of blue earth on rock, evidently marking a canyon. To the west the only mark of note was a great white bluff, standing alone, flat-topped, with bare, sloping sides. Soon the gray obscurity ahead turned out to be snow, a driving hard storm that put Marian to another test. Burying her face in scarf and coat collar she crouched there and endured. Meanwhile time passed and likewise the miles. When the storm cleared away and the sun shone again, Marian had reached a wide, red basin, sand-sloped and walled-in by low cliffs, now shining with wet faces.

At two o'clock the Indian brought his car to a halt before Red Sandy, a trading post located high upon an immense slope of sand. The traders, two young men, were as solicitous and kind as had been the Paxtons. Marian was indeed glad to warm her frozen cheeks and ears and hands. This place was like a fort, and the quarters to which the traders conducted Marian was a loft above their store. It was warm, and somehow peculiarly fitting and picturesque with its blankets and baskets, and other handiwork. How weirdly the wind moaned outside!

From the window of this house Marian had a wonderful view that fascinated and repelled her. How desolate and dreary! The immense basin appeared to spread to all points of the compass. Ponds of water glimmered under the lowering sky. Vegetation was so scanty that bushes here and there resembled animals. Across the void rose a whorl of white cliffs, bold and bleak, worn by the elements into strange and irregular conformation. This mass of rock ended abruptly in a sheer bluff facing the south. A wide avenue of spotted desert land separated it from the rise and heave of a black flat mountain to the eastward. Marian saw the almost level line of this tableland wander away into the distance, gradually to disappear in the north. And following the horizon round towards the west Marian suddenly sighted a dim purple and white dome. For long it held her gaze, not alone because of its beauty. It called. It did not seem real, so deep was the purple, so ethereal the white.

"Is that a mountain?" she asked one of the traders.

"It shore is," he replied. "That's old Nothsis Ahn. It's worshiped, by the Indians."

Marian went back to the car, where the Indian sat waiting for her. Almost she resented this swift passage across the desert. It left no time for realization, let alone contemplation. One more moment she gave to Red Sandy. It had beauty, but how austere! There was no life, no movement. The red colors dominated, but did not stand out. They merged into the drab, brown, mauve, and gray. Perhaps the lowering clouds caused the effect of gloom. The silence was impressive.

On the way down across the sandy basin Marian espied dark riders approaching from around the bluff. She watched them grow until they met and passed her, two Indian men and one woman, riding shaggy ponies and packing blankets and sheepskins behind their saddles. The woman was heavy, garbed in loose, dirty garments, with dull, dark face and unkempt hair. It was only at a distance that these Indians looked picturesque.

Then there ensued an hour in which the car chugged over a sandy road, mostly uphill, with view restricted except on the eastern side. Here the long, black, flat mountain assumed nobler proportions. Bands of little horses dotted the gray-green rise of ground. An Indian rider appeared on the rim of a ridge, loping along, lending a touch of wildness and life to the scene. Presently the driver called Marian's attention to a mound of earth with a dark hole leading into it.

"Hogan. Indian house," he said. How crude and primitive! Verily the wants and the comforts of the Indians must be few.

It was only from the high places, Marian came to learn, that the incredible openness and boundlessness of the desert could be grasped. And there came a ridge summit from which she could see afar, down and across a land of prairie, on to slowly rising bare waste that swept upward to purple and black heights. These colors held her gaze. A round knob of stony hill on the left and the continuous range of mesa on her right seemed gradually to become less prominent in her sight. In another hour she learned that the black heights were forests of cedar and the purple ones were meadows of sage. Long before she reached the beautiful open patches of purple she became aware of an exquisite fragrance in the air. It grew keener, stronger, sweeter. Marian recognized it to be sage. Only how wild and strange, stifling almost, and wholly exhilarating. Here the barrenness of the desert was not in evidence. She had climbed to a high elevation. Forest of cedar and field of sage encompassed her on all sides.

If this long, twenty-mile upgrade of desert had not slowly grown from waste to verdure, from desolate, sinister badlands to noble heights of keen, sweet air and beautiful color, Marian would not have been prepared for the next phase of this bewildering country. But she had been given time. She had grown with the miles.

So that when the Indian driver sped his car down in steep break round curve and curve, out of the forest into a changed world of stone, Marian was not utterly confounded. The road stretched on through a long narrow pass, above which toward cliffs of red and gold and yellow, so lofty that she had to look almost straight up to see their rims. They seemed not to be cliffs, but stone faces of mountains. Marian gazed upward until her eyes ached.

All too swiftly ran the car and all too short was that pass. It opened out upon ridged gray desert, with the black mesa on the right zigzagging away to the eastward and the red corrugated wall of stone on the left notching its bold skyline away to the north. Ten more miles of travel removed both ramparts far to either side. And another hilltop gave Marian her first sight of Kaidab. Her letters, her gifts to Lo Blandy had been sent to this trading post. All she saw was several low, flat stone houses, a crude and dreary habitation! Yet no splendid spectacle of the whole long ride had given Marian the thrill that now shot over her.

Chapter 4

CLOSE AT HAND KAIDAB TRADING POST showed striking aspects of life and activity. Marian looked and looked, with mounting delight and wonder.

First there were a number of the shaggy Indian ponies, unhaltered, standing with uplifted heads, and black rolling eyes askance on the mail-carrier's car. Several were without saddles, having a blanket tied on their backs; one was a cream color almost pink, with strange light eyes and wonderful long mane and tail; most of them were a reddish bay in color, and there was a fiery little black that took Marian's eye.

Huge bags of burlap containing wool were being packed into a wagon by Indian freighters. And Indians were lounging around, leaning against the stone wall of the trading post. The look of them somehow satisfied Marian. Raven black hair, impassive faces of bronze, eyes of night, lean and erect figures clad in velvet and corduroy, with glints of silver and bead ornament—these circumstances of appearance came somewhere near fitting Marian's rather sentimental anticipations.

Before the open front of one building, evidently a storehouse, other Indians were packing wool in the long sacks, a laborsome task, to judge from their efforts to hold the sack erect and stomp down the wool. The whole interior of this open house appeared busy and littered with harness, rope, piles of white sacks, piles of wool and skins. The odor of sheep struck Marian rather disagreeably. The sun was hot and fell glaringly upon the red blankets. Flies buzzed everywhere. And at least a dozen lean, wild-looking, and inquisitive-eyed dogs sniffed around Marian. Not one of them wagged its tail.

White men in shirt sleeves, with sweaty faces and hands begrimed, were working over a motorcar as dilapidated as the mail carrier's. Two Indian women, laden with bundles, came out of the open door of the trading post. The older woman was fat and pleasant-faced. She wore loose, flowing garments, gaudy in color, and silver necklaces, and upon her back she carried a large bundle or box. When she passed Marian caught a glimpse of a dark little baby face, peering out of a hole in that box. The younger female was probably a daughter, and she was not uncomely in appearance. Something poignant and bright haunted her smooth, dark face. She was slender. She had little feet encased in brown moccasins. She wore what Marian thought was velveteen, and her silver ornaments were studded with crude blue stones. She glanced shyly at Marian. Then an Indian came riding up to dismount near Marian. He was old. His lean face was a mass of wrinkles, and there was iron gray in his hair. He wore a thin cotton shirt and overalls—white apparel much the worse for wear. Behind his saddle hung a long bundle, a goatskin rolled with fur inside. This he untied and carried into the trading post. More Indians came riding in; one of the ponies began to rear and snort and kick; the dogs barked; whisks of warm and odorous wind stirred the dust; the smell of sheep wool grew stronger; low, guttural voices of Indians mingled with the sharper, higher notes of white men.

A sturdily built, keen-eyed man stalked out of the post, with a hand on the Indian mail-carrier's shoulder. He wore a vest over a flannel shirt, but no coat or hat. His boots were rough and dusty.

"Take her bags in," he said to the Indian.

Then, at his near approach, Marian felt herself scanned by a gaze at once piercing and kindly.

"Glad to welcome you, Miss Warner," he said. "Been expecting you for two hours. I'm John Withers."

Marian offered her hand. "Expecting me?" she queried curiously.

"News travels fast in this country," he replied, with a smile. "An Indian rode in two hours ago with the news you were coming."

"But my name?" asked Marian, still curious.

"Mrs. Withers told me that and what you looked like. She'll shore be glad to see you. Come. We'll go in."

Marian followed him into the yard beside the trading post, where somewhat in the background stood a low, squat, picturesque stone house with roof of red earth. Her curiosity had developed into wonder. She tingled a little at an implication that followed one of her conjectures. How could Mrs. Withers know what she looked like? Withers ushered her into a wonderful room that seemed to flash Indian color and design at her. Blankets on floor and couch, baskets on mantel and wall, and a strange-painted frieze of Indian figures, crude, elemental, striking—these lent the room its atmosphere. A bright fire blazed in the open stove fireplace. Books and comforts were not lacking. This room opened into a long dining room, with the same ornamental Indian effects. And from it ran a hallway remarkable for its length and the variety and color of its decorations.

Marian's quick eyes had only time for one look when a woman of slight stature and remarkable face entered.

"Welcome to Kaidab, Miss Warner," she said warmly, with extended hands. "We're happy to meet you. We hope you will stay long."

"Thank you, Mrs. Withers—you're very kind. I—I am very glad to get here," replied Marian, just a little confused and nervous.

"You've had a long, cold ride. And you're red with dust. Oh, I know that ride. I took it first twenty-five years ago on horseback."

"Yes, it was hard. And cold—I nearly froze. But, oh, it was wonderful!"

Withers laughed his pleasure at her words. "Why,

that's no ride. You're just on the edge of real wild
country. We're going to show you."

"John, put Miss Warner's bags in the second room.
And send some hot water. After she's comfortable and
rested we can talk."

Marian found the room quaint and strange as the
others. It had a clean, earthy smell. The walls appeared
to be of red cement, adobe, Marian supposed, and they
were cold. While washing and changing her dusty
clothes Marian pondered over her singular impressions
of Mrs. Withers. She was no ordinary woman. For
some reason not apparent to Marian, her hostess had a
strong personal regard for her. Marian had intuitively
felt this. Besides, she must have been a woman used to
welcoming strangers to this wild frontier. Marian
sensed something of the power she had felt in women of
high position, as they met their guests; only in the case
of Mrs. Withers it was a simplicity of power, a strange,
unconscious dignity, spiritual rather than material. But
Marian lost no time in making herself comfortable or
conjecturing about Mrs. Withers. She felt drawn to this
woman. She divined news, strange portents, unknown
possibilities, of which hurried her back to the living
room. Mrs. Withers was there waiting for her.

"How sweet and fair you are!" exclaimed Mrs.
Withers, with an admiring glance at Marian's face. "We
don't see your kind out here. The desert is hard on
blondes."

"So I imagine," replied Marian. "I'll not long remain
'Benow—di cleash.' . . . Is that pronounced correct-
ly?"

Mrs. Withers laughed. "Well, I understood you. But
you must say it this way . . . 'Benow di cleash!'"

Her voice had some strange, low, liquid quality
utterly new to Marian.

"Mrs. Withers, you know where I got that name,"
asserted Marian.

"Yes, I'm happy to tell you I do," she rejoined
earnestly.

Marian slowly answered to the instinct of the moment. Her hands went out to meet those offered by Mrs. Withers, and she gazed down into the strange, strong face, with its shadows of sorrow and thought, its eyes of penetrating and mystic power.

"Let us sit down," continued Mrs. Withers, leading the way to the couch. "We'll have to talk our secrets at odd moments. Somebody is always bobbing in. . . . First, I meant to tell you two things—that I know will make us friends."

"I hope so—believe so," returned Marian, trying to hold her calm.

"Listen. All my life I've been among the Indians," said Mrs. Withers in her low voice. "I loved Indians when I was a child. I've been here in this wild country for many years. It takes years of kindness and study to understand the Indian. . . . These Indians have come to care for me. They have given me a name. They believe me—trust me. They call on me to settle disputes, to divide property left by some dead Indian, to tell their troubles. I have learned their dreams, longings, their religion, their prayers and legends and poetry, their medicine, the meaning of their dances. And the more I learn of them the more I love and respect them. Indians are not what they appear to most white people. They are children of nature. They have noble hearts and beautiful minds. They have criminals among them, but much less proportion than have the white race. The song of Hiawatha is true—true for all Indians. They live in a mystic world of enchantment peopled by spirits, voices, music, whisperings of God, eternal and everlasting immortality. They are as simple as little children. They personify everything. With them all is symbolic."

Mrs. Withers paused a moment, her eloquent eyes riveted upon Marian.

"For a good many years this remote part of the Indian country was far out of the way of white men. Thus the demoralization and degradation of the Indian were retarded, so far as this particular tribe is concerned. This Nopah tribe is the proudest, most intelligent, most numerous, and the wealthiest tribe left in the United States. So-called civilization has not yet reached Kaidab. But it is coming. I feel the next few years will go hard with the Indian—perhaps decide his fate."

"Oh—there seems no hope!" murmured Marian.

"There indeed seems none, if you look at it intelligently and mercilessly. But I look at this question as the Indian looks at everything. He begins his prayer, 'Let all be well with me'—and he ends it, 'Now all is well with me.' He feels—he trusts. There really is a God. If there were not I would be an infidel. Life on the desert magnifies all. . . . I want you to let me help you to understand the Indian. . . . For the sake of your happiness!"

Marian could not voice her surprise. A tremor ran over her.

"Nophaie showed me your picture—told me about you," went on Mrs. Withers, with an exquisite softness of voice. "Ah! Do not be shocked. It was well for him that he confided in me. . . . I met him the day he returned here from the East. I remembered him. I knew him as a boy, a little shepherd who refused to leave his flock in a sandstorm. I know the place where he was born. I know the sage where he was stolen. I knew the horse thief who stole him. I knew the woman who took him east and put him in school. . . . But Nophaie did not remember me. He went out to the sage slopes of Nothsis Ahn, and when he rode back he had not his white man's clothes, or speech, or name. He was Nophaie. And he rode here now and then. The Indians told me about him. He is a chief who wants to help them in a white man's way. But the Indians want him to be a medicine man. . . . Well, I saw his trouble. And when he came here I talked. I helped him with his own language. It returned but slowly. I saw his unhappiness. And in the end he told me about you—showed me your picture—confessed his love."

Marian covered her burning face with trembling hands. She did not mind this good woman knowing her secret, but the truth spoken out, the potent words, the inevitable fact of it being no dream shocked her, stormed her heart. Nophaie loved her. He had confessed it to this noble friend of the Indians.

"Marian, do not be ashamed of Nophaie's love," went on Mrs. Withers appealingly. "No one else knows. John suspects, but is not sure. I understand you—feel with you—and I know more; you'd not be here if you did not love Nophaie!"

"Of . . . course I love . . . him," said Marian, unsteadily, as she uncovered her face. "You misunderstand. I'm not ashamed. . . . It's just the shock of hearing—knowing—the suddenness of your disclosure."

"You mustn't mind me—and my knowing all," returned the woman. "This is the desert. You are among primitive peoples. There's nothing complex out here. Your sophistication will fall from you like dead scales."

Gathering courage, and moved by an intense and perfect assurance of sympathy, Marian briefly told Mrs. Withers of her romance with Nophaie, and then of her condition in life and her resolve to have her fling at freedom, to live awhile in the West and in helping the Indians perhaps find something of happiness.

"Ah! You will grieve, but you will also be wonderfully happy," replied Mrs. Withers. "As for Nophaie—you will save him. His heart was breaking. And when an Indian's heart breaks he dies. . . . I kept track of Nophaie. He had a remarkable career in college. He was a splendid student and a great athlete. I've heard that Nophaie's father was a marvelous runner. And he carried the Testing Stone of the braves the farthest for generations. . . . But what good Nophaie's education and prowess will do out here is a question. He must learn to be an Indian. Eighteen years among white men made him more white than red. He will never go back to the white man's life. . . . Marian, I wonder—does that worry you? Be honest with me."

"No. I would not want him to go back," replied Marian.

"And you said you had no near and dear ties?" queried Mrs. Withers, with her magnetic eyes on Marian's.

"None very near or dear."

"And you were sick of artificial life—of the modern customs—of all that . . . "

"Indeed I was," interrupted Marian.

"And you really have a longing to go back to simple and outdoor ways?"

"Longing!" exclaimed Marian, almost with passion, carried out of self-control by this woman's penetrating power to thrill her. "I—I don't know what it is. But I think under my fair skin—I'm a savage!"

"And you have some money?"

"Oh, I'm not rich, but then I'm not poor, either."

"And you love Nophaie—as you're sure you could never love another man—a white man?"

"I—I love him terribly," whispered Marian. "How can I foretell the future—any possible love—again? But I hate the very thought. Oh, I had it put to me often enough lately—marriage for money or convenience—for a home—for children—for anything but love? No. No! Not for me."

"And will you marry Nophaie?" added Mrs. Withers.

Marian uttered a little gasp. Again, it was not shame that sent the prickling hot blood to her cheeks, but a liberation of emotion she had restrained. This blunt and honest woman called to her very depths.

"Nophaie is an Indian. But he's a man. I never saw a finer man—white or red. . . . I think you're a fortunate girl. To love and be loved—to live in this desert—to see its wildness and grandeur—to learn of it from an

Indian—to devote your energies to a noble cause! I hope you see the truth."

"I don't see very clearly, but I believe you," replied Marian. "You express something vague and deep in me, that wants to come out. I ought not forget to tell you—Nophaie never asked me to—to marry him."

"Well, it wasn't because he didn't want to, believe me," returned the older woman. "I've seen some lovelorn Indians in my day, but Nophaie has it worst. . . . What do you think you'll do—send for him or ride out to his home?"

"I . . . I'd rather meet him out—away—somewhere in the desert," replied Marian in thoughtful perplexity. "But would that be . . . be all right? It's so unheard of—this thing I'm doing. I *want* to do it. The strongest feelings in me sanction it. But I'm sensitive. I don't want people to know. Oh, it's the cowardice and deceit of my kind."

"Certainly it'll be all right. John will take you to meet Nophaie," rejoined Mrs. Withers warmly. "And no one, except John and me, will be in on the secret. We'll tell the men and everyone who happens along that you've come out to work among the Indians."

"Thank you. That will make it easier for me until I find myself. . . . I was brazen enough when I started out. But my courage seems oozing away."

"I reckon these first days will be hard for you. But don't get blue. All will be well. You're young, healthy, strong. You've got a mind. You'll have a wonderful experience out here and be the better, if not the happier for it."

At that juncture Withers came tramping into the room.

"Say, you look like you'd be good medicine," he said, heartily, as he stood gazing, somewhat surprised and wholly delighted. "What the desert will do to that complexion! Well, Miss, a Pahute Indian just rode in. He saw Nophaie this morning and talked with him. I thought you'd be glad to hear that."

"Oh—today! So near!" exclaimed Marian.

"Shore can't call it near—if you mean where Nophaie is. Nigh on to a hundred miles."

"What did he tell you?" queried Marian eagerly.

"Not much. I just asked if he'd seen Nophaie. He said he had, at sunup this morning. Nophaie was with the sheep. It's lambing time out there. Nophaie was a great shepherd boy. I've heard before how he goes with the sheep. This Pahute laughed and said, 'Nophaie forgets his white mind and goes back to the days of his youth.' I think all the Indians feel joy over Nophaie's renunciation of the white man's life."

"May I take a look at this Pahute?" asked Marian.

"Come on. I'll introduce you," replied Withers, with a laugh.

"Yes, go out with him," interposed Mrs. Withers. "I must see about dinner."

"I don't want to be introduced or have this Pay-Paheete see I'm interested," said Marian to Withers, as they passed out of the house. "I guess it's a matter of sentiment. I just want to—to look at the Indian who saw Nophaie this very day."

"I was only joking, Miss Warner," returned Withers seriously. "This Pahute is a bad Indian. He's got a record, I'm sorry to say. He's killed white men and Indians both."

"Oh! I've heard or read that fights and bloodshed were things of the past."

"Shore you have," said Withers, with a grim note in his voice. "But you heard or read what's not true. Of course the frontier isn't wild and bad, as it was forty years ago, when I was a boy. Nor anything so tough as fifteen years ago when the Indians killed my brother. But this border is yet a long way from tame."

He led Marian through the back of the gray stone house into the store. The center of this large room was a stone-floored square, walled off from the spacious and crooked shelves by high counters. Indians were leaning against these counters. Marian saw locks of raven black hair, straggling from under dusty, crumpled, black sombreros. She saw large silver buckles belted round an Indian's waist. She heard the clink of silver money and low voices, in which the syllables predominating sounded like *toa* and *taa*. All these Indians had their backs to Marian and appeared to be making purchases from the white man behind the counter. Piles of Indian blankets covered the ends of the counters. Back of them on the shelves were a variety of colored dry goods, and canned foods and boxes and jars. From the ceiling hung saddles, bridles, lanterns, lassoes—a numberless assortment of articles salable to Indians.

"Here's your Pahute," said Withers, pointing from the doorway out into the open. "Not very pretty, is he?"

Marian peeped out from behind the trader to see a villainous-looking little Indian, black almost, round-faced, big-nosed, with the boldest, hardest look she ever saw on a human being's face. He wore a singular, high-crowned, conical-shaped sombrero, with a wide, stiff brim. It was as black as his hair and ornamented with bright beads. His garb was soiled velvet or corduroy shirt and trousers of blue jeans. His silver-dotted belt held a heavy gun. A shiny broad silver bracelet circled his sinewy wrist, from which hung a leather quirt. Altogether this Indian was not a pleasant and reassuring sight for the eyes of a city girl, new on the desert. Yet he simply fascinated Marian.

"Well, what do you think of him?" asked Withers, smiling.

"I'm not especially taken with him," replied Marian, with a grimace. "I prefer to see him at a distance. But he looks like—"

"Like the real thing. You bet he is. But to give the devil his due, this Pahute hasn't done a mean or vicious thing since Nophaie came back. The Indians tell me Nophaie has talked good medicine to him."

"What is this medicine?" asked Marian.

"The Indians make medicine out of flowers, roots, bark, herbs, and use it for ills the same as white people do. But medicine also means prayer, straight talk, mystic power of the medicine men of the tribe and their use of sand paintings."

"What are they?"

"When the medicine man comes to visit a sick Indian he makes paintings on flat rock with different-colored sands. He paints his message to the Great Spirit. These paintings are beautiful and artistic. But few white people have ever seen them. And the wonderful thing is the use of them nearly always cures the sick Indian."

"Then Nophaie has begun to help his people?"

"He shore has."

"I am very glad," said Marian softly. "I remember he always believed he could not do any good."

"We're glad, too. You see, Miss Warner, though we live off the Indians we're honestly working for them."

"The trader at Mesa said much the same, and that traders are the only friends the Indians had. Is it true?"

"We believe so. But I've known at least two missionaries who were honest-to-God men—who benefited the Indians."

"Don't they *all* work for the welfare of the Indians?"

"Miss Warner, I can't go into detail on the missionary question. If you stay out here you will learn all about it. Nophaie will tell you the Indian point of view. And the white man's point of view you will soon learn for yourself."

In these few definite words of the trader's Marian sensed anew the subtle and complex nature of this question of the missionary work on the reservation. Withers would not talk. He would not commit himself. The Paxtons had given the same impression. For this very reason Marian began to feel that there was something wrong. Indeed she remembered Nophaie's letter, which she had reread only the day before, and now began to acquire her own objective impressions of what must be a tremendous issue. And suddenly she realized that she was no longer at sea in regard to her motive or intention—she had fixed and settled her determination to stay out there on the desert.

"Miss Warner, do you want me to send a message or letter to Nophaie, by this Pahute?" inquired Withers. "He'll ride out tomorrow."

"No. I'd rather go myself," replied Marian. "Mrs. Withers said you'd take me. Will you be so kind?"

"I shore will take you," he rejoined. "I've got some sheep out that way, and other interests. It's a long ride for a tenderfoot. How are you on a horse?"

"I've ridden some, and this last month I went to a riding school three times a week. I've always been athletic. But, of course, I can't really *ride*. I can learn though."

"It's well you broke in a little before coming west. Because these Nopah trails are rough riding, and you'll have all you can stand. When would you like to start?"

"Just as soon as you can."

"Day after tomorrow then. But don't set your heart on surprising Nophaie. It can't be done."

"Why? If we tell no one."

"Things travel ahead of you in this desert. It seems the very birds carry news. Some Indian will see us on the way, ride past us, or tell another Indian. And it'll get to Nophaie before we do."

"What will get to Nophaie?"

"Word that trader Withers is riding west with Benow di cleash. Shore won't that make Nophaie think?"

"He'll know," said Marian tensely.

"Shore. And he'll ride to meet you. I'll take you over the Pahute trail. You'll be the first white person except myself ever to ride it. You must have nerve, girl."

"Must I? Oh, my vaunted confidence! My foolish little vanity! Mr. Withers, I'm scared of it all—the bigness, the strangeness of this desert—of what I must do."

"Shore you are. That's only natural. Begin right now. Use your eyes and sense. Don't worry. Take things as they come. Make up your mind to stand them. All will be well."

At a call from the interior of the store Withers excused himself and left Marian to her own devices. So, not without dint of willpower, Marian put hesitation and reserve away from her and stepped out among the soft-footed nosing dogs and the shaggy, wild-eyed ponies, and the watchful, lounging Indians. She managed to walk among them without betraying her true sensations. The ordeal, so far as the Indians were concerned, gradually became easier, but she could not feel at ease among those pale-eyed sheep dogs, and she did not lose her fear of being kicked by one of the ponies. The wool freighters interested her. They piled on the enormous brown sacks until the load stood fifteen feet above the wagon bed. Marian wondered if they intended to start off at this late hour. Presently the coarse odor of sheep grew a little too much for her, and she strolled away, past the group of Indians toward the gate of the yard. Then from the doorway Mrs. Withers called her to supper.

Chapter 5

TWENTY-FOUR HOURS AT KAIDAB WAS FOR Marian exceedingly full and prolific of new sensation.

A sunset over the deep notch between the red rampart and the black mesa to the west—trailing transparent clouds of purple and rose and white rimmed by golden fire; a strange, sad twilight, deepening into desert night with the heavens dark blue and radiant with a million stars; a walk out into the lonely, melancholy, silent emptiness; a wonderful hour with this woman who loved and knew the souls and lives of Indians; a sinking to sweet rest with eyelids seemingly touched by glue; a broken moment of slumber when the dead stillness awakened to wild staccato yelps and mournful cries; a cold, keen, invigorating dawn; and then a day of thrills, not the least of which was a horseback ride out across the sandy, green-dotted plain with an Indian boy—these somehow augmented the process of change in Marian's heart, and clarified her mind, and established the strange fact of love for the desert. It seemed like the evolution of long time. Out of these hours grew realization of the unlimited possibilities of life and joy and labor. Never before had she divined the meaning of the words: "The world is so full of a number of things."

That evening, in another and more important council with Mrs. Withers, the matter of Marian's work was discussed. They both agreed that a beginning should be made at Mesa, in whatever connection might be available at the Indian school. Marian repeated the missionary Friel's talk to her. And Mrs. Withers's failure to express surprise or disgust, or, in fact, to say anything, was illuminating, and further increased Marian's desire to learn the inside of what was going on at Mesa. It was decided that in case Marian's overtures there were futile she could come back to Kaidab and go about her work among the Indians on her own resources. Nophaie's possible wishes and suggestions were taken into consideration. Neither Mrs. Withers nor Marian, however, anticipated anything but approval from him. What he might have to tell Marian could only inspire her or drive her to greater effort. As for the language of the Indians, Marian decided she would be quick to learn enough of that to get along with the Indians, and proficiency would come with time.

Next morning Marian arose at five o'clock. Did the cold desert air have anything to do with her exhilaration? How strange the long, black, horizon line with its sharp silhouettes against the pure pale golden flare of sky! Marian's heart swelled and beat high. What sweetness life held! She was grateful for this new significance. The water had a touch of ice and made her fingers tingle. It was with real pleasure that she donned her rough, warm, outdoor garb, blouse of flannel, riding trousers and boots. She had coat and sweater and heavy gloves to go with them. But somehow the hat she had fetched did not now seem to suit the exigency of the case. It was too jaunty, too small, too much of the gulf style. Still she would have to wear it, for she had nothing else. Other necessities, much too many, she feared, she packed in a small duffle bag.

When she got outdoors the sun had risen and appeared to be losing its brightness. A gray haze of cloud overspread the sky. The wind was cold, gusty, and whipped at Marian's hair. Indians were riding into the post, and already the work of the day was under way. Withers, bare-headed and coatless as usual, was directing the packing of the mules. Manifestly, he did not wholly approve of the way the men were roping on the huge canvas rolls, for he jerked a loop loose and called out derisively: "That's no diamond hitch." And he proceeded to do it in a style that suited him. Marian could not follow the intricate looping, but she certainly saw Withers and his man stand on opposite sides of the mule, and place a foot on him while they both leaned back and pulled with all their might. No wonder the poor mule heaved and laid back his ears and looked round as if in protest. Marian thought it was strange the animal did not burst. Presently Withers espied her. Then he halted in his task.

"Say, Johnny, will you run in the house and ask for Miss Warner," he said, quite seriously.

Marian was nonplussed and then quite confused. Could it be possible Mr. Withers did not recognize her? Indeed, it was a fact that the dignity of her twenty-three years and something of her stature seemed to vanish when she put on masculine garb.

"But—Mr. Withers. I—I am Miss Warner," she said, almost involuntarily. She did not quite trust him.

A broad smile spread over his face and a twinkle shone in his eye.

"Shore I thought you were a boy," he said. "Was wondering where *such* a boy might come from. You shore look good medicine to me."

His frank admiration was pleasing to Marian. She imagined she would have much preferred to present herself before Nophaie in distinctly feminine apparel, such as she had worn when he first saw her. But it would have been out of place here, and she had a moment of happiness in the thought that perhaps Nophaie too would find her attractive in this riding suit.

"Reckon we're going to have some wind today," said Withers, as he scanned the eastern horizon. "Couldn't you put off going till tomorrow?"

"Oh, no, I couldn't," cried Marian, aghast. "Mr. Withers, you don't really mean we oughtn't go?"

"Yes, I do, but if you feel that way we're shore

going," he replied decidedly. "You may as well get used to blowing sand now as later. Have you got glasses?"

"Yes, I have my auto glasses."

"That's good. But you'll have to find another hat."

"Oh, I was afraid of this—the looks of it, I mean. What's wrong with it?"

"Shore its looks are great. But it's no good. You want a sombrero with a wide brim. It protects your face from sun and rain. You're going to get sunburned, Miss."

"That won't bother me, Mr. Withers," replied Marian. "My skin looks very delicate, but really, it's tough. I burn red, then brown."

"Well, we shall see. If you haven't a sombrero I'll dig up one for you."

Marian never experienced such an endless hour as the ensuing one before Withers was ready to start. Breakfast for her seemed a superfluous thing. Yet she was hungry. All the time she was aware of Mrs. Withers's eloquent and penetrating glances, and the subtle little smile of understanding and sympathy. This woman who loved Indians understood her, and was living with her these thrilling, calling moments of young life. Yet a haunting sadness, too, seemed to hover, like a shadow in those magnetic eyes. Withers was gay, and given to raillery, directed at Marian's boyish looks. But at last breakfast was over, and the interval of wait following.

"Marian, you're in for a hard but glorious trip. No words of mine can tell you. Nophaie's country is beyond words to describe. Remember, study of this desert will reward you. . . . Be careful on high trails. Good-bye."

Two Indians drove the pack mules ahead of Marian. Withers had instructed her to mount and ride after them. He would presently follow. To her disappointment she had been given a horse instead of one of the shaggy Indian mustangs—a short, stocky horse not at all spirited and quite ugly. But when she had gotten

astride of him, ready to try to adapt herself to saddle
and motion, she found to her amazement that she did
not seem to need to do anything. The horse started off.
He moved quite briskly. But it was not a trotting gait.
She had ridden at a trot yesterday, and assuredly soon
tired of it. This gait was new to her, and she had
imagined she knew something about horses. She felt as
if she were riding in a rocking chair that moved on a
level, if such a thing were possible. The motion delighted her.

One of the Indians was old, judging from his gray
hair and sloping shoulders. He wore a red bandana
round his head; a thin, cotton blanket, gaudily colored
like calico, covered his shoulders, and his long legs
dangled below his stirrups. The other Indian was a boy
of sixteen years, perhaps, and sight of him was pleasing
to Marian. His ebony hair waved in the wind; his darkly
brown face was round and comely; he had eyes as black
as his hair, and these together with the smiling, parted
lips showing white, even teeth, made of him a handsome youth.

To see everything was Marian's resolve. Yet just the
sight of these colorfully clad Indians and the bobbing
pack mules, made her forget to look anywhere else.
She felt the cold puff of wind, she smelled the dust, she
rode easily without any strain whatever. Then the
mustangs and mules ahead suddenly went out of sight.
The trail had led down over a steep bank. Presently
Marian reached it. She was amazed to see a deep red
gash in the earth, with crumbling walls, and a muddy,
noisy stream. Mules and mustangs were edging foot by
foot down a declivity right at the edge of the water. The
Indians rode fast into the stream, making mind and
matter fly. They yelled at the mules. Marian felt her
skin begin to prickle and her heart to beat unwontedly.
This horse of hers manifestly had no more regard for
perpendicular places than for levels. He went right
down! Marian had no easy time holding on. And
though not looking directly at the mules she seemed

aware of the sudden shortening of their legs. Also she heard a voice behind her.

"That's quicksand," called Withers from above. "Safe, but you need to hurry Buckskin."

Marian had no time even to make up her mind. Buckskin filed off the bank and floundered into the quicksand. Marian had her first fright. She felt one of his legs go in deep, then another, and another. But he kept moving, quite lively. He did not let two hooves sink at once. And once well started he crossed that muddy stream at a sharp gait, and climbed a sandy, steep trail to the top of the bank. There Marian got her foot back in the stirrup and some semblance of her composure before Withers reached her side.

"How do you like Buckskin?" he queried. Not a word about that awful place!

"I—I guess I like him a lot," she replied.

"Shore thought you would. He's a pacer. You'll ride him where you'd fall off another horse. Just let him go. He knows the trail and he'll keep up. Afraid we're in for some squalls of wind."

Withers rode ahead to the pack mules and quickened their pace. The Indians jogged on in the lead. And Marian appeared to be left to her horse and the trail and the encompassing scenery. Ahead bare hills of yellow stone loomed up high toward the overcast sky. Behind, the desert across the wash yawned wide, with level brown floor leading away to the trading post, and then swelling to bolder heave, swept away to meet the irregular mesa wall, black against the sky.

"This—this is just not happening to me," murmured Marian to herself. She would not have changed places with anyone in the world. She was free to let herself feel.

The trail led into a defile through the hills of rock. Slanting surfaces rose on both sides of her, and gradually lifted to imposing heights. In pockets and niches grew stunted cedar trees, with roots growing out of the solid rock. The wind did not strike her here, a fact she found relieving. Buckskin held to a pace that kept him within sight of the other horses ahead. On rocky places of the trail he appeared as surefooted as in the sand. Marian began to appreciate why Withers had chosen him for her. Slowly the slopes closed in, grew higher, and the trail led uphill. Marian could not see far. She now felt comfortably warm. Perhaps half an hour of a gradual climb brought Marian out on top of a ridge from which she soon saw into the distance. How splendid a scene greeted her! Withers had waited for her, evidently anticipating her delight.

"Thought you'd like this ten-mile strip," he said. "The big black rock standing out of the plain is called the Captain. And the Indians call that sharp monument you see Slim Rock That Stands High. It's twice as high as your Washington soldier monument."

Long and green and broad appeared the level hollow of desert that led to these upstanding figures, lovely and sentinel—like in the distance. Ten miles! It did not seem a third of that. Yet Marian, riding on and on, and always watching these statues of rock, soon discovered how deceiving was the distance. For a whole hour the desert did not change shape or size or color. In another hour Marian rode between them, to gaze up in awe, to marvel at the black granite grandeur of the Captain and the red sandstone splendor of Slim Rock That Stands High. And these were outposts to the gateway of desert land, beyond Marian's comprehension. She could only look and look, and ask Withers questions, and ride on and on, slowly to grow, hour after hour, into realization of the deceit of distance, and marvel of color, and immensity of the uplands, and the weird, fantastic and sublime nobility of sculptured shafts of stone.

Cold wind and overshadowing clouds, and frequent gusts of flying dust, and brief squalls of pelting sleet, passed by over Marian with no more effect than if they had never been. Something great was entering her soul. Was this the home of Indians? What did white people realize of the nature and wildness and loneliness that

had created these children of the desert? What must
dwell in the minds of a race living in this land of
enchantment?

Then, toward mid-afternoon, what Withers had
feared and predicted came to pass. "Sandstorm," he
said. "But not bad. It won't last long. Get on your
glasses, and cover your mouth and nose with your
scarf."

A pall of yellow swooped down out of the west. Dark
and weird, magenta in hue, the sun shone through this
wall of dust. The wonderful landmarks ahead were
blotted out. The sweep of this desert storm seemed
fierce and swift, swallowing up the monuments and the
plains, and moving down upon Marian with a majestic
and inevitable precision. Then it enveloped her.

Marian imagined she grew suddenly blind. And she
knew she began to choke and suffocate. She had to
breathe through the scarf, which seemed a thick band,
and permitted no air to pass. There was not enough air.
Her lungs lifted and heaved. The smell of dust seemed
as stifling as the substance of it. She felt the fine, thin,
stinging particles on face and neck. And when that
heavy front of the storm passed by Marian emerged
just in time to escape acute distress.

Riding was disagreeable still, but gradually the gusts
of whirling dust lessened, until the storm blew away
toward the eastward, enveloping the uplands there as it
had in the west. The sun came out, most pleasantly
warming Marian's cold hands and face, and lighting the
desert. Soon there came the best hour of the day, close
to sunset, warmer and without wind.

Again Withers waited for her.

"We're getting somewhere. I didn't tell you before.
This is the sage flat where Nophaie used to shepherd his
sheep. Here he was stolen. . . . Yonder under that red
mesa is the place where the thieves drove his flock.
We'll camp near it. Way over here—that great break
into the Valley of Gods. Nophaie was born there."

Withers rode on. Marian stared after him and then

down at the gray sage. She reined in her horse. Here!
Nophaie, the little Indian boy, lonely shepherd, here
stolen! A wave of emotions swelled Marian's breast.
Tears dimmed her eyes, so that the gray soft color
beneath her grew blurred and misty. She wiped her
eyes. There appeared to be no mark of stone within the
circle of her vision. A wide, gray-green, gently rolling
plain of sage led everywhere toward the upstanding
rocks, the closest of which was the red mesa Withers
had signified. Marian dismounted, and gathering a lot
of the fragrant sage she placed it in the pocket of her
blouse, and meant to treasure it always. Then with a
hand on her horse she gazed away across the plain
toward the uplands where Nophaie had been born. It
meant much to her, to trod on the earth that had
known Nophaie's boyhood feet, to see the wild rock
towers that had shadowed his birthplace. Magnificent
monuments, pillars and columns and shafts, all reflecting the gold and red of the sunset, far away and
infinitely lovely, speared the horizon line and the white
clouds. Valley of Gods!

Marian mounted and did not look back. Her heart
was full. To the fore stretched the trail, winding
through the sage. It led her under the shadow of the
ponderous red mesa, a massive butte with columns like
an organ, standing out alone in the desert, far from the
main wall of the uplands. Upon a grassy bench Withers
had made camp. Already a fire was burning. The horses
were rolling. The Indians were unpacking the mules.

"Get down and come in," said Withers cheerily.
"Find a seat and rest yourself. We'll soon have supper."

Then it appeared Marian became conscious of aching
bones and tired muscles. She was glad to rest. All that
pertained to this trip was of extreme interest to her, but
just now seemed subservient to the personal haunting
thoughts in connection with Nophaie. She forced herself to watch Withers at his camp tasks. He did not
appear to be in a hurry, yet results multiplied magical-

ly, and all in a few minutes, apparently, there was
supper steaming fragrantly, and a little tent stretched
over a roll of blankets for her bed. Camping out was
not entirely new to Marian. She had sat round campfires in Maine and the Adirondacks. But this was
different, just as the Dutch oven was a strange and
fascinating cooking utensil in her sight. It was a black
iron pot with a lid. Withers had thrown the lid into the
fire. The pot sat upon a bed of red coals, raked to one
side. Withers deposited the handmade biscuits in the
oven, lifted the lid out of the fire with a stick and set it
on the pot. Then he piled red-hot ashes over the lid;
and apparently forgot this part of the task. Marian was
curious to see what happened.

"Come and get it," presently spoke up Withers, in
his hearty voice.

"Get what?" queried Marian.

"That speech is the western call to eat."

"Oh. . . . And what's to become of the biscuits in
that black pot?"

"Young lady, after you eat some of my biscuits you
will never be happy again," replied the trader, laughing, and forthwith proceeded to knock the lid off the
oven. Marian could scarcely believe her eyes. Next
moment she was sitting cross-legged before a strip of
canvas upon which Withers spread the repast. The odor
that assailed her suddenly awakened a ravishing hunger. And Marian began her first meal out on the desert,
with an appreciation and relish never before experienced in her life. Withers served her, then the Indians,
who stood by with eager eyes, and then himself.
Marian's acute senses fixed the reality of that hour—the
picturesque Indians, the western trader, forceful and
wholesome and kindly, the fragrance of bacon and
coffee and hot biscuits, the penetrating cold wind that
swept in and blew the pungent smoke in her face, the
pleasant heat of the fire on her back, and outside of that
camp circle the vague sage plain environed by looming
walls.

"Shore there's nothing wrong with your appetite," remarked Withers in his quaint way.

"I'm ashamed of myself, Mr. Withers," replied Marian. "But my excuse is, never was I so hungry or did I taste such good things to eat. Your boast about your biscuits was not an idle one."

The trader evidently got a great deal of pleasure out of Marian's hearty appetite and her praise. Later, too, when she insisted upon doing some little share of the after-supper tasks he seemed amused and glad. Marian began to associate the simplicity of this Westerner with the bold ruggedness of force that characterized him.

Marian found she needed her heavy coat, but in lieu of that she wrapped a blanket round her, and strolled away from camp for a while. The afterglow of sunset came out on the distant walls, as if for her especial benefit. How delicate and exquisite the softness of rose and gold! They faded while she watched. Twilight seemed to last long, but at length night fell. Marian seemed alone in the desert. The place where Nophaie had been captive with his flock seemed infinitely lovely and sad. The cold wind chilled Marian, and swept by her, strangely soundless. There was absolutely no break in the silence. She felt that she could not have borne such silence for long. Great white stars fired the blue sky above the black walls. Thought and emotion and lonelir ss, such as Marian had then, would have soon driven her back to camp. But beyond these she was growing very cold, and the strange, dead darkness roused fear, and she was worn out from the long ride. So she turned toward the fire and light and the red blaze which marked camp.

As she approached, Marian had a picture etched upon her mind's eye—the bright glow of campfire, emphasizing the black windy hall of the desert, with the Indians sitting before the ruddy blaze and Withers standing with back to the heat. Rough, bold figures, singularly typical of all that pertained to western color and line, they stood out in sharp relief.

"Shore I was just going to call you," said the trader. "You mustn't stray far at night, or anytime. Reckon you'd better turn in. Tomorrow we hit that Pahute trail."

Marian crawled into the little tent that was so low it touched her head as she sat upon her bed, and making a pillow of sweater and coat she wearily unlaced her boots and slipped gratefully down under the heavy woolen blankets. She tried to think some more, to realize all that had happened, to ponder and dream over the future, but at once she was claimed by sleep.

In the morning Withers called her, and when she crawled out of the little tent it was into a wonderful darkling gray of dawn, cold and pure, stingingly sweet with its perfume of desert, with the great mesa standing clear and sharp and black against the eastern gold of sky.

"Today we climb out on top," was one of the trader's droll remarks.

An hour after starting Marian appreciated what he meant, though she was utterly at a loss to see how they could ever surmount the tremendous red wall toward which they were riding. It looked the scarred, blunt face of a mountain. The slant of broken rock that leaned against its base might be surmountable, but it did not extend far up. For the hundredth time Marian learned that what she saw at a distance was vastly different at close range.

Marks that had appeared to be scars turned out to be ledges and lines of broken cleavage and slopes of talus and masses of broken rock, through which it at last seemed barely possible to climb. The close approach to this lofty barrier was not without excitement for Marian. And when Withers led off the well-defined trail that kept to the lowlands, to take a dim rough trail which turned straight for the wall, she felt a deep thrill. This must be the Indian trail never traveled by white people.

"Here's our Pahute trail," said Withers, as he dismounted. "It heads in from cross country. I'm sorry to say you'll have to walk. Climb slow, rest often, and in bad places keep on the up side of your horse."

The Indians were climbing on foot, leading their mustangs. The mules were bobbing the packs up a zigzag trail. Withers likewise began the ascent. Marian followed, confident and eager, all the time with eyes roving everywhere. What struck her singularly was the fact that though the immense ascent appeared to be perpendicular there was really foothold upon its slope. Whenever she halted to catch her breath, which moments grew more frequent, she gazed at the Indians. They did not rest. Nor did the mules. How wonderfully that trail had been worked out, zigzagging the first long slope, then taking to ledge and crack, and then worming from side to side up a break between two craggy capes! It made Marian dizzy to look high at the rim. The Indians passed out of her sight and so did the mules, while Withers slowly got far ahead of her. Marian did not particularly like this aspect of the climb and discovered that Buckskin did not, either. She became extremely hampered and hindered by the horse climbing too fast behind her. He bumped her with his shoulder, nearly knocking her over, and he stepped upon her heels. Marian had to keep ahead of him, and on the increasingly steeper bits of trail this grew almost too much for her. Buckskin could not or would not climb slowly; and at length Marian became aware that he had to expend considerable effort to make the grade.

"Look out below. Dodge the rocks," yelled Withers, from far above her.

The zigzags of the trail had placed him directly over her, and evidently his horse had loosened stones. Marian heard them clattering down, and quickly she chose a shelving portion of wall for protection. The sliding stones passed below her, gathering momentum and more stones on the way, until the sound augmented into a rattling roar. Then it ceased.

Marian resumed the climb, with most of her confidence gone and all of her breath. People back east never saw a hill! She thought of a girl friend who used to refuse to walk on a level, let alone upgrade. And soon the sensations of warmth and breathlessness passed to those of fire and pain. A burden pressed upon her chest, and her legs felt dead. She learned that to rest long was worse almost than not to rest at all. For it grew too wonderfully good, if she halted more than a moment. So she staggered along and upward, panting laboriously, hot and wet, trying to avoid Buckskin, and to keep from looking down into the void that had become awful. The light grew brighter over her. She heard the trader's cheery call of encouragement. How endless that last step zigzag to the top!

"Fine! Shore you're there as a climber. But it's nothing to Pahute Canyon," Withers was saying.

"O-h!" panted Marian, as she dragged herself to fall upon a stone seat. She could not talk. Her breast seemed as if it were caved in. The trader's compliment fell upon most doubting and scornful ears.

"Rest a little," said Withers kindly. "And then look around. We're on the rim of Nophaie's country."

That roused Marian to a renewed interest. First she looked back at the lowlands from which she had climbed. How far below! Straight down the trail sheered, yet she had ascended it. The Valley of Gods rose prominently out of the vast stretch of desert, now visible to the eye; and the crowns of the monuments were on a level with the great wall from which Marian gazed. They belonged to the same strata of red sandstone. All that space below and between had weathered away. Worn by wind and sand and frost! This land of mystery and beauty bade fair to transform Marian. Far away these red stone gods stood up, aloof, these red stone gods, stupendous and grand. She watched them for moments, and gradually her composure and strength returned.

"Shore I'm glad to see you take to the look of this

desert," observed Withers seriously. "Most people
don't. Though of course very few ever have the luck to
get such view as this. What I mean is, all we have here
is wonderful country. Indians, horses, birds—what few
living things there really are seem absolutely not to
exist, because we seldom see them. So there's nothing
to look at but the vastness—nothing to think of. That is
why an Indian is great. He's like his surroundings."

"I don't—know what I feel—and couldn't tell—if I
did," replied Marian. "I want days and months here
. . . yet afterward—could I ever be happy again?"

"Places have more to do with happiness than people," rejoined Withers. "Well, let's be drifting. We've
only climbed the first step up this stairway."

And then Marian dreaded to look toward the west.
Yet she was impelled. Huge and beetling, wild with
fringe of green trees, another wall obstructed the sky.
It was close, and northward it broke off abruptly.
Withers was riding off through a forest of cedar trees.
Marian got on her horse, not without some sharp pains,
and followed the trader, deeming it best to keep him in
sight. The trail was dim. In that bare ground, however,
Marian believed she could have followed the fresh
tracks of the horses in the lead.

This bench of fragrant green forest soon led to the
base of a rocky rise, where Withers waited for her.

"Just let Buckskin have free rein," he said. "I'll keep
an eye on you. And say, I saw where Indian horse
tracks cut in on this trail. I'll bet our Pahute you
admired has gotten ahead of us. If so, Nophaie will be
on his way to meet us before sundown this day."

Marian tried to drive thought of such a contingency
out of her mind. It stormed her and left nothing of
sense to meet the ever-increasing requirements of this
ride. She wanted to see all, and not dream the hours
away. She yearned for this meeting with Nophaie, yet
dreaded it.

Withers held back now and accommodated his progress to Marian's. She felt relieved to have him near,

though she did not want to talk. Withers, however, had
little to say, considering time and distance. They began
a long climb up over bare yellow rock, wavy, hummocky, ridgy, with hills and holes, yet always bare
yellow rock that somehow permitted a labyrinth travel
towards the summit. Not wholly bare was it, for Marian
saw dwarfed cedars growing in niches where dust and
water had given growth to a seed. Half a mile this
strange slope ascended, at length reaching the level of
the huge abutment of stone Marian had first noted from
the rim below. She seemed now on the very summit of
the uplands. Yet this was not true. There were farther
and higher points to the westward. To the north the
view offered wide contrast with long, black ranges of
mountains rising to peaks of white.

"Look back and down," exclaimed Withers with a
ring to his voice. "I've been here only once, yet I never
forgot *that*—and never will."

From this height Marian found the spectacle to be
immense and baffling—league on league of gray-green
desert—the red ramparts on each side of the portal to
the Valley of Gods—and between these wide sentinels
the pinnacles of grandeur and mystery and light—
sacred to the Indian. She felt the uplifting of her spirit.
Could anyone be dead to this? What was nature if not
eternal? There were moments of life transcendent in
revelation to the roused mind. Nophaie had made gift
to her of this sublimity and never would she be the
same as she had been. Soon she would behold him—the
Indian she loved—through whom had come deep
thoughts and stirrings of her heart, and now the birth of
nobler understanding. Nature flung its immortal task in
her face and she learned her first lesson in humility.

Chapter 6

FROM THAT VANTAGE POINT OF EXCEEDINGLY wide range Withers led away to the west, ascending one step of the bold corner of bluff, and then traveling along at the base of a shelving wall, in the shade of which were rich green growths. Damp cold atmosphere here assailed Marian. The cause of this appeared to be banks of snow filling the hollows under the wall. A crusting of red dust covered the snow.

Marian reveled in riding the kind of trail here presented. It was soft red earth, without rocks or deep washes, and it wound along the bold corners of the wall, under the looming shade, through thick piñons and cedars, with always a changing scene out across the wild uplands. The last quarter circle round that wide-ended wall sent the creeping cold sensations over Marian, for the overhanging sections of crumbling cliff above and the abrupt opening of an abyss below, a sinister chasm a thousand feet deep, made this part of the trail a perilous one.

Then once more Marian rode out into the sunlight, with level, open desert ahead. The Indians and pack mules were in sight, going into a dark-green forest of cedars and piñons, larger and richer than those below. Mile after mile this forest rolled westward, rising to plain of purple sage. Beyond the horizon of deep color rose a black and white dome of a mountain that Marian believed she recognized as Nothsis Ahn, the first sight of which she had obtained at Red Sandy. As she rode westward this mountaintop dropped below the horizon.

Marian began to find the saddle and stirrups and motion most uncomfortable things. The easy gait of

Buckskin very likely had saved her up to this hour. But now the riding had commenced to tell upon her. Grateful indeed was she for the stretch of good country, for she had feared the trails more than growing discomfort. Indeed, she sort of gloried in her aches and pains. Despite a hot sun the air was cold. And it grew to hold such dry, sweet fragrance that Marian felt in it a kind of intoxication. By and by all the landmarks of stone dropped out of sight. There appeared to be only undulating forest of green interspersed with patches of purple. Nevertheless a gradual ascent was evident, and a gradual increase in size of trees and green of foliage and fragrance of sage.

The sun climbed high and burned hot. A warm breeze, burdened with the sweet incense of the desert, blew in Marian's face. She rode on, losing track of time. No weariness or pang could deaden her enthusiasm or interest, or that haunting and recurring surety of the growing nearness of Nophaie. There were live creatures to watch on this endless, rolling plateau— dark blue jays that uttered singular, piercing cries, and lizards that darted across the red, bare earth, and hawks that sailed low looking for prey, and rabbits that scurried away in the sage.

It was hunger that reminded Marian of the passing hours and discovered to her that she had ridden until noon. Five hours of steady riding! At four miles an hour she had in all covered twenty miles. She wondered if Buckskin was tired. He paced on, steadfast and leisurely, as if distance or time or sun were nothing to him. Marian had recourse to her sandwich and bit of chocolate, and a drink from her canteen, therein to be rendered grateful and thoughtful for such simple things. It was the need of anything that made it precious. When before in her life had a dusty, black-crusted biscuit seemed at once a pleasure and a blessing? How often had she no taste for chocolate! And as for water and its wonderful, refreshing power, she had known nothing. There must be a time then for food, for drink to mean a great deal. And if for these, why not for all things?

As Marian rode on, pondering thoughts thus evolved, all at once she looked up to see a tremendous gash in the green-forested earth ahead. Withers, on foot, was waiting for her on the brink of a chasm. Far across Marian saw the opposite rim, a red-gold, bare-faced cliff, sheering downward. She was amazed. The very earth seemed to have opened. As she rode up to Withers the chasm deepened to astonishing depths and still she could not see the bottom. The trader halted her before she got to the rim.

"Pahute Canyon," he said. "And it's bad medicine. You've got to walk fast. Because the horses can't go slow and I'll have to head them. Be sure to keep me in sight. Otherwise you might lose the trail."

Marian dismounted and handing her bridle to the trader she walked to the rim. A ghastly and naked glaring canyon yawned beneath her, tremendously wide and deep, bare of vegetation and blazing with its denuded and colored slopes.

"White people don't get to see Pahute Canyon," said Withers, as he gazed from beside her. "It's the wildest and most beautiful in the West. Reckon it'll be shore a spell before automobile tourists will drive in and out of here, eh?"

He laughed grimly, with some note of gratification in his voice. Marian felt speech difficult. She was astounded. Pictures of grand canyons could not convey any adequate conception of what was given by actual sight.

"Wonderful! Fearful!" exclaimed Marian, feeling the strange drawing power of the depths. "Oh, it seems impossible even to—to *slide* down there."

"Well, let me get down a ways with the horses before you start, so you won't roll stones on me," said the trader. "Then you'd shore better come a-sliding, if you want to see Nophaie today. We've got to rustle to make the other rim before dark."

"Do . . . do you really believe . . . he'll meet us?" queried Marian.

"I'll gamble on it. . . . Be careful you don't sprain your ankle on these loose stones."

With that Withers looped the bridle of Marian's horse over the pommel, and started him down. Buckskin sent the stones cracking. Then the trader followed leading his own horse. Marian watched them for a moment; assuredly they had to descend rapidly or lose their equilibrium. From farther down in the depths soared up the mellow voice of the Indians, evidently calling to the mules. Cracking of rocks, and sliding rattles attested to the nature of that descent far below.

Marian took one long, thrilling gaze at the opposite rim where she had been assured Nophaie might meet her. It seemed a most fitting place for this meeting so fraught with significance for her. A green-fringed, red-gold canyon rim, bold and beautiful, lofty and lonely as the crags of eagles—it was indeed an outlook for the Indian to watch and wait. When Marian let her gaze slowly wander down from that rim she was struck with the stupendous height and massive formation of the canyon wall. Five miles distant it was, yet it looked so high and sheer and immense that she could not repress a cry. If she had to climb that to see Nophaie this day! The idea seemed absurd. She did not possess wings. How beyond comprehension were these Westerners, red men and white men, who conquered the obstacles of nature!

Under the colossal wall lay a flat of yellow sand, through which a bright, winding stream, like a white thread, meandered along shining under the sun. The stark nudity of that canyon floor was relieved by several clumps of trees, richly green in foliage. It was a light green, forming these trees to be other than evergreens, and that summer had come down in those depths.

Then Marian's gaze returned to the declivity at her feet. The angle was forty-five degrees and the trail was a narrow line of loose rocks. Marian drew a deep

breath and essayed the start. But loath to take the
plunge that would permit no more gaze at length and
breadth of this wonderful canyon, she halted to satisfy
herself and make the spectacle hers forever. The declivity was almost straight down, rough, boulder strewn,
and far below apparently shelved out into a zone of
colored earths, worn into corrugations. Northward the
canyon widened into a vast amphitheater of most
exceedingly wild nature with slopes and walls and
benches and lines of strata and slides of rock, and
numberless fan-shaped facets of clay, forming a mosaic
of red, yellow, purple, gray, and violet, glaringly bare
and bright under the sun.

Pahute Canyon had all that had made the Valley of
Gods an unforgettable memory-picture, and moreover
it had the strangeness of desolation and decay and
death. Nature had her moods and here was ruthless
despoilation of the face of the earth. Marian could not
see any reason why the beautiful plateau of cedar and
piñon should have been riven by this catastrophe of
time. Yet what else could have uncovered those intense
mineral colors; which at the very least had served to
charm the Indian's eye, and furnish his paints.

Reluctantly Marian turned away from this vista of
canyon beauty. She had not taken half a dozen steps
before she forgot all about the scenery. She became
suddenly and violently aware of the treachery of loose
rocks and of the hard matter of contact with them. That
first fall hurt her considerably, especially bruising her
elbow; and it also hurt her vanity. She started anew,
more careful, and soon found herself wildly clutching at
the air, and balancing on rolling stones. This time she
saved herself. But she had a good scare. Caution would
not do on this trail. She had to step lightly and swiftly,
to be off a loose stone before it could turn with her.
There was a thrill in this descent, and she began to grow
reckless. Action liberated her spirit, and the faster she
progressed the less she felt fear. At sight of the worst
places, long slants of low rock on a bed of soft earth,

she halted long enough to select a line of rocks and then she tripped down, faster and faster, growing more surefooted with practice. Once she saw the horses and Withers far below, working out over ridged red earth. As she went down, either the trail grew easier or she did better; and despite sundry knocks and several slips she began to get fun out of it. The race for her was to keep her balance. Down and down she zigzagged, growing out of breath. The slope of boulders sheered out, affording less precipitous descent. Stones as large as houses lay everywhere. Presently Marian ran out of this boulder zone upon red earth, still steep but affording safer and easier going. When she gazed upward, to see the red rim far above, she could scarcely believe her eyes. Little steps, but many of them, made short work of distance! It was an achievement that she felt proud of as she ruefully rubbed her bruises. Then she ran on down the easy stages over soft ground, soon to find Buckskin standing, bridle down dragging in the trail. Withers waited a little way ahead. Marian mounted, then to become conscious that excitement had kept her from realizing both pain and fatigue. She rode in to meet Withers.

"You're no tenderfoot," he said gaily.

"That's all you know," retorted Marian. "My feet appear to be intact, but I assure you I have some tender *places.*"

"Did you slide some?"

"I did. . . . And I could surely give pointers to some baseball players I've seen."

"Get on and ride now. Don't be scared of the jump-off places in the trail below. Just hang on."

"Do you know, Mr. Withers, you have the most wonderful and easy solutions to these trail problems? Just hang on!"

The trader laughed and turned his horse to the descent. Marian let Buckskin have free rein. The clay slopes below presented a strange varigated appearance and seemingly stood on end. Red succeeded to yellow and yellow to violet and that to pale chocolate. The horses slid down places so steep that Marian could scarcely keep her seat in the saddle. Some places Buckskin just slid down. These always meant a deep wash to cross with a climb up the opposite side. Buckskin would not climb leisurely. He usually jumped the washes, and before Marian could establish herself properly in the saddle again he was loping up the bank. The result was mortifying to her and sometimes harmful and not wholly without panic. Withers's admonition was faithfully acted upon by Marian, though not always without frantic and violent measures. Nevertheless she had moments of thrill and pleasure, intermingled with the other sensations. It seemed she was descending into the very bowels of the earth. How deep this canyon! Though early in the afternoon the sun just tipped the western wall. Marian grew extremely tired just holding on, and was indeed glad when the last incline led down to a sandy wash, that, in turn, opened out into the canyon floor.

The stream which from above had appeared a thread of silver now proved to be a shallow and wide flow of chilly water, into which horses hurried to drink. Withers got off, lay flat and quenched his own thirst. The Indians had halted beside one of the clumps of green trees and were talking to another Indian who was on foot.

"Take a rest in the shade of these cottonwoods," suggested the trader. "You'll need all your strength climbing out. I see some Pahutes."

Not until Marian had ridden across the sandy flat almost to the cottonwoods did she observe other than the one Indian. Then she saw an Indian woman with a child sitting somewhat beyond the clump of trees. Upon dismounting Marian searched in her pockets for something to give the child, and found a piece of chocolate that had escaped her at lunch time. With this she approached the two.

A fire was smoldering on the sand. Two cooking

utensils sat nearby, each with remnants of food adhering to it. The woman was young and rather pretty, Marian thought. She wore a dark dress of some thick material, a bead necklace round her neck, and silver bracelets studded with turquoises, very crude in design. The child appeared to be a girl of almost three years, tiny of form, with little dark frightened face. The mother showed a shyness that surprised Marian. Indeed, there was something wild about these two natives of this canyon, especially in the black tangled hair of the little one.

"Here," said Marian, with a smile, proffering the chocolate. It amused her greatly to see that despite an unmistakable fright the child flashed out a brown hand and snatched the candy. Then she shrank closer to her mother, as if to hide behind her. Marian wanted to stand there and make known her friendliness, but out of kindness she turned away. Her presence was assuredly a source of fear to the child and extreme embarrassment to the mother. From the shade of the cottonwoods Marian watched them, with wondering interest and sympathy. No hogan or shack or habitation of any kind appeared to be in sight. But that this place was home for these Indians Marian had no doubt. She saw the flat ground was a corn field, and that the Pahute's man, now talking to Withers, carried a crude-handled shovel. What a stalwart Indian! He was young, and little there was about him to connect him with those dirty, slouching Indians Marian had seen at Mesa. As she looked he raised a strong, capable hand, pointing with singular grace and expressiveness, and slow-meaning movement, toward a point above and beyond the canyon. It was a beautiful gesture.

Withers came to Marian.

"The Pahute whose tracks we saw crossed here early this morning. He's shore to meet Nophaie. And he'll tell Nophaie the same he told this Indian here."

"What?" queried Marian, catching her breath.

"Benow di cleash on the Pahute trail," replied the trader, with a smile.

"That may be strange to these Indians. But it won't be to Nophaie!"

For answer Marian rose, averting her face, and went to her horse. As she reached for the bridle she saw her gloved hand tremble. Strange indeed was the hold she had on herself, but she could no longer trust it.

Once more she fell in behind Withers and the Indians. They rode up the canyon to a break in the wall, where they turned upward. The mouth of this gorge was narrow and jagged, opening back into the mountain of rock. To gaze up over the long jumble of broken cliff, far to the apex of that notch, made Marian's blood rush back to her heart.

Withers allowed her to ride for quite a long distance. A sandy bank ran under the right wall. Running water dashed over the rocks at the bottom of this gorge and cottonwood trees, with foliage bright green and fresh, shaded part of the trail. Soon the rocks began to encroach upon that sand strip. Marian saw the Indians above her on the left, toiling over the weathered slide.

At a crossing of the stream Withers bade her dismount. He filled her canteen. Marian found the water cold and fine, free of acrid taste, and very satisfying.

"You should drink often," he said, as he watched her. "You'll dry up in this desert. Well, shore you're a climb ahead. Go slow, be careful. Rest often. You can't miss the trail."

With that he started up a ledge of soft blue rock, leading Marian's horse. His own was evidently in charge of one of the Indians.

Marian gazed aloft, with something of shock and awe. She actually saw a wedge of blue sky, fitting into that red notch far above her. This gorge dug deeply back into the solid earth, and sides and floor were one bewildering jumble of rocks of every size and shape. She felt impelled to gaze upward, but the act was not

conducive to encouragement. Besides, it gave her a
crick in her neck.

The climb she began with forced husbanding of
strength and a restraint to her eagerness. Time enough,
if she ever surmounted this frightful steep, to think of
Nophaie! In spite of what Withers had said, Marian had
little faith in her hopes. Tomorrow, perhaps, she would
meet Nophaie. With eyes seeking out the tracks of the
horses and marks of the trail Marian slowly lent her
energies to the ascent. This trail must have been very
old, she thought, judging from unmistakable ruts worn
in ledges and places where avalanches and weathering
slides had not covered it. At every convenient rock to
sit or lean upon she rested. In half an hour she found
the gorge opening wide, bowl-shaped in the center,
with slopes of broken rock leading up on all sides.
Another half hour apparently made little progress
toward the distant rim, yet it brought her to solid rock.
All below now appeared the slanted floor of this gorge,
choked with the debris from the cliffs above.

The trail kept to the left side and led up toward the
face of an overhanging mountain of ledges, walls, juts,
and corners, the ensemble of which seemed as unscalable precipice. Marian had climbed an hour, just to get
started. Moreover, the character of the ascent changed.
She became fronted by a succession of rocky steps,
leading up to ledges that ran in right angles with the
trail, and long, narrow strips of rock standing out from
the slope, all bare and smooth, treacherous in slant and
too hard to catch the nails of her boots. How the horses
ever climbed these slippery places was a mystery to
Marian. But they had done so, for she saw the white
scratches made by their iron shoes on the stone.

More than once Marian heard the Indians and Withers working far above her. The clang of a hammer rang
out with keen metallic sound. She had observed a
short-handled sledge on one of the mule packs; now
she understood its use on the trail. Withers was cracking rocks to roll them, and breaking the corners of

jutting cliff to permit the mules to swing by with their packs. She welcomed these periods, for she had long rests, during which she fell into dreams.

When she ascended to the points where trail work had been necessary she had all she could do to scramble up. And her hands helped as much as her feet. An endless stairway of steps in solid rock, manifold in character, with every conceivable angle and crack and sharp point and narrow ledge. Mostly she feared the narrow ledges. For if she slipped on those it might mean the end of her. Treading these she dared not look over into the abyss, now assuming dreadful depths.

This toil took Marian not only far upward but far back into the gorge. The sky began to lighten. The ragged red rim above seemed possibly attainable. Below her shadows of purple began to gather under the deep walls. Her watch told the hour of five o'clock. Marian feared she had made too leisurely a task of it, or had rested too long. Still, these had been her orders from Withers. But the long climb all alone, the persistent exertion, the holding back of emotions, the whole time increasingly fraught with suspense had begun to weaken her. Resting long might have been advisable, but she could not do it. At every risky place she grew nervous and hurried. Once she lost her footing and fell, to slide hard against a projecting rock. That hurt her. But the fright she suffered was worse than the hurt. For an instant she shook all over and her heart seemed to contract. Suppose she had slipped on one of the narrow ledges!

"Oh! This is . . . new and . . . hard for me," she said, panting. "Mr. Withers shouldn't . . . have trusted me . . . to myself."

She realized she had been thrown afar her own resources. If she had not been equal to this climb, Withers would never have left her. That moment alone there in the gorge, calling upon all her courage and reserve force, was one Marian felt to her depths. She scorned herself, but she recognized natural fear—an emotion she had never felt before in her life. She conquered it. And resolutely, but with trembling lips she had to bite to still, she began to climb again.

Once more the character of the slope changed. The solid gleaming granite gave way to soft red sandstone, and the long reaches of ledge and short steps to wide zigzags, the corners of which turned on promontories that sheered out over the depths. Marian found the going easier here, and if she had not been worn out she would have climbed well. As it was, she dragged her weary feet, slowly, step after step, up the long slants of trail.

Six o'clock by her watch and the gold of sunset on the far points of the rim! It seemed only a short climb now, from every turn, yet she did not get there. Nevertheless, weary and almost desperate as she was, the moment came when the strange glamour of that canyon stole over her. Perhaps the sunset hour with its gold gleams high and purple shadows low could be held accountable for this, or the sublimity of the heights she had attained. Wild realm of solitude! Here must the eagles clasp the crags with crooked claws.

Slowly Marian toiled round a zigzag corner on a bare promontory. She paused, her eyes on the incredible steps she had ascended. Her breast heaved. A cold wind from above cooled her hot, uncovered brow.

Suddenly a cry startled her. Piercingly high and strange it pealed down, and the echoes from the canyon walls magnified it and clapped it from cliff to cliff, until it died weirdly far below.

With uplift of head Marian swept the rim above. An Indian stood silhouetted against the gold of sky. Slender and tall, motionless as a statue, he stood, a black figure in singular harmony with the wildness and nobility of that height.

"Nophaie!" whispered Marian, with a leap of her heart.

He waved his hands aloft, a slow gesture, significant and thrilling. Marian waved her sombrero in reply, and tried to call out, but just then her voice failed. Wheeling away with swift strides, shot through and through with a current of fire, she began the last few zigzags of that trail.

Endless that last climb, unattainable the rim! Marian had overreached herself. Dizzy, half blind, with bursting heart she went on, upward, toward Nophaie. She saw him dimly as in a dream. He was coming. How strange the light. Night already? Vaguely the rim wall, marred and rocked, grew darker.

No, she had not fainted. Not for one second had she wholly lost sense of that close, hard contact, of an arm like iron around her, of being borne upward. Then— one long moment—not clear, and again she felt the bursting throb of her heart, that pang in her breast. Her breath came and went in hurried little gasps. The dimness left her eyes. She saw the gorge, a blue abyss, yawning down into the purple depths of Pahute Canyon. But she could not see anything else, for she was unable to move. Nophaie held her close, her cheek against his breast.

"Benow di cleash!"

"No-phaie!"

There was no other greeting between them. He did not kiss her, and his close clasp slowly loosened. Marian rallied to the extent of being able to stand and she slipped away from him, still holding his hand. The Indian she had known as Lo Blandy had changed with the resignation of that white man's name. Dark as bronze his fine face had grown, lean and older, graver, with long sloping lines of pain, not wholly hidden by his smile of welcome. His eyes, black and piercing with intense light, burned into hers. Unutterable love and joy shone in them.

"No-phaie . . . you have . . . changed," she said, breathlessly.

"So have you," he replied. An indefinable difference in the tone of his voice struck Marian forcibly. It was lower, softer, with something liquid in its depth, some-

thing proving that his mother tongue had returned to
detract from the white man's.

"How have . . . I . . . changed?" murmured Marian. Her pent-up emotions had been eased, if not
expressed. The great longed-for moment had come,
strangely unlike what she had expected, yet full and
sweet. Slowly she was realizing.

"Still Benow di cleash, but woman now, more than
girl. . . . It's the same face I saw first at Cape May,
only more beautiful, Marian."

"At least you've not changed Lo Blandy's habit of
flattery."

"Do not call me that," he said, a somber look
momentarily shadowing the gladness of his eyes.

Marian hesitated. She was trying to realize him, to
find him again as she had known and loved him. But it
was not easy.

"Must we get acquainted all over?" she asked seriously.

"You must."

"Very well. I am ready."

"Then you have come to work among my people?"

"Of course," replied Marian simply. "I've come to
do what you want me to."

Love and loyalty spoke unmistakably in her voice,
and in the gaze with which she met his piercing eyes.
For an instant, then, Marian trembled in a consciousness of his gratitude, of his sudden, fierce desire to
gather her to his breast. She felt that, and saw it in the
slight leap of his frame.

"You are noble. You prove my faith. You save me
from hate of the white race," he said, sonorously, and
loosening her hands he took a long stride toward the
rim, and gazed away across the purple canyon.

Then Marian had her first real sight of him. This
appeared but a shadow of the magnificent form of the
famous Carlisle athlete Lo Blandy. Thinned out, lean
and hard he looked. He wore soiled corduroy and
velveteen and silver-buckled belt and brown moccasins.

His black hair was drawn back and bound under a red band that encircled his head. This garb, and the wonderful poise of his lofty figure against that background of wild canyon, removed him immeasurably from the man Marian had known as Lo Blandy. If there had ever been anything untrue or unreal about him, it was gone now. He satisfied some long, unknown yearning in Marian's heart. Even the suggestion of the tragic was not discordant. What was in his soul, then?

"I'm glad for what you think I am," she said, stepping to his side. "For what you say I do. . . . And I want to . . . to make you happy."

"Happy! Benow di cleash, this is the first happy moment I have ever lived—since I was a shepherd boy—Nophaie down there with the sheep. Happy, because, Indian as I am, I know you love me."

"Yes, I . . . I love you, Nophaie," she said, low, unsteadily. She wanted him to know again, at once.

Hand in hand then they gazed out across the purpling depths and the gold-rimmed walls, to the vast heave of desert beyond. The sun set while Marian watched and divined the strange exaltation of the moment. Incalculable was to be her blessings, the glory of loving, and forgetting self, the work that was to be hers, the knowledge of this lonely and beautiful land, seen through the eyes and soul of an Indian. Marian marveled now that she had ever hesitated or feared.

"Come, we must go," said Nophaie. "You are tired and hungry. Withers will make camp some miles from here."

"Withers!" echoed Marian, with a little laugh. "I had forgotten him—and camp—and that I ever was hungry."

"Do you remember how you used to hate clams and love ice cream, back in those Cape May days?" he asked.

"Yes, and I haven't changed in that respect," she replied gaily. "You do remember, don't you? Well, sir, how about Jack Bailey?"

"Your dancing lizard. I am jealous again to hear you speak his name."

"Nophaie, after you went away there was no more cause. I have been ridiculously true to you."

Marian felt too that she was wildly happy, and quite unlike herself in some wild desire to torment Nophaie and break his reserve. Always she had felt this Indian's strength, and womanlike, half resented it. She found him stronger than ever, harder to reach, in spite of the love in his eyes.

His mustang was the largest Marian had seen, a wild, shaggy animal of a tan color. When it came to getting upon her own horse again she was not above the little feminine vanity in her hope to make a graceful mount before Nophaie. But she indeed made a sorry one, for almost all her strength was gone. Then they rode side by side through a fragrant level land of piñon and sage, with the afterglow of sunset lighting the western sky. The romance of that moment seemed an enchantment of her dreams. Here was the glooming hour, and a beautiful place of the desert wilderness, and the Indian lover whom she recognized as her equal. His color and his race were no hindrances to her respect. She talked a little while of their last times together at the seashore, and then of friends of hers whom he knew, and lastly of her home, in which she no longer seemed to fit happily. Nophaie listened without comment. When, however, she broached the subject of her arrival in the West, and her reception by the Withers, she found him communicative. Withers was a good man, a trader who helped the Indians, and did not make his post a means to cheat them. Mrs. Withers was more to the Indians than any other white person had ever been.

Presently, the thickening twilight was pierced by the bright blaze of a campfire. And Marian followed the Indian down into a shallow ravine where a gleam of water reflected the blaze and the dark branches of cedar trees. Withers was busy at the supper tasks.

"Well, here you are," he called out cheerily. "Marian, you're a little white through your sunburn. Get down and come in. Did you climb up Pahute Canyon? Ha! Ha! I kept an eye on you. . . . Nophaie, turn Buckskin loose, and lend a hand here. Shore we'll soon have this lady tenderfoot comfortable and happy."

Marian thought she might be a good deal more comfortable but scarcely happier. It was about all she could do to drag herself to the seat Withers made for her. The warmth that stole over her, and languor, would have ended in sleep, but for the trader's hearty call: "Come and get it."

"I'm afraid you'll have to bring it to me," replied Marian. "If I get up I'll fall down."

Withers and Nophaie served her, and she discovered that exhaustion and physical pains did not destroy hunger, or in her case, keen enjoyment of the meal. Nophaie sat beside her, the light of the campfire playing upon his face. The other two Indians came for their supper, soft-footed and slow, and they sat down to eat.

After the meal Withers and Nophaie made short work of what tasks were left to do. The two Indians appeared to mingle with the encircling darkness. For a moment the low, strange notes of their voices came back to Marian, and then were heard no more. Withers erected the little tent under the piñon near the fire, and then drawled: "Shore I reckon that's about all." Then bidding Nophaie and Marian good night, he discreetly retired to his own bed under an adjoining piñon. The night silence settled down upon the camp, so lovely and sweet, so strangely full for Marian that she was loath to break it. She watched Nophaie. In the flickering light his face seemed impassively sad, a bronze mask molded in the mood of sorrow. From time to time he would lift his face and turn his dark gaze upon Marian. There she thrilled, and felt a warmth of gladness wave over her.

"Will you stay with us tonight?" she asked, at last.

"No. I will ride back to my hogan," he said.

"Is it far?"

"For you, yes. I will ride back to meet you in the morning."

"Is your . . . your home at Oljato?"

"No. Oljato is down in the lowland. Some of my people live there."

"People? You mean relatives?"

He replied to the negative, and went on to tell of his only living kin. And he fell to talking of himself, how he had chosen this wildest and loneliest part of the reservation because he wanted to be far away from white people. It was a custom of the tribe for the women to own the sheep, but he had acquired a small flock. He owned a few mustangs. He was the poorest Indian he knew. He did not possess even a saddle or a gun. His means of livelihood was the selling of wool and hides, and working for some of the rich Indians in that section. He had taught them how much better corn would grow in plowed land. He built dams to hold the spring freshets from the melting snows, and thus conserve water for the long period of drought. What his tribe needed most was to learn ways that were better than theirs. But they were slow to change. They had to see results and therefore he did not find a great deal of work which was remunerative.

It had never occurred to Marian that Nophaie might be poor. She remembered him as the famous athlete who had been highly salaried at Cape May. Yet she might have guessed it. The white people had taught him to earn money in some of their pursuits, which he had renounced. Poverty had always seemed a hideous condition. Marian had never known real luxury and did not want it, but as a child she had been in need of even the simple and necessary things of life. Perhaps to the Indian poverty was nothing. The piñons might be his roof and warmth, the sage-covered earth his bed, the sheep his sustenance. Marian hesitated to voice her sympathy and perplexity. She could help Nophaie. But how? Maybe he did not want more sheep, more horses, more clothes and blankets, a gun and a saddle. Marian felt that she must go slow. Nophaie's simplicity was striking. And it was easy for her to see that he had not been well fed. His lean face and his lean form were proof of that. Had she ever dined at the Bellow-Stratford Hotel with this very Indian? Incredible! Yet no more incredible than this hour there on the lovely desert, with a flickering campfire lighting Nophaie's dark face! How much stranger was real life than the fiction of dreams!

After a long silence, which Marian yearned to break but could not, Nophaie rose and touched her hair with his hand.

"Benow di cleash, your eyes are heavy," he said. "You must sleep. But I shall lie awake. I will come back with the sunrise. Good night."

"Good night, Nophaie," murmured Marian.

Would he bend to kiss her? She had treasured and remembered his kisses, few as they had been. But he moved away, silently, his tall form dark against the pale, starlit sky, and vanished from her sight.

Long Marian sat there, fighting sleep, fighting to stay awake to think of this place and Nophaie and her love, and what must be the outcome. Fatality hovered there in the night shadow. In Nophaie's look and voice, and the condition he confessed, she had read catastrophe for the Indian. Yet Marian could not be unhappy. She divined her power to give; and that Nophaie, stoic, nailed to his Indian martyrdom, would not wholly miss the blessedness and glory of love.

Marian repaired to the little tent and its bed of blankets. How good they felt! What a wonderful relief to stretch out and lie still! Sleep soon must deaden the throbbing of pulse, the aching of muscle, and burning of cheek. But would not her thoughts of Nophaie persist even in her dreams? Shadows of branches cast by the firelight moved on the walls of her tent, weird and strange. A low wind rose to moan in the piñons. The desert seemed to brood over her.

Chapter 7

Upon awakening next morning Marian realized how dearly she must pay for her horseback rides and climbs on foot. Breakfast had to be kept waiting for her, and Withers expressed both solicitation and amusement.

"I may look funny, but I don't feel funny," complained Marian, with a rueful face. "How will I ever live through this trip? Oh-h-h! those awful trails straight down and up!"

"We'll not go back by Pahute Canyon," replied Withers. "Now you eat all you can and walk round some. You'll find you feel better."

Marian was so sore and stiff that she had not the slightest faith in what he said, yet upon following his advice she found he had spoken truly. Notwithstanding this fact when she came to mount Buckskin she had an ordeal that left her smarting with pain. There was nothing to do but endure until gradually the exercise warmed her blood and eased her pain. At the end of which she began again to have interest in her surroundings.

The slow heave of piñon and cedar forest reached its highest ridge after perhaps an hour of riding. The sun was then high, and it lighted an enormous country of purple sage and clumps of piñons and yellow mounds of rock, now clear to Marian's gaze. How strong the sweet scent of sage! And seemingly the whole quarter of the west swelled and bulged into a superb mountain, rising to a dome of black timber and white snow. Away to the northward rose the dim, faint outline of a red-walled desert chaos.

The splendid spectacle, the fragrance of sage, the cold air, so untainted, the marvelous purple of the undulating desert, here no longer dominated by naked expanse of rock or forest of green—these stirred in Marian the emotion of yesterday. How wild and free! This upland appeared verdant, a beautiful surprise of the stark and naked desert. The same loneliness and solitude reigned over it, the same intense and all-pervading light of sun, the same mystery of distance, the same incomprehensible magic of nature.

Withers waited for her, and as she rode abreast of his position he pointed far down and across the purple plain.

"Nophaie is riding to meet us," he said. "Show me what good eyes you have."

Eagerly Marian strained her gaze in the direction he was pointing but she could not see anything that resembled a horse and rider.

"Oh, I can't see him," she cried.

"Farther to the left. There, in line with that clay-colored bluff under the mountain. Keep your eyes close down along the sage . . . Two moving dots, one white, one black."

"Yes! Yes! I see those dots. But how tiny! Can they be horses?"

"Shore they can. Nophaie is riding the black and driving the white. I'll bet there's a present for you. Nophaie has one fine mustang, I've been told. But he never rode it into the post."

"For me? You think so? That would be wonderful. Oh, will I be able to ride it?"

"Some of these Pahute ponies are well-broken and gentle. I don't think Nophaie would give you anything else."

Marian had use for her eyes from that moment on. She rode with gaze searching for the moving dots. Sometimes she lost them, and had difficulty in finding them again. But gradually they grew larger and larger until they assumed the form of horses, loping gracefully across the sage, lending wild and beautiful life to that lovely desert. The time came when she clearly saw Nophaie, and after that when she recognized him. Then she made the astonishing discovery that the white mustang had a long, black mane and tail, flying in the breeze. At closer view Marian thought she certainly had never seen any horse so beautiful. At sight of the Indians and the mules he halted, standing on a ridge, head up, mane flying. Then Nophaie caught up with him and drove him down into the trail, where he swerved to go round the mules. He pranced and tossed his head and whistled. His hooves rang! They were like bells on the stones. Marian now saw that he was almost pure white, of medium build, and well-set up, with black mane and tail reaching almost to the ground. These alone would have made any horse beautiful. It appeared, presently, that his wildness was only a spirit of youth and temper, for he evinced an inclination to trot along with the other horses. Nophaie's mount, however, was a really wild creature, a black, shaggy stallion, powerfully built, but ungainly, that had a halter round his nose as well as bridle.

Nophaie's greeting to Marian was in his Indian language, the meaning of which was unmistakable. His smile and handclasp would have been enough to make her happy. Then, indicating the white mustang, he said, "I've brought you one of my ponies. He's Pahute, and the gentlest and best-gaited horse I've seen out here."

"Oh, thank you, Nophaie. How beautiful he is! You are very kind indeed. . . . Gentlest, did you say? He looks as if he'd jump right over the moon."

"He wants to run, and he's thoroughbred, but you can ride him," replied Nophaie. "Would you like to try him now?"

"I'd love to, but Nophaie I—well—it's just all I can do to stay on this horse at the present moment. Perhaps tomorrow I will feel up to it. . . . How far to your camp, Nophaie?"

"I never think of distance as miles. Riding at this gait

we'll get there at noon. Suppose we lope ahead. That will rest you."

"Lope! Withers says 'just hang on' and now you say lope. Very well, I consign my poor aching bones to your machinations."

A touch and word from her were all Buckskin needed. Indeed, he seemed to be both surprised and pleased. He broke into a long lope that Marian found to her amazement a most agreeable change of gait, and altogether delightful motion. It changed everything, her sensations, the scenery, the colors and smells, the feel of the wind. Nophaie loped beside her, outside of the trail, through the sage. How sweet to Marian the cool fragrance blowing hard in her face! Her blood began to race, her nerves to tingle. Always she had loved to go fast, to be in action, to feel her own spirit and muscle in dominance of the moment. This was beyond her wildest dreams. She could ride. She really had not believed it. On and on they loped, each horse gradually warming to the work, and at last settling down to a steady, swinging gait that covered ground swiftly. Marian imagined there could be no place in the world more beautiful than this boundless sage plain, purple in color and heavy with its dry, sweet tang, lonely and wild, with the great mountain to the fore, and away across the distance the strange, calling, vast and naked desert of rock.

That ride intoxicated Marian. There were in her unplumbed depths of feeling. When at the end of three or four miles Nophaie called for her to pull Buckskin to a walk she found herself breathless, utterly reckless, and full of wild longings to race on and on, to capture this new, exquisite joy just liberated, to range the desert and forget the world.

"Oh! Splendid!" she cried. "I . . . never knew . . . what a ride . . . could be. . . . You must race—with me."

They slowed to a walk, and rode side by side. Marian awoke to the realization of a stinging happiness. Could it last? What was the cause? Herself, Nophaie, their love—these did not account wholly for that new significance of life. Then she remembered what Withers had said: places have more to do with happiness than people. What did he mean by that? She told Nophaie this remark of the trader's and asked for an explanation.

Nophaie did not reply for some moments. "People are false. Human nature is imperfect. Places are true. Nature itself is evolution—an inexorable working for perfection."

His reply made Marian thoughtful. How strange, coming from an Indian. For a moment she had forgotten that Nophaie had been almost as famous for his studious habits in college as for his athletic prowess. She must learn from him and in that learning perhaps realize the strange combination of his Indian nature developed by the white man's intellect. Could any such training be other than tragic? Marian divined what she had not knowledge to explain.

They rode on across the undulating sea of purple, for a while at a walk, talking, and then breaking again into a lope, and from that to slower progress once more. For Marian time ceased to exist or else it stood still.

The baa-baa of sheep suddenly pierced the quiet air.

"My flock," replied Nophaie, answering Marian's quick look.

"Where?" she asked eagerly.

"In the cedars there. . . . Benow di cleash, here is the home of Nophaie."

Marian's keen eyes swept the half circle of country indicated by Nophaie's slow, impressive gesture. She saw that they had ridden down miles and miles and miles of gentle slope, which ended in a vale marked by richer luxuriance and purple of the sage, by clumps of beautiful cedar trees, and by isolated red and yellow mounds of rock. Above loomed the great mountain, now close enough to dominate and protect. A bare, rock-floored stream bed meandered through the vale, with crystal water gleaming on smooth inclines and tinkling over little falls. A column of blue smoke rose from among the cedars. Marian could smell that smoke, and it brought rushing to memory of the delight she always had in burning autumn leaves. A brooding summer solitude and peace hung over this vale.

Nophaie led Marian in among the cedars. They were not numerous enough to make a forest, yet they furnished all that was needful to make this spot absolutely perfect in Marian's eyes. For her campsite Nophaie chose a very large cedar, with branches spreading over a little sliding fall and pool in the stream. The rock-floor of the stream appeared to be solid as granite and as smooth as glass. The ground under the cedar was soft and brown and fragrant. Indian paintbrush, with its vermillion hue, vied with white and purple primroses.

"Here I have thought of you many and many an hour, and dreamed, and tried to pray," said Nophaie. "We will put your tent here, and your bed here, for you must sleep in the open, unless it rains. . . . Come now, rest awhile, then you can meet Maahesenie, my relative. You will see my hogan and my sheep."

Nophaie helped her out of the saddle, a service she welcomed, for she was very near exhaustion again, and he arranged a comfortable seat for her in the shade of the old cedar with the beautiful pool of amber water at her feet.

"Cold snow water from Nothsis Ahn, my Mountain of Light," he said.

"Nophaie, fill my canteen," she replied. "Oh, how thirsty I am!"

When she had drunk deep of that pure water, so cold it had to be taken slowly, she understood another meaning of the desert.

Nophaie unsaddled the horses and turned them loose. A shaggy, gray animal came bounding to him. Marian thought it a wolf, but it was a dog.

"Here's Taddy, my shepherd, and he looks like the Taddy of my boyhood. Taddy, go to Benow di cleash."

He ordered the dog to go to Marian. She held out her hand and called: "Taddy." He advanced slowly, obediently, and without fear or distrust. But in the pale, strange eyes shone a watchful, inquisitive light. This dog was like the soft-footed canines Marian had feared at the post. But he permitted her hand to pat his fine head. Marian had been used to vicious dogs and fawning dogs and jealous dogs, all of which were as unlike Taddy as if he had really been a wolf. He was as curious about Marian as she was about him, and vastly less inclined to friendliness.

Nophaie came to look down upon Marian, with something soft and glad in his dark eyes.

"Benow di cleash, to see you here—to have you come for my sake!" he exclaimed, with emotion he had not shown before.

"Nophaie, it is as good for me as for you," replied Marian.

"That could not be," he replied, with a grave smile. "Your soul is not in danger."

"Nophaie!" she exclaimed.

But she offered no word in explanation of his subtle speech, and bidding her rest he strode away, with the dog beside him. Marian was left alone. The shade was cool, making it needful to cover herself with her coat. A drowsy buzz of bees or flies mingled with the murmuring and dreamy low song of the stream. They seemed to lull her thoughts and burden her eyelids. She fell asleep. Upon awakening it seemed to her a long time had elapsed, for she felt wonderfully rested. But she could not have slept long. Withers and the Indians had arrived with the pack outfit, and were making camp some little distance away. It was Nophaie who brought her duffel bag and roll of bedding. Withers followed carrying tent and axe.

"Shore you look comfortable," was the trader's

greeting. "Isn't this sage-cedar country great? I've never seen any part of the desert to equal this."

"A land where it is always afternoon," interposed Nophaie, with his eyes on Marian.

"Quote all the poetry you want to," she said languidly. "I refuse to be surprised by you again."

The two men erected the tent on one side of Marian, and spread the canvas roll with the blankets on the other.

"Young lady, you'll see the stars and get your nose nipped tonight," observed Withers.

"Nipped? By stars—or what?" she queried.

"By frost," he returned. Then seriously he continued, "I love this purple sage upland. I've come here often, though not by the Pahute trail. You wouldn't dream this fine open country jumps off over here, down into the most terrible broken desert. Rocks, canyons that are impossible."

"Yes, I would. I saw where," replied Marian.

"Well, I'm going to ride over here some ten miles south, round the corner of the mountain. There's an old Pahute lives there," continued Withers. "I buy a good deal from him, and he buys from me. He's rich and an old scoundrel. He salts his wool. Now only few Indians do that."

"Salts his wool? What does that mean?"

"He spreads his wool out in the sun and covers it with salt. The salt draws moisture from the air and melts into the wool, making it almost twice as heavy."

"Withers, I've persuaded Etenia not to do that anymore," spoke up Nophaie.

"You have! Well, by golly, I'm shore glad, as much for Etenia's sake as mine. I like him. He's an industrious, intelligent Indian. The blankets of his women are the best we buy. Nophaie, he's wealthy. I should think he would go shares with you in some sheep deal."

"Yes, he would," replied Nophaie, "but he wanted me to marry his daughter, and when I refused he grew very angry. Said I had an Indian body and white man's mind."

"Humph! that's pretty serious," returned Withers, soberly, and shouldering his axe he turned toward his camp.

"It is serious, Nophaie?" asked Marian.

"I'm afraid so—for me."

"Why? Because you can't . . . can't marry or because of what this Indian thinks?"

"Both. You see my position is hard. My people are proud that I have renounced the white man. But they expect me to fall at once into their ways. I tried. I have failed in many things."

Thought-provoking indeed were these words to Marian; and she began to get a glimpse of the problem before her.

"I'm rested now," she said, rising. "Take me to see your hogan and Maah—whatever you called him."

Beyond the stream some hundred or more yards, in an open space of higher ground, stood a large beehive-shaped mound of red earth with a column of blue smoke rising from the center of its round roof. At nearer view Marian saw that the earth had been plastered thickly over a framework of wood. The open door faced the east.

Nophaie spoke to her in his Indian tongue, something she sensed to be ceremonious and indicative of the sacredness of his act in bidding her enter. She stooped to go in. A smoldering fire occupied the center of this habitation called a hogan, and the smoke from it seemed to float round and round to drift at last up through the hole in the roof. This roof was a marvel of ingenuity and skill, being constructed of heavy trunks of cedars planted in the ground, and affording support for the many heavy branches that together formed a concave network to hold the covering of red earth. How substantial and strong this Indian edifice! Something about it impressed Marian with a significance of its long adoption by the tribe.

A few iron and stone utensils lay scattered beside the fire. A haunch of meat hung from one of the posts, and beside it on the ground lay a sack of flour, with some boxes and tins that evidently contained food supplies. Besides these, there were two beds in the hogan, one on each side of the fire, close to the wall.

"Which bed is yours?" asked Marian, unable to restrain her curiosity.

"Here," said Nophaie.

His action designated an Indian blanket and a sheepskin with the woolly side uppermost. Obviously, the former was Nophaie's coverlet, and the latter his mattress. Marian thought of the hard bed of the Spartans. So Nophaie slept there! She forced her gaze to search farther, to the end that she saw only an old coat, a leather pouch studded with silver buttons, and a worn hunting knife. These then were Nophaie's possessions and this was his home. Suddenly Marian's eyes blurred and smarted. Was that all because of the acrid wood smoke and the heavy, pungent odor? Whatever the causes Marian realized she could not have remained there for five minutes longer. Nor could she utter one word as to her feelings or impressions.

"I sleep out under the cedars a good deal, but Maahesenie doesn't like that," said Nophaie.

"Let me see your sheep," rejoined Marian. She did not speak, nor did Nophaie, while they were threading a way through the tall sagebrush, the long, light green, purple-tinged sprigs of which reached to her shoulder. She stripped a tiny branch and crushing the soft leaves she pressed them to her lips and nostrils. How bitter the taste, how like a drug the intoxicating sweetness of fragrance! She saw purple berries on the cedar trees, and a golden, dustlike powder upon the foliage. Then she heard the baa of sheep and bleat of lambs.

Soon Marian emerged from the zone of cedars into the open sage, and here her sight was charmed by a flock of sheep and goats, and many lambs. If Nophaie had only a small flock, Marian wondered what a large one would be. No less than several hundred was her calculation of their number. Most of them were white, and many were black, and some were brown. The lambs all appeared as fleecy white as wool could be. They played round Marian's feet and had no fear of her. The baaing and bleating were incessant and somehow struck pleasantly upon Marian's ear.

Then she observed another Indian, tall and gaunt, with stoop of shoulders and iron-gray hair. He folded a thin blanket round him as he walked toward her. What a record of life was his face! Years and storms and the desert!

"Maahesenie—Benow di cleash," said Nophaie.

"How do?" returned the Indian, extending a brown hand to Marian.

She shook hands with him and greeted him, not however without hesitation over the pronunciation of his name.

"White girl come far?" he asked, with slow, curving arm extended toward the east. His English was intelligible.

"Yes, very far," replied Marian.

"Saddle heap hard seat—huh?" he queried, with a twinkle in his eyes.

Marian nodded and laughed her affirmation. What sharp sight these Indians had! From a distance this Maahesenie had observed in her walk the evident telltale truth of how the saddle had punished her. Moreover, besides keen eyes they also had a keen sense of humor. This old Indian was laughing at her. But when he addressed Nophaie it was with dignity and gravity, and his gestures made known to Marian the fact that he was talking about her. When he ended Nophaie led her back toward the camp.

"What did he say about me?" she asked, very curious.

"I didn't get it all. You see my mother tongue comes back slowly to me. But I got enough to make you vain.

He said, 'Eyes of the sky and hair of the sun.' Then something about your skin being like a sage lily."

"Well, bless him!" exclaimed Marian, in delighted surprise. "And what's a sage lily?"

"Most beautiful of desert flowers. They grow wild in the deep canyons."

Marian slept again for a couple of hours and awoke to feel somewhat eased of pangs and weariness. The afternoon was far spent, waning in a solemn glory of light and peace. Marian listened to the hum of bees and the murmur of water. Gentle stream and colorful sage! The cruelty of nature and life did not seem to abide in them, yet a few moments of sharp-eyed scrutiny made known to her tiny denizens of both, seeking to destroy. Mystery of mysteries that living creatures must prey upon other living creatures! Where was God in such nature? If species preyed upon species why not man upon man?

"I declare," murmured Marian, suddenly aghast at her thoughts, "this desert is giving me the queerest ideas."

Withers called her to an early supper. Nophaie sat with her, and the other Indians sat opposite, all of whom did justice to the extraordinary meal served by the trader. "Well," he said, "my plan is to eat all the grub quick at the beginning of a hard trip. That builds up strength to finish."

After supper Nophaie walked with Marian, singularly thoughtful and sad. Suddenly he pointed to a distant, cone-shaped mound of stone that appeared to have a monument on its summit.

"I want you to climb there with me—tonight or tomorrow," he said.

"Take me now," she replied. "But why there particularly?"

"I want you to see my Marching Rocks from there—and my Mountain of Light."

"Nophaie . . . you want me to climb there . . . just

because they are beautiful?" she queried, keen to divine the subtlety of his words.

"No. But because seen from that height they give one strength."

"Strength?" she echoed. "For what . . . do you need strength now?"

He seemed to shudder and shrink, a strange, faint, vibrant convulsion, not natural to him.

"To tell you my trouble."

Nophaie's somber gaze, and the pathos and solemnity of his voice further augmented Marian's fears, and prepared her for catastrophe. His trouble must become hers. How singular his desire for her to climb to this particular height so that he could unburden himself! Their silent walk through the sage, and slow climb up a hill of smooth, bare stone, gave Marian time to fortify herself against disaster to her hopes. She also anticipated some extraordinary spectacle from the summit of this hill. The slope was steep, and ascent difficult. Looked at from their camp it had not appeared nearly so high as it actually was. They climbed from the eastern side, walking in long, zigzag slants, and resting often. Near the summit there was a depression, the upper side of which terminated in point of stone that supported the monument. This pyramid of rocks stood eight or ten feet high, and crude as it was it had some semblance of symmetry and dignity. It meant something more than a landmark to passing Indians.

"Who built it?" asked Marian.

"Men of my tribe," replied Nophaie.

"What does it mean?"

"It signifies a place for prayer. Indians climb here to pray. Never unless they have something to pray for."

"Does each Indian make his own prayer?"

"No. There are many prayers, but they are those used by our forefathers."

"Have you prayed here?" asked Marian, speaking low.

"Many times," replied Nophaie.

"Are you going to pray now?"

"Yes, to my Marching Rocks and to my Mountain of Light and to the Blue Wind."

"Will you let me hear your prayers?"

"Indeed, I want you to."

With that Nophaie again took Marian by the hand and led her up the remaining few steps to the summit of this stone hill which had obstructed the view.

"Look, Benow di cleash," he said.

Marian did as she was bidden, suddenly to become transfixed and thrilling, motionless as the monument upon which she rested a reverent hand. And as she gazed Nophaie began his prayer.

> "Marching beautiful Rocks,
>   Part red and part white,
>   With light falling on you from the sky.
>   The wonderful light!
>   I give you this,
>   This is a prayer for you.
>   On this day make my foot well,
>   Make my leg well,
>   Make my body well,
>   Make my face well,
>   Make my soul well.
>   On this day let me rise from my bed,
>   Let me not have fever,
>   Let it be well before me,
>   Let all that I see be well,
>   Let me believe now all is well."

Marian listened as she gazed, and felt that forever on her memory would be limned the splendor and the strange phenomenon of the apparent life of this weird land of Marching Rocks.

Below Marian a cedared plateau, gray with grass and sage, led eastward toward bare mounds of rock, isolated and strangely set, with semblance to great prehistoric beasts. Scattered and striking they led on over the wide, green plain, round and bare and huge, to move forward, to march on, to be impelled, to be endowed with might and majestic life. Marching Rocks! Van of the army of naked earth, vast riven mass of rock, rising and spreading from north to south, marching down from afar, driven by the dim slopes and immense heave of mountains! All that sublimity of desert was veiled in sunset haze.

"Benow di cleash, the sculptor who carved those Marching Rocks is the wind," said Nophaie. "Listen to our prayer."

> "Blue wind, beautiful chieftess,
>   Send out a rainbow by which let me walk,
>   Blue clouds, blue clouds,
>   With your shoes let me walk,
>   Blue clouds, with your leggings make me walk,
>   Blue clouds, with your shirt let me walk,
>   Blue clouds, with your hat let me walk,
>   Blue clouds, make it dark behind me,
>   Blue Wind, make it light before me,
>   Earth Woman let it rain much for me,
>   By which let the green corn ripen.
>   Make all peaceful with me."

Then Nophaie bade Marian sit down and lean against him beside the monument.

"We will watch the sun set over the desert," he added. "Sunset—the fulfillment, the glory, the end of the Indian's day! White people do not rise to see the breaking of the morning light. And they do not care to watch the declining sun. But for Indians these hours are rituals."

To the west, where Nophaie directed Marian's rapt gaze, the scale grew grand, and a supreme manifestation of nature's sculpturing. The purple shadows now began to define the canyons, and lift the wavy knolls of red rock. From out of that thick sunset haze of the direct west swept majestic escarpments, level and dark,

to overshadow the world of carved and graven Marching Rocks. Farther around, beyond the blazing center
of the west, began the black jagged uplift of Nophaie's
Mountain of Light. It sheered up to a round white-
patched, black-fringed dome. The pure snow and lofty
pine held dominion there.

Every moment the spectacle changed, and out over
the wasteland there was chaos of light and color. The
purple shadows turned to black; the reds and yellows
grew less intense. Vast rays of light slanted down from
the broken sunset clouds. Marian's emotion increased
with the growing transformations. Before her eyes
stretched a belt of naked earth, two hundred miles long
and one hundred miles wide, curving from east to west.
No human sight was adequate to grasp its tremendous-
ness and its meaning. Eye of eagle or condor, most
delicate and powerful of all organs of vision, must be
limited here. There was no movement of anything—
only the illusion of the Marching Rocks—no sound,
nothing but the stark, upflung nakedness of the earth,
beyond comprehension to the human mind, exalting to
the soul. A world of naked rock, and cedar, and sage
for the Indian! Marian cried out in her heart in pity for
the Indians that eventually must be driven from this
world, so still, so solemn, so awful, yet a refuge and an
abode of life.

The dark walls of granite grew dusky red; the
Marching Rocks moved like mammoths, majestic evidences of the ages. Distance was made clear by the
lifting of haze, the canyoned shadows, the last piercing
light of the sun. It seemed that a million facets of
chiseled rock caught this dying glow of sunset and
reflected it, throwing the marvel of light upon the
clouds. The shadows lengthened and widened and
deepened. Marian's sense of color and proportion grew
magnified or dwarfed, she could not tell which. Thousands of rock ridges, facing the sun, marched down to
meet it.

The air grew chill. Farthest away across the riven

rock a grayness blotted out the horizon. The splendid landmarks seemed to be retrenching themselves, receding, dying with the sunset. Every moment seemed more solemn than that preceding. It was a place not meant for white man. Yet how beautiful! The great light was fading. Over most of the rocky area the strange, gray shadow encroached while Marian gazed; only to the eastward did the bright gleam of sunlight face upon the highest faces of the Marching Rocks. Again the rays shot slanting from out the rifts in the clouds, growing strong and glorious, strangely lighting for the moment the horizon peaks of white. Then all that far east, as had the north, paled and darkened. It was a blight. It spread towards the sunset. Low down ruddy gleams suddenly caught the van of the Marching Rocks. But that beauty of radiance was ephemeral. It was going— going—gone. The ball of half-clouded fire tipped the slope of Nothsis Ahn, and the chasms became veiled in a haze of rose. Nophaie's mountain grew dark and clear against the steel blue sky. All the upland in its shadow seemed bathed in ethereal light. Strange change! How cold! The sun was sinking. The desert darkened. Only a disc of the sun remained, still overpowering, still master of the day. It was sinking farther. The day was nearly done. How rosy the tips of the stone hill! Then the radiant disc of white fire vanished. The sun had set. A golden glow on cloud and sky marked the place where the sun had gone down. The earth of naked stone seemed to gather power, to rise, to come out clear and cold, to reach for the encroaching twilight.

Marian turned to Nophaie and said, "I have seen. I feel all you feel. . . . Now tell me your trouble."

Nophaie rose, lifting her with him, and towered over her, his face as she had never seen it. Mystery and grief, age and strength came out in the bronzed lineaments; and his eyes were terrible. Marian imagined she saw the soul of the Indian.

"*I am an infidel!*" he said hoarsely.

The shock of intense surprise sustained by Marian precluded her utterance.

"I did not know this when I came back to the reservation," Nophaie went on, as if passion-driven. "I tried to return to the religion of my people. I prayed—trying to believe. But I cannot. . . . *I am an infidel!* I cannot believe in the Indian's God—I will not believe in the white man's God."

"Oh, Nophaie!" gasped Marian, suddenly released from stunning surprise to consternation and horror. "Your faith . . . will come back."

"Never. My white teaching killed it. That is the curse of the missionaries. The Indian's religion is best for him. The white preacher kills the Indian's simple faith in his own God—makes him an infidel—then tries to make him a Christian. It cannot be done. There is not one real Christian Indian on the reservation."

"Why . . . that is terrible," replied Marian. "But you—Nophaie—I am distressed. Oh, do you mean you have no belief in a future life?"

"An infidel has no faith."

"But yours will come back. It must. I will help you. Surely your religion is as good as mine. No one realizes more than I the necessity of faith in God and immortality. What good could life be without them? Nophaie, we must strive and pray for yours."

"Marian, cannot you understand?" asked Nophaie, in pathetic earnestness. "The knowledge forced upon me by white people—my intelligence—makes it impossible for me to believe in the Indian's religion."

"Impossible!" echoed Marian.

A silent and impressive spreading of his hands, gesture of impotence and helplessness, fixed in Marian's mind the immutability of Nophaie's spiritual catastrophe. The certainty of it pierced her heart. Sorrow for him succeeded to resentment and anger at the white people who had done his soul this injury. Nophaie's soul had as much right to its inheritance of

ideals and faiths as any white man's. Why should the
white preachers of the eastern college take away an
Indian child's faith in his God? Why should the white
missionaries on the reservation undermine the Indian
youth's religion? Marian supposed that in their fanatical egotism they imagined they were doing better for
the Indians. But were they? Nophaie's case seemed
indisputable truth that they were doing incalculable
wrong. Marian could not bring herself to the point of
wanting Nophaie to accept the white man's religion. If
she had been in his place she would not do it. But how
to help him!

"Let us go down before night falls," said Nophaie,
taking her hand.

With careful little steps Marian essayed the descent
of the stone hill, which in the gathering darkness was
more difficult. An infinite melancholy pervaded the
gray, silent desert. A campfire blazed out of the
shadow of the cedars. And by the time a level had been
reached twilight had enfolded the sage.

"Nophaie, listen to my plan for work among your
people," said Marian. And forthwith she briefly told
him the result of her interviews with Mrs. Withers.
Nophaie not only expressed approval but also gratitude; and was particularly desirous of her finding a
place at Mesa, in the school.

"You can do so much good," he said. "The young
Indian girls will love you. And as soon as you can speak
their language you will influence them against evil.
They are primitive children. There's one Indian girl you
must look after. She is Gekin Yashi—the Little Beauty.
She is fourteen years old and large for her age. I know
her father, Do etin—the Gentleman. He is a fine old
Indian. He approves of the school but he hates the
missionaries. Morgan, the missionary in control at
Mesa, is after Gekin Yashi. Her father told me, and
then I got her to tell me. . . . Marian, this exemplifies
what is so damnable and loathsome about these missionaries. Not *all* of them, mind you, but *most* of them,

the shams, the fakes, and especially this missionary, Morgan."

"Nophaie, you don't mean to tell me . . . to expect me to believe these missionaries . . . some of them even . . ." Marian broke off in heat and shame, unable to complete her query.

"Yes, I do mean it," he replied, with fierce, dark passion. "And it calls for the spilling of blood."

"Good God!" burst out Marian, in unutterable disgust. "I should say it does. . . . Nophaie, I begin to understand you."

"That's good. Now tell me, you will stay here a little? So we can ride and climb and talk?"

"Yes, I'll stay two days. Withers cannot spare more. . . . Ride? I'll race you through the sage. . . . Then I'll go back to Kaidab, then to Mesa, where I'll begin my work, for you, Nophaie. You will come to Mesa?"

"Yes, I'll ride there every week. But we must meet in secret, somewhere out in the desert. The agent Blucher has only seen me twice, but he took instant dislike to me as soon as he learned I was an educated Indian. He is bad medicine, Marian. Blucher and Morgan run the reservation and the school, not for government or Indians, but for themselves. You will see through them."

"Then you'll come every week," rejoined Marian gladly. "Oh, that will be fine. And you think I must meet you secretly? I am not ashamed, Nophaie. I am proud of . . . of my friendship with you."

"Blucher and Morgan must not know you meet me," declared Nophaie. "You could not stay there after they found out. You'll soon understand why. I'll ride to Kaidab in ten days and find out from Mrs. Withers what you've done at Mesa. Then I'll write you and tell you when I'll come."

"And how and where to meet you? I'll have my white pony, you know. I can ride out on the desert."

"Yes," he said simply.

With this most important matter understood Marian

once more felt a warmth and stirring along her veins, a regurgitating of that happiness which had been suddenly crushed by Nophaie's disclosure. She would get to see him often! That was the shibboleth of her joy, the inspiration to her endeavor. Would not her love for him and faith in him somehow gladden the dark days of his martyrdom? For she considered his life no less.

The desert night settled down, cool and still, with a blackness of shadow over sage and cedar, and the velvet sky effulgent with its myriads of white stars. Marian walked beside Nophaie, hand in hand, through the sage toward the flicker of campfire. A coyote wailed its cry out of the silence. Marian felt more than the fullness of her heart. The sage, the rocks, the murmuring stream, the desert night seemed invested with a spiritual power, a breathing soul.

Chapter 8

THAT YEAR THE SUMMER RAINS CAME LATE, just in time to save the upland country from severe drought. Nophaie's people all attributed the coming of the black thunderstorms and the down-dropping veils of moisture and the rainbows curving over the desert to the efficacy of their dancing prayers. But Nophaie could not believe this.

Up under the brow of Nothsis Ahn these rains were cold even in August. Sometimes sleet fell, pattering on the sage, whitening the flat rocks and patches of red earth, and crusting the woolly backs of the sheep. Maahesenie, who tended the flock during Nophaie's frequent absences, was exposed to these cold rains. Indian as he was he did not seek shelter. The rain was good, even if it was cold. And when Nophaie returned from Kaidab he found his only relative seriously ill of a malady that had grown with the years.

Tending the flock in the rain and sleeping in wet clothes had brought back Maahesenie's rheumatism in more severe form. Nophaie feared that he had gotten home too late. Maahesenie, relieved of his responsibility, went to his bed a very sick man. At that altitude the nights were cold, and even in daylight Maahesenie's bed in the hogan was far from as warm as it should have been. Nophaie made a warm and comfortable bed of sheepskins and blankets, but his sick relative would not stay in it. The bed he had always been used to was what he wanted. Nophaie had brought him new blankets from Kaidab, and the first Pahute who passed got these blankets in a trade for some tobacco. Nophaie undertook to instruct his sick and contrary relative.

"Maahesenie, you have what white medicine men call rheumatism. It is a disease of the blood, affecting joints and muscles, and is caused by exposure to cold and wet. You must keep very warm and dry."

Maahesenie looked at Nophaie as at a younger man who spoke idly of things he did not understand.

"Maahesenie is victim of the Evil Spirit," replied the Indian. "Maahesenie thought evil thoughts. A whirlwind, traveling from right to left, which is the wrong way, struck Maahesenie when he did not know the prayer to say. And it caused his body to be twisted. Maahesenie must have medicine to straighten him. Maahesenie must smoke the medicine in a jet pipe which the medicine man carries in his medicine bag."

Therefore Nophaie had to ride forth across the uplands to fetch a medicine man of the tribe. This old Indian accompanied Nophaie, but held no communion with him. Plain indeed was the fact that he would rather have been alone in the hogan with Maahesenie to administer to him. He gave Maahesenie the jet pipe to smoke, and when that custom had been observed he took some salt from his medicine bag, and wetting this in his mouth he mixed it with the ashes from the pipe. Then he proceeded to rub this upon Maahesenie and to massage him, meanwhile chanting what Nophaie recognized as the Wind Chant. Nophaie approved of the massaging, and it reminded him of how the football trainers used to work over him. Well he knew what was good for sore muscles.

The medicine man's next treatment was to procure flat rocks from the stream outside, and to pour different-colored sands from his medicine bag upon these rocks. He was a wonderful artist. These maneuvers in sand soon took the form of symmetrical figures, over which the medicine man mumbled impressive and weird incantation. This done he brushed the sand from the rocks, and gathering his effects together he left the hogan and went on his way.

Nophaie was not amazed to see Maahesenie very

much better and able to get up. Probably if he had been a young man it would have made him well. But he was old, and used up, and no faith could wholly banish disease. Next day he again fell victim to ague and to the slow, twisting knot of his muscles. He gave up then and in somber and silent stoicism awaited the end. Nophaie divided his time between Maahesenie and the sheep.

One day, nearly a month after Maahesenie had been stricken, a Pahute rode into camp with a letter for Nophaie. The Indian had ridden from Kaidab in ten hours. Nophaie took the letter, which had been typewritten, and was without address or signature. Yet, singular at first glance as this seemed, he knew who had written it and that it was important. Rewarding the Indian courier and asking him to stay, Nophaie repaired to the solitude of his favorite cedar and spread out the letter.

I have ridden three times to our meeting place, once each week on the day set, and have been disappointed, and worried and distressed that you did not come.

Today I met Withers at the trading post and he told me Maahesenie was dying. I am very sorry, yet relieved in that I now know what has detained you. Withers said he would wait while I wrote this letter to you and take it to Kaidab and send it to you by special messenger. He is very kind and good. You may trust him in every way. So I am writing here in the trader's office, pretending the letter is for Mrs. Withers. Believe me, caution is imperative. I am already deeply involved in the secret, underhand workings of this dreadful place.

Do not send me any more letters through the mail. If you cannot come to meet me—and I'll ride out every week on the day we set—do not send letters unless you can in care of Withers. It is not safe. My mail from the East has been opened. I doubt not that my letters home have been opened.

Some of them were never received by my aunt and friends. At first I put this down to the idle curiosity and jealousy of the clerk in the post office. He has done me the honor to press his attentions upon me, which I didn't accept. But I know now that he is merely a tool of Blucher. No letter of importance sent east to government or missionary board would ever get by this agent, unless favorable to him and Morgan. I suspected this, and fortunately I have written nothing home except my own personal interests, mostly concerning people there.

Two weeks ago Blucher asked me to do office work for him several hours each day after my regular duty at the school. I was glad to oblige him, but I insisted on one afternoon for myself, which, of course, is the time I am to meet you. Blucher apparently thinks well of me. I heard him arguing with Morgan. He called me a tow-headed doll and laughed at Morgan's hint to watch me. He said I minded my own business and did not hobnob with the men or gossip with the women. Then he heard me tell Friel where to get off. You remember the annoyance this Friel has caused me. Since I have been in the office Friel has had more opportunity to approach me. He is vile. I am afraid, my friend, that I shall have to ask you to scalp him. To my mind that is exactly what he deserves, and the act should be performed just as he begins to preach to the Indians. They hate him. Never in a hundred years would they believe one word he preaches or says. How can these missionaries lie to the Indians, cheat them in money deals, steal their water and land, and expect to convert Indians to Christianity? They do *worse* than these things, as you knew and told me, and which I could not believe until I got the confidence of the Indian girls. I can talk Nopah now and understand very well.

This duty in Blucher's office has been prolific of much information for me. I see, hear and read a great deal more than my work calls for. I feel justified in this. I am out here in your interest. Blucher is German. He is deeply concerned over the war in Europe. He hates England and he hates America. I know how to serve him to my own interest. But Morgan is suspicious of everyone. He really is in control here. He boasts of having put the "steam roller" under eleven former superintendents of this reservation. How he has the power to do this I have begun to find out. When any new government employee or missionary comes here Morgan loses no time in his peculiar politics. By his lies and persuasions he influences the newcomer to his side, and if he is successful, which he usually is, he proceeds at once to lay some kind of a trap for that person. A frame-up, you know, instigated by him and carried out by his henchmen. If he fails then he at once takes violent hatred of this interloper and begins the same kind of cunning to have him or her ousted. He really has something on Blucher. That would not be difficult for an intelligent person to find. For instance the half-breed Noki Indian Sam Ween is Blucher's interpreter. Blucher pays Sam twenty dollars a month, when he pays him. at all. I asked Sam. And I saw in government papers the amount appropriated by the government for Blucher's interpreter. But Morgan has something more on Blucher than the little matter of stealing from Uncle Sam.

All of which leads to the point of this letter. Morgan's most important emissary is Miss Herron, the matron of the Indian girls. She was a former missionary. Ask Gekin Yashi or any one of the Indian girls what Miss Herron is to Morgan.

I have now the love and trust of Gekin Yashi. She is not only the little beauty her name signifies but she is sweet and good. I have talked much with her, and though very shy and afraid she tells me her troubles. Miss Herron hates her. And my interest in Gekin Yashi has incurred Miss Herron's enmity towards me.

Now the situation as regards Gekin Yashi is this. Morgan is after her. He talks religion to her, and to us teachers he speaks of Gekin Yashi's intelligence and that he could soon make a Christian of her. But Morgan's interest in Gekin Yashi is *not* to make a Christian of her.

Do etin, the father of Gekin Yashi, will not allow her to go to Morgan's house or chapel. There is no rule to enforce this, and both Morgan and Blucher are angry at Do etin. Morgan has influenced Blucher to have a rule enforced whereby Indian girls are compelled to go to Morgan's chapel to hear him preach. This rule, I understand, is about to go into effect. I fear it will cause trouble among the Indians.

But the rule will come and Morgan will have his way. Gekin Yashi is so afraid of Morgan that she actually shakes when I speak of him. The only way I can see to save Gekin Yashi is for you to steal her away from this school and hide her in one of those wild canyons until Morgan forgets her. This will save Gekin Yashi, but not the next little Indian girl who will be unfortunate enough to attract this white missionary of God. You understand, of course, that you incur risk in attempting such a plan. Risk of your life! Risk not only of jail but of your life! Mine may be a foolish plan, for it is certain that Indians in Morgan's employ could track you wherever you hide Gekin Yashi. But I could not think of any other plan.

This is a long letter, my love, and Withers is waiting. My personal messages must go until I see you, which I hope indeed will be soon.

Nophaie pondered over this letter and reread it only to become more somber and thoughtful. The plan suggested by Marian had occurred to him also, and now in the light of her revelation he decided he would risk stealing Gekin Yashi from the school. But he was tied here to the bedside of his dying relative and there appeared to be every reason to hurry to Mesa. It could not be done. Maahesenie was closer to him than Gekin Yashi.

Nophaie waited, with his burdened heart growing heavier, and while shepherding the sheep he resolved in mind plans to rescue Gekin Yashi and safely hide her. It would be easy to hide her from white men, but almost impossible from Indians. Yet he must try.

Maahesenie died one night while Nophaie slept. Although he had expected this, the actual fact was a shock. More of Nophaie's Indian nature came out in the presence of death. His people were all afraid of a dead man. And from this stiff, ghastly mask of bronze the spirit had fled. Where had it gone? Where was it now? The mystery of death was as great as the mystery of life. Were not the strange beliefs and faiths of the Indian as credible as those of the white man? But here, in this solemn, stirring moment as in all the hours past, Nophaie felt aloof from the soul of this dead Indian.

Nevertheless Nophaie paid stern and strict observance to the burial custom of the tribe. Indians of his own tribe came to view Maahesenie, but left him for Nophaie to bury. The Pahutes who rode by that day halted to express their sympathy, and then rode on. Nophaie had forced upon him the fact that the Nopahs did not care to bury their dead. They shirked it whenever possible. Their burial ceremony lasted four days and they could not eat until it was over.

Nophaie had assisted at the funeral services of several of the tribe. He knew what to do, though he could not recall most of the prayers and chants.

First he dressed Maahesenie in his best garments and moccasins and silver. Then he set about the difficult labor of digging a grave with only an axe and sharpened cedar sticks for implements. He worked all one day at this, keeping the sheep near at hand.

Next day Nophaie, according to the custom of the tribe, broke a hole in the hogan. The dead body of Maahesenie must not be taken through the door. And it must be carried in a perfectly straight line to the grave. Nophaie spent a long time over the accuracy of this line, until he believed it was as straight as an eye of an Indian could make it. Then he wrapped Maahesenie in his best blanket and carried him out and lowered him into the grave. Nophaie's next duty was to cover the dead man and fill the hole level to the sage. Maahesenie's saddle had then to be split and laid upon the grave. Likewise his kettle had to be broken and deposited there, and the other cooking utensils habitually used by him. This breaking was performed to liberate the spirits of these necessary utensils so that they could accompany Maahesenie to the Happy Hunting Ground under the earth. Following this ceremony Nophaie went out into the sage to bring in Maahesenie's horses, three of which must be sacrificed. Rigidly as Nophaie desired to conform to the Indian's rituals he had to fight himself all the way. Maahesenie's horses were not many and three of them were all Nophaie could find near at hand. They were young and beautiful and full of the joy of life. What a pity to kill them! Why kill them at all? The hardest task Nophaie had since his arrival in the Indian country was to lead these three horses up to Maahesenie's grave and there kill them. One of them even had to be bridled so that Maahesenie could easily catch him in the other world.

Sunset of that day found Nophaie's tasks ended, except to destroy or burn the hogan. He waived this last custom of the tribe, but he did not enter the hogan and never would again. He erected a brush shelter under the cedar where Marian had slept. Night found him alone, except for the shepherd dog Taddy, and the sheep. Long into the dark hours did Nophaie lie awake. He was the last of his family and he would never have a child. The burden of his life pressed hard upon him then. The great breathing spirit of nature all around him was as true to him as any spirit the Indians might have worshiped. It was there—the mysterious power—the eternal thing—the infinite. Life went on. The soul left the body. Did it perish or live again in some other state? Nophaie could not answer that as an Indian. He must answer it as an atheist. That was the curse of his tragedy, the bitter gall of this cup he must drain. For since his advent on the desert his Indian soul and white man's intelligence had merged in one beautiful thing and in one only—a love of all nature. Sage and mountain, the gleaming red walls and purple canyons—gahd, the cedar tree and choe, the spruce, the bright face of desert flowers—these were a part of his very being. He felt the spiritual power in the rocks and he gloried in the mighty sweep of the bow-winged eagle. His Indian nature made him singularly acute in all his sensorial perceptions, but he could not think in the Indian's way.

At dawn next morning Nophaie rode out into the sage on the trail to Mesa.

Some few miles from the eastern slope of Nothsis Ahn he sheered off the trail to visit a Pahute camp where he engaged a boy to tend his sheep during his absence. The Pahutes were glad to see Nophaie and made him welcome. They were rich in sheep and horses; their wants were few; they lived peaceful and contented in the loneliness of their desert home. They never saw a white man, except on the infrequent trips to trading posts. Nophaie had forced upon him the beauty of their lives. If some of the older men saw the vision of the future and the doom of the Indian they showed no sign of it. But Nophaie saw it, and rode on his way sad and pondering, wishing that he, too, could be as happy and self-sufficient as they.

His route lay through the range of the prosperous old Nopah chief whom Withers had accused of salting wool. Etenia, the Wealthy, had words of sympathy for Nophaie's loss of kin, and forgot his reason for discord.

Nophaie did not tarry there long. He saw anew, however, the evidences of Etenia's wealth—a stone hogan of imposing proportions, corrals, and cultivated fields, thousands of sheep and droves of horses, water in abundance, and all around the wide cedared rolling country hogans of his people. Etenia had all any Indian could wish for. Yet the only thing Nophaie envied him for was that simple faith which had been handed down from his forefathers.

Nophaie loped along the sage trail, with the cool fragrances of desert in his face, the wide, green-clumped expanse of purple open to his eye. How immeasurably far apart he felt from the people who lived there! Every day brought more bitter proof. When he conversed with Indians he used their language, but when he thought, his ideas were expressed in his mind by words of English. For long he had striven to conquer this. But it was impossible. Any slow, deliberate thought expressed in Indian words was intelligible to him, even natural, yet never did it convey the same meaning as the white man's language. That was Nophaie's tragedy: He had the instincts, the emotions, the soul of an Indian, but his thoughts about himself, his contemplation of himself and his people were not those of the red man. As he saw the beauty of this wild, lovely land, and the rugged simplicity of the Indian, his marvelous endurance, his grand childlike faith in the supernatural and the immortal, so likewise he saw the indolence of this primitive people, their unsanitary ways of living, their absurd reverence for the medicine man, their peculiar lack of chastity—and a thousand other manifestations of ignorance as compared with the evolutionary progress of the white man. Indians were merely closer to the original animal progenitor of human beings.

Nophaie did not easily yield the supremacy to the white man. There were many ways in which he believed an Indian superior. He thought of Maahesenie's resignation to death and how he had lain down to meet it.

"My son," he had said to Nophaie, "do not stand over me to obstruct the sunlight. Go out with the sheep. My day is done. Leave me alone to die."

How incalculably more selfish and ignoble the custom of the white man! Nophaie remembered a time in the East, at Cape May, when he was playing baseball and living among white people—how a dying man was kept alive by nitrate of amyl five days after he should have been dead. Five days of intolerable anguish forced upon him by living, but misguided relatives! The Indian knew better than that. He had no fear of death. The mystic future held its promise. Life hereafter was a fulfillment of the present. The white man hated to let go his hold on material pleasures; the red man loved the belief of his spiritual metamorphosis. Nophaie confessed the incalculable benefits of his education, but deplored the destruction of the faith of his childhood.

That day, as many times before, he came upon the Testing Stone, lying along the trail. It stood about two feet high and was bulky. This was the stone that made a brave of a boy. There were many stones like this one scattered over the Indian country, the boys of every family tugged and toiled over them, day after day and year after year, until that wonderful time came when they could lift and carry them. It took years to develop and gather such strength. When an Indian youth could lift that stone he had become a brave. When he could carry it he was a strong man. If he could carry it far he was a giant. This exercise explained to Nophaie why an Indian could carry a stump of a spruce or the whole of a cedar down the mountainside.

Nophaie dismounted. He could not pass by this Testing Stone. It flaunted in his face a heritage of his people. Strength of manhood! The might revered by the gods! Power of arms that brought the beautiful light to the dusky eyes of Indian maidens!

Drawing a deep breath and bending down, Nophaie encircled that stone with his arms and heaved to the uttermost of his strength. He lifted it. He moved it a little way. And then its ponderous weight dragged him down, loosed his hold, and left him wet with sweat and labored of chest. Bitterly he gazed down at this proof of the Indian sinew. Scornfully he remembered his triumphs of the football field, the college records so lauded by his white comrades. Any youth of that desert was as strong as he. And to the men of the Nopahs he was as a pigmy. Maahesenie in his prime had lifted that very stone to his shoulder and had carried it for one hundred steps.

Nophaie rode on his way, and thought of Benow di cleash, and watched the changing panorama. Suddenly his horse rounded a cedar tree and shied at a monument. Nophaie had often seen this pile of stones, but never had it halted him until now. It had peculiar significance for him. Whenever an Indian passed that way, bent on a hunt or a quest involving peril, he gathered a sprig of cedar from the tree, and laying it on the monument he placed a stone over it, and spoke his prayer.

Nophaie yielded to the instinct that impelled him to reach for a sprig of cedar. He added his stone to the monument and spoke a prayer for his adventure. The idea seemed beautiful to him. He was the Indian chief faring forth on an enterprise of peril. The dream—the fancy—the faith of the red man! But futile was his simple and instinctive abnegation of the white man's knowledge. Swiftly it flashed back to reveal the naked truth. His quest was to save the soul of Gekin Yashi. He would be too late, or if not too late, he could only delay a crime and a tragedy as inevitable as life itself.

Eight hours steady riding cross-country brought Nophaie to the crest of the great plateau from which he saw the long, green lines of poplar trees that marked the location of Mesa. Far removed was this country from the sage uplands surrounding Nothsis Ahn. Bare, yellow, sandy desert, spotted with pale green, and ridged by lines of blue rock, swept and rolled away on the three sides open to his gaze. Heat veils rose waveringly from sand and smoke; and the creamy white clouds rolled low along the dark horizon line.

Some wind-carved rocks of yellow marked the spot Nophaie and Marian had chosen as a rendezvous. There was cool shade, and shelter from rain or blowing sand, and a vantage point from which to watch. Marian was not there, nor did her white mustang show anywhere down the long, bare slope toward the poplars. The time was about the middle of the afternoon, rather early for Marian. Therefore Nophaie composed himself to wait.

By and by his vigil was rewarded by sight of a white horse gliding out from the green, and heading toward his covert. Nophaie watched Marian come. She had learned to sit a saddle as an Indian. Nophaie felt the shadows lift from his soul, the doubts from his mind. Always sight of her uplifted him. More and more she was a living proof of many things—the truth of love and loyalty—the nobility of white women—the significance of life being worthwhile for any human creature—the strange consciousness of joy in resistance to evil, in a fight for others, in something nameless and hopeful, as deep and mystical as the springs of his nature. How could he be a coward while this white woman loved him and worked to help his people? She was a repudiation of all his dark doubts. To think evil was to do evil. For the hour, then, Nophaie knew he would be happy, and would part from her somehow strengthened. Nothing could cheat him out of the wonder of her presence.

At last she rode into the lane between the yellow rocks, and waved a gauntleted hand to him upon the shady ledge above. Dismounting she tied the white mustang to a knob of rock, and climbed to Nophaie's retreat. He helped her up the few steep steps, and holding her hand, he knew she would have come straight into his arms if he had held them out to her. Never before had he so yearned to enfold her, to yield to a strong, shuddering need of her. But he owed her proof of her ideal of the Indian. She had once called him her noble red man. Would he let any white man be more worthy of that word?

But five weeks had changed Benow di cleash. Did the light-colored blouse and divided skirt, instead of the usual mannish riding garb constitute all the difference? As she talked on and on Nophaie listened, and watched her. What had become of the fair skin, so like the pearly petal of a sage lily? Her face was now golden brown, and thinner, and older, too, except when she smiled. Only the blue eyes and hair of gold now held her claim to Benow di cleash. Her form had lost something of its former fullness. The desert summer was working upon her; the hot winds were drying up her flesh. And in repose of face there was a sadness that added new beauty and strength to her. Nophaie could accept this devotion to him and his people only because he saw that she was growing to nobler womanhood. In years to come she would look back upon this time and Nophaie without regret. He had vision to see that and it permitted him to be happy with her.

Then she passed from news of her friends in the East to matters at Mesa, and naturally as was her way, she told humorous things that had delighted her in the Indian children. The school brought out as many funny things as pathetic. Nophaie was pleased with the progress she had made in the Nopah language, and yet he had a strange and unaccountable regret at hearing her speak it. From reminiscence of the Indian children she shifted to an account of the intrigue at Mesa, involving friends she had made there, a young Texan and his wife, who were in trouble owing to the machinations of Blucher and Morgan.

Nophaie knew the Texan, whose name was Wolterson. He was a government stockman and his duties were to ride out over the ranges to instruct the Indians in the care of sheep and horses and cattle. What little Nophaie had heard from the Indians about Wolterson was all to his credit. This heightened Nophaie's interest in what Marian had to say, and he soon gathered the truth of Wolterson's case, which held something of significance for him.

Wolterson had come to the desert in search of health. He was a cattleman and received an appointment from the government to be inspector of Indian stock on the ranges adjacent to Mesa. Being a young man of fine southern family and highly recommended, he at once incurred the dislike of the superintendent. When he asked Blucher what his duties would be, that individual succinctly replied: "Ride around," and that was all the directions he ever got. He mastered the work solely by his own energies. Morgan solicited the good offices of Wolterson through Miss Herron's overtures to Mrs. Wolterson. As soon as the Woltersons discovered conditions patent to all old residents of Mesa those overtures fell flat. Then began the insidious, underhand, undermining work against Wolterson.

"After I'm gone today," concluded Marian, "I want you to ride down and see Wolterson. Then ask the Indians about him. Soon Blucher will trump up some charge against him and call an investigation. Unless Wolterson can disprove it he will be dismissed. Then we'd lose a good friend of the Indians. Wolterson has befriended Do etin. That is the real cause of Morgan's enmity."

"And—Gekin Yashi?" asked Nophaie, in slow reluctance.

"Safe and well, yet," replied Marian, in glad eagerness. "The mills have been grinding as of old, but not so fast. Morgan has been to Flagerstown. Blucher has been wrangling all his time with his henchmen—Jay Lord, the Mormon, Ruhr, and Glendon. I don't hear much, but enough. It's mostly about Wolterson now and something about the land and water mess stirred up by the Nokis at Copenwashie. Friel has got a patent to the land once owned or at least controlled by the Nokis. Blucher, of course, aided Friel in this deal, but now true to the twist in his brain he is sore about it. . . . The edict has not gone forth compelling the Indian girls to go to Morgan's chapel after school hours. But it is certain. . . . I have had talks with Gekin Yashi. She is ready to run off. We contrived to get permission for her to visit her father. Wolterson is dipping Do etin's sheep and this morning Gekin Yashi rode out to the hogan. She's there now and will remain over Sunday. You can go out there at night and make your plans to meet her as she rides back alone."

"Do etin will be glad," said Nophaie. "Is Wolterson in the secret?"

"Yes. He approves. But we must not let him have a hand in it."

"I shall take Gekin Yashi to a Pahute in the Valley of Silent Walls," rejoined Nophaie, thoughtfully. "But few Nopahs know this place. It is down under the west side of Nothsis Ahn, deep in the canyons."

"Valley of Silent Walls," mused Marian. Then she flashed at Nophaie: "Will you take me there some-day?"

"Yes, Benow di cleash," replied Nophaie. "But you run a danger."

"Of what—whom?"

"Me!"

Marian flushed under her golden tan and her eyes searched his. Nophaie dropped his gaze, that alighting upon her brown hand, saw it tremble and then clench at her glove.

"Nophaie, you . . . you are jesting."

"No. I think I am telling the truth," responded Nophaie. "Someday the savage and civilized man in me will come to strife. My Valley of Silent Walls is the most enchanting—the wildest and most beautiful place—the loneliest in all this desert. Walls of white and red, so high you cannot see their rims—running snow water, flowers and grass and trees! If I ever got you down there I might never let you go."

"Well, you frighten me," said Marian, laughing. "I see that you still retain some of your brutal football training. . . . But if all goes well, take me there to visit Gekin Yashi. Will you?"

"Could you get away from here?"

"Nophaie, I will never be permitted to work long at Mesa," replied Marian. "Someday Blucher will awake to my two-faced nature. For I have certainly used woman's wits to fool him."

"Well, then I will take you to my Valley of Silent Walls."

Marian placed her hand on Nophaie's and looked up into his face and then down, with evident restraint of emotion.

"Nophaie, Gekin Yashi loves you."

"That child! Why, she has seen me but a few times," protested Nophaie, painfully reminded of Do etin's proposal that he marry his daughter.

"No matter. She has seen you enough. These Indian girls mature early. Gekin Yashi is not yet fifteen, but she is a woman in feeling. I think she is very lovable and sweet. She is quite the best scholar in the school. I have spent all the time possible with her. Believe me, Morgan is not the only venomous reptile around Mesa. Gekin Yashi is Indian clear through, but she has sense. She likes the ways of good white women. I have taught her that when a white woman loves she holds herself sacred for the man who has won her."

"Marian, are you thinking that the way for me to save Gekin Yashi is to marry her?" inquired Nophaie.

"It might be," murmured Marian tremulously, "if . . . if you . . ."

"But I do not love her and I cannot marry her," declared Nophaie. "So much has white education done for me."

After that no more was said about Gekin Yashi. Nophaie felt a great throb of pity and tenderness for this white girl. How she inspired him to mastery of self, to beat down the base and bitter! Something of gaiety and happiness came to her in the closing moments of that meeting. Then the time arrived for her to go. Lightly touching his face with her hand she left him, to run down the declivity, and mount her mustang. Once, as she was galloping away, she turned to look back and wave to him. Her hair flashed gold in the sun. Nophaie watched her out of sight, with emotion deep and strange, half grief for the fate that was his, half exaltation that miserable and lost Indian as he was this woman of an alien white race made him a king.

Chapter 9

At the upper end of the long, poplar-lined avenue that constituted the only street in Mesa, the Woltersons occupied a little stone house built by the earliest founders of the settlement. A grove of cotton-wood trees surrounded a tiny reed-bordered lake where ducks swam, and swamp-black birds and meadowlarks made melody. Here was rich, dark green verdure and cool shade and a sweet, drowsy breath of summer, blowing in from the hot desert.

On the other side of the Wolterson house was a garden that bordered on the spacious playground of the Indian school.

Nophaie watered his horse at the thin swift stream that ran down from the lake through the Woltersons' garden, and along the fence to the orchards. The sun was westering low and the heat of the day was dying. Down at the other end of the long avenue Nophaie espied Indians and mustangs in front of the trading post. He went into the open gate of the Wolterson place and let his horse graze on the rich grass bordering the irrigation ditch.

"Howdy, Nophaie," drawled a slow voice. "Shore am glad to see you."

Nophaie returned the greeting of the Texan, speaking in his own tongue. Few white men on the reservation had ever heard him speak English. Wolterson was a young man, tall and lithe, with a fine, clean-cut face, bronzed by exposure. He did not appear to be rugged. His high-heeled horseman's boots and big sombrero were as characteristically Texan as his accent.

Nophaie dropped the bridle of his horse and took a seat near where Wolterson was damming up an intersection from the irrigating ditch. He tossed a cigarette case to Nophaie, and then went on working. Indians rode by down the avenue. A freighter's wagon, drawn by six mustangs and loaded with firewood, lumbered along with the driver walking. Bees hummed somewhere in the foliage and the stream murmured musically.

"The Nopahs think well of you and your work," said Nophaie presently. "You're the first stockman they ever praised. If you are brought before an investigating committee I'll get Etenia, and Tohoniah bi dony, and several more influential chiefs to testify for you."

"Shore that's fine, Nophaie," declared Wolterson. "I'm giving you a hunch I'll need them."

Nothing was said about Gekin Yashi. Wolterson spoke of his plans for dipping sheep over the ranges as far as Etenia's place. Nophaie and the Pahutes of that upland country must drive their flocks down there. Grass on the lowlands had begun to grow, so that the Nopahs would not have to range so far. Then Wolterson informed Nophaie that the government was going to instigate a blood test of cattle and horses, as the latter, especially, showed evidence of tuberculosis.

"Any horse or steer that has become infected will have to be shot," said Wolterson seriously. "Now isn't it going to be hard to convince the Indians of the necessity of this?"

"Yes. I'm afraid it can't be done," replied Nophaie. "Is there a real necessity of testing stock for this disease?"

"I think so. I have sent my approval to Washington. But I dislike the prospect of trouble with the Indians. . . . Nophaie, would you be willing to help me by explaining this test to your people?"

"I will, if you can convince *me* of its need."

"Well, when the order comes I'll ride first to your

range, and you shall see me make tests. Has Etenia many cattle?"

"Not a great many. They are all healthy."

"Nophaie, they may look healthy and still have tuberculosis."

At this juncture the little Indian boys and girls began to pour out of the big red dormitory like a stream of blue gingham. Nophaie noted that only the children from three years to five or six years of age appeared to be in evidence. They were a scampering, silent little horde, playing without the noise characteristic of white children. They spread over the playground to the number of several hundred, making a scene of color and animation. Several little boys came along to peer through the wire fence at Nophaie. They looked healthy and well cared for, and certainly were cleaner than any Indian boys he had seen. How stolid they seemed! They gazed at Wolterson with blank, black eyes, and at Nophaie with scarcely more of interest.

Nophaie also observed that two of the school teachers were out on the grounds with the children. They did not approach near enough for Nophaie to see them well. Then Mrs. Wolterson appeared, coming into the garden, wearing gloves and carrying a trowel. She was a striking young woman, dark as an Indian, beginning to show the effect of desert wind and heat. She had a pleasant greeting for Nophaie. He saw her glance run over the three Indian boys and beyond to the playground, as if she was looking for someone.

"Here comes Marian with Evangeline," she said, as if pleased.

It was then Nophaie saw Marian leading a little Indian girl towards them, and he got the impression that this meeting was not as accidental or casual as might appear to others. The two teachers were watching Marian. And Nophaie, roving his sharp eyes around, caught a glimpse of a woman's face in a window of a house across the avenue. This appeared a busier thoroughfare now. Indians were riding out toward the desert. Some of the older schoolboys were playing ball. Three Indian workmen passed by carrying long shovels over their shoulders.

"Shore," drawled Wolterson, with eyes on the avenue, "and here comes the champion liar of the reservation."

"Bob, don't say that," said Mrs. Wolterson quickly. "Somebody might hear you. The very trees have ears, not to speak of these Indian boys."

Nophaie saw a heavily built young man, roughly clad, typically western in corduroys and boots and sombrero, swinging with rider's gait up the avenue. Upon sighting the group in the garden he swerved, and tilting back his sombrero he lounged against the gatepost. His face was brown and broad, rather coarse, with thick lips and prominent eyes, wine dark in color.

"Howdy folks," he said, with a slow grin. "You ain't really workin'?"

"Howdy, Jay," responded Wolterson. "I don't get much time except of evenings."

"Why, you seem to have all the time there is," returned the other, dryly, with satire. "And look who's here—the handsome Mrs.—Bob, I calculate to find me a wife like her."

This was the first time Nophaie had ever seen Jay Lord, the Mormon, one time known as a trader on the reservation and now apparently employed by Blucher. Careless, easy, cool, with his air of devilish insouciance, this leering Westerner did not enhance Nophaie's respect for the white man. Sight of him, so palpably other than the good-natured friend his familiarity assumed, roused something latent and dormant in Nophaie.

"Jay Lord, you're a sad flatterer," observed Mrs. Wolterson.

"Sad? I reckon not. I'm happy," he replied, and sauntered into the garden. His bold gaze fell upon Nophaie, and he addressed him in Nopah.

"Say, ain't this the Carlisle Injun?" he inquired of Wolterson, seeing that Nophaie paid no attention to him.

"Carlisle? Who's that?" drawled Wolterson.

"Aw, come off," retorted Lord, in disgust. "I mean the Carlisle Indian School where this redskin went. You know as well as anybody."

"Jay, shore I don't know anything."

"Right. You spoke wisdom once. An' I reckon the less you know the safer, hey?"

Then Lord espied Marian, who had come up to the fence, leading the little Indian girl. Mrs. Wolterson went over to them, answering Marian's greeting. Lord doffed his sombrero and waved it low, crude in his assumption of a dignified salute, yet dauntless in his admiration.

"I reckon I'll hang round awhile," he said, as he approached the fence and hung over it. "Why, who's this here little girl? Aren't you an Injun?"

"I'm not," piped up the little girl, in astonishingly good English, "I'm Miss Evangeline Warner."

"Ho! Ho! Listen to the little Injun girl," replied Lord, with a loud laugh.

"Jay, please don't tease Eva," asked Mrs. Wolterson appealingly. "All the men tease her, just because she's so bright. But you will spoil her."

Nophaie had heard of this three-year-old prodigy. Her Indian mother had been glad to get rid of her, yet showed great pride in Eva's fame. For some strange reason the child, who was a full-blooded Indian, had taken remarkably to the white people's language and ways, and after two years hated the very name of Indian. She was a sturdy child with heavy round face and black staring eyes and straggling black hair, neither in appearance nor expression any different from the other little Indian girls. Nophaie roused to a strong interest in Eva.

"No, I'm not—I'm not," declared Eva, vehemently, and she kicked at the wire fence.

"Never mind, Eva," said Mrs. Wolterson, as she knelt down to take the little girl's hand. "Say your go-to-bed prayer for us."

Evangeline appeared wholly devoid of the shyness characteristic of Indian children.

"Now I lay me down to sleep,
    I pray the Lord my soul to keep,
    If I should die before I wake,
    I should worry!"

Jay Lord roared his laughter and Wolterson, too, enjoyed a laugh.

"Why—why, goodness gracious!" exclaimed Mrs. Wolterson, divided between horror and mirth. "Evangeline, where did you learn those last words?"

"From one of the men, that's sure," said Marian. "I never heard her say it that way before." Then she stooped to Evangeline and peering into the little dark face she shook her gently. "Eva, you will get spanked. Say your prayer over again—the right way. Remember . . . you will get spanked."

Very soberly the little Indian miss eyed her teacher.

"Now I lay me down to sleep,
    I pray the Lord my soul to keep,
    If I should die before I wake,
    You will get spanked!"

Before Marian could protest or even before the men could laugh, a loud voice, of peculiar timbre, rang out from behind.

"Shut that brat's mouth!"

Nophaie knew before he wheeled that the speaker was Morgan, the missionary. And he had closer view of this man than ever before.

"Come, Eva," said Marian, hurriedly, and rising, she led the child away.

"That sounded a heap like the Old Book, now didn't it?" rasped out Morgan, glaring about him.

Nophaie saw a matured man of medium height, thick bodied, with something slack in his physical makeup. He had a smooth face the striking features of which were pale eyes the color of ice and a long, thin-lipped, tight-shut mouth. He had a big nose, somewhat of a reddish hue, and his complexion was an olive tan rather than the healthy bronze peculiar to the desert. Morgan seemed not to be an outdoor man. His was a strange, strong face with an intense cast of thought or will, a deeply lined face, especially in the furrowed frowning brow. He was magnetic, but it seemed a magnetism of strife of mind, a dynamic energy of brain, a tremendous mental equipment. All about him breathed of intolerance.

Jay Lord was the first to answer Morgan. "Sounds like one of them schoolmarms, to me."

"Mr. Morgan, I am sure Marian could never have taught Eva that," interposed Mrs. Wolterson. "Why— she was shocked. So was I."

The missionary might not have heard her, for all the sign he gave.

"Wolterson, the agent tells me you drove Gekin Yashi home this morning."

"Yes, sir," replied the stockman, leaning on his shovel, and slowly lifting his gaze.

"How's come?" jerked out Morgan.

"Wal," drawled the Texan, "if you mean what did I have to do with it—Blucher gave Gekin Yashi permission to visit her father. I am dipping sheep out at Do etin's. Had to haul supplies this morning. Gekin Yashi rode on the wagon. That's all."

"Humph! When's she coming back?"

"I don't know. She said she hoped her father would keep her home."

When the missionary's restless glance fell upon Nophaie it became fixed. Nophaie met that glance. One of the qualities he had not absorbed from his long association with white people was their habit of dissimulation or deceit. Something emanating from this missionary called to the depths of Nophaie. Not the old racial hatred of red man for white foe! It was a subtle, complex instinct, born of the moment. Leisurely Nophaie rose to his tall stature, and folding his arms he gave Morgan eye for eye.

"Are you the Carlisle Indian?"

Nophaie did not feel that he was required to answer.

"Sure he's the one," put in Jay Lord. "They call him Nophay or somethin' like."

"Can't you speak English?" demanded Morgan sharply. "Let's hear some of your eastern lingo."

"I would not have to speak English very well to do it better than you," replied Nophaie, in his low, level tones, perfectly enunciated.

"Wha-at?" blurted out Morgan.

Nophaie eyed him with inscrutable meaning and did not vouchsafe any more.

"Have you ever been to my church?" went on Morgan.

"No."

"Well, then, I want you to come."

"What for?" queried Nophaie.

"To hear me preach. To learn from the Old Book. If you speak English as well as you brag you can carry the word of God—of Christianity home to your heathen tribe. Teach them how to get to Heaven."

"We have no desire to go to your Heaven," returned Nophaie. "If there really is such a paradise as you preach all the land will be owned by missionaries. And the Indians would have none to grow their corn and hay."

"You think you're smart, don't you?" snarled Morgan.

"Morgan, the stupidest Indian on this reservation is smart enough to see through you."

"Bah! Your tribe of gut eaters are too ignorant to see anything, let alone the white man's religion."

"The Indian's own religion is infinitely better for him than the white man's."

"Humph!" fumed the missionary. "Did you learn that at Carlisle?"

"No, I learned it upon my return to my people. What is more, I learned there is not one single real Christian Indian on the reservation."

"That's a damned lie," shouted Morgan, growing purple in the face.

"What do you know of the Indians out there?" demanded Nophaie, pointing to the desert. "You have never been out in the desert, unless to ride in an automobile to visit one of your missionary friends."

Slowly the color left Morgan's face and there was visible a contraction that suggested a powerful effort of will to control fury and amazement. When he had himself in hand amazement still was his predominant expression. He had encountered an Indian beyond his widest experience. That sudden check, that sudden restraint showed Morgan's depth. He could retrench. Nophaie read his craftiness. Also he received subtle intimation that this missionary must be a composite of knave and fanatic, an unscrupulous usurper who had no illusions as to his honesty, yet was a visionary zealot who believed he was an apostle.

"What do *you* think you know of me?" he demanded.

"Only what the Indians say—and what I can see," returned Nophaie, in subtle scorn.

"I have been missionary here for over fifteen years. The Nopahs are harsh. They are slow to appreciate my work."

"No, Mr. Morgan," retorted Nophaie. "You have it wrong. My tribe has been *swift* to appreciate your work. Don't try any of your religious talk on me. It is all bunk. . . . You are not a missionary."

"Insolent heathen!" ejaculated Morgan, choking so that the thick folds of flesh on his fat neck worked up and down.

"A missionary is a *man* sent out by church or society to propagate religion in the sincere hope and faith that an alien race will be saved," continued Nophaie. "It is a mistaken sincerity—a futile generosity. Emerson, who had the greatest intellect ever developed in America, vowed he would never give a cent for missionary work. . . . If you were a real *man* you might help the poor Indians. You might teach them better ways to build, cook, harvest, irrigate, shear their sheep and store their corn. You might teach them sanitary laws. You might, by example, show them how a white man works with his hands. But you do not work. Your hands, I see, are softer than Mrs. Wolterson's—if she will permit that doubtful compliment. . . . No, Mr. Morgan, you are not a builder. You are a destroyer. And whatever else you are it is certainly not a missionary."

Morgan's egotism was stronger than his restraint—his outraged sovereignty could not all in a moment be silenced.

"I . . . I'll put you in jail," he said, with hard expulsion of breath.

"What for? Telling the truth," rejoined Nophaie, in lofty scorn. "This is a free country. I am an American. An honest Indian!"

"I'll haul you up for this," threatened the missionary, lifting a shaking hand.

Swift as light Nophaie leaped out of his statuesque posture, so suddenly that both the missionary and Lord recoiled, as if from attack. Certain it was that Morgan's face paled.

"Haul me into court," returned Nophaie piercingly. "Haul me before your investigation committee! I would like nothing better. I will have Indians there, and *real* white men to listen. . . . Do you get that, Mr. Morgan?"

But the missionary shirked an answer, and with somber glance sweeping away he drew Lord with him and passed out of the gate, down the avenue. Lord's voice, low and hoarse, came back on the breeze.

Thereupon Nophaie turned to Wolterson and his wife. The Texan's habitual calm appeared to have been broken.

"Shore you gave him hell," he said, breathing deep. "You could have knocked him down with a feather—and me too. . . . About the happiest few minutes I ever passed in Mesa!"

But Mrs. Wolterson appeared pale and distressed.

"Oh, he was mad," she whispered.

"Shore I never saw Mr. Morgan upset like that," returned her husband, with a slow grin. "He just couldn't believe his ears. . . . Nophaie, take a hunch from a Texan. Somehow and someway this missionary will injure you. He has had to suffer an unparalleled affront before other people. Besides, he actually was afraid of you—amazed—furious—then afraid. I felt it. I've long studied this man. And I can't prove much, but I feel he is capable of anything."

"Morgan is a coward and liar. I wonder that some Indian has not killed him long ago," said Nophaie. "It proves the patience and the restraint of my people."

"Nophaie, I've lived among violent men," rejoined the Texan soberly. "Don't underrate Morgan. He's been long in power here. He's arrogant—malicious. I'd put nothing beyond him."

"Well, to be forearmed is half the battle," replied Nophaie, as he turned to his horse. "I'll not ride to Mesa anymore in daylight, nor let Morgan know I'm ever here."

It was long past dark when Nophaie reached the hogan of Do etin. A fire still burned and in its flickering light sat the father of Gekin Yashi, a man little beyond middle age, stalwart, deep-chested, with massive head and great rolling eyes like those of an ox.

Nophaie saw that he had been expected. Bread and

meat and drink were tendered him. While he ate hungrily his host smoked in silence. Do etin was not rich in horses and sheep, as were most of his neighbors, nor was he a chief. Yet he occupied a position of respect and dignity in the tribe, by reason of his intelligence. Gekin Yashi was his only child. Do etin's range had long been a grassy flat in a shallow canyon watered by a never-failing spring. Nophaie looked round in the shadows of the hogan for Gekin Yashi and her mother, but they were not there. Perhaps Do etin waited upon him to go into council, and had sent his women to a hogan of relatives near at hand.

By and by Do etin broke his silence. He gave his consent for Gekin Yashi to go with Nophaie and approved of that procedure. But he doubted it would be possible to hide his daughter for long. Nophaie should not at once incur risk of government punishment by marrying Gekin Yashi or letting it be found out that he had hidden her away. Do etin believed the white man's education good for the Indian boys and girls. It taught them to help their parents in new and better ways of living. But the religion forced upon them was not acceptable, and the ruin of Indian girls by white men employed on the reservation, especially by missionaries who used their office to take advantage, was the basest and blackest crime of the many crimes the white race had perpetrated upon the red.

Do etin went on to tell of the confessions made to him by Gekin Yashi—of Blucher's enmity toward her father—of Morgan's haranguing at her—of the matron's forcing upon her menial labors when she should have been in school—of brutality to the Indian children —how all the milk and fruit, which should have gone to the children, was used by Blucher and his associates.

Nophaie brought the information of Blucher's new ruling, the enforcement of which, soon to go into effect, meant that the Indian girls must go to Morgan's chapel to hear him preach.

Do etin showed intense passion and vehemence.

"Never shall Gekin Yashi go to Morgan! Never shall Do etin let the white missionary make his daughter a whore!"

After this outburst he was long silent, pondering, brooding, manifestly doubtful of the future. Something pathetic and impotent about Do etin touched Nophaie to pity.

"Do etin, we are in the power of the white man," he said, earnestly. "There are good white men who believe in justice to the Indian. But most of them are bad. We must look far ahead. The white race will never wholly absorb the red. If that were possible it might be well for both. But the Indian will merely be pushed back upon the barren lands and eventually swept off the earth. These things we strive against, as the Nokis fight being cheated out of their water and land, or as our efforts to save Gekin Yashi—these things are nothing but incidental to the whole doom of our people. We must resist, but the end will come, just the same."

"Yes, it will. But who will fight? Only one Indian, here and there, whose heart has not been crushed."

Do etin bowed his massive, dark head, and the somber firelight shadows played over his still form.

"Nophaie, you come with the white man's vision of the future," he asserted.

"Yes. You were taught to see with your heart. The white education taught Nophaie to see with his mind."

"The sun of the Indian's day is setting," replied Do etin mournfully.

In the clear, cool, gray dawn Nophaie waited out on the desert for Gekin Yashi, as it had been planned she would come.

Eastward the darkling light on sand and shrub lifted to the long blue wall of rock that cut the plateau, and above it flared the pale gold herald of sunrise. The desert was as still as death. Nophaie waited, at last fixing his gaze down the gradual slope to a point where Gekin Yashi must appear. She came into sight, a slim,

dark figure on a gray mustang. Nophaie felt a thrill in
that moment. Deep in him old Indian instincts survived. He was the Indian brave waiting for his Indian
maiden. The desert stretched there vast and lonely.
Mountain and mesa, vale and canyon, the long, greasewood dotted ridges, the green soap-weed, the innumerable stones, and the sands of the wastes—all seemed to
cry voicelessly of the glory of Indian legends of love.

The sun rose, now shining upon Gekin Yashi's raven
black hair, upon the face that was like a dark flower.
Two months had changed Gekin Yashi. And never had
he beheld her in other than the blue-gingham uniform
of the government school. She wore now the velveteen
and silver and beads and buckskin common to her
tribe. As she reined in the little mustang beside Nophaie her dusky eyes flashed one shy, frightened, yet
wondrously happy glance at him, then were drooped
under dusky lashes. Her bosom heaved. Gekin Yashi
could not hide her love, perhaps did not want to.
Nophaie mourned in his heart his unworthiness and the
futility of his life.

"Daughter of Do etin, listen," he said. "Nophaie is
the Indian with the white man's mind. He has come
back to help his people. He is Do etin's friend. He loves
Gekin Yashi, but as a brother. Nophaie will never
marry. . . . He will take Gekin Yashi far into the
white-walled canyons, to the Pahutes, and hide her
there. And always he will be her brother and try to
make her as the white girl Benow di cleash, teaching
her what is evil and what is good."

Nophaie rode away with Gekin Yashi to the northward, avoiding all trails, hiding as best he could their
tracks, searching the desert with keen eyes for Indian
riders he wished to avoid. As sunset came he turned to
the hogan of a Nòpah he could trust. Next day the black
slopes of Nothsis Ahn loomed on the horizon. Gekin
Yashi gradually found her voice and came at last to talk
to Nophaie. Thus he had opportunity to study the effect
of the government school upon an Indian girl. Most of

what she had learned was good. Some of it was bad. When she went back to her home and married, to have children of her own, she and they must certainly be the better for her schooling. Nophaie saw that as a fact, provided she could return to Indian ways. In the long run many educated Indian girls and boys might change the squalor and improvidence then natural to their elders. It relieved Nophaie to settle this question in his mind. Education then for the Indian was good. The fault in the system then and the terrible wrong to the Indian girl was something false in the enforcement of an alien religion, and the abasement of virtue that seemed to come inevitably by association with white men. The simpleminded, worshipful Indian maiden, primitive in her instincts and unsustained by any moral law, was merely prey for beasts of white men. White race and red race could not mix. If the red man was inherently noble, a dreamer of the open, a fighter of imaginary foes, a warrior against warrior of another tribe, a creature not meant for civilization, then the white man was a step above the Indian in evolution, past the stage of barbarism, steeped in a material progress of the world, selfish and intellectual, more pagan than the Indian, on the decline to a decadence as inevitable as nature itself. For Nophaie saw clearly that nature was the great law. The Indian, even the barbarian, was nearer the perfection that nature worked so inscrutably for. The individual must perish that the species might survive. Nature's ideal was strength, virility, fecundity, long life, all physical. If nature was God then the only immortality of man lay in his offspring. How bitterly every channel of Nophaie's thought led to his consciousness of being an infidel!

In three days Nophaie reached the Pahute camp under the brow of Nothsis Ahn, believing that the few Indians to whom he had trusted Gekin Yashi would keep her secret. It cost him all his sheep to engage these Pahutes in Gekin Yashi's service. They could not leave their range and go into the deep canyons for an

indefinite period without being well paid for it.
Nophaie had not thought of that, but he gladly gave up
his flock. It was much harder to say good-bye to Gekin
Yashi. "Nophaie! Nophaie!" she called, as he rode
away. Her cry pierced his heart. What was it that he
saw in her dusky eyes? Shadow, indeed, of the Indian's
doom! He rode back to cheer her, to speak for once
words that he could not swear were truth. Then he rode
out again. *"Nophaie!"* Her faint cry pealed out over the
sage. But he did not look back.

Chapter 10

FROM THE HOUR NOPHAIE GAVE UP HIS SHEEP to the Pahutes in payment for their care of Gekin Yashi he became a nomad—a wanderer of the sage.

With responsibility removed from his life he was no longer tied to his lonely upland home—a fact that at first seemed grievous. But he was soon to discover how his loneliness had been a kind of selfishness which had kept him aloof from his people. In the past he had spent only a small part of his time among the Indians, and that upon his rides to Kaidab or to Mesa and return. How little had he really helped them compared to what he might have done! Looked at now he found this owing to his love of being alone, of wandering with his sheep in the sage, of brooding over his strange life; and also to the sensitiveness with which he realized that though he could go among his people he could not become a part of them.

A few rides from hogan to hogan showed Nophaie that his status among the Nopahs had undergone a remarkable change. Not at once did he grasp what it was to which he must attribute this welcome change. At Etenia's home, however, the subtle fact came out in the jealousy of Etenia's daughter—she and all the Nopahs had learned of his abduction of Gekin Yashi. Nophaie was much concerned over this discovery, for it augured ill for the seclusion of the Little Beauty of the tribe. But upon consulting the old Indian he learned that the news had traveled far and wide across the ranges, from rider to rider, from hogan to hogan, from lip to lip. Soon every Nopah on the reservation would become ac-

quainted with the great feat of Nophaie, who had stolen
Gekin Yashi from the missionaries. Nophaie had been
born of chieftains: he was now a chief by wisdom and
valor. The spirit of the Nopahs still lived. The glory and
the dream were gone, but there still lived a man of the
olden time, a master. Etenia swore there was not one
Indian in all the tribe who would betray Gekin Yashi.
Perhaps some of the sneaking, crawling Nokis, in fear
of Morgan and Blucher, would trail Gekin Yashi to her
hiding place. But every Nopah gloried in the deed of
Nophaie. He was a hero. All the greater Indian now
because he had used his white man's brain to save the
maiden of proud Do etin!

"Nophaie will marry Gekin Yashi now," concluded
Etenia, and all his enmity seemed gone. He honored
Nophaie and feasted him, and had his braves sit round
the hogan fire and sing the beautiful Nopah legends of
love and courage. Nophaie was powerless to correct
this impression that had gone abroad. All Nopahs and
Pahutes, too, took it for granted that the Little Beauty
was destined to be Nophaie's wife. All in a day, it
seemed, his fame had been transformed. Every Indian
knew Nophaie's story, and all the aloofness and scorn
and distrust engendered by his white education would
be now as if they had never been.

Etenia knew his people. Of all the white race Indians
hated most the missionaries—those men who lied in
one breath and preached of Jesus Christ in another.
Nophaie had put into actual deed the secret longing of
every Indian. In a week of riding over the country
Nophaie had impellingly forced upon him the truth of
Etenia's judgment. Indian boy, maiden, brave, chief,
medicine man—all revered him. The Nopahs had been
warriors. There still survived in them worship of the
strong, the courageous, the fighter. The youths of the
tribe looked up to him as one whom their elders held to
be a master, one whose greatness would one day be
told to them.

Nophaie rode far to keep his next appointment with

Marian at Mesa, and for the whole hour of their meeting he talked of the change that had come through his taking Gekin Yashi away from the power of the missionary. Telling her seemed to clarify the vague and strange conceptions of what had happened to him. Then her instant joy was uplifting.

"Nophaie, now your great opportunity has come," she said, with glad and earnest eyes on his. "You can be a power among your people. But keep secret—that you are an infidel."

"I will," he replied. In just those few words she illumined the wondering, brooding subjectiveness of his mind. Whatever he was, opportunity now smiled upon him, and it seemed great. He would be listened to and followed.

"Now let me talk, for soon I must go," said Marian. "No one suspects you. All they know at the agency is that Gekin Yashi has disappeared. Blucher did not care. But Morgan was furious. I heard him raving. This will make bad blood between them. And Do etin will suffer. I fear for him. He was summoned to the office, and I was there when they questioned him. What a grand old Indian! He thrilled me—so calm, so somber and aloof, before those men. He answered every question put to him, yet he seemed not to lie."

" 'Do you think she ran off?' demanded Morgan.

" 'Yes,' answered Do etin.

" 'Where?'

" 'Gekin Yashi's tracks led north off the road to Mesa—and disappeared in the sands.'

" 'You'll help us find her—get her back?'

" 'No.'

" 'Yes, you will. And you'll send her to my church.'

" 'Do etin will die before he send Gekin Yashi to the missionary.'

" 'Why—you damned heathen?' shouted Morgan, beside himself."

Here Marian drew a quick breath, as if the memory of that moment had shocked her.

"Do etin drew himself up and seemed to expand. His eyes were terrible. . . . 'Do etin will never let the missionary make his daughter a whore!' Morgan drew back to strike Do etin, but Blucher prevented that. And Do etin stalked out. I have never seen a man look as Morgan did then."

"Marian, let me tell you, Do etin said exactly the same to me," returned Nophaie. "But to throw that in Morgan's face!"

"Oh, I fear for Do etin," cried Marian. "They will do him harm. I *know* it. . . . After Do etin left Morgan ordered me out of the office. 'Get out, you white-faced cat!' he shouted. And he pushed me out and slammed the door. I heard him say: 'Blucher, when we find this Indian hussy you've got to enforce that rule. And if Do etin doesn't put his thumb mark on my paper it'll go bad for him. And *you*'ll get the steamroller!' Blucher replied: 'The hell you say?' And Morgan yelled back: 'Yes, the hell I say! I've put that steamroller under eleven former agents of this reservation and I'm good for a full dozen. Me, and the Old Book back of me are just that strong!' Then they quieted down and I could not distinguish what they said, but they were talking for a long time. I think you ought to advise Do etin to move to the very farthest point on the reservation."

"He would not go a step," replied Nophaie.

"Then indeed I fear for him," said Marian. "It was the look of Morgan—the tone of his voice. The terrible nature of the man seemed unmasked. Blucher, too, is growing harder. He is under a strain. I think the war in Europe is in his mind."

Nophaie returned by way of Red Sandy, where at the trading post he was surrounded by Nopahs he had never seen before and made to realize his importance. The trader there was buying wool at fifty cents a pound and complaining about the scarcity of it. The Indians did not need money. They were not making any blankets. Nophaie was struck with the evidence of prosperity and independence exhibited by these lowland Nopahs. None of their silver trappings were in pawn to the trader, which was an unparalleled sign of good times.

Riding off across the sand to the northward with some of these Indians Nophaie covered twenty miles and more before he dropped the last horseman at his hogan door. Everywhere the gray-green benches were spotted with flocks of sheep and little bands of mustangs, and cattle. At every hogan the women crowded to the door to peep out at him, smiling and whispering. One old squaw elbowed her way out.

"Nophaie, look at Nadglean nas pah," she said, with great dignity, "who tended your mother at your birth. Nadglean nas pah washed your eyes. She lives to see you, Nophaie, the Warrior. . . . Come, feast with us."

Nophaie stayed there, keen to learn of his mother, grateful to feel stealing over him a closer touch with his people. By nightfall, when the feast was served, the hogan had no room for more Indians. They ate for hours and sang until late in the night. The occasion seemed one of honor and joy to these Indians who delighted in Nophaie's company. Many a dusky eye shone the brighter for his words.

Next morning he rode on his way more impressed than ever before with the prosperity and happiness of the Nopahs. It seemed he now could reasonably calculate that all the twenty thousand Nopahs of the reservation were in the high tide of well-being. Almost his hopes rose to a point of believing what Nadglean nas pah had said: "Now all is well." Only the wise old men like Etenia and Do etin saw the future. Most of the simpleminded Indians lived on in the present, taking their wealth as a matter of their worthiness; eating, sleeping, riding, shepherding the days away, unmindful of the handwriting of the white man like a shadow on the sage.

Night overtook Nophaie on the crest of the great heaving slope that led to the upland country. He had made a shortcut from Shibbet taa, westward toward

Etenia's range. His horse was weary. Nophaie turned it loose in the sage and made his bed under a thick-branched cedar. For his meal he ate meat and corn given him at the last hogan.

All that was truly Indian in him beat in his blood and stirred in his soul here in the solitude and the loneliness. He was miles from any trail he had ever ridden. Only sight of Nothsis Ahn could give him his bearings. He was lost in the desert, reckoning with a white man's reason, but the red nature of him whispered he could never be lost. He lay down on cedar boughs, with a saddle under his head, a blanket over him, and peered up at the white stars. The silence was of the desert locking its elements in repose. There was no sound, no life but the breath of nature, the penetrating power of an invisible spirit hovering over all, abiding in the rocks, floating in the fragrance of the sage.

For long Nophaie lay with the absorbed senses of the Indian tranced in their singular capacity of absolute thoughtlessness. He did not think. He felt. He had this Indian inheritance, unknown to the white man. Though he did not realize it in a thinking act he was unutterably happy while this trance lasted. He saw. The vast, star-studded dome of blue sky arched over him, endless, boundless, only obstructed by horizon line. He saw the shooting stars gleam across the heavens. He saw through the blue depths to the infinite beyond. He saw the shadow of gahd, the cedar, against the sky; and the gray obscurity of the sage and the dim hills, spectral, like hills in the dawn of the earth. He smelled the dry pine-scented dead and fallen leafage under him, the woody cedar, the taint of gophers in the holes of the dusty ground, the fragrance of the sage, the faint hint of rain wafted on the still air from far-off storm, the horse odor of his saddle, the warmth of his body. He tasted the breath of living things and the death of the desert, all in the bits of cedar and sage he unconsciously chewed. His ears drank in the sounds of the silence—nothing but the vast, low thrumming of nature, which might have been the beat of blood in his breast. And he felt all the deathlessness and immortality around him, the link between his living frame and the dust of bones of his simian progenitors, felt life all about him, in stones and woods, in the night shadows, in the mystic dim distance, felt the vast earth under him and the measureless void alone as parts of his being.

Then across his idle, vacant, opaque mind suddenly shot thought and memory and image. He saw Marian's beautiful face, the crown of golden hair, the eyes of azure blue. His love surged up, like a flood undammed. And he remembered he was Nophaie, wanderer of the sage, outlaw of his people, an infidel, without home or kin or flock, the poorest of Nopahs, doomed to illusion, beating his life out against the bars of alien hate.

Upon reaching the upland pasture under Nothsis Ahn, Nophaie herded his horses into a band, and drove them out on the Pahute trail. Next night he camped down in the deep canyon with the family who lived there, finding in this remote place that his fame had arrived before him. Welcome was his in every Indian habitation. At sunrise he headed his horses up the overhanging colored slope of earth and rock, out on the cedared flats, down into the monument country where Oljato and the range of his boyhood called with poignant sorrow and regret, and across the red and yellow desert to Kaidab.

"Sure, I'll buy your horses," said Withers, in reply to Nophaie's query. "What will you take for them?"

Nophaie hesitated a moment, then named a figure.

"That's not enough," replied Withers. "I'll give you five more on each horse. What'll you take—cash or trade?"

Nophaie took part of the deal in new outfit for himself, which included a gun.

"Reckon you're going to do what Blucher told Wolterson, 'Ride around,'" said Withers, with a laugh. "You can do some riding here for us. I'm glad you came. Mrs. Withers was about to send for you."

Nophaie wondered what the trader's wife could want him for, unless something in connection with Marian. Also he was curious to see if she had any knowledge of his rise to fame among the Indians through his taking Gekin Yashi from the school. Mrs. Withers was glad to see him and was eager to hear news of Marian, but she had heard nothing of his abducting Do etin's daughter.

"Nophaie, I would like you to help us here in a little job—our kind of missionary work," she said presently. "Do you know this half-crazy Indian we call Shoie?"

"No," replied Nophaie.

"Well, he claimed to have bewitched a squaw who died. And he has told two other squaws that he means to work his spell upon them. The first one, Nolghoshie, the loping woman, got to thinking about this, and she fell sick. I'm afraid it will kill her. I want you to help me get Shoie to say he will remove his spell. Then ride over to Nolghoshie's hogan and tell her. The other squaw is the wife of Beleanth do de jodie. He is a rich Nopah and a good man. I'm afraid his wife will also get to brooding about this spell. We want to tell her that it's what you called Morgan's preaching."

"What was that?" inquired Nophaie curiously.

"Bunk!" exclaimed the trader's wife, with a twinkle in her eyes. "That word has spread all over the reservation. I've had a dozen Indians ask me what 'bunk' meant. You see, loudmouthed Jay Lord told it in the trading post at Mesa, before some Indians. That's how it got out. I wouldn't commit myself to calling Morgan's preaching bunk but that sure describes the talk of Shoie."

"I thought Jay Lord was one of Morgan's right-hand men," observed Nophaie reflectively.

"No, he's Blucher's tool. For that matter they all hate each other. Now, will you stay here at the post for a few days and help me to deliver these squaws from Shoie's spell?"

"Mrs. Withers, do you really believe these Indian women can fall ill and die of such a thing?"

"Believe it? I know it. It happens often. To think evil is to be evil, for an Indian. If you can make any Indian think a thing it is true for him."

"Yes, I know. But I never heard of a half-crazy Indian casting a spell."

"Nophaie, it will take years before you learn the superstition of your people. You never will understand wholly. Remember, you have lived your life away from them."

"I can influence this Shoie," he replied, and then briefly related what had happened in Wolterson's yard at Mesa, his interview with Do etin, his taking Gekin Yashi away into hiding, and the strange reaction of his tribe.

Mrs. Withers grew intensely animated, almost excited, and she seemed at the halfway point between elation and anxiety.

"So *that* was it!" she exclaimed. "I've been wondering about this sudden interest in you. Well, Nophaie, there is no other single thing you could have done to establish a great name for yourself among the Indians. That will put you high up. So in one way it is good, for no matter what the agent and missionary do your name is made. But it is bad in other ways. They will get Gekin Yashi. Some of the Nokis will trail her. If Blucher finds out your part in it he will arrest you. And when they do find Gekin Yashi I wonder how Do etin will act."

Thereupon Nophaie told of Do etin's anger and his stern ultimatum.

"That is very bad," she said, gravely. "Do etin can't keep Gekin Yashi from going to Morgan's chapel, once that rule is put into effect. You see the Indians are really prisoners on this reservation. They have to obey the government. If they don't they will be forced to . . . That is bad. Do etin will never break his word or give in. It means jail for him—or worse."

Nophaie took some time over the selection of his outfit, especially the gun. He felt himself a novice in the use of firearms, and after considerable deliberation he decided a small weapon he could conceal if desirable, or carry on his belt, would be best for him.

"Here's your man Shoie," said Withers, coming into the post.

Nophaie approached this Indian with interest, and something of disgust, and yet with a strange, vague reluctance. This last must have emanated from the early mental associations of Nophaie's boyhood, intimations of which often stirred him to wonder and doubt.

Shoie appeared to be an Indian of perhaps twenty years of age, a big-headed brave with bushy hair, from which he derived his name. His face might have impressed a superstitious squaw but Nophaie saw it as that of a vain, sullen Indian, lacking in intelligence. Shoie's garb was not that of a prosperous Nopah.

He was evidently flattered to be singled out of the group of Indians, and showed the same deference for Nophaie that had become universal. Nophaie affected to be impressed with Shoie, bought cigarettes and canned fruit and cakes for him, and spent quite a while with him before broaching the subject of Shoie's spell of bewitchment. Then Shoie denied that he had cast a spell upon any squaw. But after some persuasion he confessed it, saying these women were possessed of evil spirits which he wanted to exorcise. Nophaie at length got him to say that he would remove the spell.

Nophaie decided at once to ride out to the hogans of these Indians and take Shoie with him. When Mrs. Withers had been informed she asked to see Shoie, and conversed with him for a moment.

"Maybe it will work," she said to Nophaie, "but I have my doubts. Shoie is much impressed. He thinks he's a big fellow. He sees that he can make himself felt. Now what will happen is this. He'll do as you want today. But tomorrow or some other day he'll tell the Indians he has put back the spell. You see he's just demented enough to make the superstitious Indians afraid of him."

Nolghoshie, the loping woman, lived out across the desert, in a canyon that opened into the mountain mesa. Hogans were numerous under the looming wall of this upland. Nophaie made rather a ceremonious visit out of this trip, talking with Indians, and asking some to accompany him. Nolghoshie owned many sheep. She was an expert blanket weaver. Her husband had gone off to some other part of the reservation. Nophaie found her tended by female relatives or friends. Before he entered the hogan he called these women out and told his errand, indicating Shoie, who stood by, hugely alive to his importance. The women were glad; they cast dark and fearful glances at this Indian possessor of witchcraft. Nophaie thought best not to take Shoie into the hogan with him.

Nolghoshie lay on her blankets, a squaw still young and not uncomely, and for all Nophaie could tell she looked perfectly healthy. But she was sick in her mind.

"Nophaie has brought Shoie. He is outside," said Nophaie impressively. "He will take away the spell."

The squaw stared at Nophaie and then at her attendants, all of whom nodded vehemently and corroborated his statement. The effect on Nolghoshie was magical. Her face lost its set, solemn gloom. Her eyes dilated, and she sat up. Nophaie talked to her for a few moments, assuring her that the evil spirit had departed and would not return. Nolghoshie grew better even while he was there. Nophaie left, marveling at the effect of thought upon the mind and body of a human being.

He rode with Shoie to the far end of that pasture land, some ten miles to the westward of Kaidab. Beleanth do de jodie was at home, much concerned about his wife. She was very ill. The medicine man had done her no good. Nophaie had audience with her also, and saw at once that it was precisely the same kind of case as Nolghoshie's, only this squaw had thought herself into a more dangerous condition. Nophaie was not sure that he reached her understanding. But she, at least, showed no sign of improvement. Nophaie went out to find Beleanth do de jodie pressing presents upon Shoie, an unwise proceeding, judged in the light of Mrs. Withers words.

Next day a messenger arrived in Kaidab with news that Beleanth do de jodie's wife had died. This gave Nophaie a profound shock. He exerted himself in every possible way to keep Nolghoshie from finding out. In vain! Her own attendants, in spite of advice and importunity and threats, told her of the death of the other woman who had been under Shoie's evil spell.

Nolghoshie fell back into the panic of superstitious fears. Nophaie besought her with all the eloquence and persuasion he could command. She only grew worse. Then he galloped off in search of Shoie. At last he found him, on the very moment bragging he had put back the spell upon Beleanth do de jodie's wife, and intended to do the same for Nolghoshie.

"Come back with me," demanded Nophaie. "So that Nolghoshie may hear from your own lips the spell is broken."

"No!" returned Shoie, sullenly, with an uplift of his bushy head.

"You will come," replied Nophaie, sharply, and he dismounted.

The Indians present, all except Shoie, rose in respect to Nophaie. And old chief, who had evidently been listening, put his head out of a hogan.

"Nophaie is master," he said. "Shoie is an Indian with twisted mind. He is not a medicine man. His spell is a lie."

Nophaie knocked Shoie down and beat him, and dragging him to his feet shoved him back to his horse.

"Get up," he ordered.

Nophaie forced the bleeding and frightened Indian to ride with him to the hogan of Nolghoshie. But they arrived too late to lend any light to that darkened brain. Nolghoshie was raving.

Nophaie drove Shoie off with a threat to kill him if

ever again he claimed to cast a spell of witchcraft on an Indian. Upon Nophaie's return to Kaidab with the news, Mrs. Withers expressed sorrow but not surprise.

"I knew just that would happen," she added. "Nolghoshie will die."

And next day came the messenger with news of her death and that none of the Indians would bury her. Nophaie took this duty upon himself.

Chapter 11

MARIAN WARNER BELIEVED THAT SIX MONTHS of intensive work in close contact with missionaries, and diligent study of every book she could get on the Indian problem, had given her a fair understanding of the weighty question. To this observation and study she brought as keen and critical and unbiased a judgment as was possible for her. Emotion did not govern her judgments. Strange and poignant as her feeling was, through her relation to Nophaie, she kept it from clouding her vision or narrowing her mind or obstructing her sense of justice. Something about the desert and its primitive peoples had sharpened her intelligence, changed her whole outlook on life; something about the missionary relation to the Indian stunned her with its incredible falsity through bad missionaries, its pitiful futility through good ones. To her conception the majority of missionaries were bad, and they made almost useless the efforts of those who were good.

It was Marian's belief that the singular situation was a result of three things—government rule, missionary intrigue, and the isolation of the Indians on reservations in the desert.

Agents were appointed by the government; missionaries were there only by courtesy. The whole relation between them, and the fate of the Indians, lay in what kind of men they were. Political influence sent many men to be superintendents of reservations, but few of them were efficient. Failure in other walks of life was not a great asset for success in a most complex and difficult field. The very ablest and finest of men would meet with work needing all their acumen and broad-mindedness. The bigger they were, it seemed, the more complicated their positions. Possibilities of the Indian were unlimited, but so also were the difficulties of helping him. It was, however, pretty safe to assume that agents did not accept appointments for love of Indians or yearning to do good. Marian got the complete history of a dozen agents before Blucher, and often when she should have been sleeping she was writing these records down. The one agent among these whom the Indians respected and liked, who bade fair to help them, did not last long with the redoubtable Morgan.

Most of these agents had been hopelessly out of their element. They were holding down an irksome job—out there because they had failed in the East or for poor health or because they had political influence enough to gain a job they were not equal to, or in some instances to get away from an environment that regarded them askance. Some there were who had honestly tried hard to adapt themselves to this work, only to find it beyond them. But from the point of view of Indians and missionaries and employees of the government, and especially of the traders, almost all of the agents were failures. Probably the subtle, complex situation was too much for any man of ordinary attainments.

The missionaries were there on their own volition and through the influence of church, and solely by the courtesy of the government.

A popular idea of missionaries seemed to be that because of their chosen calling they were above reproach. They could not do evil. But this was a terrible blunder. The whole Indian service was hindered and burdened by the imposters and charlatans who were masquerading as missionaries. The weak-minded and weak-lunged preachers who came next in order were just as inefficient as the shaman, just as derogatory to real true missionary work among the Indians. Every post had a dozen or more of these parasites, of most every church denomination. It was only fair to do justice to the priests, who at least were kind and helped the Indians, and who perhaps came nearer to real missionary work. Thus they were thrown together to exist on the money donated by churches and mission boards and societies and private philanthropists.

Years of earnest study and love were of cardinal necessity in learning to understand the Indians' needs. Even an honest missionary of sense and character had a tremendous task on his hands. What then had those shallow, slight, and miserable men whom accident or disgrace or failure or misplaced religious importunity or selfish greed had made so-called missionaries? Utterly futile! Vain oblation!

The Indian's conception of religion is beyond the comprehension of most missionaries. He thinks in symbols. His God is Nature. The Indian feels God in sensorial perceptions of an immense and mystic spirit of life and death about him. All that occurs in nature are manifestations of a supreme being's control of the universe. To these he prays and chants. He prays to the sun for heat to warm him and melt the snow, and bring back the green to corn and fruit. Out of the soft earth spring the bread that he eats, the grass for his flocks. It nurtures life. Snow, rain and dew, the frost and the wind—these come from the Great Spirit. The sliding avalanche, the thundering flood, the splitting crash of lightning, the blizzard, and the torrid, leaden-hazed day of summer, the yellow sandstorm, swooping along with shriek and moan—all the phenomena of nature have direct and personal connection with the Indian's inner life. His head is in the clouds. He walks with shadows. He hears the silent voices. He is mystic. He is closer to the earth than white men. His vision is enchanting. Beauty, color, melody, line and curve, movement and fixity exist for him. From the tree comes the bow, from the flint the arrowhead, from the beast the sinewed string—from physical things about him all the needs of his material life. From the invisible center of his surroundings breathes the potency of creation, the divine essence, the secret. At sunrise the Indian stands entranced in adoration of the renewed burst of light, facing the east, with his prayer on his lips. At sunset he watches the departing glory of the lord of day, silent, rapt, his soul absorbing that golden effulgence, and his prayer ending, "Now all is well."

Only the few men and women who have spent long years in the Indian country, with open minds and hearts, can grasp adequately his symbolism, the poetry and beauty of his unuttered thought, the worship of nature that is his religion.

The good missionary, the one of a thousand, the man who leaves home and comfort and friends to go into a lonely, hard country, burning with zeal to convey the blessing of Jesus Christ to those he considers heathen— armed with a printed book and full of tract speeches, the platitudes of preachers, the "words of religion"— honest and sincere and confident—this missionary has little or no conception of the true nature of his task, of the blindness with which he is afflicted and must eradicate, of the absurdity of converting Indians in little time, of the doubtful question as to the real worthiness of his cause, and, lastly, of the complications fomented by other missionaries, and employees of the government, the cliques, the intrigues, the inside workings of the machine. How little does the world outside a reservation know of the tremendous and staggering question of the relation of missionary to Indian? The good missionary's life is a martyrdom, his fight against the parasitical forces noble as it is futile, and his task of transforming the Indian's religion of nature to the white man's creed one well nigh impossible.

The bad missionaries, which includes the great majority, are Bolshevists. Like old women gossips they carry tales and stir up dissension with agents and assistants, with traders and Indians. Every fool of an Indian finds in them a welcome ear, and every wrong or fancied wrong is magnified and used to further their interests, to furnish proof of their activity.

Least of all do the majority of these missionaries, good and bad, understand the desert and its meanings, its subtle influence upon life, its inscrutable ruthlessness and ferocity.

Missionaries, with other white people, born to a life in civilization and comfort, are thrown here and there in little communities all over the desert reservations. They work or idle as suits their natures, but they live. They are unconsciously affected by their environment. The desert is wide, open, vast, free, lonely, silent, fierce and violent, hard and cruel, inevitable as nature itself. The sun is no respecter of people who live in places not meant for them. Winter and summer the great, vast light, the glare of the sun, is terrible. It is not to be endured by people with white skins. The God of the Indian, at least, did not intend white men for the desert. The Bedouin, the gaucho, the Indian all have dark faces—the pigment of their skins was created to resist sunlight. For months the heat is torrid, incalculable in its effect upon mind and blood. In the spring the simoon blows—piercing winds, flying walls of sand, days and days of yellow palls of dust, irritating to eyes and souls of white people. The storms are fierce, sudden, violent, like the nature of the desert. The winters in the high altitudes, on the open waste, are bitter and long and cold.

The elements, loneliness and solitude, the great emptiness, the endless encroachment of the desert invariably and inevitably work upon the minds of white people. Were their hearts in this life and their hopes for a future lived on the desert the effect on character, as well as physical being, would be vastly different. But mostly they hate the wild country that holds them for the time. Thus deterioration is sure, both bodily and mentally. Always in sparsely uninhabitated places, especially in wastelands where the elements make life stern, men and women find self-interests and human weaknesses growing magnified. They go back in the scale of progress. Hate is more of hate, love is fiercer, jealousy, greed, cowardice, selfishness stalk out from under the thin skin of civilization and grow rampant. Endurance brings out the weakness or strength of any man. Self-preservation is the first law of life, and on the desert this instinct comes to the fore. But few men, and those the lovers of the open and who welcome the hard life, ever grow nobler for contact with the desert. That some men and women do grow wonderful through a strange evolution wrought by desert life is proof of the divinity that is in them. These are closest to the Indian. But those who deteriorate have the excuse of being unfortunately placed in an environment that brings out the frailties of the human family.

Not improbably this elemental influence explains in part the wrong perpetuated upon Indian women by white men.

Whatever missionaries might have been back in civilization, out in the wild country they are confronted with life in the raw. They react to it just as subtly as other men. The only reason they are more culpable than other men is because their office as ministers of the white gospel gives them a peculiar opportunity and advantage, which to use is utterly base.

But in all justice the truth is that the Indian girl is strangely and pitifully susceptible. She is primitive. She has still the instincts of the savage. Her religion does not make for sophistication, does not invest her with a protection universal in white girls. Her father, perhaps, is a polygamist. Her mother does not teach her the restraint of instincts. There is no strict observance of moral law in the tribe. She does not think evil because in her creed to think evil is to be evil. She is shy, dreamy, passive, though full of latent fire, innocent as an animal, and indeed similar to one. Her mind is a treasure store of legends and lore, of poetry and music, of maiden enchantments, but her blood is red and hot, and she is a child of the elements.

Chapter 12

MORGAN PUT THE LETTERS IN A DRAWER OF HIS desk and locked it.

"I've got the Old Book behind me," he muttered, with a sibilant note of exaltation in his voice.

Then he gathered together a number of typewritten pages, all soiled, with the dirty thumb marks of Indians at the bottom. These he placed in an envelope, sealed, and addressed it, and placed it in his pocket to give personally to the Indian mail carrier. Morgan never entrusted his communications to the post office at Mesa. Pondering a moment, with his fat fingers thrumming on the desk, he had an intense and preoccupied air. The furrows on his brow knit into a knot.

His office adjoined the chapel where he preached to the Indians. It was not a severe and austere room by any means. Color and comfort were exceedingly in evidence. There was a significant absence of anything of Indian design. This study had two other doors, one opening into his living room, the other out upon a back porch.

Presently Morgan got up and went to the open window. The September morning breeze bore a hint of melting frost. The summer was waning. Already the orchard showed the gold and bronze colors of autumn. But out beyond the sweep of desert seemed as changeless as it was endless. That wide expanse of green and yellow, with the dark, rugged lines of canyons in the distance, and the stark areas of clay and rock, seemed an encompassing barrier. Morgan had no love for the open spaces.

His first visitor that morning was Jay Lord. The heavy-booted, lazy-striding Mormon entered familiarly without removing sombrero or cigarette, and his bold face wore a mask of a smile. His dusty garb attested to recent travel.

"Howdy, Morgan," he said. "I got back last night. Haven't seen Blucher yet. Reckon I wanted to see you first."

"Did you find out anything?" queried Morgan.

"Wal, yes an' no," returned Lord. "I can't prove what Blucher wants. Them Pahutes are sure close-mouthed. But I've a hunch the Carlisle Injun Nophay had a lot to do with Gekin Yashi's disappearance."

"So had I that hunch," retorted the missionary darkly. "Blucher didn't want to send you. He doesn't care now the girl has been brought back. But *I* care. And I want examples to be made of Do etin, and whoever rode off with Gekin Yashi."

"Reckon you'll never prove anythin' on either Do etin or Nophay," said Lord dryly. "You'll just have to frame them."

"Jay Lord, I don't like your talk."

"Wal, if you don't like it you can lump it," drawled the other. "I told you I was ready to work for your interests, in the dark. An' so I am. But don't call spades hearts to me. I've been ten years rustlin' round this reservation."

Morgan's pale eyes studied the blunt nonchalant Mormon, with that penetrating, somber gaze of a shrewd man who trusted no one.

"Very well. We'll call spades spades," replied Morgan, succinctly. "I need you. And you want to replace Wolterson. I'll see that Blucher puts the steamroller under him. And I'll pay you besides."

"How much?" asked Lord laconically.

"What it's worth to me," snapped Morgan. "I don't pay men before they work."

"Ahuh! Wal, we understand each other. An' is my hunch about Blucher correct?"

"What is that?"

"Wal, you wasn't particular clear, but I sort of got an idea you wanted more on Blucher, so you could steamroll him when it suited you."

Morgan deliberated. The way his hand closed tight betrayed his realization that he was dealing with a shrewd, unscrupulous man whom he must bind and hold.

"You're no fool, Jay Lord. That's why I want to keep you here at Mesa. . . . Now tell me why you believe this Carlisle Indian had something to do with Gekin Yashi's disappearance?"

"Wal, the day after she was lost I rode across the mesa," rejoined Lord. "I found where Gekin Yashi had rode off the trail. An' I searched round till I saw moccasin tracks in the sand, an' hoss tracks. I've been a hoss tracker all my days, an' there wasn't a wrangler in my country who could beat me. I jest got down on my knees an' made a picture in my mind of them moccasin tracks an' hoss tracks. Then I measured them. I trailed them tracks all day, till I seen they were goin' straight north. Then I came back."

"Well, go on," said Morgan, impatiently. "The Nokis did as well as that."

"Sure. But it took them long to find out what I knew right off—that they'd lose the trail when they came to the sage and the flat-rock country up towards Nothsis Ahn."

"Yes, but if the Nokis lost that trail how did they eventually find Gekin Yashi?"

"Wal, I found *that* out this trip. Your Nokis didn't find Gekin Yashi. The Pahutes who had her brought her to the camp of the Nokis."

"Humph! Pahutes? This is queer. Were these Pahutes afraid?"

"Not of you or Blucher," replied Lord, with a sardonic grin. "It came about this way. There's a half-nutty Nopah named Shoie. He's a spellbinder. He heard about these Pahutes having Gekin Yashi hid deep in the canyons. Of course all the Nopahs knew that. Wal, this nutty Injun sends word by a Pahute that he had put his spell upon Gekin Yashi to kill her. He'd already killed two Nopah women with his spell. The Pahutes are more superstitious than the Nopahs. They fetched Gekin Yashi out to the Nokis who were huntin' her."

"Well!" ejaculated Morgan. "And how do you connect the Carlisle graduate with this?"

"Wal, that's the funny part, hard to prove to anybody but myself," responded Lord, scratching his head. "While I was up in that country I found out where Nophay had lived an' buried his relation. Sure, it's a wild country. But I rode across it, an' I finally found Nophay's hogan. I searched around for hoss tracks and moccasin tracks like them I had pictured in my mind. An' I found them, plain as print. I found clean-cut moccasin tracks on the grave of Nophay's relation. I recognized that track. An' on the way down here I asked a Nopah who buried Nophay's relation an' he said Nophay. . . . Now, Morgan, that's my hunch. It doesn't prove anythin', except to me. I *know* who stole Gekin Yashi away."

"That's proof enough for me," returned Morgan somberly. "Lord, you're a sharp fellow. I didn't appreciate you. We'll get along. . . . Now, don't tell Blucher this about the Carlisle Indian. . . . Go now and do Blucher's bidding. Keep your eyes and ears open. And see me often."

Morgan intercepted the mail carrier and safely deposited the precious affidavits of his zeal in that trusty Indian's pocket.

The missionary then made his observant way up the shady avenue of tall poplars toward the agent's office. Morgan was light-footed. He stepped softly, though not from any instinct like the Indians. Manifold indeed were the intricacies of his habit of life. As he mounted the high porch steps he heard voices. Friel and the Warner girl! Morgan paused to listen.

"Let me alone," the girl protested wearily.

The sound of scraping chair on the floor followed, then swift, soft steps, and a man's voice, with a quick note, rather hoarse. "Marian, I can't let you alone. Don't you know when a man loves you?"

"No, I don't—if the man's you," declared Miss Warner. "I don't *want* to know. . . . Mr. Friel, I've long despaired of you showing any instincts of a gentleman, but I didn't think you would attack me."

"Nonsense. I only wanted to kiss you."

"Your intrusion—your words are an insult," returned the girl, with spirit. "And your . . . your trying to hold me is worse."

"Didn't I ask you to marry me?" he said banteringly.

"Yes, and your proposal had not the ring of sincerity. Even if it had, I would have refused you. I tell you once more. No! I don't care for you, I couldn't care for you."

"But I can make you care," he responded.

"Mr. Friel, I wonder you can be such a . . . a fool," retorted Miss Warner, in anger. "Do you imagine me to be one of these simpleminded Indian girls?"

"I think you're adorable," he returned, "and I'll make you pay for calling me a fool. Of course I am—to be so crazy over you . . . come here, golden hair!"

"Oh! You . . . you . . . " burst out the girl.

Morgan strode to the door and entered. Friel was trying to enfold Marian Warner in his arms and she was thrusting him back.

"Hah! Excuse me, young folks," said Morgan, with severe levity. "Am I interrupting a love scene?"

"You are not!" cried Marian, hotly, now jerking free of Friel. Her face was red. Her dark blue eyes blazed. Her bosom heaved. For the first time Morgan thought this blond girl handsome. Dark women only appealed to him.

"So ho?" he ejaculated, with pretension of surprise. "What was it I interrupted then?"

"Mr. Morgan, you can judge for yourself," replied the girl, with trembling hands at her disheveled hair.

"This man sneaks in here while Mr. Blucher is out. . . . I despise him. I think he's the cheapest, most offensive cad I ever saw. I'm not in the least afraid of him. I don't run to get out of his way. But I will not stand his . . . his . . . "

"Attacks, I suppose you mean," interposed Morgan, as the girl paused breathless, and at loss for a word.

Friel confronted Morgan in suppressed agitation. He was a tall man, not yet beyond middle age, thin and nervous, with lean face of pale wolfish cast.

"See here, Morgan, you're damn quick to grasp at things, aren't you?" he rasped out, sneeringly. "You sneaked in here yourself."

"Miss Warner, this is serious, but I acquit you of blame," said Morgan, paying no attention to the irate Friel. "Where is Blucher?"

"He went to the dormitory to consult Miss Herron."

"Please go for him. Don't mention this unfortunate . . . affair. Leave that to me. I'll see you are not attacked again."

When Marian had left Friel roused from his momentary angry consternation, and he fell into a fury. For a moment he was beside himself, flung his arms, tore at his hair, and choked in his utterance.

"Friel, this is a serious charge," declared Morgan.

"Trump it up! Hatch something! Frame one of your damned tricks on me," exclaimed Friel, in low, hoarse passion. "Bah! I'm onto you. How you jump at anything to further your nefarious ends! I'm in love with that girl. You interrupted my lovemaking. That and nothing more!"

"Friel, I'd like to believe what you say," replied Morgan caustically, "but Miss Warner's plain talk proves you're either a liar or out of your head."

"My heavens! It was her temper, I tell you. She knows I didn't mean her harm," protested Friel.

"No, she didn't. And neither do I. Suppose I call an investigation by the mission board? If Miss Warner testified to her convictions, and if I told what I saw, you would be rather seriously involved, now wouldn't you?"

Friel gave the head missionary one comprehensive glance, keen and malignant, and somehow impotent. Then his whole demeanor changed. Manifestly he had been surprised by Morgan in the expression of amatory advances he did not deem criminal, and next he had fallen prey to perfectly natural wrath. But now he had suddenly lost his excessive irritation, his impulsive and explosive fury.

"Investigation!" he echoed slowly. "You wouldn't call one on me?"

"I've been your friend here. I've kept you here on the reservation. This behavior of yours is not becoming to a missionary. And your ranting at me did not sound like music to my ears. I might call an investigation by the board."

"You *might*," returned Friel sarcastically. "Which means you won't just so long as I stand hand in glove with you?"

"Precisely. You remember that little irregularity of yours, concerning the testimonials—the thumbprints of Indians who didn't know they were signing away their land and water rights? For land you now have a patent to?"

"Yes, I remember, and most decidedly I remember the idea did not originate wholly in my brain."

"That you cannot prove," replied Morgan tersely. "So I think you'll be wise to stand on my side of the fence. Here comes Blucher. Not a word of this!"

Morgan locked the door of Blucher's private office. He did not need more than sight of the agent's face to see that the German's twist of mind was at work.

Blucher was stocky of build, light-complexioned, broad of face, with the Prussian look. Intolerance!

"What's the trouble?" asked Morgan, and it was certain he lowered his voice.

Blucher's gray-blue eyes dilated and suddenly appeared to gleam dancingly with little arrows of flame.

"What's *your* trouble?" queried the agent, with a laugh. "You're stewed up, same as I am."

"Don't talk so loud," replied Morgan, with significant look and motion at the door of Miss Warner's room. "I don't trust that girl. My Noki says he saw her at the Castle Rocks talking to our Carlisle Indian. If it's true I can see through a good deal. But I'm not so sure of that. The Noki wasn't close to them. But we're cautious now."

"Suppose it was true?" asked Blucher, interested.

"It was that educated Nopah who stole Gekin Yashi from the school."

Blucher vibrated to that.

"Who told you? How do you know? What—"

"Never mind how I get my facts. I know. That's enough."

"But what you know doesn't satisfy me," returned Blucher testily. "I like Miss Warner. She's a fine girl. I can't see one fault in her. What's more, she's a great help to me. I'd miss her."

"I'm not suggesting you give her a ride on my steamroller," rejoined the missionary. "If she's valuable, get all you can out of her—until we know for sure. And meanwhile be cautious."

"How're we going to know for sure? We've read some of her letters. But they didn't prove anything to me. I think you're overcautious."

"Not me. Those letters of hers gave me an idea. She lived in Philadelphia and spent her summers at the seashore. She wrote of seeing baseball games there. Now I've learned that our Carlisle graduate was one of the most famous athletes the eastern colleges ever developed."

"That Indian!"

"Yes, that Indian," rejoined Morgan. "I'm not likely to forget the sample he gave us of his education. That Nopah has brains. Well, I'm wondering if Miss Warner might have known him in the East. I'll write to my Philadelphia friend and ask him for more information, especially if this Carlisle Nopah played baseball at the seashore."

"Why not cut straight to the heart of a problem?" queried Blucher impatiently. "You work in the dark."

"It's never wise to show your hand."

"Let's not waste opportunity. I'll have Miss Warner in here," replied Blucher.

The missionary raised a warning hand, restraining the agent.

"Wait a moment." Morgan's pale cast of thought grew more intense. "All right. Fetch her in. But let me question her. I'll take a chance."

Blucher, unlocking the door, opened it and called, "Miss Warner, please step here."

She came in, quiet, composed, but a keen eye could have detected a slight constriction of her throat, a glistening dilation of the pupils of her blue eyes. Morgan assuredly saw the slight signs of agitation. He fixed his cold, icy gaze upon her face.

"Miss Warner, you deny you're a friend of the Carlisle graduate Nophaie, that you meet him secretly?"

The girl's golden tan seemed to recede leaving a clear pallor on cheek and brow. A quick breath escaped her. Then she flushed dark red, her eyes blazed as they had blazed at Friel, her head went up in dauntless spirit.

"Mr. Morgan, am I to understand that I am a hireling to whom you are privileged to put such personal questions?" she flashed at him, in counter query.

Morgan made a slight motion of his hand, as if for Blucher to dismiss her. Manifestly he had been answered to his satisfaction.

"*Do* you deny?" interposed Blucher.

"I would not deny any implication whatever made by Mr. Morgan," the girl returned loftily.

"Very well. That will do," said Blucher, waving her to the door, which he closed and locked after her.

Morgan signed him to draw a chair closer, and he whispered, "It's more than I suspected. Your doll-face

is a deep, clever woman. She meets the Indian. Maybe
she's in love with him. Absolutely, she's not what she
seems."

The agent stroked his chin and gazed with abject
wonder and disgust at the missionary.

"Morgan, you look for rottenness in every man and
woman because your mind is rotten," he said. "I don't
believe what you think about her."

Morgan's stout body jerked a little, as with the
propelling of blood in sudden anger. And the lowering
cold shadow of his eyes might have been thought-
provoking to a less stolid man that Blucher.

"I usually find what I look for," rejoined the missionary. "Let's drop the Warner woman for the present.
How about the Wolterson case?"

The agent unlocked his desk and produced letters
and papers.

"Wolterson is about ready for your steamroller,"
said Blucher grimly. "All my reports have gone
through. Here's a copy of a letter to Wolterson from
Commissioner Salisbury, Department of the Interior at
Washington."

Blucher spread a paper covered with handwriting in
lead pencil and he read:

Robert Wolterson
Through Supt. Mesa Indian School

Sir:

   Reports indicate that your services as stockman
are not satisfactory; that you lack energy and
initiative; that you boast you can make a living
without work; that you are wholly inattentive to
your duties and have no interest in the welfare of
the Service; that you spend your time in idleness,
loafing around your quarters, at different trader's
stores, or taking pleasure trips; that you almost
invariably remain in bed after the other employees

are at their work; that you have neglected the agency stallions, which were in your care, to such extent that one of them died; and that through your negligence a young heifer recently died.

You will be given ten days from the receipt of this letter to show cause, if any, why you should not be transferred or dismissed from the Service. Your reply should be submitted through the Superintendent within the time specified.

Re'sp
Otto Salisbury

"Humph!" ejaculated Morgan. "That's not much of a charge against Wolterson. What was his reply through you?"

"It's too long to read. Take this copy with you. One thing sure, Wolterson makes a strong case, and just about proves it. More than that he has bobbed up with influential friends in Texas, one of them a senator. The best we can expect is that Wolterson will be transferred to some other point on the reservation."

"That will do. What we don't want is an investigation out *here*. Wolterson is sharp enough to get that Carlisle Indian down here, with a lot of Nopahs who know things. . . . I see this Indian and Wolterson, his wife, Miss Warner, the trader Withers, all in a clique to oust you."

"If me why not you?" queried Blucher darkly.

Morgan waved a deprecatory hand, singularly expressive.

"You're only the superintendent."

"And *you* have the Old Book behind you, yes?" demanded Blucher scornfully.

"I have the Rock of Ages behind me. I can't be moved."

"Missionary Morgan, do you really believe what you say?" queried Blucher.

"I know," said Morgan, with finality.

"Hell! You and your Old Book will go smash some day—the longer you last the harder you'll smash."

"Perhaps. But you'll not be here to enjoy it," retorted Morgan. "We get off the issue . . . I think we need to make further charges against Wolterson. I suggest you involve him in this kidnapping of Gekin Yashi."

"It won't be necessary. Wolterson will be through here when I approve his transfer. I advised his dismissal, but evidently that was a little strong."

"So much for him," mused Morgan, gazing deeply into space. "Before we get on to the Do etin case let's thrash out this matter of the Indian young men being permitted to get into the girls' dormitory at night."

"Isn't that my affair?" inquired Blucher. "Are you superintendent of this school and reservation?"

Morgan's reply was neither negative nor affirmative. It was a silent study of the face of the agent.

"I got the truth of it," Blucher began slowly.

"From what source? Miss Herron told me all she knew before you heard of the goings-on."

"You *think* she told you all," retorted Blucher, with malice. "As a matter of fact, she lied. I believe she had something to do with those Indian youths stealing into the dormitory."

It was Morgan's turn to show amazement and skepticism.

"Miss Herron was a missionary before she became matron of the school," declared Morgan, as if the bare statement of such fact refuted any possibility of culpability.

The superintendent stared. Then he laughed outright. Evidently this interview was not wholly irksome.

"What's that to do with it?"

"It has all to do with it," replied Morgan. "Miss Herron has the responsible duty of looking after the moral welfare of the girl students."

"Bah! Morgan, can't you call things by their proper

names, at least to me?" queried Blucher. "What you mean is that this particular matron was put in her job by you. Therefore, she is responsible to you. Responsible to *you,* yes, for the moral welfare of these Indian girls—and for accurate record of what goes on, so that *you* could be kept posted."

Morgan made a gesture which seemed to intimate that Blucher's talk was Sanskrit to him.

"I can't prove anything on Miss Herron, so there's no need of my giving reasons for what I believe," went on Blucher.

"Yes, there is," returned Morgan sharply. "*I* am responsible for Miss Herron. And any word breathed against her must be substantiated with facts."

Blucher did not appear so dense that he was unconscious of being dominated by this missionary. Nor was his impotence a lack of courage or wit to resist. There was something else.

"Facts? Well, the first fact I established is that this night-visit business has been going on for a long time."

"How long?"

"Ever since you first evinced interest in Gekin Yashi," returned Blucher significantly.

Significance appeared to be lost upon Morgan. "So? Then say about six months."

"Yes. Last spring, about the time this began, one of the Indian girls died very mysteriously. Some sort of convulsion. Well, another girl has just been put in the maternity ward. These are facts. Ruhr, one of my policemen, caught a dozen Indians—young men of the reservation, *not* of the school—coming out of the dormitory late at night. And you know how Miss Gale started the investigation by telling us Gekin Yashi had run to her room for protection. This happened only a few days after Gekin Yashi was brought back to the school. Now Gekin Yashi told me, through my interpreter, Sam Ween, that several times before she left the school she had run to *Miss Herron* for protection.

. . . Funny now that your conscientious matron did not report that to the superintendent?"

If the missionary strove to keep his face from being a study he did not altogether succeed. Blucher took a cigar from his desk, and lighting it, puffed a few times, all the while watching his visitor.

"Morgan, I know you and others credit me with the blockheadedness supposedly common to Germans," continued Blucher. "But I'm not so thick that I ruin everything. . . . I suspect, mind you, I *suspect* that Miss Herron did not lie awake at nights praying for the protection of Indian girls, especially of Gekin Yashi. I know beyond a doubt that Miss Herron was glad when Gekin Yashi disappeared. Also I know from Miss Herron's own lips that she strongly disapproves of the rule making it compulsory for the Indian girls to go to your chapel. . . . Are any of these facts illuminating to you?"

"Not particularly," returned Morgan, with a heavy expulsion of breath. "But the goings-on of these young Indians prove they are heathen and will stay heathen until they are Christians."

"Which will be never," declared the superintendent.

The missionary was not proof against this outspoken repudiation of his entire work in the Indian field.

"I have many converts," he declared, haughtily, with the blood rising to his temples.

"Morgan, your converts are illusions of your fertile brain," said the German contemptuously. "You show a paper to an Indian. You pretend to read what is not there. You say to this Indian: 'Have you not learned from my sermons? Have you not accepted my God?' And the Indian replies, 'Yes.' What he means is, 'Yes I have *not!*' And you get his thumbprint on your paper and send it to your mission, your church. The poor, deluded fools back in the East think you are a great missionary."

"Blucher, what you think of me and what I think of

you are not the issues at present," said the missionary
deliberately. "By and by we are going to clash. But just
now we've serious business that necessitates unity."

"Yes, I know," grunted Blucher, "and I hate to get
down to it."

"If you don't make examples of Do etin and Nophaie
your authority on this reservation will absolutely
cease," declared Morgan impressively. A singular force
emanated from him. He radiated strong suggestiveness
of will.

"Damn that old Indian!" exclaimed Blucher, with
sudden passion. His face set like that of a bulldog. "I'll
make him consent to that rule or . . . or . . ."

"You'll never make him do anything," interrupted
Morgan. "You don't know Indians. Do etin will keep
his word. He'll never consent to Gekin Yashi coming to
my church."

"I don't blame him a damn bit for that," retorted
Blucher, brutally. "But Gekin Yashi is not the point
with me. Do etin has bucked me. He has opposed me.
He will make me look weak to all the Indians. But how
to make an example of him, unless . . ." He paused in
dark significance.

Morgan leaned forward to whisper tensely. "*Unless!*
You have it. . . . Send Ruhr, the policeman, Glendon
and Naylor at night to arrest Do etin. But they *are not*
to arrest him. They will return with news to you. Do
etin refused to consent to the new rule of the government. He resisted arrest. He fought. . . . He was
shot!"

"For once we agree," whispered Blucher in reply.
His set face had grown pale. "And how about the
Carlisle graduate?"

Swift as light the missionary snapped his fingers, but
the lifted hand shook before Blucher's strained gaze.

"That educated Indian is the most dangerous man,
red or white, on this reservation," hissed Morgan.

"Then it's settled," replied Blucher.

"Send your men after Do etin tonight," added the missionary.

"Yes, the sooner the better. And that compulsory rule goes into effect right now."

Morgan hurried across the wide avenue toward his house. He strode as a man who would be dangerous to meet on a narrow footway. Apparently all he saw was the hardpacked sand upon which he trod.

In his study sat the Indian whom he had expected— Noki, a slim, tall, very dark man with straight black hair, and eyes of piercing sharpness. This Indian's last service to Morgan was the bringing back of Gekin Yashi. Long had he been the missionary's spy and tool of craft.

Morgan gripped his arm and dragged him to the couch, there to force him down, and loom masterfully over him. Moistening his lips Morgan began in hoarse whisper of singular potency.

"Noki, tonight you pay your full debt to the white man of God. . . . Go to Do etin's hogan. Be there just at dark. Let the Indian see you, but not the white men who come. Watch these white men go into Do etin's hogan. Steal close and listen to what they say. Trust to the darkness. Listen to that council. Remember every word you hear. And watch—see every move. When the white men go away you hurry back to me."

The Noki's sloe-black eyes shone with something more than comprehension. The Nopahs were heredi- tary foes of the Nokis. This Indian stared solemnly, then he said, "Let the white man speak again."

Deliberately, but with abated breath, Morgan whis- pered again his directions.

For a long time after the Indian had left Morgan sat motionless in his study, locked in thought, his brow a congested mass of furrows. What bound him there was a habit of mind—a recourse to invention to meet every possible future angle, to fortify against the unexpected, to hide the machinations of a master strategist, to satisfy a monstrous egotism. No still, small voice pierced the conscience of this man of God.

At last he arose, muttering half aloud, "That for sure puts the steamroller under Blucher. But it's not enough. . . . As for me, I have the Old Book behind me!"

Chapter 13

MORGAN STAYED UP UNTIL A LATE HOUR THAT night, expecting the Noki to return with news of what had actually happened. But the Indian did not come. The missionary grew rather toward a conviction that nothing unusual had occurred. So at midnight he put aside the Bible he had been studying and went to bed. His slumbers were not disturbed by nightmare or visitor.

Next morning, while at breakfast, Morgan had a caller—the old man who had been the government farmer at Mesa for years. His short, wedge-shaped figure seemed energized by rugged vitality; his features were a record of the desert.

"Mr. Morgan, the Nokis down at Copenwashie are raisin' hell with me," he began.

"Yes? What for? And when you address me, pray do not be profane."

"It's a dry season. All but two of the springs have failed. The Nokis haven't enough water for their alfalfa. Friel gets the water first for his land. That's what the Nokis are sore about. An' I'm sayin' they've got reason!"

"Why do you come to me? I deal with the souls of Indians, not their water rights."

"Wal, Friel's missionary deals are most with their water rights," replied the farmer bluntly. "Now my stand is this. The Nokis are industrious farmers. They've worked hard in that alfalfa. An' I don't want to see it burn up. Friel said what he did was none of my business. I want the Indians to have more of the water that belongs to them."

"Belongs to them? How do you figure that?"

"The Nokis were here before either the Nopahs or the whites."

"That's nothing. The water belongs to the government. And Mr. Friel has a patent on land and water from the government. I couldn't do anything, even if I wanted to."

"Friel has no horses suffering for hay or water. He *sells* his hay. The Indians need good hay and plenty of water. They can't send their horses out into the desert to live on soapweed and greasewood. These Nokis are freighters. They freight supplies from Flagerstown. That's how they earn their living. . . . They're not gettin' a square deal."

"Go to Blucher," replied Morgan.

"I just left him," returned the farmer. "He wasn't interested—sent me to you. I reckon he was upset by his men havin' to kill an Indian last night."

"That so? I hadn't heard," rejoined Morgan, with no especial interest. He might not have been aware of the gray desert eyes bent upon him.

"Wal, it was owin' to some new rulin' or other Blucher ordered," went on the farmer. "Do etin refused to obey, as I heard the story. When Ruhr with his deputies, Glendon an' Naylor, tried to arrest Do etin he fought—an' they had to kill him."

"That was unfortunate," said Morgan, gravely shaking his head. "But Indians must learn to obey."

"Mr. Morgan, would you be good enough to have Friel ease up on the water?" asked the farmer earnestly. "He's usin' more than he needs. An' we haven't had a lot of rain at Copenwashie."

"No. Such a request from me would imply that I shared your opinion as to Mr. Friel's wastefulness, which I don't."

"Ah-huh!" ejaculated the government man, and abruptly turned on his heel. His heavy boots thumped on the porch. Then he was gone.

In the course of that day Morgan heard many ver-

sions of the killing of Do etin. He read Blucher's brief
statement to the officials at Washington; he asked for
the distressed Marian Warner's knowledge of it; he
heard Ruhr tell how it had happened, and also Glendon. He showed grave concern as he met the stockman
Wolterson and asked what he had heard about it. All
stories were substantially the same, precisely what the
school policeman and his deputies had reported first to
the superintendent and later told to other government
employees. There was no excitement or any particular
comment. The death of an Indian was nothing. But
when Morgan asked Jay Lord what he had heard, the
Mormon added a few trenchant words of his own to the
reiterated story: "Wal, that's what *they* say!"

Late that day Morgan received the Noki spy in his
study, the windows and blinds of which were closed.
And peering down into the dark, inscrutable face of
this Noki who hated Nopahs, Morgan heard a long
story, told with all the singular detail of an Indian's
subtle and faithful observance, a story strangely and
vastly different from all the others concerning Do etin's
tragic death.

The shadows of night were creeping over the desert,
deepening in the wide canyon where Do etin had his
hogan. Noki hid along the trail, behind the sandy
hummocks with their tufts of greasewood. The rats had
ventured out of their holes. A hawk sailed low with his
sharp head bent, seeking prey. Already the sheep were
settling down for the night in their stone-walled corral
under the bluff. Now and then came a soft baa-baa on
the cool wind. From the shadows wailed the hungry cry
of a coyote. Flickering campfires widely separated
made bright points down in the gloom.

By and by Noki left his hiding place and passing
down into the canyon he went to one hogan and then
another. He was asked to eat and if he needed help to
find his horse. Noki assumed a mysterious air, important, yet full of reticence. All the time he kept his sharp
eyes on the ridge where the trail passed down to Do

etin's hogan. Here the last flare of the golden afterglow silhouetted the brush against the sky. When Noki espied three horseman ride across that clearness of sky he left his hogan and hurried down the canyon, stealing like a shadow. But he did not try to avoid Hotalie nez, the tall singer, a Nopah he well knew. Noki did not heed the Nopah's call, nor did he heed that he was followed. Soon he heard the soft pound of horses' hooves. Then voices of white men! He stole on, through the brush, until the bright light from Do etin's hogan showed the white men dismounting at the door. They went into the hogan and Do etin's squaws came out. The blanket over the door dropped to shut in the light. Noki strode by Do etin's women, who were whispering in alarm. Then Noki ran. His keen ear caught swift rustle of brush and thud of moccasin behind him. He halted. Hotalie nez, the tall singer, loomed over him. Noki whispered one word that told of peril, and looked no more at the Nopah.

Noki glided to the hogan, meaning to peep under the blanket covering the door. But gleams of light low down from Do etin's hogan showed it to be one not wholly covered with earth. There were holes between the cedar poles. Noki crept like a cat to the hogan and peered in.

A bright fire burned. Do etin's women had built a fire to burn down to a bed of coals, the better for cooking. Noki saw Do etin rise to his feet, and extend his hands in the greeting of hospitality.

"White men are welcome in Do etin's hogan," he said, in Nopah.

Ruhr advanced first into the circle of firelight, then Glendon and Naylor.

"Howdy, Do etin—shake hands," said Ruhr, in the white man's tongue.

With dignity and friendliness the Indian extended his hand. Ruhr grasped it, and suddenly pulled with all his might.

"Now—roughhouse him—quick!" he called, low and hard, to his followers.

But Do etin wrenched loose. With powerful heave he flung Ruhr across the hogan against the wall. Glendon and Naylor then grappled with Do etin. They wrestled with him and in the struggle kicked over the cooking utensils and sent the firebrands scattering. Do etin only strove to free himself. This the two men helped him to do—one with a blow, the other with a shove. Do etin staggered back and half turned. Then out of the gloom beyond the fire circle Ruhr shot—once—twice—three times. The heavy reports boomed in the confined space of the hogan. Do etin swayed, and fell without a word.

"Has he croaked?" queried Ruhr hoarsely. "See! Hurry! One of you mess up the place."

Glendon knelt beside the still figure while Naylor kicked utensils around, scattered the fire and food supplies. The hogan filled with smoke. The light grew dim. The figures appeared shadowy.

"Sure. He's dead," whispered Glendon.

"Come—beat it," replied Ruhr.

They lifted the blanket before the door, and filed out.

It was again night, and one of those nights set for the Indian girls selected by Morgan to come to his chapel to hear him preach. This missionary had not mastered the Nopah language; he had merely been among the No-pahs and Nokis so long that he had acquired a use of their tongue sufficiently to make his meaning clear.

"Your tribe is under control of my government," he harangued at the still, dark faces. "You must learn to obey the white man. Your people are too old to learn. They are heathen. Their God is no good. Their religion is no good. Your parents have no chance for Heaven. They are steeped in ignorance and sin. They will burn forever in Hell's fire.

"You girls are now like sores healed over with all under the skin rotten. That girl Naspa, who died—she was full of sin. That was why she died. If she had accepted the religion I offered her she would now be in

Heaven. But she would not put her hand in mine, so she went to Hell. And there she burns!

"Heaven and Hell are places. Most of the things you do and believe now will send you straight to Hell when you die, unless you take my religion. My Word from the Great Book! The fox made the Nopah Indian, and the fox is the lowest of beasts. As you are now, each of you is like a big, ugly sore. The school doctor, the medicine man makes medicine over it, and it looks fine from the outside. But under that coat it is still a sore, full of rot and pus. So are you Nopah girls rotten at the heart. You think if you can put on bright clothes so you will appear fine on the outside you are all right. For this you are going straight to Hell!

"You must forget the songs and the legends and the prayers of your people. Indians are heathen. They must accept the white man's way, his clothes, his work, his talk, his life, and his God. Then someday the Indians will become white in heart."

Thus the missionary preached for an hour to those still, dark faces. Then he dismissed his congregation, but at the door of the chapel he drew one Indian girl back.

"Gekin Yashi—you stay," he said, as he held her. "I will preach to you alone, so you can spread my word to your sisters."

This Indian maiden did not have a still, dark face. It was pale and agitated, yet beautiful with its contour, its great dusky eyes, its red lips. She was trembling as the missionary led her back from the door. Suddenly he pushed her into a seat and towered over her, strung in all his body, obsessed with his fanaticism.

"Gekin Yashi, do you know your father is dead?" he asked, in harsh, sharp voice.

"Oh—no, sir," the girl faltered, sinking back.

"He is. . . . He was killed last night—killed because he fought the white men who went to arrest him. But it was sin that killed him. He would not obey."

The missionary paused. Gekin Yashi's sweet and

youthful face slowly changed—quivered with tears streaming from her tragic eyes—and set in a strange, dull expression of fear, bewilderment, and misery. Then her dark head drooped.

"You ran off to the Pahutes," went on the missionary. "Who took you?"

Gekin Yashi made no answer.

"It was Nophaie. He will be shot the same as your father, unless you confess your sin and then accept my religion. . . . Speak! Did Nophaie take you away?"

"Yes," she whispered. "But your men brought me back. But Gekin Yashi has . . . not sinned. She is like the white girl Benow di cleash."

Then the missionary thundered at her.

"Yes, you have sinned. You are all sin. Only the Word can wash you clean. Bid me speak of it—pray for you to Jesus Christ. . . . I will save you from the ice pits and the fire caves of Hell. . . . Tremble in your fear! Fall on your knees, you daughter of heathen! Hate that false nature worship! Love Jesus Christ! Love me—the white man of God! Promise to do what I tell you!"

The Indian girl lifted her face, and then her little brown hand that fluttered like leaves in a storm.

"Gekin Yashi—promises," she breathed almost inaudibly. "Gekin Yashi . . . will . . . love . . . Jesus Christ—and you!"

Chapter 14

MARIAN, WHILE WAITING FOR THE DISMISSAL she expected every day, worked on as if no untoward thing had happened. But in reality nothing was left for her save a morbid curiosity in the affairs of this government school and her faithful, stubborn, unquenchable desire to help the Indians.

The autumn days wore on close to winter—wonderful, keen, clear days with the desert imperceptibly changing its hue. At night the wind mourned outside her sleeping quarters and moaned in the poplar trees. By day the sun shone in a cloudless sky, blazing over the desert, a flooding, all-embracing light.

No more did Marian ride out to Castle Rocks. No more did she have the thrill and joy of meeting Nophaie. Neither he nor she had any proof that his life was in danger, but they suspected it, and they knew his liberty was threatened. Nophaie had entrusted one letter to Withers and another to a Nopah sheepherder, both of whom delivered these missives through Wolterson. A note of despair and of love rang through Nophaie's wild words, troubling her soul, yet somehow inexpressibly sweet. Separation made him desperate. He needed her. And Marian, in her growing poignancy, longed to go to him, to be his wife. She would have lived in a hogan. Yet even in her longing she realized the nobility of the Indian. She was not meant for a hogan—to raise her children in a mound of earth, like a troglodyte. Infinite respect for Nophaie had added to her love. He was a man. How passionately she burned to prove to the world what an Indian could be! Somehow she would prove that, if not by her own modest pen, then by the power of someone to whom she could tell her story. Nophaie, the same as she, was waiting for

185

developments, perhaps for the hour of her dismissal. Meanwhile his entreaty was for her to hold on and keep her courage, and do what good she could in her own way. Most of all what sustained Marian was the cry of his heart for her.

So she waited, and the weeks passed. And as they passed her experience with the Indian children widened, and her knowledge of the hidden wheels of this government machine grew by leaps and bounds. But the ideal she had cherished so sentimentally, so impulsively, faded away as an illusion, and the hopes she had entertained day by day turned themselves to bitter ashes.

Between her and Gekin Yashi had come a strange, cold, somber shadow, like that in the Little Beauty's dusky eyes. Marian refused credence to the fears her intelligence prompted. Circumstances had altered her opportunities to be with Gekin Yashi. These came now but seldom. Miss Herron's enmity was open and scarcely possible to combat. The matron was all-powerful in the school. Moreover, Gekin Yashi no longer received Marian with shy, sweet gladness. The Indian maiden had aged. She had frozen. She listened, but did not respond. She seldom raised her eyes. Only rarely did Marian penetrate her reserve. Never again would Marian hurt Gekin Yashi by mentioning Nophaie. And another illuminating reaction of Gekin Yashi's was her reply to one of Marian's appeals. "Oh, no one ever tells me beautiful things!" Marian wondered was all Gekin Yashi's pathos due to the loss of her father?

As winter approached, and the war in Europe extended its claws farther and farther over the world, and especially towards the United States, Blucher indubitably leaned more to an obsession of the rights of Germany. Marian typed many of his letters. As this catastrophe of war slowly spread its dark shadow over the nations, threatening surely to envelop America, Blucher let slip the mental note of lesser things. He could scarcely put his mind on the tasks before him on the reservation, let alone solve their problems. Thus he grew lax in caution, at least so far as Marian was concerned. Nor was he guarded in speech with anyone. One afternoon a number of the government employees were in Blucher's office, the door of which stood open. News had arrived in the mail of various angles of the war, mostly favorable to Germany. The talk of the men was general, though forceful enough, until all at once Wolterson spoke out: "Shore somebody ought to shoot that Kaiser."

Blucher started up as if he had been struck; and if ever a man's face was charged with concentrated passion his was then. He actually addressed Wolterson in German, and then, seeing how all the men stared, he grew red and blurted it out in English.

"Would you shoot the Emperor?"

"Well, wouldn't you?" drawled Wolterson.

"I certainly would not," snapped Blucher.

The Texan's reply rang out minus the drawl. "Shore *I'd* like to."

Blucher suddenly seemed to see in Wolterson something vastly more inimical than the sordid, petty interests of a government reservation for Indians.

What Blucher's reply was, if he made any, Marian did not hear, nor did she get another look at him. From that hour, however, she dated a fixed change in Blucher. A tremendous force changed the direction of his mind, so that his weaknesses were as if they had never been. Marian pondered over this and also over a remark made to her by Wolterson. "If the good old U.S. has to go to war with Germany, life will shore be hell for us on this reservation."

Meanwhile, Marian's observations and convictions grew with the passing of time. What a great deal she would have to tell Nophaie upon their next meeting!

Missionaries on the reservation did things in an underhanded way, which kept at white heat a feeling of bitterness among government employees. Morgan was a master in this Machiavellian game of politics. Some of the employees were not adversaries of the missionaries, although they had been brave enough to take exception to extraordinary statements made to the Indians. Girls had been taken from the reservation, during the absence of the agent, and sent to another state to attend Bible School. Morgan had been seen repeatedly on the school fields and at the school stables, and in other isolated places, talking earnestly to enemies of Blucher. On one occasion, a trader who was not in any way connected with the Agency or the Mission had an errand of business which took him after dark to Morgan's home. When he rapped on the door of the lighted study he heard someone run from the room into another part of the house. And not for several moments did the missionary open the door.

Gossip did not prejudice Marian, though she always gave it an attentive ear. Facts were all that she recorded, and some of these savored of the rank. One of Morgan's missionaries happened to go into a trader's store when there happened to be a rush of business on. He volunteered his services as extra salesman, and was caught helping himself out of the cash drawer. Some of the missionaries were in the habit of visiting Indian women in their hogans. The Indians talked freely of this and gave the names of the missionaries. One of the Mennonite missionaries went to Flagerstown and represented to a large supply company that he had helped build a fence round a cattle range just off the reservation, and he demanded one hundred dollars for his services. The money was paid. Later this company found out that the missionary had not lifted a hand in the work.

Most significant of all Marian learned was the singular fact that letters written to Washington, and to the Mission Board, were not only never answered, but never received by the officials to whom they were addressed. The chief of all the Nopahs, a most intelligent Indian, wrote through an interpreter a letter to Washington, telling and substantiating facts important to the government and to the reservation. He concluded this letter—a copy of which Marian read and considered a remarkable document—by asking a question: "Is this reservation a reservation for Missionaries or for Indians?" No reply was ever received.

Marian had great difficulty in learning the real deep significance of the Indians' religion. The Nopahs prayed to the Sun, Moon, Stars, Wind, Thunder, Lightning—anything beyond their understanding and all of which they symbolized. They recognized the unseen power which sent the sun each day, and the warm winds and the cold, and all physical phenomena. They heard the idea that God was a person and abided in a particular place, but they argued if there was a personal God and a material Heaven, there would be a road leading to it. They believed there was a physical life for spirits of the good, which belief accounted for their custom of sending with the dead the best horses, bridle, saddle, belt, beads, gun. Tools of all sorts were sent—the spirits of the tools—everything that was sent along for the spirit of the dead man had to be killed so that they could go along. Nopahs believed that spirits of evil persons went into animals here on earth—into the coyote, bear, cougar, snake—and this was the reason why the Indians seldom or never killed these creatures.

Marian's personal observances magnified along with the others. Yet keen as was her curiosity she avoided some things that would have been easy to see, the same as she avoided listening to the older Indian girls when they tried to tell her about the matron and the missionary. On the other hand there were incidents she did not care to see, yet could not help seeing. At the midweek religious service Morgan slapped the Indian boys who did not remain quiet while he ridiculed the beliefs of their people. Morgan often reported the children to the matron with instructions that they be punished. Marian had seen several instances of Miss Herron's punishments. She compelled children to bend forward, hands touching the floor, or to stand erect, with hands lifted

high, for as many minutes as they could endure it. Not
unusual was it for a girl to faint under this punishment.
One day some Indian boys ran across the porch of
Blucher's house. Marian saw the agent run out, catch
one of them, knock him down, and kick him after he
was down. The little fellow did not rise very readily.

Another day, early in December, when despite the
bright sunshine, there were ragged edges of ice along
the irrigation ditches, Marian was hurrying by the cellar
door of one of the storehouses. Through the door she
saw two tiny Indian boys trying to assort a huge pile of
potatoes. It was very cold down there in the cellar and
the potatoes were covered with frost. The boys were so
cold they could not speak and could scarcely hold a
potato in their little hands. Marian took them to the
engine room, where they could get warm. Then she
reported the incident to Blucher, who insulted her for
her pains.

By a process of elimination Marian arrived at a few
proofs of the compulsory school education being bene-
ficial to the Indians. Perhaps ninety-nine out of one
hundred students returned to the old life, the hogan
and the sheep. They could not help but carry ideas of
better life, better methods, better management. They
could understand English and knew the value of money
and of a trade. So that whether they liked it or not they
were somewhat better equipped to meet the inroads of
the white man. These advantages, however, were negli-
gible, especially in the case of the Indian girls, when
compared with the disadvantages of the compulsory
school system. Marian inclined more and more to the
conviction that the whole government school and reservation system was wrong.

These weeks of comparative inaction for Marian and
the dearth of news from Nophaie and the apparent
indifference of Blucher and Morgan to her presence as
an employee of the government in no way lulled her
fears, and certainty of ultimate dismissal. The powers
were intent on matters of more importance. On the

contrary, Marian grew brooding and nervous, and was troubled by strange portents impossible to define. She felt that something was about to happen.

And one morning, when Miss Herron, her hard face pale and agitated, came running into the office Marian felt a shock. Her intuition had prompted her aright.

The matron ran into Blucher's office, the door of which was open.

"Where's Morgan?" she asked shrilly. "I can't . . . find him."

"What's wrong?" queried Blucher, with a frown of annoyance at this intrusion or disruption of his thought.

"That Carlisle Indian . . . forced himself into the school room," cried Miss Herron. "He scared me out of . . . my wits. He's dragged Gekin Yashi into the hall, where he's talking to her. I heard Morgan's name . . . then I ran out . . . over to his house—to tell him. . . . Oh, that Indian looked terrible."

"Nophaie!" ejaculated Blucher. Manifestly that Indian name conjured up swift and bewildering ideas. Blucher looked mightily concerned. When Miss Herron started to run out he detained her: "You stay right here—and keep your mouth shut." Then he grasped at the telephone.

The shock to Marian had kept her standing just where she had been when Miss Herron entered. Shuffling soft footsteps that she recognized as Morgan's gave her another shock. Then the missionary entered. Certain it was he did not know of the presence of Nophaie. But his glance at Marian, and then sight of Miss Herron in Blucher's office told him something was amiss.

"What—why are you here?" he demanded.

"Shut up!" interrupted Blucher. "Morgan, there's hell to pay. Your Carlisle Indian is here with Gekin Yashi. . . . Hello—yes, this is Blucher—where's Ruhr? Not there? Where is he? Find him quick."

Blucher slammed down the receiver of the telephone and glared at Morgan. Marian could only partially see the missionary's face, and what she saw was pale.

"Morgan, that Indian is with Gekin Yashi now," said the agent, hoarsely. "Your friend Herron here heard him speak your name."

"What's it mean?" the missionary blurted out incredulously.

"I don't know, but I wouldn't be in your boots for a million," replied Blucher sardonically. "Have you got a gun?"

"No."

"Well, the Old Book won't be behind or in front of you now!"

"Lock the door," shouted Morgan, wheeling. He shut it hard and turned the key.

Marian had a glimpse of his face and somehow sight of it roused her. She peered through the open door, out into the yard, toward the dormitory. A tall Indian was running fleetingly toward the office. Marian thrilled to her depths. Had she not seen that magnificent stride? This Indian was Nophaie, running as she had seen him many a time—running with the incomparable swiftness that had made him famous on all the eastern college fields. Before she could draw another breath he had reached the porch steps to mount them in one pantherish bound. His moccasined fe⋅ᵗ padded on the floor. Then he flashed in upon her, somehow terrible. A soiled handkerchief, folded narrow, and spotted with blood now dry, circled his brow and black hair. His eyes seemed to pierce Marian.

"I saw Morgan come in," he said. "Is he there—with Blucher?"

"Oh, yes," gasped Marian. "They're locked in. You mustn't . . . Oh!"

Nophaie pulled a gun from somewhere, and lunging at the locked door he shoved his foot against it with tremendous force. The lock broke. The door swung in. Nophaie bounded across the threshold.

Marian, suddenly galvanized into action, ran after him.

Miss Herron lay on the floor in a faint. Blucher sat

back in his chair, mouth agape, eyes wide. Amazement had begun to give way to fear. Morgan was ghastly.

Nophaie, with his right hand, held the gun low. It was cocked and it had an almost imperceptible quiver. With his left hand Nophaie significantly touched the bloody bandage round his head.

"Do etin's murderers did not give me that," said Nophaie. "They came three times to find me. But they failed. It was your Noki who ambushed my trail and shot me. . . . I have his confession."

Neither of the accused could utter a word. The Indian's menace was unmistakable, as inevitable as it was terrible.

"Morgan, I thought well to get Gekin Yashi's confession also, so I can kill you without the compunction white education fostered in me."

The missionary gasped and sagged against the wall. Blucher, livid and fearful, began to stammer incoherently.

Marian felt a tremendous sensation in her breast. It seemed to lift her. It passed, and she found herself burning deep within, suddenly unclamped from that icy terror.

"I am going to kill you both," said Nophaie.

With that Marian shut the door behind her. Then she got between Nophaie and the men, facing them. She realized what she had to do and was equal to it.

"Keep quiet. I will save your lives."

Wheeling to Nophaie she went closer to him, with one hand going to his shoulder, the other forcing down the leveled gun.

"You must not kill these men."

"Why not? Blucher had his men murder Do etin. Morgan has murdered Gekin Yashi's soul."

"That may well be true," responded Marian. "It's not a question of justice. If you shoot them you will go to the gallows."

"Yes, if I were caught. And then I would like to tell in a courtroom what these men are."

"Nophaie, you would not be believed except by a few who could not help you."

"Then I'll kill them in revenge. For Gekin Yashi—for my people!"

"No! No! You are above that, too. It's only your passion. There is no *good* to be accomplished. The evil these men have done will earn its punishment. Don't kill them."

"I must. There is no justice. Your government is not honest or fair with the Indian. It never was and never will be. Politics, money, graft—these are the assets of the Indian Bureau. Not to save the Indian! These reservations are not for Indians. They are desert fields, isolated wastes with which a few white men induce the government to appropriate fifteen million dollars, that they may keep their fat useless jobs. . . . The whites have educated me. And all I know cries out to kill these devils. I must do it."

"But you are the man I love," cried Marian, driven to desperation by his cold truth, by the remorselessness of his just wrath. "You are the *man.* I don't care what color you are. . . . It would break my heart if you became a murderer—a fugitive from justice—and if . . . if they hanged you, I'd die! My God, Nophaie, for the sake of my love—for me—let these men live. Think of what I've done for you—what I am *willing* to do for you. I'll marry you. I'll live with you. I'll spend my life helping your people . . . if . . . if only you . . . will not . . . spill blood."

She embraced him, clung to him, weakening at the end of her long appeal.

Nophaie let down the hammer of his gun. "That is different," he said, and though his speech had the accent and courtesy of the white man, the look of him, the loftiness was Indian. "You cannot purchase their lives by sacrificing your own. But for your *sake!* Benow di cleash, hold my gun."

Trembling, Marian accepted the heavy weapon, wondering the while what he meant to do. She began to throb and thrill. His look, his demeanor, the very radiation of him had undergone a remarkable transformation. The deadliness, the something foreign to Marian's conception of him, had vanished. Strangely he recalled Lo Blandy.

"Gentlemen, this girl of your race has saved your lives," he said. "I meant to kill you. . . . But not even she, or your government, or the God you pretend to worship, can save you wholly from the Indian."

Then with swift violence he turned upon Morgan, and in one singular, powerful motion, in which his whole body appeared to participate, he shot his knee up into the missionary's prominent abdomen. The blow made a sodden sound not unlike a heavy beat upon a drum. Morgan crashed against the wall, his head struck hard, his mouth spread wide, and a tremendous expulsion of breath followed. All the wind had been kicked out of him. As he sank to his knees his face grew hideous. His hands beat the air.

Next, in one bound Nophaie leaped upon the desk and from that right down on Blucher, breaking the chair and sending the agent hard to the floor. Nophaie did not even lose his balance. How light, supple, wonderful his movements!

Marian could not have cried out or moved to intercept him to save her life. She was in the grip of an absolutely new and strange and terrible spell. Nophaie no longer meant to kill; he meant only to hurt. And that liberated something deep in Marian's blood. It seemed to burst and shoot in fiery currents all over her. The Indian's actions fascinated her. How strange that he never made a move to strike Blucher, who was cursing in fury and terror, trying to get up! But he could not. Nophaie kept kicking him down. Every time the German got to hands and knees Nophaie would swing a moccasined foot. He kicked and he shoved. And then it appeared he was plunging Blucher nearer and nearer to Morgan, whose convulsions had evidently gained him some breath. Another kick sent the agent hard against the kneeling missionary, knocking him over.

"At Carlisle I learned a great many white men's tricks," said Nophaie, with grim humor. "And one of them was to kick. College men claimed I could kick a football harder and farther than any other athlete who ever lived. And when I kicked with my knee, they carried somebody off the field. Now since I scorn to soil my heathen red hands on such dirty beasts as you I must resort to kicking."

And without particular violence or rancor, he kept up this game of football until both men were disheveled, bloody-nosed wretches. Suddenly he ceased. Marian saw then that Miss Herron had revived and was sitting up. Nophaie looked at her with the same disgust that the men had inspired in him.

"I ought to kick you, too," he said. "But I have a white man's education." Drawing Marian out of the room he closed the door, and took his gun from her shaking hands.

"Don't be frightened, Benow di cleash," he said, with a strong, tender arm around her. "You saved me again. I can do nothing but love you more—and go back to my canyons. . . . Don't worry about what Blucher and Morgan will do. They are cowards. They will not speak one word of this. If you get dismissed, go to the trader's house. I beg of you, stay on the reservation yet awhile. Send me word through Withers. Good-bye."

"Oh, Nophaie," cried Marian, trying to find her voice.

He glided out upon the porch, looked to right and left, and then leisurely trotted down the steps, down the path to the road. Marian espied his horse tied to the fence near the gate. She expected to see men running from all directions. But there were none. Marian's heart slowly moved down out of her throat. She saw Nophaie mount his horse and lope away.

Chapter 15

DEEP IN THE CANYONED RECESSES OF THE rock-ribbed earth, far beneath the white dome of Nothsis Ahn, Nophaie established his refuge in one of the almost inaccessible niches of his Canyon of Silent Walls.

He had packed supplies in from Kaidab and had left the post with an arrangement whereby any letters from Marian and more supplies would be sent once a month by a trusted Pahute.

Nophaie held dear to heart and conscience Marian's appeal that he not become a murderer. And it seemed the only way he could escape spilling blood was to hide himself in the canyons, there to spend the winter months, and to wait. He had little fear of Blucher's hired policemen finding him here. Long before they could get near the only entrance to the Canyon of Silent Walls they would have lost any possible trace of him. Between his retreat and the upland plateau of Nothsis Ahn lay many miles of labyrinthine canyons, and the great western roll of the Marching Rocks. There was no trail over these hills of marble. The smooth, wind-worn slopes left no trace of hoove or moccasins. Many were the perilous precipices along which wound the only course over this range of wind-carved mounds. The last Pahute hogan stood on the cedared brow of the upland slope, thirty miles in an air line, three days exceedingly toilsome travel up and ever upward out of the rocky depths.

Nophaie penetrated to the farthermost corner of one of the canyoned wings of the valley; and here where the foot of white man had never trod, under gleaming white walls lifting to the sky he pitched his camp. It was a place of all places for the lonely Indian. The upland

country was now in the grip of winter. Down here the
grass and moss were still green, the willow and oak
leaves had thinned out yet many were left, fluttering
gold in the sunlight, and the cottonwoods tenaciously
clung to their autumn hues. Flowers still bloomed on
the benches where the sun lingered longest. Bees and
beetles buzzed throughout the noonday hours. Choe,
the spruce tree, beloved by Nopahs, could be seen
standing black and slender far up on the snow-
margined brow of Nothsis Ahn, but down here in the
valley gahd, the cedar flourished, and kept its everlasting rich green. Tolie, the blue jay, sacred to Nopah
ceremonies, had come down off the mountain to spend
the winter where the heat of the sun was reflected from
lofty walls. Mockingbirds heralded the late sunrise with
bursts of melody. Shy, wild little birds, nameless for
Nophaie, darted among the willows above the murmuring stream, now and then uttering melancholy notes.
And from the high niches and crannies pealed down the
sweet, strange, piercing twitter of the canyon swift, a
bird that pitched downward like the gleam of an arrow.

Nophaie had reasoned that if there was anything to
help him now in his extremity it was communion with
his soul, and mastery of his physical self, here in the
shadow of these lovely, silent walls. If arrest for assault
threatened him out there on the reservation he could
not have gone on long working among his people.
Besides, more than arrest surely threatened him. The
wound from Noki's treacherous bullet had scarcely
healed. So that there were several reasons why it was
well for him to hide, to be alone, to await some mystic
issue which was written. He would escape his enemies;
he would be free of the cold winter that bound all
Indians to their hogans; he could live in utter freedom
here in this beautiful valley; he could dream and think
the hours away, facing his soul, finding himself, growing away from that fierce hatred, realizing some melancholy happiness in the sweetness of love for Benow di
cleash.

Nophaie's valley resembled somewhat the shape of an octopus, except that the main body was narrow and crooked, and the arms extended far and winding. This body was about a mile in length, and the larger arms were much longer. Innumerable ramifications on a lesser scale cut into the cliff walls everywhere. A thousand undiscovered and untrodden nooks and corners, caves and caverns, cliff dwellings and canyons in miniature assuredly were lost in the intricacies of this valley. The great curved arm that cut deep into the bulk of Nothsis Ahn was a tremendous canyon in itself, lofty-walled as its head, opening wide at its juncture with the main body, margined by wondrous, shining, smooth walls waved like billows, red and yellow in hue, and crossing the valley proper to narrow again and lift its ramparts to the sky. Through this canyon ran the stream of water, and its course was one of ruggedness. That stream in flood, swollen by suddenly melting snows on the mountain, had cut a deep and devious gorge, and had carried a million boulders on its way. It had dug a dry riverbed of rocks. Gravel bars, sandbars hid their white surfaces amid the boulders, and cottonwood trees stood up among them, and willows shaded them. Thickets of reeds and matted brush and long, coarse-bladed grass made impenetrable barriers to the wilder recesses. This canyon showed most the forces of the elements and it was a wilderness.

Nophaie seemed driven to explore, to seek, to search, to climb—especially to climb here and there, high and low, for a height that was unattainable but to which he must aspire. All Indians loved lofty places. And Nophaie was like an eagle in his love of the lonely crag and the wide outlook. The silent walls close at hand had no greater fascination than those beyond ascent. Time would surely come when they would speak to him. These dreaming walls had a voice for others beside the red man—for all humanity. But it had to be waited for and earned. Nature was jealous of her secrets. She spoke only to those who loved her.

Rest and calm returned to Nophaie, and then the days seemed to merge into one another, to glide on and on toward a nameless and wished-for end, an unveiling of the future.

The day had been unusually warm for that time of year. At sunset, when Nophaie climbed the high, cone-shaped knoll in the amphitheater of the valley, there was still heat on the smooth rock. He felt it through his moccasins, and when in climbing he touched it with his bare hand the contact was pleasant. A partially overcast sky and an absence of wind had kept out the cool air from off the mountain.

Nophaie reached the round summit and there he reclined, not happy, but still less haunted by his giants of shadow and unrest. Bees or beetles went humming past him, evidently on a line toward the higher cedared part of the valley. These belated toilers made the best of daylight.

The overcast sky broke but slightly in the west, and that only enough to send a faint rose color to the tips of the great white towers. Through the gap to the north Nophaie saw the dim purple rim of a distant mesa. The long slow twilight was one of the strange and beautiful features of this Canyon of Silent Walls. Sunset came early because the insulating walls stood up so loftily that before the day was done they hid the westering sun. So the waning light lingered long. Nophaie watched the faint rose fade and the gray shadows rise. What he longed for eluded him. He had only the strange joy of his sensorial perceptions.

Before darkness enveloped the valley he descended from the knoll, walking on a long slant, surefooted as a sheep, sliding here and there, down and down into the boulder-strewn ravine, where indeed night had fallen. There beside the stream he was halted by sounds not heard before—the strange croaking of canyon frogs. The unusually warm day had brought summer again to the denizens of the canyon. But the croaking of these frogs was weird and weak, as if they had only half awakened. One uttered a faint hoarse rattle, another a concatenated twang, another a kind of bellow, at widely separated intervals. Then followed a few trills, neither high nor sweet, yet somehow melodious. With the cool night wind these songs of belated summer ceased, and Nophaie heard them no more.

But that little he had heard was good for him. While he sat there on a huge boulder the night fell black. He felt the sadness and tranquility of the hour, and realized that many such hours must be his, out of which might come some alleviation of his sorrow.

Above him the rounded wavy lines of the knolls loomed dark, and beyond them towered the canyon walls with crags against the sky. No blaze of stars illumined the heavens. There was no blue. From the shadow under him there rose a sweet music—tinkle and babble and murmur and splashing and gurgling of swift water over stones. It accentuated the loneliness and silence of this isolated rent in the earth. Nophaie's people and the world of white men seemed far away and not necessary for him at that hour. Time spent here would teach Nophaie the superfluity of many things— perhaps resignation to his infidelism and the futility of love. The silent walls, so like great eyelids full of dreams, the deep shadows, the haunting memory of the trilling frogs, the soft, cool breeze, bringing breath of snow, the vast black heave of the mountain of rock, and the infinite sky above, more mystic without its trains of stars—these brought a sense of the littleness of all living things, of the exceeding brevity of life.

Nophaie's emotions gradually grew deep and full. That bitter and hateful mood of the past slowly lost its hold on him. He seemed to be stripping off the clutch of a half-dead lichen from his soul. The oppression of the wonderful overhanging rocks—a sense surely that had not been Indian—left him wholly. Noble thoughts began to form in Nophaie's mind. His work left un- done, his duty to his people, his responsibility to a

white woman who had blessed him with love, must be
taken up again as the only rewards of his life. Emotion
uplifted Nophaie and intelligence combated selfishness.
Yet always sadness dominated, an ineradicable sadness
now because there had come to him a tremendous
realization of the mastery and tragedy of nature. Any
human nature was a fascinating study; his own in
contact and relation to his people was a sorrowful
thing; here against the loneliness and solitude of this
wilderness it was forced out stark and naked. He
seemed an animal with a soul—the necessity to eat and
no longing for life—the power to re-create and no right
to love—the seed of immortality in him and no belief in
God.

But strangely a hope seemed gestating in Nophaie's
soul, trying to be born. More and more he felt its
stirrings deep within him. It was like that fleeting
conception of aboriginal man he sometimes caught
when he narrowed his eyelids and looked at nature as if
he were the first human to evolve from the ape. It was
as ephemeral as the moment in which he felt but did not
think. It had to do altogether with the physical. In
nature then was not only the secret, but also salvation
for him, if any were possible. What he yearned to reach
was the God of his forefathers. This surely was a
worship of nature, but not as he saw nature. The spirit
of dead men did not go into rocks and trees and clouds.
Was there a spirit that went anywhere? Nophaie saw
through superstition. In Indians it was ignorance—the
need of worship of supernatural things—of powers
greater than human. But if there were a spirit in man
that left his dead body, might there not be a spirit in
nature infinite and everlasting? Nophaie's stirring hope
was that he had really begun to hear the voices of the
silent walls. Not morbid fancy, not sentiment, not
lonely, brooding, erotic love, not the fear of death and
the blind strengthening of false faiths, not anything but
intelligent grasp at the soul of nature! Scientists would
not grant nature a soul. But wise as scientists were

they could not solve the riddle of life, the extent of the universe, the origin of time, the birth of man, the miracle of reproduction. Their deductions were biological, archeological, physiological, psychological, metaphysical—many things, but not one of them explained the something, the life, the soul in the vocal cords of a mockingbird. Could any scientist explain why a sage lily strangely changed the instant after it was plucked? Nophaie was at war with the intellectual forces that had robbed him of his religion. There was something in these dreaming, silent walls, these waiting, brooding, blank walls, these wind- and water-sculptured stone faces of the ages. So he wandered under their shadow, he watched them at dawn, in the solemn noonday light, at sunset, and in the black canopy of night. So he climbed over them and to their summits, and high upon one to see another.

Nophaie was sitting up high in the center of the amphitheater and the hour of sunset was nigh.

An intense hue of gold crowned all the rounded rims and domes that faced the west, out of which poured a glory of sunset light. High on the white towers of rock the gold was red; higher still on the snow of Nothsis Ahn it was rose. Away across the gap of the valley, northward, loomed up the great mesa, veiled in lilac haze. Faint, soft, dying lights attended the waving slopes under the ragged crags that touched the colored sunset sky. Clouds floated there—fleecy, like wisps of coral in a turquoise sea—cumulus, creamy white edged by silver, mushrooming in rosy columns—clouds of pearl and alabaster, and higher in the intense blue, smoky wreaths of delicate mauve, and bossy, beaten masses of burnished bronze.

Every moment there had its transfiguration. Every moment seemed endless in its gift to the recording soul. This was the living world of nature and its change was one of the elements of its marvelous vitality. The beauty and the glory might have existed only in Nophaie's mind. But they were tangible things. The light fell golden upon his hand. All the valley was full of luminous glow, moving, changing, rays and shadows, a medium of enchantment. An eagle, bow-winged and black against the luminosity of the sky, swept across the field of Nophaie's vision, flashing like a streak of darkened light, to plunge into the purple depths beyond the walls. It gave life to Nophaie's panorama. It gave him a strange joy. From the lofty tower above the monarch of the heights had shot downward like a thunderbolt, free, alone, beautiful, wild as the wild wind, to gladden Nophaie's sight, to add another thrill to his hope.

Nophaie knew not the prayer to say there upon his rounded altar of rock. Not one Nopah of all the tribe would have been so wanting! But he breathed one of his own.

"Glory of sun at dying day,
　Beauty of cloud in the sky,
　Splendor of light on the crag,
　Passionless god of nature
　　　　　Make me as thou.

"Lend me thy gift.
　Teach me thy secret.
　Give me thy spirit.

"Eagle of the marvelous flight,
　Shade of the purple height,
　Ray and veil and mystic glow,
　Blue of heaven and rose of snow,
　　　　　Come to Nophaie.

"Come all things of heaven and earth,
　Come out of west and north and east,
　Come from the blowing wind,
　Come from without the silent walls,
　　　　To the lost and lonely soul
　　　　　and call me thine."

Nophaie turned to face the east, the sacred direction of the sun-worshiper. Grandeur of the west must be reflected in the east. Rounded rocks, waved on high, billowing higher to the rims, in velvet tones of red and lavender, heaved to the loftier walls. Where the setting sun struck the wall faces in full light it painted them a vivid orange red. Deep shadows made sharp contrast. Crevices and lines of cleavage hid their purple mystery from the blaze of the sun. They lifted the golden surfaces, contoured them with edge of violet. The Canyon of Silent Walls had been flooded with transforming hues. It shone upon a thousand surfaces of gold and red, with undertones of steps, leading up and up, stairway of the gods, to the castellated towers above. Gray towers, white towers, tinged with gold, rugged and spired, crowned this horizon wall of rock, and led Nophaie's gaze onward to the south where the grand north wall of Nothsis Ahn was emblazoned with the cataclysmic scars of ages.

Of all the silent walls insulating Nophaie's valley this was the loftiest and the most aloof, the one most calling, the wall of weathered slope of avalanche, of the green-black timber belt shining in the sun, of the pure white dome of snow. Here were the unattainable heights. Baffled and haunted, Nophaie could only withdraw his gaze down to the twilit-canyoned amphitheater beneath him and build over in his sight this magnificent speaking wall of rock, this barrier of stone, this monument of nature, this beautiful face of the mountain of light.

Beneath Nophaie there was shade of canyon depths —the dark cedar clumps, the blank gray thickets, the pale boulders, all growing obscure and mysterious in the purple twilight. Where the base of the lower wall began to sheer upward it was dark, carrying on its face the conformation of the western walls that cast the shadow. Darkly the wavering edge of shade stood out with startling distinctness against the deep red, sunset-mirrored cliffs beyond. Perceptibly this dark line of shade crept on high. As the sun sank lower the shadows of all intervening walls rose like a tide, and the radiance moved upward. There was no standing still of these contrasting bands of light and darkness. They moved and their color changed. A flock of canyon swifts swept glitteringly down from the heights, like flying sparks of golden fire, and darted into the shadows, perhaps to the warmer shelves of rock for the night. Sweet, wild, and faint twittered out their notes.

The red walls sheered up to those of gold, where line and regularity broke into a thousand cliffs, corners, benches, caves, a vast, half-circular mountain front of rock where niches were fringed by stunted cedars and arches festooned by clinging lichens. An army of cliff dwellers might once have dwelt on that great slope. A mile wide and nearly as high was this one wall of belted gold, rugged, jutted, jagged, buttressed, terraced and crowned by cornice of white crags. Only winged creatures could ever rest on those towering pinnacles. They belonged to the condors and the clouds—towers like idols of the gods, golden at the base, white as clay above, with ruddy crowns pointing to the broad black belt of Nothsis Ahn, and the rose-white dome of snow.

Wall columnar as the rolling, lofty cloud of the sky! Nophaie gazed upward lost in contemplation. Of all gifts the gift of sight was best. But the eye of mind saw into the infinite. This insurmountable wall which barred Nophaie resembled him inasmuch as it lifted its face to the firmament. And while he gazed the sun went on with its miracle of transfiguration. Life of color, spirit of glory, symbol of eternal change! This enchantment of a moment was the smile of nature.

Nophaie pictured the wondrous scene from above; he imagined he had the eye of the soaring eagle. Underneath that strong vision lay the dark canyons, the red knolls, the golden walls, a broken world of waved bare stone. High on one of the rounded hills of rock stood a lonely, statuesque figure of man—the Indian—

Nophaie—strange, pitifully little, a quivering atom among the colossal monuments of inanimate nature. He was the mystery of life thrown against that stark background of the age-old earth. Like a shipwrecked mariner on his spar-strewn sinking deck, the Indian gazed up at the solid and enduring mountain. Bright stone-face of light! Silent wall with a thousand walls!

All Nophaie's profound worship of the elements, his mastery of will and stern projection of soul, his sublimity of hope, the intense cry of his spirit for light—more light—light of God like this glorious light of sun—left him standing there on the height, alone in the solitude, with burden unlifted, with the passionless, pitiless, ruthless, all-pervading, and all-concealing eyes of nature on him in his abasement.

Days passed into weeks and time was naught. The north wind roared on Nothsis Ahn and storm clouds lodged there, black, with dropping gray veils. But down in the Canyon of Silent Walls there was neither winter cold nor wind. Nophaie sought the sunny walls and dreamed in their reflected heat. Only one arm of the canyon still remained unexplored and he had left that for some task of energy and action to fall back upon when his spirit ebbed low.

One day, from far down the canyon, pealed and echoed the call of an Indian. It startled Nophaie. He had forgotten the Pahute whom Withers was to send with supplies. He had forgotten that and more. Surely there would be news of the world beyond these silent walls, of the reservation and of the affairs at Mesa—last and the only one all-imperative, word from Benow di cleash.

Nophaie ran. It was the fleetness of an Indian, but the gladness of a white man. Almost scorned that eagerness, that strange knocking at his heart. The solitude he had sought seemed to stand out clearer now, an enemy to his intelligence. Lonely canyons were abodes for barbarians, savages, Indians—not for men with developed thought. The work of white men should ever be to help the increasing progress of the world toward better life. But he was not a white man. So as he ran his thoughts multiplied.

Nophaie found the Pahute in the main arm of the canyon. He had brought a pack mule heavily laden. Nophaie led him to his camp, and there unpacked the mule, and cooked a meal for the Indian, and learned from him that white policemen had sought him all over the reservation and had returned to Mesa. No other news had the Pahute, except that the trader at Kaidab had told him to get to Nophaie on this day: "Jesus Christ Day," added the Indian with a grin.

"Christmas!" exclaimed Nophaie, and strange indeed were his memories.

The Pahute left early in the afternoon, saying he wanted to get over the Marching Rocks before nightfall. Nophaie was again alone. Yet how different the loneliness now! There were packets and packages in that pile of supplies which, despite their outside wrappings of burlap and paper, did not bear the hallmark of an Indian trader. Nophaie felt rich. It struck him significantly that he was unutterably glad. But was it not a certainty of messages from Marian? That assuredly, yet he could not be sure it was all! Unpacking the heavier parcels first Nophaie found that the trader had added considerable to the monthly order. Then there was a bundle of lighter weight, more carefully packed, and inside was a tag upon which was written in English, "Merry Christmas from Withers outfit."

Nophaie tried to be annoyed at this, but he could not, and he found that what irritated him was the happy greeting in English. "I am an Indian," muttered Nophaie. Yet he did not speak that in the Indian language. "Christmas gifts and greetings," he added, "and I am glad." Indian or not he could not help his feelings. It was kind of the Withers family to remember the educated Indian in his lonely solitude. Nophaie found cigarettes, matches, chocolate, raisins, chewing gum, a clasp knife, a little hand axe, a large piece of tanned buckskin with needles and thread, and woolen socks and a flannel shirt. Withers had guessed his needs and had added luxuries.

Then with hasty fingers Nophaie opened the smallest packet that he had guessed was from Marian. Inside the heavy paper was more paper, and inside that water-proofed cloth, and inside this a silken scarf all neatly folded round a soft, flat object. Nophaie unfolded the scarf to behold a large, clean, thick, white envelope upon which had been written one word: Nophaie. Marian's handwriting! A thrill went over him. There were illusions, but also there were realities. No moment of life that did not bring happiness to some mortal!

He put the letter aside, and opened the second packet, larger, flatter, more strongly wrapped, encased in pasteboard. He expected to find a photograph and was not disappointed. But before he opened the cover out dropped an envelope containing snapshot pictures of Marian taken at Mesa with her own camera. The best picture was one of her riding the white mustang he had given her. They were all good pictures, yet not one of them seemed like the image he had in memory. The desert was hard on Marian. But when Nophaie opened the large envelope he had strike him like a blow a beautiful likeness of the fair face he loved and remembered so well. This was a fine photograph, taken in Philadelphia, probably some little time after he had left the East.

"Benow di cleash!" he murmured, and all the white flowerlike fairness seemed to flash in a beautiful light from that pictured face. Gazing he forgot for long the other presents. When he opened them he found books, magazines, late newspapers, pads and pencils and envelopes, a small hunter's sewing kit, a box of medicines, bandages, candy, nuts and cakes, and last of all, a watch with radium numerals, and a buckskin fob, decorated with Nopah buttons. She had not forgotten to include in all this loving munificence some token of the Indian. That thrilled him as nothing else had.

One by one he handled these gifts and pondered over the effect they had upon him. Beyond peradventure of doubt these established the connection between him and the world of white people. Eighteen years of his life, the forming and fixing period, had developed to such things as these, and not those of the red man. He might starve naked in a cave of the canyons, with nothing representative of the white race near him, but that could not change facts. He was more white than red. He loved Marian Warner. Her gifts made him happy. The isolated solitudes of the desert were good for his soul and body, but they could never wholly satisfy.

Chapter 16

NOPHAIE CARRIED MARIAN'S LETTER TO HIS favorite resting and dreaming place. Not on the heights did he care to read her message, but in the amber shadow of the silent walls.

This place was a strange one, a narrow section of canyon, where the west wall leaned to meet the cavernous eastern wall, the lofty red rims of which showed a blue ribbon of sky above. Here the canyon turned sharply to the left and then to the right giving a strange impression of stupendous leaning walls. At the base of the cavernous cliff ran the murmuring stream of clear green water. Banks of moss and grass stood out from the wall, dry, odorous, and gray. The leaves of the cottonwoods were not yet devoid of their autumn hue. Any sound here was weird, hollow, ringing, melodious, and echoes magnified all. Nophaie found his accustomed seat and with mounting beat of heart he opened Marian's letter. Was he really there—lonely outcast Nopah in the solitude of a silent canyon—holding in his hands the letter of a noble and loving woman of a hated race?

Dearest Nophaie,

Greetings on your Christmas Day! I could not be happy without sending to you my greeting, my love and my gifts. May these find you well. May they assure you at least of the constancy of Benow di cleash. I cannot, even on Christmas Day, believe wholly in the spirit: "Peace on earth—goodwill to man." Not when the one I love, whom I know is worthy, is hidden in the wilds, persecuted by men of my color!

If I could write you a whole volume I would never be able to crowd in all. My dismissal came quite some time after your visit. In fact I ran the office until Blucher and Morgan came out of seclusion. Then I got the "steamroller" all right, and without my month's pay! I'm grateful for that, because it gives me an excuse to go back to the office, which I have done regularly since I came here to stay with the Paxtons. They are very kind to me, and allow me to pay my board. I help out in the trading store sometimes where I keep up my study of the Indians. Here I get another angle on the reservation.

As far as I am able to tell nothing has yet leaked out in Mesa about that football match you had with Blucher and Morgan. I will never get over that day. Never will I trust myself again. If you were an Indian I was a *savage*. I just swelled and tingled and burned with fiendish glee every time you kicked one of the—footballs. My only regret rises from the fact that I never saw you play real football in the college games that made you famous.

My last interview with Blucher and Morgan was a nightmare. Blucher was poison. Morgan tried to intimidate me and drive me off the reservation. He said—but never mind what he said. The Indian police have returned from their search for you—I imagine. But you will do well to lie low for a while. There is a seething volcano under this particular part of the reservation. The Woltersons expect dismissal any day. All communication to Wolterson comes *through* the superintendent. Why, I could run this reservation better than the government does it. The whole Indian Service, if judged by this arm of it, is merely a gigantic political machine. But that you know.

I suspect that Blucher is greatly concerned about the possibility of the U.S. being drawn into war with Germany. There is indeed a grave possibility of that very thing. You will see the latest news in the papers I send. These came today with the mail carrier from Flagerstown. Read them carefully. You may be a Nopah, but you are also an American. One of the truest of Americans—the red-blooded species! German militarism threatens not only the peace of the world but also the freedom. If war is declared I trust you will tell the truth to every Nopah on this reservation. For I absolutely *know* that Blucher will oppose any Indian help to the United States Army. I read a letter he wrote to a German in New York. He was typing it himself and when someone called him *I read it.* If I could only have secured a copy of it or have remembered it. But I was excited—shocked. Blucher is all German. If war *is* declared the situation here on this reservation will be a terrible one. Think how to meet that, Nophaie.

I have seen Gekin Yashi but once. She was in the school yard near the fence as I passed on my way here from Woltersons'. I got close to her before she saw me. Her face has altered strangely. It gave me a pang. For a second I felt that I could tear and rend. . . . When she espied me she *ran.* I called, but she paid no heed.

The Indian girl who was put in the maternity hospital here recently gave birth to a child. She will be sent to Riverside—separated from her baby under the mandate of studying for five years before she can have it. Indian women *love* their babies. I hear Blucher has sent the father to jail. Various and weird the law of this reservation school!

I have no plans. I am waiting. You may be sure I'll not leave the reservation. I might be taken off, but they'll have to carry me. This winter is no great problem. I need rest and I want to write some.

Later, if nothing comes up here, I might go out to
Kaidab. In the spring I hope to see you. I want you
to know that I meant what I said in Blucher's office
the day you confronted him and Morgan there. I
would be happy to marry you and share what I
have with you, and your life and work among your
people. I have the means for a start. And we can
work. I ask only that we spend some part of each
year in California or the East. I have vanity enough
not to let myself dry up in this desert air and blow
away!

Time and trouble change character, do they not?
I am the stronger for what has come to me out
here. The desert is terrible. It destroys and then
builds. I never knew what light was—the wonderful sun—and wind and dust and heat—stars and
night and silence—the great emptiness—until I
came to the desert. Perhaps so with love!

Somehow I will endure the long silence, for you
must not risk writing me yet. I will dream of you,
see you among the rocks. Always, as long as I live,
rocks and walls of stone will have thrilling and sad
significance for me.

Benow di cleash

Nophaie gazed in seeming terror at the stupendous
wall of stone opposite. He could not see either of its
corners or its base. Solid rock, impenetrable and
immovable and insurmountable! The temptation that
confronted him now was just as much a wall, a barrier,
an overpowering weight.

Benow di cleash loved him. She would marry him.
She would share all she had as she would share his life.
Live with him! Belong to him alone!

The fact was a staggering blow. Here under the
accusing eyes of his silent walls he felt as he could never
have any other place. Loneliness had augmented his
hunger for a mate. Nature importuned him for her
right. And suddenly Nophaie found himself stripped

bare of all ideals, chivalries, duties, of all the false sophistries of his education, of the useless fetters of his infidelism.

Human being, man, Indian, savage, primitive beast —so he retrograded in the scale. As a human he aspired to martyrdom, as a man he sacrificed love, as an Indian he steeped his soul in noble exaltation, as a savage he felt only the fierce race of hot blood, as a primitive beast he struggled in the throes of hereditary instincts, raw and wild, ungovernable—the imperious and inscrutable law of nature.

While he lay motionless as that mossy bank it seemed the elemental, the natural, the mindless automaton of living flesh must win. There was nothing else in life. This staggering bundle of nerves, vessels, organs, blood and bone that constituted his body had millions of cells, each one of which clamored for its right to completion, expression, reproduction. Death to cell, organ, body, man, individual, but life to the species! This instinct that Nophaie strove to kill was the strongest of all forces in the universe.

One terrible moment Nophaie lay there under the walls that seemed to thunder the meaning of nature. Then he sprang up to force this living body of his, this vehicle he abhorred, this beating, burning frame of blood-veined muscle, into violent and sustained effort, into exhaustive physical activity that must bring subjugation of the instincts which threatened his downfall. He must win now—in this hour—or lose forever. Thought, reflection, reason, argument—these faded in his consciousness like pale vapors of mist when the blazing sun rose. Before he could think he must subdue something in him, a hydra-headed, multiple-lunged, insatiate instinct to project his life into another life. Nophaie refused that species of self-preservation. If it was instinct that maddened him and instinct that he fought, it was also instinct that sent him out to move, to run, to climb.

There were none of his race to see him, to bring their

medicine men to exorcise the evil spirits which possessed him. Only the silent walls had eyes to watch him in his terror.

Nophaie ran. He leaped the brook. From boulder to boulder he bounded. Along the grassy benches, under the looming ledges, over the washes, through the thickets, up the canyon he sped with that incomparable stride of the Indian runner trained under the great masters of college athletics. Strange place for the famous athlete who had delighted the crowds, who had heard their trampling, pealing roar when he ran! The white man had trained him—the white man had educated him. But it was now the Indian nature that gave Nophaie the instinct to run away from himself.

He halted at his camp long enough to lay aside the precious letter from Benow di cleash. He did not want to soil that white paper with its beautiful and appalling words of love. All his life he must keep them. And he feared them now. Again the shuddering of his flesh, the burning of the marrow of his bones! Out he ran, straight for the notch of the canyon, with wild eyes on the white-towered wall of Nothsis Ahn. No Indian had ever surmounted that wall. But Nophaie would surmount it or perish in the attempt. To see afar over the desert, to pray and to absolve himself the Indian had always climbed high.

Nophaie's moccasined feet padded softly over the bare stone slope. He ran up the long, wavy, red mound, and from its round dome, where often he had watched the eagles and the sunset, he put his keen vision to the task of finding a way to climb the north face of Nothsis Ahn. There were a hundred intricate zigzag ascents up that mountain wall, not one of which seemed possible for man.

Down the waved knoll Nophaie ran, light and sure as a wildcat, and over the wide area of bare rock to the main base of the wall.

There he began to climb in a long slant, up the brown, smooth incline, veined and striped, and around the headed corners, and back to a long slant in the other direction, up and up by these zigzag courses, to the curved and rolling rim of red, where began the vast slow heave of the white amphitheater.

All this slope was windswept bare, soft to the foot, a white stone that disintegrated under force; and it was like a rolling sea slanted on end. Levels, mounds, benches, ridges, holes, gorges, all rounded and smooth, with never a crack or cutting edge or loosened fragment passed by under Nophaie's swift steps. Impetuosity and passion drove him. He climbed on gradually slowing to the steeper ascent. From far below this white amphitheater had appeared what it was not. Its dimensions magnified with approach. A line of cleavage seen from below was on nearer view a great wide dip in the ocean slope of rock. Nophaie's detours consumed miles of travel. To and fro across the corrugated face of this mountain wall he traveled, always climbing higher. A rare cold atmosphere, thin in oxygen, further slowed his efforts. Climbing grew hard. He no longer ran. He sweat, he burned, he panted. He saw only the stone under his feet and the gray looming towers above, still seemingly as unattainable as ever.

Along the last circling ledge of the amphitheater he worked around to the bold rugged bluff, surmounted it, and climbed into a world of cliffs, precipices, promontories, sharp and jagged and jutting in strange contrast to the waved and heaved ascent he had accomplished. Here he had exercise for the eye of an eagle, the leap of the mountain sheep, the surefootedness of the goat. Far back on the other side of the towers he worked, finding them still high above him, still unscalable. On and upward he toiled, and at last reached a point where the huge, white-towered abutment joined the bulk of Nothsis Ahn. Nothing of this was visible to eye below in the valley. He had ascended to the white crags that stood out and up to hide all but the dome of the mountain. Nophaie pulled himself up, he let himself down, he leaped fissures, he crept along abysmal chasms blue in

depth, he rimmed the base of crags, and climbed
around and between them.

Out of the zone of white pillars and turrets at last!
Level with the nests of eagles! Nophaie stood at the
base of the weathered slope of Nothsis Ahn, the track
of the avalanches, the tilted level of loose rocks; and he
looked almost straight up to the green band of timber
and the glistening dome of snow. If climbing had been
difficult and hazardous before now it was approaching
the impossible. Nophaie sent the rocks sliding below
him; he started the slides into avalanches. He loosened
the slopes above him. He performed miracles of agility,
speed, and endurance. Like the Indian masters of
the legends, he consorted with eagles, bounded
with the feet of the wind, swung on the edges of the
clouds.

Snow and spruce halted Nophaie, a forest of evergreens, matted and webbed into impenetrable wind-
falls, buried deep in the white ice of the heights. He
could not go higher. At the edge of snow line, on a gray
brow of rock, he built a monument, so that it would be
visible to the eye of an Indian from below. But he
offered no prayer to the god of the mountain.

In the piercing cold of that altitude, blown upon by
the strong north wind, Nophaie gazed out and down
upon the naked earth below. Dim, abysmal, obscure
the depths from which he had toiled! Beauty and color
were naught. Distance was lost. The great canyons
were dark purple threads. Over all the immensity of
ghastly desert brooded a spirit of desolation and death
and decay. The sun blazed down a terrible truthfulness
of light.

What Nophaie had climbed so desperately for
seemed never to have been. He had spent the forces of
his nature—the physical instincts. For that hour, perhaps forever, he had conquered. On the heights came a
regurgitation of emotion, a flashing back of thought.
There was blood on the worn edges of his moccasins;

his fingernails were worn to the quick. The ache in his bones, the pang in his lungs, the deadness of his muscles attested to the nature of that climb. Hours could be measured as years!

Long after dark that night Nophaie dragged his bruised and weary body into camp, there to crawl into his bed and stretch his limbs, as if never to move them again. Sleep and rest, for days and nights, restored his strength, yet he knew that climb had been the supreme physical effort of his life. The strain of a hard football game had been as nothing. A hundred-mile ride across the desert had been as nothing. Likewise Nophaie realized that he could never again climb the north wall of Nothsis Ahn. Powerful, fleet, sure, agile, enduring, keen-sighted and Indian-sinewed as he was, these faculties did not alone account for that superhuman task. The very inspiration for the climb had receded somehow, dimmed and paled back into the secret and mystic springs of his nature. But as the days and nights multiplied in the shadow of the silent walls Nophaie learned that the noble proof of his love for Marian was not in surrender to it. He would not drag her down to his level. Utterly impossible for him was a life among white men. He had been wronged, robbed, deprived of his inheritance. He saw the incredible brutality and ruthlessness of white men toward his race. He saw that race vanishing. He was the Vanishing American. He had no God, no religion, no hope. That strange hope born there in the canyon had been burned out in the fire kindled by Marian's offer of love. Nature had deluded him. She had been a veiled, beautiful face lifted to him.

The silent walls heard Nophaie's denial—and how strange a light gleamed on their faces! Benow di cleash loved him and he must break her heart. But grief would give her strength that his burden could never give. Nature in her inscrutable way had drawn Nophaie and the white girl together; and no doubt that merciless nature divined a union which would further her evolutional designs. Nature recognized no religion, no God. Nature desired only birth, reproduction, death, in every living creature. Love was the blind and imperious tool of nature. How could love endure with age and death?

Days passed into weeks and weeks into months. Three times the Pahute came, and three times a white, thick letter stormed Nophaie's soul, yet left him stronger.

He measured the passing of winter by the roar of wind on the slope of Nothsis Ahn, by the circling back of the sun, by the earlier dawns, by the hot days and the peeping of frogs at nightfall. He lived that swiftly flying time in his simple camp tasks, in wandering and climbing as if the unattainable would one day be his, in dreaming of Marian and writing thoughts and experiences for her, in study of the nature of his stone-walled retreat.

Not until a late day of his sojourn there did he explore the one remaining arm of canyon. What was his amazement and regret to find it beyond comparison with any of the others.

Three miles or more of exceedingly rough travel brought Nophaie to a point where this canyon changed its color, its height and width, its bed, its skyline, its every feature. Nophaie christened it Canyon of Gleams. Its hue was the strange one of pale marble in the moonlight; its height sheer perpendicular and incredible; its width six feet at the base, gradually widening in V-shape to perhaps fifty feet at the top; its bed was solid, smooth, grayish rock hard as iron, worn into deep, smooth ruts by the rushing stream; and its skyline was a long, even, straight lane of blue as far as Nophaie could see. No bird, no lizard, no beetle or bee, no frog or insect, no living creature or sprig of vegetation crossed Nophaie's vision. The hollow reverberating mocking voice of the stream was the only sound that could be heard. There was no wind. The uneven stream bed gleamed, the water gleamed, the walls gleamed, the bank of sky gleamed.

Nophaie penetrated this gigantic split in the vast bulk of rock until his progress was impeded by a further narrowing of the canyon and a depth of water that made it necessary to swim, if he went on. By placing a foot on each wall and hitching himself up Nophaie reached a height from which he could see that the canyon extended a long way, with increasing obstacles. Did he hear a faint roar of waterfall? He determined to swim through there someday when the water lost its edge of ice.

This Canyon of Gleams grew to have an insatiable fascination for Nophaie. He wandered there often, never to find it altogether the same. The hollow bellow of water never changed. But all else! No sunlight ever penetrated that colossal rent. At night it was so black he had to feel his way out to the open part. Afternoon seemed the most wonderful there, by reason of some conformation of the rims above reflecting a thick, rich, tangible, gleaming light with tinge of gold. The gleams of water and wall were as mutable as the shades of sunset. Here Nophaie felt least the encroachment of the white man, the dominance of his knowledge, the loss of faith, the sacrifice of love, the imminence of unabatable grief.

The vast walls pressed close upon him, to give him the fear they might suddenly slip together and bury him forever in the bowels of the rock-ribbed earth. They were not dead things, these walls. They had a spiritual power, and were more beautiful than paintings. Indeed, they seemed to be painted windows through which the soul of nature gleamed. Silent, always silent to Nophaie, yet full of unuttered voices! The Indian in him was comrade of the rocks. The earth was his mother. And all the sands of the sea and grains of the desert were rock; the vast upheaved magnificence of Nothsis Ahn was rock, and the desert. The earth itself was rock and rock its foundations. Therefore the solid wall was his mother and the gleams were her smiles and the silence her unutterable voices.

Spring! The water of the brook swelled and lost its green for hint of yellow; the frogs changed their peeping to solemn croak and sweeter trill. The white primrose and the lavender daisy bloomed in sunny places. Blades of grass shot up as if by magic and the cottonwoods lost their gray!

Nophaie grew restive. The hold of the silent walls lessened. In him were contending tides. Silence and solitude had dragged him to the verge. Forgetfulness, and the thoughtlessness of the Indian, had closely infringed upon his memory. Nature had importuned with all her insidious and supreme mastery over the senses. Hate and infidelism had trampled in vain on his soul. He was still free.

The day came when a loud call awoke the drowsy echoes of the silent canyon. It startled Nophaie. That had not been the voice of an Indian. Had the long solitude worked upon his mind? Nophaie ran to the wide gateway between the red walls. He saw horses, mules with packs, an Indian, and then out from the shade of a cedar strode Withers, mopping his heated face.

"Howdy, Nophaie," he said, with smile and earnest gaze. "You look fine."

Nophaie stirred to the warmth of the trader's close handclasp. He returned it and that was all his response. Utterance seemed difficult. Long had his voice been silent. Besides, Withers bore a look of intense strain. He was thinner, older. A suppressed passion seemed rampant in him.

"Come out of the sun," asked Withers, turning. "It's hot. And I've ridden hard."

Nophaie followed him to a seat on a flat rock in the shade. The moment seemed to hinge on strange events. The trader's presence might mean that which must add to Nophaie's burden.

"Throw saddles and packs right here," said Withers

to the Indian who had come with him. "Nophaie, where is your horse?"

"Gone," replied Nophaie. "I have not seen him for a long time."

"I figured on that and I fetched one for you."

"Withers, why did you bring me a horse?" queried Nophaie, conscious of an inward tremor.

"Because I think you'll hit the trail back with me," replied the trader significantly.

"Has anything happened to Marian?"

"Sure, a lot's happened. But she's okay—well and fine."

"Withers, it's a long, rough ride here. You've got strong reason for coming yourself. Tell me."

"Strong! Wal, it sure is strong," retorted the trader, grimly.

"Why did you come?" demanded Nophaie.

"War!" flashed Withers.

In one bound Nophaie was on his feet, transfixed and thrilling.

"No!" he exclaimed.

"Yes, by God!" returned the other, and he too rose from his seat. A steel-gray flinty light shone from his eyes.

"Germany—and the United States?"

"Nophaie, you've said it!"

"Blucher—and the Indians?" Nophaie's voice was quick and ringing.

"I haven't a damned word to say about Blucher," burst out Withers passionately. "But I'll tell you a few facts outside the reservation. . . . For weeks Germany has torpedoed American trading vessels, threatened and bullied President Wilson, insulted the American flag. . . . Then she sunk the *Lusitania* with American men, women, and children aboard. . . . Then she sent submarines to our very shores. . . . The President and Congress have declared war!"

Nophaie recalled Marian's letters. How certain passages now seemed limned on his memory in letters of fire! German militarism! Downfall of civilization! Death of freedom! Slavery of Americans! By every right and law and heritage he—Nophaie—was the first and best blood of America. The depths of his whole soul roused to strange, fierce passion.

Withers held out a shaking hand.

"My son has gone," he said thickly. "Already! He did not wait for the draft."

"Draft! What is that?"

"A new law. A war law. Every young man between twenty-one and thirty is called to army and navy, to fight for his country."

"Will this draft affect the Indians?" queried Nophaie sharply.

"No. They can't be drafted. But the government has appealed to all Indians to register. That means, as I understand it, an enrolling of the names and numbers of Indians, their horses and stock, so that the government can have this information for reference, for some use that is not clear to me. We're all drawn into the war—whites and Indians. But no Indians can be compelled to go to war."

"Can they go if they want?"

"Yes. And the call is strong for Indians to enlist."

"I will go!"

Withers forced that shaking hand down on Nophaie's shoulder where it gripped hard. For an instant speech was beyond him. How strange the agitation of his rugged face! The unplumbed passions of the man had been upheaved.

"Nophaie, you don't *have* to enlist. You are nothing to the people of the United States. They have wronged you."

"I am an American," replied Nophaie sonorously.

"I didn't come to ask you to go to war," responded Withers, in earnest passion. "But I came to tell you *this*. . . . The Nopahs are being lied to. They did not understand the idea of registering. They are being made to believe it's a ruse, a trick to get their names, their thumb marks on paper. They are being deceived into believing this register is only another white man lie, and if they sign they can be drafted. . . . Old Etenia met me on the way here. He said: 'If the Big Chief at Washington wants my young braves for war why did he not ask them to go? The Nopahs have been warriors. But never have they been forced to fight!' Another old Indian said, 'Let the Germans kill all the Americans. Then we can get our land back and live in peace!' Nophaie, this tribe of yours numbers over twenty thousand. They must not be made to believe they can be unjustly driven to war. The truth must be told them. This false rumor of government treachery, this damned propaganda must not spread further."

Nophaie understood why the trader's lips were sealed as to what he knew. Marian had prepared Nophaie for understanding of this fostering of hostility among the Indians.

"I will tell the Nopahs the truth," he said. "I will take Indians with me to war."

Chapter 17

Nophaie bade a long farewell to his Canyon of Silent Walls. At the eastern portal—high above the narrow defile between ragged cliffs—he gazed down at the green valley with its wavy confines of red, and fixed that picture on his memory forever. A faint, cold sensation—was it tremor or sinking of heart?—went over him. Was it mystic portent of evil prophecy that he would never again dream under those silent, gleaming walls? He cast out the vague thought.

He and Withers made a record ride to the camp of the Pahutes, where they stayed overnight. Nophaie began his ministrations there. None of the few Pahute men present, however, came within the prescribed limits of the war demands.

Another day brought Nophaie and the trader across the upland sage to the range of Etenia. The old Nopah had sons and relatives, and more horses and cattle than any other Indian in this quarter of the reservation. It was important that he be persuaded to accede to the act Withers had called registration.

Nophaie found himself received with a respect and deference which presupposed the fact that during his hiding he had gained in prestige. It augured well for the success of his new work among the Indians. Nophaie sought council with Etenia, which was granted; and the old Indian asked the honor of the trader's presence. Nophaie had gone over in his mind an exhortation he believed to be honest, eloquent, and persuasive, and which he believed would appeal to the Indians. This he delivered to Etenia with all the force he could muster.

The old Nopah smoked in silence. He had been deeply impressed, and could not at once reply to such a strong discourse. At last he spoke.

"Nophaie sees with the mind of the white man—far and wide. He should sit in the councils of the Nopahs. Etenia believes and will register his name. He will sell cattle and horses to the government. He will say to his sons, one of you shall go fight for America, for the white people, for the land where they keep us. Etenia will say his sons shall draw lots for him who is to go to war."

That night Etenia had all his sons and relatives at his hogan in honor of Nophaie and to hear him speak. He ordered a feast to which Withers was invited. They ate and made merry and sang. Then the old Nopah rose to address the assembly. He was solemn and austere, darkly impassive, chieftainly in his dignity.

"Sons—and sons of my people—Etenia has come to many years. He has worked hard and he is rich. He owes no white man so much as a silver button. He owes no Indian. . . . Etenia has not the wisdom of the gods. He cannot heal like the medicine men. Etenia's age make him want to trust younger man. Therefore has he heeded Nophaie.

"Our white Father at Washington has declared war on a wicked people far across the broad water where the sun rises. These wicked people are warriors. They have long worked at the arts of war—they have long made guns and bullets and powder to prepare for war. . . . For three years now they have fought their neighbors—the white people who have sought to live in peace. And they are driving these good peoples out of their homes, killing men, women, and children. They will win the war unless our white Father at Washington sends many young warriors across the broad waters.

"Lies have been told us. Etenia's sons do not have to go to war. The white men who have spread such lies are snakes in the grass. Their forefathers belonged to that wicked people who practice war. They are not American. They are not friends of the Indian.

"Etenia's people are asked to register, to give their names to the government, and the number of their horses and cattle. Etenia believes Nophaie and the white trader. These men are not liars. Nophaie will ride over the ranges to carry truth to those who are being deceived. Etenia will register and he tells his sons and all Indians to follow in his footsteps. He will give one of his sons to go to war with Nophaie."

Then Nophaie rose to make his address, deeply stirred by the words of Etenia. And with ringing voice he damned the evil force at work on the reservation, and brought home to the dark, still-faced Nopahs the truth of the real danger that menaced them. He did not appeal directly to the Indians to enlist. But he finished his speech with a trenchant statement of his own stand.

"Nophaie will go to war. He will fight for the English, who are forefathers of Americans. Nophaie and all the Nopahs are the first of Americans. He will fight for them. And he will believe he is fighting no more for the white people than he is fighting for the Indian and his land."

When lots were drawn among the sons of Etenia it turned out that the youngest, the favorite of the old Nopah, the joy of his declining years, must be the one to go with Nophaie.

"Etenia says it is well," declared the father, with lofty pride.

At Kaidab there was a crowd of Indians, and an unrest and excitement totally new and strange to the trading post.

Nophaie found the white people stirred and upset, under the stress of an emotion that none could control. Nophaie talked with all of them. The trader's wife showed the strain of worry, and a mother's fear for her son, and a suppressed anger and concern over the Indian situation. The Indians were excited. They collected in little groups and talked. Every hour saw more Nopahs ride into the trading post. And Nophaie found them sullen, distrustful, and hard to approach. But for his late rise to the dignity of one worth listening to he could not have gotten their ear at all. A subtle and powerful influence had been at work among them. Nophaie had guessed its origin and he discovered how and by whom it was being done. He realized at once that he had been too late to influence the Indians in a body, and would have a difficult task to persuade them to register, let alone go to war. Nevertheless he did not allow this unfortunate circumstance to deter him from his great task.

At the outset of his activities there he encountered Shoie, the binder of evil spells on Indian women. Nophaie was about to pass him in contempt. But suddenly he halted. This Indian was young, strong, a keen scout, a wonderful breaker and tracker of horses. His mentality might be one to adapt itself readily to war. Nophaie meant to leave no stone unturned.

"Shoie, I am going to fight for the Americans," he said, in the Nopah tongue. "You are a warrior. Will you go with me?"

"Shoie will fight for Nophaie," replied the Indian, with a gleam in his dark eyes.

For days Nophaie haunted the trading post and importuned the visiting Indians. His dogged efforts earned success, but nothing that satisfied him. Always he got the attention and the respect now due him; only he encountered the wall of doubt that once raised in an Indian's mind was almost impossible to break down. One old Nopah said: "All white men are liars!" Another Indian said: "No white man can lie to me twice."

The government idea of registration met with a subtle and powerful check. Nophaie could not learn from any Indian just what was the content of the hostile propaganda. He guessed, however, that the idea of registering had been falsely represented to the Indians, and it was just such an idea that would stick in their minds.

Nophaie decided a wiser plan for him would be to ride out over the reservation and head off this German propaganda. He had intended that in any event, but now he saw he must make haste, yet he was loath to abandon Kaidab with only seventeen Indian names promised for registration and only three for service. Withers's comment on this was significant.

"Nophaie, you've done well."

At this juncture Nophaie received another letter from Marian, and it acted as a spur. Affairs were at white heat in Mesa—all relative to the war. Nophaie had been long forgotten by the authorities. It would be safe for him to do his utmost to counteract German influence among the Indians. Marian knew he would do his noblest and then go to France to fight for his country and for her. "It comes down to that," she wrote. "The women of America are in danger of the Hun!" She had spent some time at Flagerstown and was as well and strong as she had ever been. There now would surely be work for her on the reservation. The war had opened avenues for women. But whatever work fell to her lot he was to understand that she would come to him, if he could not come to her, before he went to training camp. Somehow her words made Nophaie's heart swell with the thought of the part he could play for her in war.

And there was a concluding passage in the letter that made his blood boil in fury against the sordid malignity of those in control at Mesa. Nophaie read this passage over again.

"My beautiful white mustang Nopah is dead! He had to be shot. Oh! It nearly broke my heart! Wolterson has been compelled to make blood tests for tuberculosis in Indian horses. He said he never would have touched Nopah. But Blucher saw my horse and *ordered* the test. Wolterson made it and reported Nopah's blood perfectly healthy. All the same Ruhr came over and shot him."

Nophaie rode out into the desert on his mission, and few were the hogans he missed. It would be impossible for him to cover all of the reservation, and he did not have many weeks before he must report for service. But he rode fast, far and late. Most of the Nopahs in that vicinity now had heard of his stand and were ready to listen to him. Every name added to his list strengthened his cause. As slowly as this list grew likewise did his influence. If only he could have forestalled the German! Nophaie thrilled to his heart. He could have led a regiment of Nopahs—strong, young, fierce, hard-riding desert-bred Indians to war. The thought of being too late was sickening. It goaded him on to ride faster and farther to find Nopahs who had not been deceived.

One after another, as the days passed swiftly, he found young braves who would be guided by him. He gave these instructions and knew they would keep their word. Of the hundreds of Nopahs he approached only one here and there would listen. Those who yielded to his persuasion were mostly free young men, sick of reservation life and restriction. Grateful for their falling in line to swell his list, Nophaie rode on and on. Many a mustang he left spent at a hogan in exchange for another willingly lent him. Never a Nopah but accorded him welcome at nightfall. His quest was that of a warrior and a chieftain, even though his people could not follow him.

Thus, as time flew by, fleet as the hooves of Nophaie's mustangs, he gradually worked into territory new to him, far across the great mesa to the est, where he was not known. Here he had less trouble to find converts. Only the country appeared sparsely inhabited by hogans! The active propaganda had not taken root among these Nopahs.

One afternoon near sunset Nophaie reached a small trading post kept by a squaw man. The last Indian Nophaie had interrogated had bidden him ride in haste to this post. Mustangs to exceed a score in number were standing haltered and loose before the squat, red-stone house. But no Indians were in sight. Dismounting Nophaie went to the door and looked in. He saw the backs and black-banded sombreros of a crowd of Indians all attentive to the presence of a white man sitting on the high counter. That white man was Jay Lord.

Nophaie stole in unobserved and kept behind the Indians. He listened. Lord was lighting a cigarette. Evidently he had either paused in his harangue or had not yet begun. The careless air of the erstwhile Jay Lord seemed wanting. Nonchalance did not rest upon his round, dark face this day. Indeed, Nophaie was quick to grasp a weary and furtive irritation. And the strain that showed in all white men's eyes these days was not wanting in the Mormon's.

"Indians, listen," began Lord, in fluent Nopah. "Blucher has sent me out all over the reservation to tell you not to register. Don't put your names or thumb marks on any paper. If you do your horses and cattle will be taken and you will *have* to go to war. There's no law to compel Indians to fight. You can't be forced to go. But if you sign papers—if you register—the government will have you bound. Then you've got to go. This register order is not what it seems. It's an old government trick to fool you. You've been fooled before. Listen to your real friends and don't register."

When he concluded his harangue there followed an impressive silence. Then an old Nopah, lean and wrinkled and somber, addressed the speaker.

"Let the white man tell why Blucher sends him. If the government lies to the Indians—to make warriors of them—then Blucher lies, too, for he is the government."

"Blucher is a friend of Nopahs," replied Lord. "He does not think the registration is honest. The government has made a law to *drive* young white men to war. It does not hesitate to *cheat* the Indians for the same reason."

The ensuing silence of a moment seemed pregnant with the conviction of the Indians. Presently another of them moved forward. He leaped on the counter. He too was old, a scar-faced Indian, with fierce dark mien. He shook a sinewy hand at the young men before him.

"Hagoie will kill any Nopah here who registers!" he thundered.

That appeared to end the speech-making, for all the Indians began to jabber excitedly. Nophaie took advantage of the moment to slip outdoors. Twilight had fallen. He walked to a corral near the house and sat down out of sight to wait for darkness and to think. He did not intend to let Lord get away from that post without being confronted. He had noticed the Mormon was packing a gun. Therefore it would be policy to surprise him. Nophaie argued dispassionately that he had good cause to kill Lord, not to consider the possibility of self-defense.

In twos and threes the Indians came out of the trading post to mount their horses and ride away into the gloom of the desert. Soon Nophaie felt that he could trust going close to the house. At an opportune moment he approached and leaned in the shadow of the stone wall. More Indians came out, until there appeared only a few left. Then as Nophaie had hoped for, Jay Lord came out the door with the squaw man. The latter was speaking. Evidently Lord was going to see about his horse.

"I'm married to a Nopah squaw—shore," said the trader, with a hint of wrath, "but I ain't no Indian, nor fool, either. I didn't like your talk about this register order."

"Ahuh! Wal, be damn good and certain you

keep your dislikes to yourself," growled Lord. "Otherwise, you won't last long here."

The squaw man retired into his house and the Mormon strode toward his horse.

Nophaie glided after him. Then just as Lord reached for his bridle he must have heard something for he stiffened. Nophaie pressed his gun against Lord's side and said low and sharp, "Don't move your hands. If you do, I'll kill you."

"Nophay?" ejaculated Lord hoarsely.

"Yes—Nophaie."

"Wal—what you want?"

"Listen. . . . I heard your talk to the Indians. I know now what has influenced them all over the reservation. It's German propaganda, and you're Blucher's mouthpiece. You're no better than a German yourself. You're a traitor. Do you hear me?"

"Hell! I ain't deaf," growled Lord, straining to hold himself stiff. His face now made a pale blotch in the gloom.

"Lord, this talk of yours is *treason*," went on Nophaie. "Do you have to be told that by an *Indian?* If I had time I could get Nopahs and white men, too, who'd help me prove your guilt. But I want all my time left to undo your dirty work. I'm going to war—to fight for *your* country. . . . Now, here, if you don't quit spreading these propaganda lies of Blucher's I'll ride to Flagerstown and enlist. Then I'll come back on the reservation. I'll be an American soldier, outside the law. Blucher can't touch me or hold me . . . and I'll kill you—Lord—I swear I will! Do you believe me?"

"Wal, I reckon I do," replied Lord gruffly. "An' if you want to know, I'll give you a hunch I'm damn glad to be scared off this job."

"Just the same, get on that horse and keep your back to me," ordered Nophaie.

In another moment Lord, cursing under his breath,

was in the saddle. A hard, leathery thud and jangle attested to his use of spurs. The horse plunged away to be enveloped by the darkness.

Nophaie stayed at the squaw-man's house for two days, and all his earnest talks to the Indians who visited the post failed signally to overcome the insidious propaganda spread by Jay Lord.

To Nophaie's dismay he found that the farther he penetrated into this part of the reservation the colder the Nopahs met his solicitations.

Hot weather came. The desert summer lay like a blanket over sage and mesa and sand. All the mornings dawned cool and pleasant, with the sky clear and blue, the sun a glorious burst of gold, and the desert a rolling open land of color. But as soon as the sun tipped the eastern mesas the heat veils began to rise from the sand. Towards noon white creamy clouds rose above the horizon, to mushroom and spread and grow dark, eventually to let down the gray winding curtains of rain. Each thunderstorm had its rainbow; and there were times when Nophaie rode down a vast shingle of desert with rainbows and storms on the horizon all around him while upon his head the hot sun fell. Many a storm he weathered, grateful for the gray wet fallout of which he emerged drenched to the skin.

At length Nophaie headed his horse back toward the west and the country he knew best. One whole day he rode along the rim of a deep blue canyon, before he could cross. Many a day he went hungry, and slept where night overtook him.

At the Indian villages east and south of Mesa, Nophaie ran into conditions not heretofore experienced by him. As the taint of white civilization began to be more pronounced here so was the agitation incident to the war. Nophaie did not find the groups of excited Indians sympathetic to his cause. These Nopahs close to the borders of civilization and the railroad were markedly different from the Nopahs far to the north. Rumors had been spread all over that section— enforcement of the draft, confiscation of stock and wool, seizing of all firearms. Blucher's minions had done their underhanded job well. Nophaie saw more drunken Indians in short time than he had ever seen before in all his rides over the reservation. Many were selling wool to the traders, in a hurry to dispose of it. Prosperity was at its peak. But an ominous shadow hovered over the desert. The Indians seemed to feel it. Their work was neglected. Crowds of Indians rode into Flagerstown, to return with their minds chaotic. The fever of the whites communicated itself to the red man. The medicine man predicted dire troubles for the Nopahs.

Nophaie's passionate dream of leading thousands of Indians to war had to be dispelled. His tireless labors resulted in upwards of two score Nopahs signing their thumb marks to his paper. Word came to him from various sources that Indians were enlisting in the army, but he could not verify this until he got out of the desert. A terrible bitterness at the government worked on him. In wartime, what was the secret of holding a German enemy to an important post, where he could undermine the faith of thousands of Indians who would have made great soldiers? What stolid ignorance and blindness on the part of government officials! Blucher was guilty of treachery and treason. He had been just keen enough to grasp the fact that these Nopahs could and would fight for America. And he had deceived them, adding to their already weary disgust at false-hood after falsehood. Nophaie saw the truth in all its appalling nakedness. He realized what might have been possible with the proud, fierce, young Nopahs. A great page of American history—an Indian army joining the white man in battle for liberty—would never be writ-ten. Nophaie had the vision. He loved his people. He knew their wonderful qualities for war. They might have made—they would have made—a glorious record, and have paid the government good for evil. Heroism for injustice! They would have earned citizenship in the United States. What magnificent opportunity lost! Lost! Nophaie's heart burned with hatred for the German who had ruined the noblest opportunity that had ever confronted his people.

"I should have killed Blucher," muttered Nophaie. "No service I can render now will ever be one-thousandth as great as that would have been."

Nophaie rode into Mesa, there to take farewell of Marian. Long he had dreaded this and thrust it from his mind. But now with his work ended, and the near approach of the date set for him and his Nopahs to enlist, he had to think of her.

Much as he yearned to see Marian he was greatly relieved to learn from Paxton that she was in Flagerstown, and would expect him there. She left Nophaie a short note, telling him where to find her, and she entreated him not to tarry long at Mesa.

Nophaie had need of that entreaty. Never in his life had he been victim of the dark and terrible mood now fastened upon him. The wrath roused in him by the murder of Do etin and his ambushment by Noki, and the tragedy of poor little Gekin Yashi had not been the same as this now so murky and hot in his soul. The idea of war had liberated something deep and latent in Nophaie. The menace to the seaboard of the United States, which he remembered so well; the encroachment of an utterly unscrupulous enemy that well might raze the hogans of his own race, burn the sage, and make quarries of his beautiful walls, had stung and roused in him the instinctive savageness of his nature.

It was in this mood that Nophaie reached Mesa, and the pathos of Marian's letter and the proximity of Blucher and Morgan only added fuel to the smoldering fire.

Nophaie made no effort to hide. He was in reality an American soldier. He had ridden thousands of miles in the service of the army. No reservation jail, no jail at Flagerstown could hold him now. Freely he mingled with the Indians at the trading post. An unusual number were there, some drunk, all excited, and a few were bound for Flagerstown, on the same errand as Nophaie. The mail carrier had two of them engaged as passengers, and readily agreed to take Nophaie. It was a five-hour run by automobile. Nophaie thrilled to his depths. Five hours only—then Benow di cleash! He gazed from the stone step of the trading post, out across the sand and brush of the mesa, away over the stark and painted steppes of the desert to the upflung, black-peaked range of mountains. Benow di cleash would be there. Already the sun had begun its western slant, and when it touched the horizon rim he would see the white girl.

Ought he not see Gekin Yashi? The thought flayed him. No! That would be the last straw added to the burden of his hate for Morgan and Blucher.

Nophaie took no part in the jabbering of the Indians around him, but sat back behind them on the stone steps, his sombrero pulled down to hide his face. There he smoked his cigarette in silence, brooding and dark in his mind. When school recess time came and the Indian boys ran to and fro like blue-ginghamed little automatons, Nophaie watched them from under the brim of his sombre-ro. What would be their future? And then when beyond them, through the fence he espied the brown-faced black-haired little Indian girls, each of them a Gekin Yashi for some Nopah, he looked no more. Visitation of the Hun could hardly add to their tragedy!

An automobile thrummed up the road from Copenwashie and stopped before the trading post. Two white men beside the driver occupied it. One of them was Blucher. Had that round bullet face thinned out?

Nophaie felt the leap of his blood. Blucher and his companion got out of the car, and climbed the stone steps, in earnest conversation not distinguishable to Nophaie. But as the superintendent passed to enter the trading post Nophaie could have reached out a long arm to touch him.

Kill him now! The whisper ran through Nophaie's being. It was a flame. Almost it precluded thought. Could he serve his America or his own people in any better way than to kill this German? No! All Nophaie's intelligence justified his passion. What matter if civilization beyond the confines of the desert knew nothing of this man's iniquity? Nophaie knew. What matter if the callous and mighty government machine never knew—or knowing would not care—or blind in its red tape and infinite ignorance hanged Nophaie for his deed? Nophaie knew. There were things outside of reason or self-interest. But the face of Benow di cleash rose in Nophaie's reddening sight, and he was again master of himself.

Presently Blucher and his attendant came out, accompanied by Paxton, who appeared to be talking about flour he had exchanged for wool. Blucher stood a moment at the doorstep. Again Nophaie could have reached him. And all the burning fires of hell in Nophaie's heart were smothered into abeyance by his love for a white woman. Just to save her pain he sacrificed the supreme and only savage lust of his life. Once he was all Indian. How easy to kill this man! What inexplicable emotion quivered to the thought! To rise—to fling his sombrero—to thrust a gun into this traitor's abdomen—to eye him with the eye of Indian ruthlessness and white man scorn—to free passion in the utterance: "Look, German! It is Nophaie! And your last vile moment of life has come!"

But Nophaie gave no outward sign of the terrible storm within him. It passed, like a wind of death. And he marveled at the strange chances of life. Here stood

this Blucher, utterly unaware of the presence of the
Indian who had no fear of anything, who had waived
murder by the breadth of a hair. Evil men there had
been and still were in the world—men who knew the
perils of life and had the nerve to gamble with them—
but Blucher was not one of these. Morgan was a
stronger man, as he was a greater villain, yet he, too,
was blind. Dead to something righteous and terrible in
the souls of some men! The agent of the government
and the missionary of the church were but little
and miserable destroyers, vermin of the devil, with all
their twisted and deformed mentality centered upon
self.

Before sunset that day Nophaie was in Flagerstown
and had dispatched a note to Marian. Before he started
to meet her he had enlisted at the recruiting station and
was a soldier of the United States Army.

At the end of a street near the outskirts of town
Nophaie found the number he was hunting for. And as
he mounted the porch of the little cottage Marian
opened the door. Fair golden flash of face and hair! He
did see clearly, stumbling as he went in. Her voice
sounded strange. Then they were alone in a little room
with vague walls. Dread he had felt at prospect of this
meeting, but he had not understood. He only wanted to
spare her pain. This woman now, holding his hands,
gazing with strained, dark eyes of agony up at him was
remembered by her beloved fair face, but something in
it was strange to him.

"Benow di cleash!" he said unsteadily.

"Nophaie—lover—my Indian! You are going to
war— Oh, God!" she cried, and threw her arms around
his neck.

Even as Nophaie bent to her white face, now flaming
red, and to her lips, he gasped at the meaning of her
singular abandon. One word had been enough. War!
And he pitied her, and loved her as never before, and
understood her, and clasped her close, and kissed her

until she sank against him, pale and spent. To him her kisses, with all their sweetness of fire, called to his own lips only an austerity of farewell. Long ago, in his Canyon of Silent Walls, he had fought his battle against love. Here he was as strong, tranquil, grave as she was weak and passionate.

"Nophaie . . . when do you . . . go away?" she whispered.

"Tonight, at ten."

"Oh! So soon? But you go first—to training camp?" she queried breathlessly.

"Yes."

"You might not be sent abroad."

"Benow di cleash, do not have false hopes. You *want* me to go to France. I'm fit now to fight. And it will not take long to make soldiers of my Nopahs."

"That means the . . . the front line . . . the trenches . . . scout and sharpshooter duty—the most dangerous posts!" she cried, with a hand going to her mouth.

"Indians would not court the safe places, Benow di cleash. We are going—sixty-four Nopahs, most of whom I enlisted."

Then he told her of his long rides and his importunities to beat Blucher's influence, and of his failure. She warmed to that and in her anger at the treachery of the agent and her pride in Nophaie she passed by the more poignant moment of this meeting.

"I knew he was pro-German," she said, with flashing eyes. "Yet, strange to say, he has strong friends here. Oh, this little town is out of its head. What must Philadelphia or New York be now?"

"If the Indians are excited, what must white men be?" replied Nophaie. "All this war feeling is bad, wild, terrible. But I have nothing to lose and everything to gain. I—"

"Nothing . . . to . . . lose!" she cried, suddenly sobbing, and again her arms flashed round his neck.

"Nophaie, you have *me* to lose. . . . Don't you love me still?"

"Love you! Child, you are beside yourself," he replied tenderly. He saw the havoc of war in this girl's breaking of reserve and intensity of emotion. "Only today I proved my love for you, Benow di cleash."

"How? Not to me, not yet."

He told of the incident where Blucher passed within reach of his arm, at a crucial moment when all the savagery of Indian nature was in the ascendant, and he had denied it.

"Only thought of you kept me from killing him," he concluded.

"*Me!* I'd have been glad," she returned, with again that strange blaze in her eyes.

Nophaie realized anew that the white girl now presented a complexity of character perhaps beyond his comprehension. She, who had been the one to save Blucher's life, now would have gloried in hearing of his death through her lover. This war spirit had unsettled her mind.

"Nophaie, let me follow you to New York—to France," she begged.

"Let you follow me! Why, Benow di cleash, I couldn't prevent you, but I implore against it."

"I would never disobey you. Let me go. I can become a nurse, do Red Cross work, anything."

"No. If you want to obey me—give me happiness—stay *here* and go on helping my people until I come back—or—"

"Don't say it," she cried, and shut his lips with hers. "I can't bear the thought. Not yet. Maybe some courage will come to me after you are gone. I love you, Nophaie. A million times more since I came out here to your country. The desert has changed me. Listen, after you leave I will go east for a while. But I promise I will come back here and work—and wait."

"All is well, Benow di cleash," he said. "I feel that I

will come back. . . . Now let us go outside and walk. I cannot say good-bye to you inside a house."

Gold and purple clouds attended the last ˋteps of sunset—a magnificent panorama along the western slope of the mountain range. At the end of the lane a low rocky eminence rose, the first lift toward the higher ground above the town. Stately pine trees grew there. Wide apart, rugged and brown, with their thick green tops, they appealed strangely to Nophaie. A solemn and beautiful and splendid emotion came to him as he walked under them with Marian. Strength seemed to have passed from him to her. She was growing calmer and assimilating something of his faith, of the mystic in him.

The warm summer air floated away, and the cool wind from the mountain took its place. The rosy afterglow of sunset faded into pale blue. A lonely star glimmered in the west. The great still pines grew black against the sky.

"Benow di cleash, when the Indian says at the end of his prayer, 'All is well,' he must mean that what must be is best. Your missionary never interprets any prayer as a submission to life, to nature. The white prayer is a fear of death, of what comes beyond. I have no fear of death, nor of what comes after—if anything *does* come. The only fear I have is for you, and such of my people as Gekin Yashi. Women of any race are marked for suffering. I deplore that. It is one of my atheistic repudiations of the white man's god. There is enough physical suffering for women. Just last week when I stayed at a hogan I saw an Indian woman die in childbirth. . . . You must understand how gladly I welcome a chance to forget myself in a righteous war. I know the nature of fight—what violence does to the body—and if it does not kill me it will cure my trouble. Perhaps over there I may find the God I could not find in my silent canyons. Then there is the man—the Indian of me—rising up fierce and hard to fight. If all Germans are like Blucher I want to kill some of them. . . . You must not have one unhappy hour on account of my going to war. Think of me as an American soldier. Physical pain is nothing to me. I have played football with injuries that would have laid white men in the hospital. I welcome this chance to justify the Indian. Any Indian not steeped in his ancestral blindness and ignorance would be as I am now. So I bid you not be unhappy. If I live to come back to the reservation, *then* you may have cause to be unhappy about me. For I know the war will bring misery and poverty and plague to my people. But be glad now that with all my misfortune I can rise above it and hate, and fight for you and your people. Love of you saved me from the dissolute life so strangely easy for the Indian among white people. It saved me to strive against my infidelism. And it has uplifted me to believe I may come somewhere near the noble Indian you have dreamed me."

Chapter 18

AFTER NOPHAIE'S DEPARTURE MARIAN FELT as if the end of all had come. She had not looked beyond this last meeting. And now with the poignant and stinging experience in the past she seemed lost and brokenhearted. She fell into a terrible depression, out of which she struggled with difficulty. The desert called her; the promise to Nophaie was a sacred obligation; but she could not at once return to her work among the Indians. She decided to go back east for a while.

The hour she arrived in Philadelphia she realized that outside of her need of change and the pleasure of old associations there was other cause for her to be glad she had returned.

Philadelphia, like other great cities, was in the throes of a nation preparing for war. The fever of the war emotion had seized everyone. The equilibrium of the staid and tranquil city of brotherly love had been upset. Marian found her relatives as changed as if many years had intervened between her departure and return. They had forgotten her. Each was obsessed by his or her peculiar relation to the war. The draft of a son or brother or nephew, the seeking of war offices, the shifting of trade to meet the exigencies of war demands —all these attitudes seemed personal and self-seeking. Many of Marian's acquaintances, young men under thirty, in one way or another avoided the clutch of the service. The baseness of this was thrown into relief by the eagerness with which others enlisted before the draft. Young women were finding the world changed for them. Every opportunity appeared thrust upon them, even to the extreme of donning khaki trousers and driving ambulances in France. Marian could have found a hundred positions, all more remunerative than any she had ever had. It was a time of stress. It was a time of intense emotional strain. It was a time when the nobility and selfishness of human nature vied with one another. It was a time that tried the souls of mothers. It was a time which called forth strange, deep and far-reaching instincts in young women. It was a time when drafted soldiers misused the glamour of their uniforms.

Marian had her own reasons for being personally and tremendously stirred by the war. That made her charitable and generous in her judgments of others. But the wildness and unrestraint she could not condone. She could not blame any girl for heedlessly rushing into marriage with a soldier—for she had yearned to marry Nophaie—but she was affronted and disgusted by the abandon she saw in so many young people. The war had given them a headlong impetus toward she knew not what.

Yet Marian felt this strange and terrible thing herself. Why did her heart swell when she saw a soldier? Why did her eyes dim when she saw from her window a tramload of soldiers speeding towards New York? The spectacular sale of Liberty Bonds, the drives, the bazaars, the balls, the crowded theaters, the enlistment of half the graduating class of the University of Pennsylvania—in the midst of all this strange, exalting atmosphere Marian found her reason for being glad she had come home. No American should have failed to see and feel these days. The desert had isolated and insulated Marian, until it had seemed she was no longer a part of the great republic. She had as much reason as any woman—except mother of a soldier—to be terribly drawn into the chaos of wartime. Whenever she thought of Nophaie a shuddering possessed her internal body and she was sick. Yet there was a pride in him that was growing infinite.

Marian did her bit in the way of buying and selling bonds, and in Y.M.C.A. and Red Cross work. But for her promise to Nophaie to go back to the reservation she would have gone, like so many young women, to extremes of war enthusiasm. The urge to go to France was something hard to resist.

Nophaie's letters were few and far between, and not what they had been out in the desert, but upon them Marian lived and sustained her hope. In September she went to the seashore to get away from the humidity and tainted air of the city, which, since her sojourn out west, she could hardly endure. And she needed rest. She went to Cape May and haunted the places on the beach where she had been with Nophaie.

The restless, bright Atlantic! Marian bathed in the surf and spent long hours upon the sand. This period was restful, yet it was singularly acute and living. The grand roll of the breakers, the thunder and boom, the white cordage of foam and the flying spindrift, the green heaving sea far out—these elements seemed to be understood better and appreciated more through her memory of the desert. But she loved the desert most; and every day the call of the wide-colored wastes, the loneliness, and something she could not define, rang more subtly in her ears.

So time flew by, and autumn began to decline into winter. It took more time for Marian to dispose of what little property she had, and following that came a letter from Nophaie telling her when he was to sail from New York to France. Marian went to New York in a vain hope of seeing him. But all she had of him was the sound of his voice over the telephone. For this she was unutterably grateful. The instant she had answered his "hello," he had called piercingly: "Benow di cleash?" Then shaking all over the little booth, she had listened to his brief words of love and farewell.

She was one of the throng of thousands of women on the Hoboken docks when the huge liner left her moorings. Thousands of faces of soldiers blurred in Marian's sight. Perhaps one of them was Nophaie's. She waved to them and to him. She was only one of these thousands of women left behind to suffer and endure. This was harder for Marian than the farewell in Flagerstown.

White fluttering sea of waving handkerchiefs! Flash of ruddy, boyish faces! These meant so much. They were so infinitely more than just incidents of life.

The keen, bright winter sun shone down on the dock of weeping women, on the huge liner with its tan-colored fringe of human freight, on the choppy, green-waved Hudson River, and the glitter of the imperial city beyond.

Marian returned to Philadelphia with her spirit at lowest ebb and for once in her life fell prey to an apparently endless dejection. Besides, the cold wet climate was hard on her health after the dry, bracing desert. She suffered a spell of illness, and when she recovered from that she saw it best to wait for spring before starting west. Meanwhile she went into war work. All of her notes on the reservation and the Indian school remained untouched. She had not the heart to rewrite them for publication. She read newspapers and periodicals on the war until her mind was in a chaotic state. Once, at least, she was stung into specific realization and an agony of suspense.

A newspaper printed a report of French operations along a river at the front. For some reason not stated it was important that observations be kept from the end of a certain bridge, long under German gunfire. For three days a soldier had stood motionless; whitewashed to resemble a post, at the exposed butt of that bridge. He was successful in his observations and had not drawn the gunfire of enemy. But he died from the strain and the whitewash. This scout was an American Indian.

"He . . . he might have been Nophaie!" whispered Marian, in torture.

In April Marian received a reply to a letter she had written Mrs. Wolterson.

King Point, April 3

Dear Marian,

I am long indeed in replying to your most welcome and interesting letter. But you will forgive me, for my excuse is work, work, work. Imagine! Out of six white people and thirty little Indian children, *I* was the only one not down with the influenza.

First your account of the goings-on of people in the East, and all that war stuff, stirred me to thrills, made me long to be home—for I, too, am an Easterner—and yet caused me to thank God I am out in the open country.

We were transferred here, as you already know, and left Mesa without regret, except for our few true friends there. We are fortunate to be retained in the service at all. The wrong done my husband by Blucher and Morgan was not undone and never will be.

Blucher, you will be glad to hear, had a sudden check to his pro-Germanism. Something or somebody frightened him. My friends write me that his reactions to this fear, whatever it was, resulted in him applying himself to reservation work. But he will not last much longer as superintendent. He will get the "steamroller."

Morgan, however, goes on his triumphant way with his Old Book behind him. What a monster that man is! It is utterly inconceivable that such a fanatical devil could have such a post. It all shows the power of the idea of religion—of missionary work. Morgan is a missionary of Hades! His latest stunt will interest you. Ramsdell, the cowboy missionary, was one of the few really good and helpful missionaries whom the Indians ever recognized.

You will remember that Ramsdell's way of work did not appeal to Morgan and his cronies. I suspect they feared Ramsdell was really acquiring influence. Robert, my husband, many a time came across Ramsdell *helping* the Indians. He worked with them, digging ditches, plowing, planting, and building. Ramsdell was a good mechanic and he tried to teach things to the Indians. Then he did not thrust his religion down their throats. Hell's fire and all that bunk had no place in his talks. More significant, perhaps to the Indians, was the fact that Ramsdell never had anything to do with Indian women. He was a rough diamond, a hard-riding parson, but as Robert says, "Shore the real thing." Well, Morgan called one of his investigations, his tribunals. He and two of his missionary colleagues constitute the Mission Board. They brought Ramsdell to their court, and accused him of being a leader in Heathenism. This charge was based on the fact that he dressed in Indian costume for the entertainment of Indian children. Another charge was that he was too friendly with the traders to be a true missionary. He was dismissed. So rolls on the Christian Juggernaut! Sometimes I do not wonder at the utter incredulity and scorn of the Indians.

Here is a bit of news that comes closer to us. Gekin Yashi has again disappeared. The report went out from headquarters that she had again run off. But my correspondent in Mesa does not believe it. No attempt was made to trace Gekin Yashi. If she had run off she would have been tracked.

None of the policemen have left Mesa. I know what I think and so does Robert. But it seems best not to trust my suspicions in a letter. Someday the truth will come out. Alas, for the Little Beauty of the Nopahs! When I think of her, and the child prodigy Evangeline, and noble Nophaie, I am sore at heart. King Point is not at all like Mesa. I loved

Mesa, despite what I suffered there. This place is high up on the desert, over seven thousand feet above sea level. It is bleak, barren, bitter cold, and the winds are terrible. The snow last winter blew level with the sand. It did not fall! But yet there is beauty here. Great red bluffs, covered with cedars, and sand dunes forever changing with the wind, and yellow mesas, and long white slopes of valley. But the solitude, the cold, and the mournful winds are dreadful. Influenza swooped down on us late in winter, a very fortunate circumstance. Had spring not come, I believe the whole population of some thirty-six would have been wiped out.

As it was, everybody but myself fell sick. Can you imagine my labors? I had them all to myself before a doctor came, and then after he was gone. The poor little Indian children—they were so sick! I hardly had time to eat, let alone sleep. And when relief came it was none too soon for me.

I have no direct information regarding influenza ravages at the other points on the reservation. But I understand it hit the Nopahs pretty hard. I never saw any disease like this. I dread the return of winter. Warm weather kills the germ or whatever spreads this sickness. If it should come early in winter, I shudder to think what might happen out here on the reservation.

You wrote in your letter of returning sometime. We are glad to hear this news. Mrs. Withers wrote me that she had received a letter from Nophaie from France, and that he said he had seen you on the pier at Hoboken, just before his ship sailed. But you did not see him! How strangely things happen! I have two brothers at the front in France. When I think of them I think of Nophaie.

All good wishes to you, Marian, and let us hear from you.

Sincerely,
Lillian Wolterson

Marian went back to the Indian country prepared to carry on personal interest in the welfare of
the Nopahs.

It had been her good fortune to meet an estimable
woman philanthropist who was at that time sending
money to missionaries on the reservation. Two of these
Marian knew, and one of them was Morgan. She told
the generous woman that she did not believe a single
dollar of her donations ever reached the Indians. The
wealthy philanthropist was incredulous and opened her
eyes wide at Marian's revelations. She had influence in
Washington and knew the president of the Indian
Mission Bureau in the state of New York. Marian
interested this woman to the extent of getting her
support in the probable need of securing permission to
pursue her work on the reservation, independent of the
agent there.

At Flagerstown Marian rented a little cottage out
near the pines, from which she could see the green
slopes and gray peaks of the mountains. This time, with
knowledge and means to set about her task, she
provided a comfortable place to come to, during visits
from the desert.

Marian's first trip on the desert was out to King
Point, where she spent a profitable day with the Wolter-
sons. King Point was as cool and pleasant in summer as
Flagerstown, but Marian found instant antagonism in
the head of the Indian school there, making any project
of hers rather out of the question. Besides, there was
no place to stay. The school was a small branch of the
main system, and no Indians lived in the near vicinity.
The missionary there had been stationed by Morgan.
He was a nonentity, judging by the replies he made to
Marian's queries. And his wife seemed to regard
Marian with ill-disguised suspicion.

To Marian's regret she found matters not happy for
the Woltersons. Blucher's enmity had a long arm.
Wolterson had encountered the same underhanded

tactics that had been in operation at Mesa. Moreover, the altitude and the cold, and the poor quarters furnished by the government, had not improved his health. Marian advised him to leave the Indian service.

"Shore I've got to," he drawled, "but I hate to quit just now. Looks like I'd been driven out."

Before Marian left she received a suggestion from Wolterson that made her thoughtful. He told her about the little settlement of Nokis at Copenwashie, how they were growing poorer in water and land, and had a hard winter ahead of them.

"Shore they'll not be able to feed their stock," said Wolterson.

"Why?" inquired Marian.

"Because they have less land than formerly and very little water. They can't raise enough alfalfa."

"Why less land than formerly?"

"Friel and Leaman have gotten most of the Indian's land."

"Oh, I remember. But *how* can they do that? It seems absolutely unbelievable to me."

"Listen and I tell you," replied Wolterson. "First, the missionary elects the particular piece of ground he wants. Then he gets the superintendent to report to Washington that this land is not needed by the Indians. It is *always* the best piece of ground. The government grants the use of a little tract of land upon which a church may be built. Soon it is further reported that this is not sufficient for the missionary to raise garden and hay. Another tract is available and this is also turned over to the missionary. After a time the missionary applies for a patent to this land. Friel has got his patent. Leaman is pretty close to getting his. Others are pending. With the land the missionary gets a supply of water for irrigating, and often in addition he gets a good spring, and this much water is simply taken from the Indians. Water on the desert is limited. Last year was dry. This one may be drier. And there you are."

"Well!" ejaculated Marian. "So that is how missionaries acquire their lands?"

"Shore it's an old story, all over the world," rejoined Wolterson. "I have an uncle who went to Hawaii. He was a rancher, and thought something of settling in the Pacific. He said all the rich planters in the Hawaiian Islands were descendants of missionaries who had gotten land from the natives. Oh, this Old Book stuff is great for missionaries, if they don't happen to be Christians!"

Marian had planned to go next to Kaidab, but influenced by the incentive of Wolterson's suggestion, and a dread of seeing just yet the beautiful sage uplands labored by Nophaie, she decided first to look over the field at Copenwashie. The Paxtons at Mesa gave her a warm welcome, and between them, for the sake of a subterfuge that might be wise, they arranged a basket and blanket buying job for her.

Copenwashie lay down on the edge of the mesa two miles or more from the government post. At any time it was a barren, desolate outlook, and in summer under the leaden haze of heat it was surely mercilessly inhospitable to a white person.

The Nokis were agricultural in their pursuits, not nomads like the Nopahs. The two tribes had long been inimical to each other. One old Noki woman, who was so old she did not know her age, had told Paxton she could remember when the Nopahs could ride down on the village and throw Nokis over the cliffs. Their houses were flat-roofed and built of stone and adobe, cool in summer and warm in winter, a very great improvement on the hogan of the wilder Nopah. In many cases rude corrals adjoined the houses. The several lanes of the village, were upon Marian's first visit, colorful and active with burros, dogs, chickens, cows, and Indian children. A keen tang of cedar smoke filled the air. It brought to Marian's mind the campfire of the upland country. Thin, curling columns of blue smoke rose from invisible holes or chimneys.

Marian went from door to door of these little low houses and asked to see baskets. She saw stoves, beds, sewing machines common to white households. The rooms she got a peep into were whitewashed and clean. The Nokis were short in stature, broad-faced, resembling a Japanese more than a Nopah, and the women all appeared to be heavy. They spoke some little English, but they were reserved and shy. Marian was hard to please in style of baskets, but she paid the price asked without haggling. Thus she carefully felt her way along the line of procedure she had adopted. When she left the village and ascended the slope to the level of mesa she looked back.

The place seemed a jumble of little rock and mud huts perched on the very edge of a precipice. Below lay a wide green valley with Indian laborers at work and threads of water running to and fro. Across the valley rose a red and yellow bluff, rising out on the ghastly desert. To the right of where Marian stood loomed an imposing structure of stone, built by masons, two-storied and with a tower. This was the home of missionaries. Somehow Marian resented its presence there. She was looking at it with an Indian's eye. She thought of the cowboy-missionary Ramsdell, who had slept and lived like the riders of the open. Knowing what she knew, Marian had difficulty in restraining more than prejudice.

Paxton had driven her down to Copenwashie, and said he did not approve of her walking unattended. So Marian adjusted herself to a slow progress of passing the time and winning the confidence of the Nokis. But there were other demands upon her time—study, reading, writing letters, keeping in touch with all pertaining to the war. The heat of mid-day was after all not unendurable, and she got used to it, though she endeavored to stay indoors during those hours. She hired the Indian mail carrier, who remembered her, to carry her letters to Flagerstown and to do her errands. Three or four times a week she visited the Noki village. On each trip she bought baskets, and she left candy and dolls and musical toys with the children. When a Noki woman asked her if she was a missionary, Marian thought she had gained a point in her emphatic negative.

She anticipated embarrassing situations and prepared for them. Jay Lord sat on the trading-post steps during the summer evenings. Morgan had asked somebody what that "white-faced cat" was doing back on the reservation. Friel had learned of her presence. But so far Marian had been clever and fortunate enough to avoid meeting either of them face to face. She did not care, however, when that might happen.

If happiness could have been hers it might have come to her here on the desert that had somehow changed her, and in the work she had chosen. But she could not be really happy. Nophaie wrote but seldom. He was "somewhere in France." His letters were censored, and he wrote so little of himself. Marian lived in constant dread that she would never hear from him again—that he would be killed. It did not torture that he might be injured. For she knew he was an Indian to whom injuries were nothing. She could not break the morbid habit of reading about the war. She had terrible dreams. She hated the Germans more and more. Even the tranquility of the desert, its wonderful power to soothe, did not help her with this war emotion. She seemed to be doing all these things while she waited. Life did not stand still but her heart seemed to. She endured, she made the most of her opportunities among the Nokis, and she tried not to fail in faith and hope. But the long, hot summer dragged, relieved only by one short visit to the cool mountain altitude of Flagerstown.

With the end of summer there seemed to be an end to the uneventful waiting monotony of her life.

Withers called for her one day and packed her off in his car to Kaidab. His wife was not very well and needed a change of climate and wanted Marian to take a short trip with her to California. Marian gladly consented, and while preparations were under way for this journey she rode horseback, and climbed high on the black mesa to try to get a glimpse of Nophaie's country. All she could attain was sight of the red pinnacles of the monuments of the Valley of Gods. But she was grateful for this much.

Looking across that wild and wonderful desert of upflung rocky ramparts and green reaches of lowland, Marian thought of the Indian boy who had been born there, who had shepherded his flock in the lonely solitude, listening to the secret voices of Indian spirits, who was now fighting in France for the white man and for America. Marian's old strength seemed to flow back to her heart. She had been sick, lonely, brooding, weary for Nophaie. She needed love. But she realized her utter selfishness in contrast to Nophaie's nobility. Just a sight of the upland country revived her earlier spirit. She must not be found wanting. Every day added to this renewal of courage and with that, and the cooler days, there came a quickening of her energies.

Withers found the time propitious for a short absence from Kaidab. His partner Coleman said business would grow poorer instead of better. The decline of the Nopahs' fortunes had begun. Price of wool had been steadily falling. There was no demand for baskets and blankets. The Indians had been prodigal of everything. There were no stores laid away. And they misunderstood the decline in price for their wool while the price of all the trader's wares soared higher.

"They're facing the hardest winter they ever had on this desert," concluded Coleman.

"Wal, you're talkin'," responded Withers thoughtfully. "And if that 'flu' disease strikes the reservation when cold weather comes it's good night!"

"Will the war never end?" sighed Mrs. Withers.

"End? It's ended now. The Germans are licked. They're stallin' for time right now," retorted the trader, with fire in his eyes. "They'll never go through another winter. I almost wish they would not show a yellow streak. France has got their number. Marshal Foch ought to be allowed to wipe the Germans off the earth. If he isn't, the Germans will trump up some trick, and they'll come back in the future, worse than ever."

Withers's son Ted had gotten to France, but he was still among the reserves, back of the front line, and that fact evidently irritated the Westerner. He wanted his son to fight. Mrs. Withers, on the other hand, was grateful for the chances that had so far spared her only son. The sister of this boy shared her father's aggressive ideas. Marian had grown war-weary. The whole terrible, incredible, and monstrous riddle revolved around Nophaie. And she had not heard from him for many weeks.

The last day of Marian's stay at Kaidab she prevailed upon Miss Withers to ride out and climb the highest point available. Withers sent one of his Indian riders with them. They had a long, hard, and glorious ride. From the brow of a great divide Marian saw the whole vast reach of the Valley of Gods—the red sentinels of the desert—lonely and grand against the haze of distance. She saw the dark organ-shaped mesa under the shadow of which Nophaie had been born. Then far to the westward, up and up over the giant steps, she caught a glimpse of green-cedared and purple-saged uplands, and above them the huge bulk and dark dome of Nothsis Ahn.

Marian felt a tremor that was more than a thrill. Her breast heaved, her sight dimmed. Wild, lonely, beautiful land of sage and canyon! She loved it. The clearest teaching of her life had come from its spell. She longed to climb the endless and rugged trail to Nophaie's silent walls. They were not silent for her.

This day had been full, poignant, resurging the old flow of emotions. As Marian rode across the level stretch of gray desert before Kaidab the sunset was gilding the rims of the distant mesas. Rose and lilac hazed the breaks in the walls, and the waste of sand and grass waved away under a luminous golden light.

Withers was waiting at the gate for the riders. His face wore an excited, eager, and happy expression, such as Marian had never before seen there. What could have broken this intrepid Westerner's reserve? Marian experienced a sensation of weakness.

"Get down and come in," he called. "Come a-rustlin' now. I've got news."

Marian tumbled off some way, and ran at the heels of Withers's daughter, who was crying, "Oh! Dad's got a letter from Ted!"

So indeed it turned out to be. Mrs. Withers had been crying, but was now radiant. The trader fumbled over many sheets of paper, closely covered with writing.

"Sis, you can read all of this afterward," he was saying. "Ted's all right. Fussin' because he won't see any real fight. He says what I told you all—the Huns are licked. *Whoopee!* You know I wrote Ted months ago and asked him to find out about our Indians. I'd given up hoping. But he's found out a lot, and I'll read it. Marian, your Nophaie has got the Distinguished Service Medal! *What* do you know about that?"

Marian could not have spoken then to save her life. She seemed locked in sensation—mute in the sweetest, richest, fullest, most agonizing moment in her life.

The trader fumbled over the sheets of paper. His fingers were not wholly steady.

"Here," he began, "this letter seems less cutoff than any we've had. Ted writes: 'I had some luck. Happened to run across a soldier who'd been in the thick of the front-line battles with some of our Indians. What he had to say about them was a-plenty. He knew Lo Blandy when he played college football. So it's a good guess Lo Blandy is our Nophaie. I got thick pronto with this soldier. His name is Munson. He hails from Vermont. He'd not only been in the front-line trenches

with our Indians, but in the hospital with some of them.
I've forgotten names and places, if he told me. This
French lingo is sure hard for me. Munson said an officer
told him there were thousands of American Indians in
the service. That was news to me. It sure tickled me.

"'A good many Indians have been killed. Whether
or not any of them were Nopahs I can't say. But the
Indian who pulled the bear-trap stunt is our own nutty
Shoie, the spellbinder. Munson said they called him
that, and he answered exactly to the description I gave.
Now it appears that every night or so Shoie would pull
a crippled German into the trenches. These German
soldiers would have either an arm or leg broken, and
terribly lacerated. Shoie never had much to say over
here. You know the Indian. But like all the other
redskins he was a wonderful scout, and therefore had
something more of freedom than the white boys. These
Indians were no more afraid of No Man's Land than of
crossing the desert at night. Shoie was watched. And it
was discovered that he pulled these crippled Germans
into the trenches in a number four bear trap, attached
to a long wire. Shoie would crawl out in the darkness—
they said he always picked the places where German
soldiers were sneaking—and set the bear trap. Then
he'd slip back to the trench to wait. When he got one
everybody along that line sure knew of it. For the
Germans hollered like hell. At that to crawl into a
number four bear trap would make any man holler. All
Shoie said was: 'Me catch-um whole damn German
army!' I guess maybe the buddies didn't hand it to this
Indian.

"'Well, there's more about Lo Blandy. Munson lay
in the hospital with him, and found out he had been
wounded four times, the last time seriously. But he
seemed nearly well then. That was three weeks ago.
Blandy—or Nophaie—was to be discharged and sent
home as an invalid, incapacitated for further service.
He had been in everything the war afforded, except
actual death. That seemed to miss him. Munson said

Nophaie was indifferent to danger and pain. Shell shock had affected him somewhat, and gassed lungs made him a probable consumptive. But to Munson he was certainly far from a physical wreck. I think Munson said Nophaie got into the great Chatoo-Therry (how'd you spell that?) mix-up, and that an officer gave him the D.S. right off his own breast. Sure some stunt for an officer, believe me!

"'Anyway, Nophaie along with other Indians must be on the way home by now. I'm sure glad. It simply was grand to hear what devils they were among the Germans. I can't remember every caring a whoop about the Nopahs. But I've a hunch that a lot of Americans, including myself, haven't ever appreciated the red man.

"'My chance of plugging a Fritz has become slim, indeed, and for that reason I'm sure homesick for you all, the smell of cedar smoke and sheep wool!'"

Chapter 19

NEWS OF THE ARMISTICE DID NOT REACH MESA until late in the afternoon of that memorable November day. It came from the lips of the mail carrier. He was not credited. Paxton rushed to the telephone to call up Flagerstown, only to find the wire down. A crowd of Indians collected around the mail carrier, and they all believed him. Only the whites were skeptical.

"Oh, it's too good to be true," said Mrs. Paxton to Marian.

"It must come soon," breathed Marian tensely. Had she not a letter in her bosom—from Nophaie—telling of the deterioration of German morale?

Paxton came striding in, half out of his wits between doubt and hope. He nearly fell over the baby. He hugged his wife, then suddenly ridiculed her hopeful assumption.

Marian went out through the store, down the stone steps, and into the crowd of Indians around the mail carrier. Both Nokis and Nopahs formed that group. Excitement was rife. They jabbered in their low, guttural speech. Marian smelled whiskey. But resolutely forcing her way in she got to the mail carrier.

He was certainly in possession of his senses. Indeed, he was somber, almost stern. If emotion held him it was deep-set.

"What have you heard?" she asked, in her own language.

"War over. Germany run—holler no more shoot— want make big council," he replied.

"Who said so?"

"All come over wire. Heap talk over wire. . . . Men run round, get drunk, white squaws yell like hell. All stop work, bells ring, big smoke pipe on lumber mill blow steam long time, no hear."

And the Indian made significant motion to his ear, and then to his head, indication of his idea of a people with whirling brain.

Marian hurried back to the Paxtons.

"Friends, the Indian is telling the truth. There's a jubilee in Flagerstown. What else but peace could account for it?"

"Oh, it's too good to be true," repeated Mrs. Paxton.

Just then Paxton's clerk came running in. He was pale, and appeared about to choke.

"Eckersall on the phone," he blurted out. *"War over!* Friel brought news—he and Leaman. They just got in from town. Everybody gone crazy."

Eckersall was the government farmer down at Copenwashie and an old Westerner not given to hyperbole.

Paxton suddenly sat down as if glad for support. His wife hugged the little baby, and cried out, "Thank God!" Marian kept silent, but she felt as both these good people.

The clerk ran back to the store, and Paxton got up to rush after him. Marian and Mrs. Paxton indulged in a few moments of heartfelt felicitations, not unmixed with tears. And these few simple reactions appeared to be the forerunners of an hour of mounting excitement. Supper was not thought of. Outside in front of the trading post the crowd grew apace, and now white faces began to mingle with the dark ones. Friel's car came humming along, and it contained three other white men and several Indians. The latter leaped off as Friel drove on. He saw Marian standing on the steps, and waving his hand he yelled, *"War over!"* Marian waved back, and this was the only time she had been glad to see the missionary. He was a bearer of blessed news. He drove on, manifestly in a hurry to get to government headquarters.

The November air was raw and cold. It chilled Marian through. She went into the Paxtons' sitting room, where she sat by the window. The trader came through and opened the window. "Don't miss anything. There'll be hell. Blucher has arrested some Nopahs. And I'll bet they never go to jail."

Marian was now all eyes and ears. The trader kept running to and fro, with his wife at his heels. She was trying to make him stay in the house. Nothing unusual, however, occurred outside for a while. The crowd swelled to upward of a hundred Indians, a motley, dark assemblage, divided into several groups, each of which undoubtedly surrounded an Indian with a bottle. The white men had drawn apart.

It had been rather an overcast day, with clouds massing in the west. Perhaps the time was yet an hour before sunset. This purple and gray curtain broke to let out a ruddy, sulfurous glow that brightened the desert, and tinged the canopied sky. There was no hue of silver or gold. Shades of red burned against the purple, making a strange, weird, yet beautiful approach to sunset.

Marian saw an Indian running down the avenue between the poplars. Some of the watching Indians shouted. This Noki evidently was frightened for he looked back, and then darted in among his fellows.

Friel's car appeared, still containing the same number. Marian recognized two of them. The missionary drove to the steps where he stopped the car and got out. Manifestly he was starting for the window to speak to Marian when one of the other men called out, "Hold on, Friel."

The missionary, halted by the peremptory call, impatiently turned back. The Indians were looking now up the avenue. Marian heard another car coming. Before it reached range of her sight four white men came hurrying along. Ruhr, the policeman, was the foremost, and the last two were Glendon and Naylor.

Marian did not recognize the second man. They had the mien of angry, excited men, yet not overbold. Then the second car drove in sight. Sam Ween, the interpreter, was driving it. Morgan stood on the running board and Blucher stood up inside. It was not a difficult matter for Marian to perceive the state of their minds. When the car stopped Morgan hopped off and Blucher filed out.

"Arrest the Indian!" he yelled.

Ruhr apparently had the least reluctance to penetrate the suddenly silent crowd of Indians, and one of his deputies, the stranger Marian did not recognize, rather haltingly followed him. Glendon and Naylor hung back, a fact that added to Blucher's exasperation. Morgan, too, edged away from the ominous-looking front line of Indians. Presently that line was broken to emit Ruhr dragging an Indian behind him—the Noki that had hidden. Blucher ran in and shackled him.

"What'd you put irons on him for, you blockhead?" called Morgan. "Indians hate irons. And I told you they were in bad mood. Some of them drunk!"

"Who's doing this?" hoarsely called the agent.

The younger and probably more intoxicated number of the Indians suddenly appeared to move in unison and to spread round Blucher and his men. They closed in, shouting.

"Let that Indian go!" yelled Morgan, with all his might.

"See him—in hell first," yelled back Blucher.

Then the crowd became noisy, violent, and decidedly threatening. Marian lost sight of the white men in the melee. She felt her pulses beat in excitement and fear. Surely the Indians were in no mood to trifle. How dark and wild their upturned faces! They surged into a knot. That, too, broke as before, only more rudely, and it let out the white men, disheveled, pale, and thoroughly frightened. The Indians had forced Blucher to unshackle the Noki he had arrested. They jeered at him.

Bottles flashed aloft, held by dark, sinewy hands. *"Whiskey!"* some of the Indians shouted, and several deliberately drank in the very face of Blucher. He was forced back toward the side of the trading post, as it chanced, near the window where Marian crouched.

"Skin stretched over stick!" yelled a Noki who could speak good English. Then both Nokis and Nopahs took up that slogan, each in their own tongue. When this outburst subsided the Noki who had taunted Blucher turned on Morgan fiercely and menacingly:

"Where's your Jesus Christ?"

Taunt, contempt, hate, and warning all seemed embodied in this query.

Then older and sober Indians in the crowd dragged the violent ones back, and away from the trading post. But plainly it was no easy task. Cooler heads prevailed, however, and it seemed that Blucher and Morgan might have escaped violence.

"What'd I tell you?" shouted the missionary hoarsely.

Blucher vouchsafed no reply. His pale, sweaty face seemed to have fixed in an expression of furious trance. Marian had a good look at him as he passed the window to go to his car. He might have been walking in a nightmare. Indians were naught to him. His strident orders and violent movements had been merely the explosion of an unabatable and terrible passion. Stolid, heavy, immovable German that he was, he had heard news to unseat his reason for this hour.

Likewise, Marian had a fleeting glimpse of Morgan's face. Did she catch a lurking, sardonic gleam, a malignant flash of eyes? Or had her sensitive imagination conjured up illusive justifications of her opinion of this man. She marveled at the missionary. As a woman she seemed to shrink from her enormous conception of him. Was she right or wrong? She would have wagered her all that his mind was an abyss as dark as Hell and that his soul was a wilderness.

Then those two men, at once so infinitesimally little

in her conception of life and so monstrously powerful to rouse the drum and beat of her passions, slowly passed out of her sight.

December came, bleak and raw, but holding off in the inclement weather that made the desert an inhospitable place for white people. Influenza was reported by the authorities on widely separated parts of the desert. No effort was made to check the disease or to minister to any Indian except the school children. But it was not considered serious.

Marian awoke one day to a realization that she had found favor with the Nokis. Long before she expected it she was welcome in the secluded homes of these strange desert people. But after all they were very human, very susceptible to kindness and goodness. They would accept charity, and presents, but a material thing was no sure way to their hearts. Marian really did not discover this until after she had won them.

Then it became clear to her that she had been under as intelligent and careful a scrutiny as she had bent upon them. She was judged by what she said and did, and by developments that verified the appearance of them. No missionary ever quite adopted her tactics, for even the Catholic priests, who were the kindliest workers, and somewhat approaching Ramsdell in their method, could not long refrain from importunity and preaching.

After Marian had acquainted herself with the actual conditions of these Indians she set to work in her own way to help them. There were babies and old men going blind from trachoma; there were children with congenital hip disease; there were always injured horsemen and sick housekeepers; last of all, the whole village was poor and growing poorer.

The war might be over, but its aftermath had just begun. There were signs that more than warranted the gloomy forebodings of Withers.

Marian never saw the government school doctor waste a ride down to Copenwashie. She brought one

from Flagerstown. And his several visits, followed by
her own ministrations, alleviated considerable distress.
When the skeptical Nokis saw there was no comeback
from this, no axe to grind, nothing but the kindness of
Benow di cleash, they subtly and almost imperceptibly
changed. The old Nokis learned to relax their somber
faces in a slight smile; the children grew glad to see
Marian, more for her presence than for gifts.

It was very hard on Marian to remain even half an
hour inside the little houses because of the acrid smoke
from the open fires. This severely affected her eyes and
even her throat. When she got out into the cold, cutting
desert wind she was always relieved. So she did the best
that she could, grateful, indeed, that her efforts were
not futile.

Paxton went out of his routine to help her. Eckersall,
in his rough, uncouth way, left no stone unturned in her
behalf. Between the two of them Marian seldom had to
make the windswept two-mile stretch up the mesa. She
did not come into contact with Blucher or Morgan, and
so far as she could tell they were not paying any
attention to her affairs. This apparent fact, however,
did not blind Marian to their possibilities. They were
like moles, burrowing in the dark.

The missionaries of Copenwashie at first made fun of
Marian. Once more Friel had pressed his amatory
advances, which Marian had met with some rather
blunt speech: "Mr. Friel, you may blind yourself with
egotistic convictions. There's no limit to mental aberra-
tion. But I think you are a liar. And I'm not exactly
flattered with your presumption that I'd marry you and
live on the land you stole from the Indians." Friel never
again made fun of her, or attempted to make love to
her. He joined the other Copenwashie missionaries in
open warfare against her influence with the Nokis. Nor
was it at all strange that their lies made Marian's
position stronger. For the hundredth time Marian
marveled at the workings of the missionary mind. The
very virtues and qualities that should have been para-

mount in a missionary appeared to be utterly lacking in most of them.

Naturally Marian's growing close relation to some of the Nokis resulted in their confidences. And by the middle of December most of the little tribe who owned horses or cattle, and especially all of the freighters, were hard pressed for feed for their stock. Marian lent money to some of the neediest. But the situation was not to be met by the little money she could spare. So she took up the matter with Eckersall.

"Reckon I seen it comin' all along," was Eckersall's reply. "The Nokis are in for a hell of a winter, if you'll excuse my talk, miss."

"How much will it cost to buy hay for the winter?" asked Marian.

"Them freighters alone will eat up a thousand dollars before spring."

"Oh, so much! I can't afford that."

"Wal, sure you can't. An' what you are doin' more'n shows up this bunch."

"Where can we get help?" went on Marian.

"Reckon I don't know. Have you any friends you could ask?"

"Hardly. I wonder if Withers could help us."

"Withers! I should say not. Why that trader is goin' broke on the Indians this winter. Mark my words. I met him at Red Sandy last week. An' I asked how about things out Kaidab way. He jest threw up his hands."

"Eckersall, who has all the alfalfa raised here this last summer?" queried Marian curiously.

"Friel has most of it. Leamon has some."

"Ah! And has Blucher any hay?"

"A-plenty. Some I raised an' the rest freighted from town."

"Well, cannot the Indians get some of that hay?"

"Humph! They'll have to pay d--- high for it. An' jest now is a bad time. Blucher is sore over the meat deal."

"What is that?"

"Wal, miss, I'm only a government employee, an' I reckon I ought to keep my mouth shut. Sure I could trust you. . . . But that's not the point. I'll tell you what I'll do. I'll go to the agent an' make a strong talk for the Nokis."

"Thank you, Eckersall. That's good of you. Maybe we can do something."

But Marian's hopes were not high. And when from another source she learned the current talk about the meat deal she was even less sanguine. It appeared that as the winter advanced Blucher had solicited meat from the Nokis and Nopahs. But he would not pay over five dollars for a beef. As a result, the Indians sold but little of their stock and the Indian children had considerably less of a meat diet. Marian knew that the government advanced more money than offered by Blucher. But he refused to pay more than five dollars. It took no clever acumen to deduct why this was so and what he did with the difference.

Several days elapsed before Marian again saw Eckersall.

"Wal, ma'am, you are on the wrong side of the fence," he complained, ruefully, in reply to her eager query.

"How so?"

"We have a hankerin' for these poor devils of Indians. . . . Miss, I went to our German agent an' I made the speech of my life. I painted the woe of the Nokis an' the sufferin' of the horses as it was never done before. I told him that he made the Nokis freight supplies from town. That he had to pay them, but didn't pay them enough. That these freighters had no other way to make a livin'. He said he hadn't any hay to spare at twenty dollars the ton. Go to the missionaries. . . . Wall, I went to Friel an' talked with him. An' he said *forty dollars* a ton! The Nokis can't pay that. So I went back to Blucher an' railed at him again. He snapped at me: 'If the missionaries want forty dollars a ton for their hay, then the Indians will have to pay forty dollars.'"

Not long after that Marian met one of the freight wagons at the foot of the mesa grade. The wagon was packed full of boxes and bales, making a prodigious load to haul through sand and up the desert hills. Three teams of mustangs were hitched to it. Six little horses! They were skin and bones. How dejected and weary and hungry they appeared! Their ribs showed like fence pickets. Raw sores had been worn by the makeshift harness.

The drivers, both young Nokis, were walking. One held the long reins; the other led at the head of the first team. They were as tired as their horses. They had walked from Flagerstown—the whole distance of nearly eighty miles—to spare their teams. Marian questioned them, and though they grinned, their replies were significant of depression.

Following that incident Marian fell upon another equally illuminating. Blake, one of the least-known missionaries, a comparatively recent gathering to the fold of those who sought to save the Indian's soul, had several times told an intelligent Noki: "Hay and grain will be provided by Jesus Christ if you believe all I tell you." This missionary left his two skinny horses to graze round the trading post. One day the intelligent Noki was driving home and in his wagon was some hay for his horses. When the Noki went into the post, the starved horses belonging to Blake approached the wagon and ate up the hay. Upon discovering the circumstance the Noki dryly remarked: "Yes, missionary off somewhere praying Jesus Christ to send hay, and his horses here steal and eat mine!"

The Nokis realized that their land was being gradually taken away from them, and this winter they had grown restive and morbid under the strain. In former years the Nokis had been allowed to raise alfalfa on a certain number of acres of the school farm, but this

year that privilege had been taken from them. If the
government was using all the hay raised, and if the
missionaries demanded exorbitant prices for theirs,
then all the Noki could do was to quit freighting
supplies. For his horses had grown too weak to pull.

Winter came at last, biting, icy, and the desert
became an open waste to dread. Day after day clouds
rose, threatening storm.

Privation followed hard on the cold heels of winter,
and many of the Noki families began to suffer. What
with lack of food for man and beast the outlook was
discouraging. Marian bought stores of supplies from
Paxton—who charged exactly what they had cost him—
but these did not go far or long.

Then came the incident that heaped fuel on the fires
of Noki resentment.

Leaman, the missionary, had made a hurried trip to
Flagerstown, where he learned that flour had gone up
two dollars a hundredweight. It so happened that on his
return trip he passed several Noki wagons going into
Copenwashie to buy flour. Therefore, in possession of
this information, he hurriedly drove to the trading posts
at Copenwashie and Mesa, and bought all the flour the
traders had, some two thousand pounds, at the old
price.

Leaman, before this incident, had won a universal
dislike for himself. It then fell out that he was to go
beyond the endurance of even these stoical Nokis.

He got permission from the agent to preach to the
schoolchildren after they had assembled in the school-
room each day. So he chose the first hour of the
morning session and talked to the children about his
interpretation of the Bible. The Nokis objected to
Leaman's taking the time from the school work to
impose his undesirable doctrine upon them, and they
complained to the agent. Nothing was done. The Nokis
grew more resentful. They roused dissension. Their
activities caused reports to be made to the government,

and an inspector was sent out. He ruled that the preaching during school hours be discontinued. But after he had gone Leaman was seen to get audience with Morgan and Blucher, with the result that he kept up the preaching during the forbidden hour.

The Nokis held council over this turn of affairs and absolute usurpation of their rights. The chief himself came to Marian and asked her to read to him the ruling of the inspector. She did so, in Nopah and in English, both of which languages he understood.

"Benow di cleash, don't you think we ought to kill him?" asked the Noki.

Marian was shocked and told him with all the force she could command that murder would only add to their troubles.

"Don't you think we ought to kill him?" the chief kept repeating to everything Marian said.

"No, no, you must not," she protested. "Try sending a delegation to face Leaman. Show him the inspector's ruling and tell him you have had white people read it."

"Don't you think we ought to kill him?" was all the chief said.

But the next day, while Leaman was preaching to the children, this delegation suggested by Marian assembled in front of the village.

It was a cold, lowering day with wind sweeping down across the desert. The village had been swept clear of snow, except in the protected corners of stone walls. Marian had anticipated some untoward event, and she had borrowed a horse to ride down early. That ride had required something of fortitude. When she neared the village she saw Nokis riding in from the Red Sandy trail. And when she reached the dip of mesa risen she had further cause for excitement.

The delegation contained all the male Nokis, and some of the other sex, with a plentiful addition of Nopahs. Marian's eyes gladdened at sight of the tall, graceful, picturesque Nopah riders, blanketed as they were. Manifestly there was something in the wind. The crowd was walking and riding toward the school. Marian followed. It was some little distance, and all the way new riders fell in with the delegation. What surprised Marian, and added to her excitement, was the apparent fact that the Nopahs were going to take part in this protest. But to Marian it looked more ominous than a formal stating of objections. The Nokis meant to stop the preaching that they considered an imposition on the time and attention of the schoolchildren.

"Leaman, come out!" shouted a clear voice, in good English. It rang in Marian's ears. Unmistakably Indian, but was it Noki? Marian had to restrain a strange agitation. She convinced herself she was nervous and overinclined to imaginings. But she felt that she could trust to her eyes, and she rode farther to within one hundred feet of the school.

The missionary did not appear promptly enough to please the Nokis. They began to shout. Someone pounded on the door. Then again the clear, high, Indian voice pealed above the others, silencing them.

"Missionary, come out or we'll come in!"

The door opened and Leaman appeared. He had the face of a missionary and just now it was red. His figure, which resembled Morgan's, seemed instinct with intolerant authority. Yet in spite of this he was not at ease.

"What do you want?" he demanded.

"Get out. Quit preaching," replied the leader, and from the crowd came shouts confirming his order.

"I won't," yelled Leaman furiously. "Blucher gave me permission to preach. I'm going to do it."

"Read the order from Washington."

The missionary waved aside the paper planted in his face. It appeared to be in the hands of a short Noki beside whom stood a tall Nopah. He wore a wide sombrero pulled down over his face. The crowd of Indians rode and pressed closer. A low hubbub of voices began to rise.

"Come. Go to Blucher. Let us hear what he says. Let us have understanding. You've got to stop preaching in school!"

"No!" exclaimed Leaman hotly. "I won't stop. And I won't go to Blucher."

One of the mounted Nokis cast a lasso, the noose of which circled Leaman's neck. The crowd shouted wildly.

"Haul him out," yelled the leader.

Then the mounted Noki rode away from the school, drawing the lasso taut, and dragging the missionary out through the crowd. His face was not now red. Both his hands clutched at the noose around his neck. Manifestly the intention had merely been to rope the missionary and drag him into the presence of the agent. But the hell of Indians as well as that of white men was paved with good intentions. A wild young Noki, mounted on a spirited horse, pulled it up until its front hooves paved the air.

"*Hang him!*" this Indian yelled in Noki.

A roar broke from the crowd. In a twinkling the somber spirit broke to let out the devil. The time was evil. Long had the war oppression and passion dammed in the breasts of these Indians. Their wrongs burned for revenge. Some of their number were undoubtedly the worse for liquor.

But one of this crowd recognized the peril of Leaman and chose to divert it. He yelled piercingly and split the cordon of Indians closing around the missionary.

That piercing yell not only silenced the angry Nokis: it gave Marian the most startling shock of her life. She recognized that voice.

The tall Nopah reached Leaman's side and his long arms grasped the taut lasso. With one powerful lunge he jerked the Noki from his horse.

That tall form! That action! Marian thought she had lost her mind. Then the Nopah, in recovering from his exertion, rose to expose his face.

Nophaie! Marian screamed the name, but no sound

left her lips. She clutched the pommel. A terrible uplift
of her heart seemed to end in bursting gush of blood all
over her.

One sweep of long arms sent the noose flying from
Leaman's neck. How ghastly livid his face! He fell
against the Indian, either in collapse or feigning faint.

"Missionary, do you see Jesus Christ?" yelled a
Noki.

His derisive call was taken up by others.

The Indian braced Leaman, shook him hard, hauled
and pushed him through the crowd, and released him at
the door of the school. Leaman staggered out of sight.
When the Indian turned to face the crowd, tall, lithe,
with singularly free stride, Marian assuredly recognized
Nophaie. He began to push back members of that mob,
once again pressing toward the schoolhouse. Other
Indians, quickened by his example, fell in line to avert
further violence, and at length the whole mass, sullen
and gesticulating, was forced back into the village.

It was afternoon and Marian waited in Paxton's
sitting room for Nophaie.

She had met Withers at the post. He had come to
Mesa with Nophaie to take her back to Kaidab. They
needed her there. Outside the dark day had grown
colder and grayer. A snow flurry whitened the ground.
The wind mourned. Withers had said Nophaie looked
well enough. No one could tell! He had reached the
reservation from a point on the railroad east of Flagerstown. Two whole days! Forty-eight hours he had been
on the desert without her knowledge! He had ridden
down to the village to find her. God, indeed, had
smiled on a missionary that day. A Nopah had saved
his life.

Would Nophaie never come? Withers had gone to
fetch him back. But Marian could not wait. If she could
only see him, feel him, make sure this was not the
madness of a dream, then she could be calm, unutterably thankful, strong to stand any shock!

Suddenly she heard a step. Soft, quick, padded

sound of Indian moccasin! Her heart stopped beating. Nophaie entered. He was the Indian of her memories.

"Benow di cleash," he said, in voice that was rich and happy.

She raised both arms and lips before strength left her. Then as he enveloped her, she needed nothing but to feel. One woman's flash of sight—the keen, dark Indian face, thinner, finer, softening in its bronze— then she could see no more. But she felt—rippling of muscles that clasped and set round her like iron bands. Pressed against his wide breast she felt its heave and pound. And his lips!

"Oh, you *seem* well! *Are* you well?" Marian was saying, later, for what seemed the hundredth time.

"Well, yes, but I'll never again climb the north wall of Nothsis Ahn," he replied with a sad smile.

"Nophaie! Oh, I am not quite myself," she whispered. "You feel strong—you look the same. . . . No, there's a strange change . . . your eyes! Nophaie, your mouth! They twitch."

"That's only shell shock," he said. "It will pass away. Really, I am pretty good, considering. The gas left me subject to consumption, but I haven't got it yet. And my old sage uplands will cure me."

Marian could scarcely believe her eyes. She had expected to see him maimed, broken, aged, wrecked, but he was none of these. Slowly she realized. Then she espied a medal on the dark velveteen shirt he wore. His D.S.! How did he win that? Was she not a woman?

"Benow di cleash, my dearest, I've not been to pink teas, like you used to drag me to at Cape May," he replied with a laugh that signalized the acuteness of her joy.

"You fought! Oh, I've heard," she cried out. "The Withers boy wrote home. He had met a soldier who knew you—told him all about you. . . . Munson!"

"Yes. We met over there. But soldiers are apt to be quiet about themselves and to praise the other fellow."

"Nophaie—forgive me—something in me demands

to know," she said, unable to repress her strange emotion. "I . . . I think loving you and living out here has made me . . . a little more American than I was . . . more Indian! Did you play football with any Germans?"

He laughed, but not in the same way. For an instant he seemed no longer Nophaie.

"Benow di cleash, I did—yes. I got into a field of Germans—scattered—running like the old football players. . . . *Only I had a bayonet!*"

Chapter 20

A MODERATION OF THE SEVERE JANUARY weather attended Marian's arrival at Kaidab.

Withers had said to her: "We're a pretty discouraged outfit, and we need a little of your sunshine. We all had the flu except Coleman; Mrs. Withers isn't her old self yet. That's the worst of this queer sickness. It leaves half its victims with some infirmity. We're going to need you and I reckon you'll be better off and shore happier at Kaidab. And if it's work you're looking for among these poor Indians—Ha!—I reckon you'll have enough. For this winter has started in a way to scare the daylights out of us."

At first Marian did not see justification for the trader's grim statements. His wife was rather pale and weak, but she was getting well, and certainly was cheerful. The son was still in France, safe now at last from the Germans. Coleman had grown thin, and somewhat somber, yet appeared perfectly well. The Indian servants were identically the same as when Marian had last seen them. She felt that she must not, however, be oversanguine as to the well-being of the Withers household. She sensed, rather than saw, an encroaching shadow.

Nophaie had no home now, except the open, and Withers forced him to accept room and board in his house. Marian was sure that one of the trader's needs of her was to help him keep Nophaie from going back to the hogans of his people, which to do in midwinter for him would be fatal.

The afternoon of Marian's arrival at Kaidab was not without something of pleasure and happiness. The dark

cloud hovered at the horizon of the mind. She herself
brought cheer and gaiety, for she felt she certainly
owed them that. Besides, the proximity of Nophaie
made her more light-headed than she would have cared
to confess.

"Marian, you should see Nophaie in the uniform he
wore when he got here," said Mrs. Withers.

"His service uniform?" responded Marian eagerly.

"Yes, and it sure showed service."

Whereupon Marian conceived an irresistible desire
to see Nophaie in the garb of a soldier. So she asked
him to put it on. He refused. She importuned him, only
to be again refused. Nophaie seemed a little strange
about the matter. But Marian did not care, and persist-
ing, she followed him into the long hall of the Indian
decorations, and there she waylaid him.

"Please, Nophaie, put your uniform on for me," she
begged. "It's only a girl's sentimental whim. But I don't
care what it is. That girl loves you."

"Benow di cleash, I hate the sight of that uniform
now," he said darkly.

"Oh, why?"

"I don't know. I didn't hate it until I got back
here—on the desert—home."

"Oh! Well, you need never put it on again after this
time. Just once for me. I want to take your picture.
Think: I have pictures of you in football suit, baseball
suit, Indian suit. And now I want one of you as a
soldier—an American soldier. Why not?"

And she was not above lending her arms and lips to
persuasion, which quite vanquished him.

"You're a white girl all right, all right." He laughed.

"White? Certainly, and *your* white girl."

Somehow she seemed to want to be unutterably
tender and loving to him, as if to make up for what she
owed him. But when she saw him stride out in his
uniform she quite lost her teasing and affectionate
mood. It was almost as if sight of him had struck her
dumb. The slouchy, loose garb of an Indian had never

showed Nophaie off. As a soldier he seemed simply magnificent. She dragged him out in the sunlight and photographed him to her satisfaction. Then all the rest of the afternoon, which they spent in the living room before the big open fireplace, she was very quiet, and watched him.

After dinner he went to his room and returned in velveteen and corduroy, with his silver-buckled belt and moccasins. Nophaie again! Marian felt glad. That soldier uniform had obsessed her. Its meaning was so staggering.

Withers seemed to throw off cares of the present and forebodings of the future. He teased Marian and he kept coaxing Nophaie to tell something about the war. Marian added her entreaties to those of the trader. But Nophaie would not speak of himself. He told about the deaths of four of his Nopahs, all in action at the front, and each story had for Marian a singular tragic significance. Then he told about Shoie, who had turned out to be more than a bear trapper of Germans. American officers discovered Shoie's remarkable gift for seeing or picking out weaknesses in the German front line, when they were driving. Nophaie said it was simply the Nopah's wonderful eyesight. At any rate, Shoie was sent out on scout duty, both by day and night. He could hide himself in apparently level, bare ground. He needed no more cover than a jackrabbit. He had the Indian's instinct of stealthiness.

From one of his scouting trips Shoie did not return. He was reported among the missing. But sometime during the fourth night of his absence he crawled back to his own trenches. A sentry stumbled over him. Shoie could not talk, and appeared covered with blood, probably seriously wounded. Examination proved that he had been spiked to a wall through hands and feet, and his tongue had been cut out. As Shoie could not write his own language or understand much of the white man's, it was difficult to find out what had happened to him. Indians of his own kind at length pieced out the probable truth of his story. He had adventured too far and had been captured. The Germans had tried to force him to talk, or to make signs in regard to his regiment and trenches. They did not understand an Indian. Shoie made faces at them. They drove spikes through his hands and feet and left him hang for a day. Then they tried again to make him tell what they wanted to know. Shoie stuck out his tongue at the intolerant Germans. They ordered his tongue cut out. And still they left him hang. That night Shoie worked the spikes through his hands, then pulled out those that held his feet. And he crawled across no-man's-land to his own trenches. He recovered from his injuries to go back on duty.

"Oh! Monsters!" cried Marian. "Could they not have killed him?"

"Benow di cleash, the Huns were like Blucher," replied Nophaie.

That was the only word he ever said against the Germans, the only time he ever spoke of them.

"And is Shoie here?" queried Marian eagerly.

"Wal, I reckon so," replied Withers. "He was in the store today, begging tobacco. Sure it's a sight when he tries to talk. The Indians are more scared of him than ever. They think he has offended the evil spirits who had his tongue cut out to punish him for casting spells. Something strange about what's happened to Shoie!"

It was intensely interesting to hear Nophaie talk of Paris, and crossing on the troop ships, and his return to New York. Marian could not be sure, but she divined somehow that women had been one of the incomprehensible side factors of the war. A flash of jealousy, like fire, flamed over Marian, only to subside to her absolute certainty of Nophaie's aloofness.

"Withers, this will interest you particularly," said Nophaie, "as it deals directly with the Indian problem. . . . In New York I ran into one of my old teachers and officers from Carlisle. He remembered me well. Was not at all surprised to see me in Uncle Sam's uniform.

And he was glad I had done something. He took me to dinner at the Astor and we talked over my school days and football records. Asked me what I was going to do, and if I'd like a job. I told him I was going home to work with my people. That made him serious. He said: 'The work needed among the American Indians now lies along the line of citizenship. This government reservation bureau is obsolete. The Indian myth is punctured. Whenever the Indians protest against attempts to civilize them it is owing to the influence of reservation officers and politicians who want to keep their easy pickings. These fakirs encourage the belief that the Indian question is still serious, and that the government must still control them. Almost all the Indians have been born under bureau administration. They have been controlled by the political bureaus. Most of them have learned to be dependents upon the government. They know nothing of white man's ways, which certainly is a black mark against the Indian Bureau.

" 'The Indian in the war service brought to all intelligent and honest American thinkers something of vital significance. The Indians did not have to go to fight. They enlisted, perhaps ten thousand of them. Many were killed. They were in all branches of the service. I am absolutely certain that these Indian soldiers were not in sympathy with the bunko game of adopting American generals into the tribe. That was only some more of the politician's tricks to keep the reservations under government control and restrict the Indian to the desert.

" 'And it is not only unjust to the Indian, but a detriment to the government and people. If never before the Indian has now earned a right to get out among white men if he wants to or to live free upon his unmolested land. If these Indian Bureau men were honest in their work to civilize Indians they would make them free and give them the right of citizenship. Suppose the government restricted all the aliens and emigrants who settle in America. They would never become real Americans as most of them do.

"The real good to the Indian has been subordinated to the main issue, and that is the salary of fifteen thousand government employees. It is a waste of money. Actually, most of it is wasted.'"

Withers then indulged in some language a good deal more forcible than elegant, and he concluded his outburst by asking Nophaie if the Carlisle official had mentioned the Mission Board.

"No. It was I who asked him about that," returned Nophaie. "And he said: 'What have the missionaries got to do with it, anyhow?' Well, when I told him how the missionary with the Old Book behind him actually governed this reservation, and governed it basely, he was dumbfounded. 'Politics and religion,' he said, 'wouldn't appear to be good bedfellows.' "

"Nophaie, how would *you* decide the Indian problem?" asked Withers. "I've been among Indians all my life. My wife knows Indians better than any other white person I've ever heard of. It's a problem with us. As old Etenia says, you've got a white mind and red blood. I want you to tell us your angle."

Nophaie leaned on the high mantel and poked his moccasined toe at a stick of wood fallen from the fire. He seemed tranquil and sad. He had a thoughtful brow. His eyes had the piercing look, the somber blackness peculiar to his kind, but they had something more, and it was much for this nameless light that Marian loved him. She seemed to see it as the soul of an Indian—a something the white man did not believe in. She was curious to see how Nophaie would answer the trader's earnest question, and did not believe he would answer at all.

"I could solve the Indian problem. First, I'd exclude the missionaries, or emasculate those who insisted on thrusting their religion upon us," he replied, with a strange, dark bitterness. "Then I'd give the Indian land and freedom. Let him work and live as he chose—send his children to school—move among white men and work with and for them. Let the Indians marry white women and Indian girls marry white men. It would make for a more virile race. No people can overcome the handicaps now imposed upon us. Not much can be done in the way of changing or improving the matured Indian. But he was good enough as he was. This Indian wants none of the white man's ways. He cares only for his desert and his people. He hates the idea of being dependent. Let him work or idle for himself. In time he would develop into a worker. The Indian children should be educated. Yes! But taught to despise their parents and forego their religion? Indian children would learn—even as I have learned. What ruined me was to make me an infidel. Let the Indian's religion alone. . . . The Indian is no different from a white man, except that he is closer to elemental life, to primitive instincts. Example of the white man's better ways would inevitably follow association. The Indian will absorb, if he is not cheated and driven. . . . I think the Golden Rule of the white man is their best religion. If they practiced that, the Indian problem would be easy."

Late that night after the Withers family and others of their household had gone to bed, Marian sat awhile with Nophaie before the glowing embers in the fireplace.

This hour really was the happiest and most beautiful in its teaching of any she had ever spent with him. The Indian veil had not yet come between his white man's education and experience. Much of his bitterness had vanished. It showed only in his reference to missionaries. If he had been great before he went to war, what was he now? Marian could only feel little, humble, adoring, before this strange composite of a man. For Marian he was now more of a lover than he had ever been. How subtle, how complex! Marian trembled a little, fearful even in her hour of bliss. Why had he let down his Indian reserve? What did he know that she

did not? If he had gotten rid of the scourge of his
soul—his infidelism—he would have told her. But she
would have divined that. Nophaie was at once closer to
her than ever, yet farther away. All she could do was to
grasp at the skirts of the happy and thrilling and
thought-provoking hour.

Next day Marian encountered Shoie. It seemed to
her that Withers tried to attract her attention from the
Indians in the trading post, but he was not successful.

She went into the store, back of the counter, and
drew closer to this Indian hero who had been mutilated
by the Germans. She did not recognize Shoie. He was
some other Indian, like the evil spirit he claimed to
possess. His face had been strangely lacerated, and he
resembled a creature distorted by demonic laughter.
Shoie was a physical wreck. His Indian garb, that
manifestly he acquired from an Indian of larger stature,
hung loosely upon him, and it was ragged. She did not
see how he could keep warm, for he had no blanket.
And he huddled over the stove. Presently he observed
that Marian was staring at him. She could not tell
whether he was angry or glad. He opened his mouth.
His scarred lips moved to let out a strange sound. It
bore no semblance to words. Yet how plain it was he
tried to speak. Only a roar issued from the tongueless
cavity. To Marian it was horrible. She fled.

Bad news arrived that day; along with more rain,
cloudy weather. Both white travelers and Nopah couri-
ers reported increasing illness in the sections of desert
they had traversed.

"It's come," grated out Withers, somber as an
Indian.

That night the desert wind mourned under the eaves
of the house. Marian could not sleep for long. How
mournful! It wailed low and rose to a shriek and lulled
again. It made Marian shiver. It had an unearthly
sound. Its portent was storm, cold, evil, plague, death,
desolation.

At dawn a blizzard was blowing. Snow and sleet and

dust sheeted across the bleak levels, obscuring the mesas. It lasted two days, and broke to raw rain that melted most of the snow. The sleet again, followed by bitter cold! The sun did not show. At night the moon and stars were hidden. A dark, leaden, rolling canopy obscured the heavens.

Nophaie rode the ranges. Neither Withers nor Marian could keep him in. And the concluding weeks of that month brought the catastrophe Withers had predicted.

The Indians were caught like rats in a trap. Their hogans were no places to fight influenza. These months already of growing poverty had suddenly culminated in a terrible situation. They had saved no money. They had only horses, sheep, and corn. The price of wool fell to nothing. Withers managed to hold the best of the blanket weavers working at a loss to himself. He kept these families. And no Indian was turned away empty-handed from the store. Meat and corn were about all most of the Nopahs had to eat, and the time came when many of them did not have that. From a prosperous people they fell in six months to a starving people, at the mercy of a disease that seemed fatal to most. It killed them quickly. Those it did not kill, it left blind or infirm, or deaf.

In February hundreds died of the disease, within a radius of fifty miles of Kaidab. Whole families were taken. For many more days the sun did not shine, and the nights were black. The Indians thought the sun and moon had failed them. The medicine men prevailed upon them to believe that the only thing left to save them was the eating of horseflesh. Therefore they killed and ate great numbers of their best horses.

One morning Coleman found a dead Nopah lying beside the stove in the trading post. He had probably hidden behind the counter while the trader was locking up. Apparently he had not been any different from the other Indians. But the influenza had attacked him in the night and had killed him.

This mystery and terrible nature of the disease

absolutely appalled the Indians. They could not regard
it as a natural sickness. It was a scourge of the evil one.
And, most certainly, it was not a sickness carried by
one Indian to another, though just as certainly it was
contagious. It struck here and there and everywhere.
Lone sheepherders, who had not been seen or met by
any Nopah for weeks, were found dead. Hogans full of
Indians were found dead. Young and old went alike,
but the strong and healthy braves in the prime of life
were killed the most quickly. Peculiarly raw and brutal
were the ravages of the scourge. It came unawares like
a lightning stroke. And the Indian suddenly filled with
palsy and fever surrendered at once. He was like a wolf
caught in a trap, stricken, spiritless, ready for death.
The proud spirit of Nopah bowed under this brand of
his evil gods.

"Influenza, pneumonia?" queried Withers scoffingly.
"Hell! It's a plague. A *war* plague! Don't I know these
Indians? Why, bad colds and pneumonia are nothing.
But this damned disease is a beast of hell. Don't talk to
me of germs. It's no germ. It strikes from the air. It
comes *down*. It must be some of that infernal gas the
Huns let loose on the world. How else can we explain
the strange way it acts? Yesterday some Mormons rode
through. They told of meeting seven Nopahs on the
trail. These Nopahs were okay. Next day they went
down in a heap. I sent men over there. Six of the
Nopahs were dead. A little boy was living, half buried
under the dead bodies. Old Etenia fell off his horse and
died in two hours. His family has been nearly wiped
out. Nopahs die on their way *here*. Do you think they
were sick when they started? That's what jars me—the
way it strikes these Indians and how quick it kills! A
white man will fight, but an Indian won't. Not this
plague! It has got his goat, as the cowboys say."

In the midst of this tragic time Withers received word
that Gekin Yashi had fallen victim to the dread malady.
A sick Indian rode in with the news, disclosing the
whereabouts of the Little Beauty. She was married to a

Nopah who came often to the post, but who had never given Withers a hint that might have cleared up the mystery of her disappearance.

"Just like a Nopah!" ejaculated the trader. "Well, Gekin Yashi is down with flu. It'll kill her, almost sure. Maybe we can get her out in time. Her husband's name is Ba ho zohnie. He's a jester. Damn fine Nopah. His hogan is somewhere up Noki Canyon. I've sent Indians with horses to the mouth of the canyon. I'll take the car. Maybe I can drive up to the Pass—maybe to the canyon. . . . Give me medicines and whiskey."

He had been talking to Coleman and his wife. Marian sat beside the fire, startled and grieved into silence. Suddenly, Nophaie entered, unfolding his blanket. His quirt hung on his wrist. Snowflakes gleamed on his sombrero.

"Oh! Here's Nophaie," said Withers. "I was hoping you'd get back. Have you heard about Gekin Yashi?"

"Yes. We must hurry. She is dying. And she has a baby."

Marian leaped up, stung into action. "Let me go with you," she entreated.

Nophaie showed less willingness to take her than Withers. But Marian prevailed upon both of them, helped by Mrs. Withers.

"Bundle up warm. Take a hot stone for your feet," she advised, "and don't get either overheated or chilled. It's a squally day—storm and shine."

"Don't count on the shine," observed Withers. "You'll have to ride against the wind. Reckon you'll not forget it."

The ride in the car, with a hot stone at her feet and heavy blankets around her and over her face, was not much for Marian to endure. But when she got into the saddle, headed toward the wind, it was a different matter.

The day was not far advanced, and the sky appeared divided into sections of lowering gray pall, broken purple clouds, and stilly blue sky. The sun shone fitfully. At the outset the cold was not bitter, though the wind cut like a knife.

Neither sad errand nor inevitable discomfort could keep Marian from being responsive to other sensations. The mouth of Noki Canyon yawned wide, a jagged, red-cliffed portal, speckled with white snow patches and black cedar trees. The bald faces of stone were glistening wet. A deep wash meandered out of the canyon. Cold and wintry as was the scene it held fascination for Marian; and though not in any degree so magnificent as Pahute Canyon it was impressive and beautiful. The towers stood up carved, cragged, creviced, yellow in the sun, red in the shade, white on the north summits.

A familiar yet strange sensation assailed Marian, something which at first she was at a loss to define. Presently, however, she associated it with the icy cutting tangible quality of the air, and from that she discovered it was a faint fragrance of sage. Again she had come in contact with the most significant feature of the uplands. But she could not see any sage and concluded it must be farther on.

The threatened storm held off and the wind appeared to be switching and falling. Marian grew fairly comfortable in the saddle, warming to the exercise. And when the clouds broke and the sun shone forth she had opportunity to see this canyon.

It appeared to be a grand, winding portal into the solid rock bulk of the upland desert. Pahute Canyon was too deep and wide and tremendous to grasp. This canyon was on a scale that did not stun the faculties. It had a noble outline of rim, exceedingly broken into spires, domes, crags, peaks, monuments, escarpments, promontories; and the side canyons, intersecting with it, were too numerous to count. That appeared its most singular feature. At one point Marian rode across a wide open that might have been classified as the hub of a wheel, from which many canyon spokes ran off in all directions. From above Noki Canyon must have had

the shape of a centipede, with the main canyon consti-
tuting the body and the fringe of side canyons the legs.

About five or six miles up the Noki there came a
change of conformation. It spread wider, the cliffs
lowered, the perspective was much better because the
former overpowering proximity was now gone. Marian
was now not so close to the canyon that she could not
see it.

Wide flats of greasewood sloped up gradually from
the steep red-earth banks of the wash. A shallow,
muddy creek, lined with shelves of dust-colored ice,
wound between them. Riding across this creek, which
had to be done several times, was an ordeal for Marian.
The ice shelves broke under the hooves of the horses;
and they had to trot through the water to keep from
miring in quicksand. The steep trails up soft sandy
banks further worried Marian. She had to grasp pommel and mane to hang on; and when she rode down,
that was worse, because she slid forward on the neck of
her horse.

"Benow di cleash, do you see there is no feed for
horses or sheep here?" asked Nophaie, turning once to
wave his hand towards the flats. "This used to be the
most fertile of canyons. Two dry years! And do you see
the empty hogans?"

Marian had not observed either of these features.
But now the fact struck her forcibly. How bare the soil!
Not a blade of bleached grass! Dead greasewood, gray
as ashes, vied with the stunted cedars and a few scrubby
oaks, in relieving the barrenness of the canyon floor.
Long slopes of yellow sand, spotted with horse tracks,
ran up from the wash. Slopes of snow showed white in
protected places on the north side.

Gradually the trail climbed, and gradually the canyon took on more of beauty and less of grandeur. The
colors grew brighter. Patches of purple sage made
wonderful contrast to the red cliffs. It seemed that this
accentuated the loneliness and desolateness of the
deserted hogans. How sad, haunting the eyelike doors,

facing the east! No more did Indian rise to stand on his
threshold, to see the sun break over the eastern ramparts! A melancholy stillness pervaded the atmosphere
of this canyon. No sound, no living creature! Winter
had locked the canyon in its grip, but there was more
than winter to hold accountable for the solitude, the
seeming death of life.

A gray moving cloud, low down, filling the canyon
thick as fog, came swooping down. It was a snow
squall. It obscured cliffs, side canyons, turrets, and
towers, yet Marian could see its upper margin, a soft
rolling gray mass, against the blue of sky.

Withers led off to the left into one of the intersecting
canyons. It looked narrow, steep-sided, gloomy, and
mysterious under the approaching storm. When the
snow reached Marian she had a few moments of
exhilaration in the feathery white pall; and then as it
came thick and cold, she protected her face and paid
attention only to the trail.

That appeared to go on end more than its predeces-
sors. Marian rode up and down until she felt she was
not sure of her equilibrium. Finally the trail took to the
bottom of a wash, on a stream bed of sand and icy
sheets and an inch of clear water. The snow squall lost
its vigor, thinned out, and began to blow away as it had
come.

Suddenly, Marian saw a strange radiance. She
looked up. The snow was still slanting down, large
white flakes far apart, and they seemed to be of some
exquisite composite hue. Blue, white, gold! Or was it
only the strange light? Marian had never seen the like.
The sun was shining somewhere and through the
marvelous moving veil of snow gleamed the blue sky.
How unreal! Then it became a transparent medium,
revealing the golden rims of the canyon above, and
magnified a tower into a Babel of mosaics. Clearer,
more amber, grew the light; and soon purple slopes of
sage rose from the stream bed, to the snow banks under
the cliffs. Here the sage gave off pungent odor too

thick and powerful to be fragrance. It was a breath, cold, spicy, intoxicating. The storm swept on, wreathing the rims and filling the narrow canyon behind. To the fore all was clear once more, blue sky, golden towers, gleaming down upon a closed notched end of this canyon. It was a wild, beautiful place, enclosed by wet-faced cliffs, fringed by black spruce, sloped in snow and sage.

When Withers rode up a bank, and into a clump of cedars to dismount before a hogan, Marian realized with a shock that she was at the end of the ride. She had forgotten its portent.

Nophaie slid off his horse, and dropping his blanket from his shoulders he stooped his lofty form and entered the hogan. Withers ordered the two Indians he had brought with him to build a fire under the cedars.

"Get down and exercise a bit," he said to Marian. "They'll soon have a fire to warm you."

"Won't you let me see Gekin Yashi?" asked Marian, with hesitation.

"Yes, but wait," he replied, and taking a saddlebag off his saddle he hurried into the hogan.

Marian had scarcely dismounted before the trader came out again, with a look on his face that made Marian's halting lips stiffen.

"Too late!" he ejaculated, a little huskily. "Gekin Yashi died in the night. Ba ho zohnie's mother must have gone sometime yesterday. And . . ."

"Someone said there was a—a baby," faltered Marian, as the trader hesitated.

"Come here to the fire," rejoined the practical Withers. "You look blue. . . . Yes, there is a baby, and it's half white, as anyone could see. . . . It's about gone, too, breathing its last. I can't do anything but stay—and bury them."

"Oh! Withers, let me go into the hogan?" asked Marian.

"What for? It's no sight for you, let alone the risk."

"I'm not afraid of sight or risk. Please. I feel it's a

duty. . . . I cared for Gekin Yashi. She was so sweet and pretty."

"Reckon that's one reason why I'd rather you remember her as she used to be. . . . By God, every white man who has wronged an Indian girl should see Gekin Yashi *now!*"

"I will never forget the Little Beauty of the Nopahs," murmured Marian sorrowfully.

"All right, you can go, but wait," went on Withers. "I want to tell you something. Ba ho zohnie was one of the best of Nopahs. He had loved Gekin Yashi since she was a kid. But she didn't care for him, and Do etin wouldn't make her marry him. Maybe she ran off from the school at Mesa—in her shame. For Gekin Yashi was as good as she was pretty. But if she did run off it was made easy for her. Ba ho zohnie found her—his brother who's with us told me—and he took her home and married her. The half-white baby was welcome, too. Now he's in there holding on to the poor little dying bugger, as if it were his own!"

It took courage to walk up to that hogan and enter. The smoldering fire was almost out. Marian saw Nophaie sitting with bowed head beside a young Nopah —the counterpart of hundreds Marian had seen—who held a four- or five-month-old baby on his lap.

Nophaie did not look up, neither did the other Indian. Marian bent down over that tiny bundle and peered into the convulsed face. How dark the Indian's hand alongside of the baby's cheek! Even as Marian gazed an indefinable changing reached its culmination and set. She believed that had been the passing instant of life. Marian felt the drawing back of her instinctive self, repelled and chilled at heart.

Beyond these sitting Indians lay a blanketed form close to the hogan. It suggested the inanimate nature of stone. Snow had drifted in through the open framework of the hogan upon the folds of blanket. Behind Marian on the other side next to the wall lay a slighter form, not wholly covered. Marian saw raven black hair and shape of head she thought she recognized.

"Nophaie," she whispered. "This—this one must be Gekin Yashi."

"Yes," replied Nophaie, and rising he stripped back the blanket from the dead girl.

At once Marian recognized Gekin Yashi and yet did not know her. Could this be the face of a sixteen-year-old girl? Disease and death had distorted and blackened it, but this change was not alone what Marian imagined she saw. Gekin Yashi's songs and dreams and ideals had died before her flesh. She looked a matured, settled, Indian wife. Marian received the distinct impression, however fanciful or morbid it might be, that the Little Beauty of the Nopahs had found the religion and love of white men as false as Hell. And she had gone back to the Indian way of thought and feeling, somber, mystic, without bitterness or hope, pagan or barbarian now, infinitely worse off for her contact with civilization.

Marian's poignant reflections were interrupted by the voice of Withers inside the hogan.

"Nophaie, the baby is dead. Make him give it up. We've got to bury these Indians and beat it out of here pronto."

Marian spread her cold and trembling hands to the fire. Somehow the trenchant words of the practical trader roused her out of the depths. Such men as Withers bore the greater burdens. He had kindness, sympathy, but he dealt with the cold, hard facts. He was making himself a poor man for this Nopah tribe and working like a galley slave and risking his life. Through him Marian saw more of the truth. And it roused a revolt in her—against weakness and a too great leaning towards idealism and altruism—and for the moment against this stark and awful plague of influenza.

Nophaie might be taken. He would be if he kept

riding the range day and night, exposing himself to both bitter weather and the disease. The fear struck at Marian's heart. It did not pass. It shook her and stormed her. If there were lioness instinct in her it raged then.

Withers strode out of the hogan accompanied by the Indians.

"Get the tools," he said, pointing to the pack he had brought.

Nophaie remained beside the hogan door where Ba ho zohnie leaned, a forlorn and strangely striking figure. He seemed a groper in the dark. Trouble and grief burdened him, like weights. He did not seem to hear the earnest words of Nophaie or see the tall form before him.

Beyond the hogan, in a level patch of sage, half-circled by cedars, Withers set the two Indians to digging graves. Then the trader approached the hogan, and wielding an axe began to chop a hole through the earthen covering and interlaced poles beneath. Marian remembered the dead bodies of Indians should not be taken out at the door. Manifestly where it was possible he did not spare himself in observing the customs of these people of the desert.

Ba ho zohnie turned away from Nophaie and went back to his dead. Marian called Nophaie to her, and she led him behind the clump of cedars, where the horses were nibbling at the sage. Nophaie's mind seemed clouded. She held his hand, endeavoring to quell her mounting excitement. The sun had come out momentarily, crowning the towers with gold. How deep a purple bloomed the sage!

"Benow di cleash, you should not have come," said Nophaie regretfully.

"I'm glad. It has hurt me—done something more than that," she replied. "I was sick—sick deep in my soul. But I'm over it, I guess . . . and now I want to talk."

"Why, you're white—you're shaking!" he exclaimed.

"Is it any wonder? Nophaie, I love you, and I'm terror stricken. . . . This awful plague!"

He did not reply, but his hands pressed hers closely, and his eyes dilated. Marian had learned to sense in him the mystic, the Indian, when it stirred. She wrenched her hands free and threw her arms around his neck. The action liberated and augmented the storm in her breast. What she had meant to express utterly, in her frenzy to save Nophaie and make him take her out of the desert, burst all bounds of woman's subtlety and deliberation. What she said or did in this mad moment of self-preservation she never realized. But she awakened to a terrifying consciousness that she had inflamed the savage in Nophaie.

He crushed her in his arms and bent to her face with eyes of black fire. He did not kiss her. That was not the Indian way. Tenderness, gentleness, love had no part in this response to her woman's allurement. His mastery was that of the primal man denied; his brutality went to the verge of serious injury to her. But for the glory of it—the sheer backward step to the uttermost thrill of the senses—deep in the marrow of her bones—she would have screamed out in pain. For he handled her, bent her, swung and lifted her, and flattened her body as might have a savage in sudden possession of a hitherto unconquerable and unattainable woman of the wilds.

Like a sack he threw her across her saddle, head and feet hanging. But Marian, once partially free of his iron arms, struggled and rose, and got into a better position on her horse. She reeled against Nophaie. She could scarcely see. But she felt release from his grip. Something checked him, and his blurred face began to grow distinct—to come closer—until it pressed against her bosom.

"White woman . . . you'll make . . . an *Indian* of me," he panted, in husky, spent passion.

It pierced Marian. What more strange, incomprehensible appeal could he have made? Yet how deep it struck! She—who had loved the nobility of him—to drag him from the heights! To use her physical charm, her power in supreme selfishness! It was damnable. It showed the inherent nature of the female. She abhorred it. Then came her struggle. Only the tragedy of this Indian man could ever have mastered the woman at that moment. Gekin Yashi, the poor, demented Shoie, Ba ho zohnie and his unquenchable sense of loss, Do etin and Maahesenie—these strange figures loomed beside Nophaie's. That was a terrible moment. She could not work her will with Nophaie. Nature had made the man stronger, but the ultimate victory was woman's. But what of the soul? Could she deny it, crush it, repudiate it? Could she rise to material happiness over the destruction of Nophaie? Love, marriage, children, the fulfillment of physical woman, was not all. For what was Nophaie striving?

"Nophaie—forgive!" she whispered, encircling his head with her arms, and pressing it closer to her breast. "I've been—beside myself. This plague . . . this death as . . . as common as the stones . . . has made me a coward. And I tried to make you . . ."

"Benow di cleash, that'll be about all," he said, raising his face, and he smiled through tears.

An hour later Withers's melancholy task had been completed. Ba ho zohnie reprised to leave with the party. Marian's last sight of him was one she could never forget—the dark-faced Indian standing before the hogan he could never enter again, peering across the graves of his mother and wife, and the ill-gotten baby he had meant to father, across the gray sage flat to the blank walls of stone. What did he see? What did he hear? Whence came his strength?

Withers grumbled as he rode past Marian, to take the lead.

"I can't do more. He wouldn't come. He has no place to sleep. Nothing to eat. . . . Heigh-O! It'll be a hard ride back. Rustle along. Get-up, Buckskin!"

Snow began to fall and the canyon grew gray as

twilight. Marian followed the others at a brisk trot. The air had grown colder. When they rode up into the open reach of the main canyon a driving wind made riding against it something to endure. Gray, dull, somber and dreary wound the Noki, with palls of snow swooping low down, roaring through the cedars. The snow was wet. It adhered to Marian's clothes and grew thicker as she rode on. She could scarcely see where to guide her horse. And she suffered with the cold.

That snow squall passed to permit wider prospect of gloomy canyon, obscured towers, white-mantled rims, dark caverns, and forlorn barren benches. Another storm, with long, gray veils sweeping the cliffs, came up the canyon. The wind and snow made a seeping whine through the cedars. As fast as Marian shook off the white covering it returned, until too weak and frozen to try any longer she gave up. Branches of cedars stung her cold face. When at last she reached the end of that ride she was indeed glad to let Nophaie lift her off the horse.

The car ploughed homeward through snow and mud, down out of the Pass into level valley. Again the gray masses of clouds spread and rolled away.

Marian saw the great tilted ledges, mountains in themselves, the tip of the lonely, black sentinel above the red north wall, the round-knobbed horizon line to the east, and the gray, cold, wet waste of the desert.

Chapter 21

THREE THOUSAND NOPAHS DIED OF THE plague, and from one end of the reservation to the other a stricken, bewildered, and crushed people bowed their heads. The exceedingly malignant form of the influenza and the superstitious convictions of the fatalistic Indians united to create a deadly medium. When spring came, with its warm sun, dissipating the strange wind of death, the Indians believed that the eating of horseflesh had saved them.

Slowly the clutch of fear loosed its possession of Marian's heart. Slowly the long spell of gloom yielded to a hope inspired by sunshine and a steady decline in the death rate of Nopahs. Yet not wholly did her old spirit return. There was something ineradicable— vague, tenacious, inscrutable—something she felt every time Nophaie smiled at her.

They all worked to alleviate the sufferings of the Indians. If the trader ever saved any money, he lost it all and more that winter. Marian's means had shrunken to almost nothing. Civilization seemed far away, absorbed in its own problems. The affairs of the reservation moved on as always. And the little circle of white people at Kaidab lived true to something the Indians had inspired in them, forgotten by the outside world.

March, with its last icy breath of winter, yielded to April with its sandstorms. The wind blew a gale one day and the next was calm, warm, with spring in the air. Only a few cases of influenza were reported, and deaths but seldom.

Yet Marian could not quite feel free. The tentacles of

a deep-seated emotion, stranger than love, and impalpable, still were fastened in her heart.

Nophaie had ridden to Oljato and when he did not return the following day the nameless thing that was neither thought nor feeling laid its cold hand on Marian's soul.

She worked on Withers's accounts that day; she wrote long-neglected letters; she busied herself for an hour over a sadly depleted and worn wardrobe; she rode horseback, out to the rocky ridge above Kaidab, and strained her eyes on the trail to Oljato.

But these energies did not allay her nervousness or quell the woman's sixth sense. She tried the trading post, which of late had been hard to bear. Hungry, gaunt Indians would come in and stand around, staring with great dark eyes until Withers or Coleman gave them something to eat. It was a starved tribe now.

Marian saw Indians carrying bows and arrows, a custom long past, which had been resumed because the hunters had sold their guns or could not buy ammunition. Wool had practically ceased its use as a means of trade. The Indians would not shear sheep for the price offered. A few goat skins and an occasional blanket were bartered over the counter. It was distressing to watch an Indian woman come in with a blanket, often a poorly made one that Withers did not want and could not sell, and haggle over a price which was ruinous for the trader to offer. In this way Withers kept alive the Nopahs of his district. They did not thank him, for none of them understood.

This day Marian encountered Shoie again, and despite the feeling almost of horror that he incited, she resolutely stood her ground and watched him. Shoie's companion was a young Nopah, very dark and wild looking, ragged and unkempt, with a crippled foot. Something about this second Indian impelled Marian's sensitiveness even more than Shoie. He was watching Shoie's signs and the contortions of his lacerated lips as he tried to convey some meaning. Withers observed Marian's perplexity and gave her his interpretation.

"That crippled Nopah is one of the few criminals of the tribe. He's the Indian who assaulted one of Etenia's little daughters. They caught him and held his foot in the fire until it was burned to a crisp. That was his punishment and he is now an outcast. I reckon Shoie is trying to say that he'll cast an evil spell over him."

Marian earned her momentary forgetfulness of self then in contemplation of these two Indians. Extremes as they were they fixed her mind on the mystery of life. A monstrosity she had seen at Copenwashie, a Noki albino Indian, white-haired and pink-eyed, hideous to behold, had not affected her as either of these two Nopahs. She compared them with Ba ho zohnie and Nophaie. But when thought of Nophaie recurred she could no longer stay in the store.

Outside it was growing cool. The sun had set, and there shone a ruddy effulgence over the tilted sections of wall in the west. Coyotes were wailing. Marian walked in the twilight. It seemed an immense and living thing, moving up out of the desert. An oppression weighed upon her. How dark and lonely the empty space out beyond! The stone-walled confines of the wasteland flung its menace at her thinking mind.

Withers appeared unusually quiet that night. His wife talked a little, in her low voice, grown like an Indian's. But the trader had not much to say. Marian sat beside the hearth, with eyes on the glowing white and gold embers. Suddenly, she was startled out of her reveries.

"What was that?" she asked.

"Horse. Must be Nophaie," replied the trader, as if relieved.

Marian sat still, listening. But she heard only a strange knocking at her heart. At length the door opened with a sweep. Nophaie! His eyes were those of an Indian, but his face seemed that of a white man. He staggered slightly as he closed the door behind him and leaned back against it. His whole body was in vibration, strung like that of an athlete about to leap. His piercing gaze left Marian's face to search the trader's.

"John, give me a room to die in!"

Withers gasped and sank back limp. His wife uttered a frightened and compassionate cry.

"It's got me!" whispered Nophaie.

Marian's terror voiced its divination of her nameless instinct.

"Oh, my God—Nophaie!" she screamed, and ran to him.

Nophaie reeled over her. Intense and terrible seemed the strain of spirit over body. He clasped her shoulders, held her away from him.

"Benow di cleash, I should have been dead—hours ago. . . . But I had to see you. . . . I had to die as—a white man!"

Marian shuddered under the strange clasp of his hands. They burned through her blouse.

"White woman—savior of Nophaie—go back to your people . . . all is . . . well!"

Then he collapsed on her and was caught by the trader. They half-carried him to his room and laid him on the bed. Then began frantic ministrations in his behalf. But little could be done for him. His jaw was locked. The fire of his face, the marble pallor, the hurried pulse, the congested lungs, the laboring heart all proclaimed the dread plague in its most virulent form.

Once in the dim lamplight, as Marian knelt beside the bed in agony, calling, "Nophaie—Nophaie!" he opened his eyes—somber, terrible, no longer piercing with his unquenchable spirit; and it seemed to her that a fleeting smile, the old beautiful light, veiled for an instant his tragic soul, and blessed her.

Then it seemed to Marian that a foul black fiend began to thrust the life of Nophaie from her. It became a battle, all unconscious on the part of the victim. Poison fires sucked at his life's blood. This was not an illness—not a disease—but a wind of death that killed the spirit and loosed devastating corruption upon the living flesh.

The trader entreated her to leave the bedside and at length dragged her back to the sitting room. There Marian huddled down before the fire, racked with pangs. Oh! The futility of Nophaie's life and of her love! Mrs. Withers came and went, softly stepping, tender of hand, to mourn into dead silence. The vines under the eaves rustled.

Sometime in the late hours Withers came to her and touched her gently. His face was alight with a strange glow.

"Nophaie . . . he . . . is he gone?" whispered Marian, rising.

"Marian, it doesn't make sense," Withers's voice was husky. "I can't explain it. He should be dead, but somehow he's not. It must be—now I think he's going to make it. But God only knows how."

"Oh, thank God," whispered Marian, suddenly, hand to tears. "Can I see him, now?"

"Wal, he's still unconscious, but the fever seems to be breaking. And I think he would want you with him now, whatever happens."

Chapter 22

NOPHAIE'S RETURN TO CONSCIOUSNESS LEFT him with fading memory of black hideous depths, where something inexplicable in him had overthrown demons.

He had expected that he would die, but now he knew he would live. Had he not welcomed death? A vast struggle had gone on within his physical being. Vaguely, it seemed that he had been in terrible conflict with the devil over possession of his soul. Haunting, brooding thought of this strange thing occupied his waking hours and lingered in his dreams.

The satisfaction of the Withers and the joy of Marian at his quick strides toward recovery gave Nophaie a melancholy happiness. They loved him. They did not recognize any barrier between him and Benow de cleash. Was there really a barrier? What was it? He spent hours trying to grasp the dim facts of former convictions, vows, duties. They eluded him. They grew dimmer. Something had happened to his soul or else the plague had left his mind impaired.

Nophaie was up and around on the fourth day after the crisis of his illness. He avoided contact with the Indians, and indeed with his white friends also, as much as that was possible without being discourteous. And they in turn appeared to understand and help him. Yet always while he sat in the warm sun of the May mornings or walked under the greening cottonwoods, Marian's eyes followed him. He felt them. And when he met her gaze at close hand there shone a beautiful glad light. It thrilled him, swelled his heart, yet he felt it to be a reckoning he must sometime deal with.

In a few more days Nophaie's vigor had returned enough to warrant his leaving Kaidab. So, at an opportune moment, when he was alone with Withers and his wife, and Marian, he spoke out about his plan.

"John, will you give me a pack of grain and a little grub?"

"What for?" queried the trader, in quick surprise.

"I want to ride off alone—into the sage—and the canyons," replied Nophaie thoughtfully.

Marian left her seat beside the fire and came to him, quite pale, with wondering, darkening eyes.

"Nophaie, are you—strong enough?" she asked fearfully.

"That will make me strong," he replied, with a smile, and he took her hand.

"Reckon it's not a bad idea," agreed Withers, more to his wife than to the others. She was silent, which in her meant acquiescence. Then he turned to Nophaie. "You can have anything you want. When'll you go? Tomorrow? I'll get your horse in or you can have one of mine."

"Yes, I'll go at sunrise, before Benow di cleash is up," returned Nophaie.

"You'll go off alone and stay alone?" queried the trader.

"Honest Injun," replied Nophaie.

"Good. Reckon I don't mind telling you I'm worried a little," went on Withers, running his hand through his touseled hair. "Ba ho zohnie has begun to play hell with the Indians."

"I knew that," said Nophaie.

"Ba ho zohnie!" exclaimed Marian. "Isn't that Gekin Yashi's husband? The young chief I saw up—there?"

"That's the Indian," rejoined the trader.

"Ba ho zohnie has the best blood of the Nopahs," interposed Mrs. Withers. "He comes from the first clan. He's really a great chief."

"Reckon that means more than I thought," said her husband. "He's inflaming the Indians against Morgan and Blucher. I hear he's . . . developed into a wonderful orator . . . anyway he has never gotten over Gekin Yashi's death. He is trying to get the Indians to rise against the whites. That's not new by any means here on the reservation. It probably will fizzle out, as all the uprisings do. But it *might* not. I just don't like Ba ho zohnie's influence. Could he be stopped, Nophaie?"

"You would have to kill him," replied Nophaie.

"Ahuh! Well, all we can do is hope nothing will come of it," returned the trader, rising.

Mrs. Withers followed her husband out, leaving Nophaie alone with Marian. She still stood by his chair, looking down on him.

"Nophaie, where will you go?" she asked.

"I'll go to Naza."

"So—far?" she ejaculated, with a little catch in her voice.

"It's not far for me."

"But why Naza . . . if it's only loneliness . . . the sage and canyons you feel you need?" she went on earnestly.

Nophaie released her hand and put his arm round her waist. He felt a little shock go over her and then a long tremble. The sweetness and meaning of her presence had never been more potent. There seemed a difference in their relation—he could not tell what. That was another thing he must learn. He felt weaker, less able to hurt her.

"Benow de cleash, I'm not sure, but I believe I'm going to Naza because it's the greatest god of the Nopahs."

"Oh—Nophaie!" she faltered. "Are you still tortured? You told me how all the Nopah gods failed you. Even Nothsis Ahn was only a gray, cold mountain, without voice or soul for you."

"Yes, I remember, Marian," returned Nophaie. "But I don't seem to be tortured or driven, as I was when I climbed the north slope of Nothsis Ahn. It's something I can't explain. I don't even know that my desire to go is anything but physical. Yet I'm in strange mood. I want solitude. And somehow Naza calls. There's light—perhaps strength for me in those silent canyons."

"Oh, if you could only find peace!" murmured Marian.

Nophaie left Kaidab before sunrise and rode out across the desert in the gray melancholy dawn. The discordant bray of a burro was the only sound to break the silence.

From a rise of ground he turned in the saddle to look back at the trading post. A white object, fluttering from a dark window, caught his quick eye. Marian was waving good-bye to him. The act was something he might have expected. Reining in his horse on the height of ground he watched for a long significant moment, while conflicting emotions burdened his heart. He would answer her surely. The little white handkerchief fluttered more vigorously. She saw that he was watching her. Then he answered with the slow sweeping gesture of an Indian who was going far across the ranges, to a place that beckoned him and from which he would soon return. He saw her face gleam from the window and he imagined the light upon it. Wheeling his horse he rode down the other side of the ridge, out of sight of the post, and forced consciousness of Marian out of his mind.

Nophaie's mount was one of Withers's best, a big, strong, mottled bay horse, easy-gaited and tireless. He did not appear to note the added weight of pack and blanket, tied behind the saddle. Nophaie felt dizzy and insecure, sensations he attributed to his weakened condition. These would leave him, sooner or later, and for the time being he walked the horse. Once out of sight of fences and cattle he began gradually to relax, to change, to shuffle off old morbid thoughts and feelings as if they had been dead scales. This journey would be the most cardinally important one of all his life. He divined that, but did not know why. Would Naza prove to be a shrine? Then he surrendered to the longing to give himself wholly to sensorial perceptions.

A pink glow suffused the steely blue sky over the eastern ramparts, leagues to Nophaie's right. Northward he could see the tip of a red butte rising above the yellow, cedar-dotted ridges of rock. The song of a mockingbird, the yelp of a coyote, the scurrying of a cottontail into the brush gave life to the desert scene. Nophaie smelled the wood smoke from Indian hogans; he saw blanketed Nopahs watching him from a cedar ridge; he heard the wild, piercing song of a shepherd moving away with his flock. He avoided the well-beaten trails, so that he would not meet any of his people. He meant not to exchange one word with a living soul while on this pilgrimage.

He crossed the deep wash, and climbing out of it, and up the wind-scalloped and rain-carved rocky slope beyond, he reached a point where he might have looked down upon Kaidab, but he faced ahead, eyes keen to catch the first sight of the great valley of monuments.

Soon he espied, from tip down to base, a massive red butte, with columns like a pipe organ, standing out upon the desert from the main wall of the uplands. It was still far but he hoped to camp there that night, and renew acquaintance with the sweet sage slopes where as a boy he had shepherded the flocks of his father. Across his senses flashed a wondering query as to why he should long to see them now, when always since his return to the reservation he had avoided those vivid scenes of boyhood. He answered nothing; he refused to reflect.

It was as if he saw the desert with new eyes. All the old landmarks appeared magnified. The walls and pyramids that for hundreds of years had been invested with the spirits of his race seemed glorified in his sight, yet they were not idols or gods to kneel before and worship. Through them his senses grasped at a different meaning of beauty and nature, time and life.

Nophaie rode down into a wide, yellow-walled canyon and out upon a green and sandy level, where the sun grew hot and the dust puffed up in whorls. The wide far-flung horizon was now lost, and he appeared encompassed by walls, sweeping and long, broken and irregular. For hours Nophaie rode on, aware of sun and wind, of the steady clip-clop of hooves, and the swing of the horse, of the open stretch of valley around him, and the red and yellow walls that seemed to travel with him. At the far end of this stretch he climbed a low pass, where a colossal black shaft of rock speared the sky, and looked down into the Nopah valley of monuments where his people had lived, and where he had been born. The spectacle held him for moments.

His destination for that day was the great pipe-organ mesa now looming grandly ten miles farther on. It guarded the entrance to the sacred valley, where each separate monument was a god of the Nopahs. Fatigue and exhaustion wore upon Nophaie. But these were nothing. Only collapse or death itself could have halted him.

When he reached the magnificent mesa, sunset was burning the walls and monuments with gold and rose. The desert floor was gray near at hand, purple in the distance. Above the red barrier which he must climb on the morrow a glorious cloud pageant held his gaze, as he leaned panting on his horse.

A thin stream of water wound shining down the sandy wash. The color of clouds and mesa flamed in it. Nophaie unsaddled the horse, fed him grain, and hobbling him turned him loose. Then he set about his own simple needs. Hunger was not in him, but he forced himself to eat. This hard journey that he was taking would soon restore his elemental instincts.

A soft gray twilight was creeping out from the red walls when Nophaie reached the spot where he had sat so many days as a boy, watching the sheep. It was a long ridge not far from the great butte. Grass and sage were thick there even as in his boyhood. The fragrance filled his nostrils, and memory, sad and sweet, flooded his mind. He found the flat red rock where he and his sister used to sit together. How long ago! She was dead. All his people were gone.

Nophaie gazed across the gray valley to a V-shaped crack in the south wall. The narrow ribbonlike stream shone winding out of this canyon. Up there, where the canyon boxed under close-looming cliffs, he had been born. Nophaie could remember when he was three years old.

"The Indian in me speaks," he soliloquized. "It would have been better for me to have yielded to the plague. That hole in the wall was my home—this valley my playground. There are now no home, no kin, no play. The Indian's deeds are done. His glory and dream are gone. His sun has set. Those of him who survive the disease and drink and poverty forced upon him must inevitably be absorbed by the race that has destroyed him. Red blood into the white! It means the white race will gain and the Indian vanish. . . . Nophaie is not yet thirty, yet he feels old. He is ruined, he is lost. There is nothing left. He, too, should vanish. This spot should be his grave. Under the sage! Death, sleep, rest, peace!"

But Nophaie's intelligence repudiated that Indian fatalism. It might be true to his instincts, but not to his mind. He was still young. The war had not destroyed him. The plague could not kill him. His body was tough as the desert cedar, his spirit as unquenchable as the light of the sun. Every day that he lived he could mitigate in some degree the misery of his race, if he chose. But his hatred—the hatred of Morgan and Blucher, of all the white men who had wronged the Indian—that was the cancer in his soul. Neither an instinctive Indian life, nor one governed by his white education could be happy while that hate curdled his blood. Then flashed the uplifting thought that the love of Marian, given him with all the wondrous strength and generosity of a white woman's heart, should overcome his hate, compensate for all his sufferings, and raise him to a state far above revenge or bitterness. She had paid him for all personal wrongs done him by her people.

But here Nophaie felt the ignominy of his bitterness. His love for Benow de cleash, her love for him, did not seem to have power over that hate. Something more was needed. And suddenly he knew this was the meaning of his strange quest—of his pilgrimage to Naza.

Long Nophaie reclined there in the gathering darkness. White stars peeped over the black ruins. The cold night wind rose and moaned through the sage. The flicker of his campfire shone against the black base of the mesa. From far across the valley came the faint bleat of lambs, sad, plaintive, significant of life on the lonely desert.

In the rosy silent dawn, with the sunrise at his back, Nophaie rode into a dim and untrodden trail that climbed from the low country, up over the first red rampart, and on across a flat region of rocks and washes, up again and farther, higher into the stretches of cedar, piñon, and sage. Behind him the great shafts and monuments rose out of the lowlands, continuing to the level where Nophaie rode in the same red stratum. Often he turned to gaze back, to see them dark and majestic against the white clouds.

Nophaie gathered strength from these surroundings, and from the spicy tang on the cool wind, and the slow-gathering sense of his agonies, like the miles, fading back of him. It was not that he was coming into his own again, though the purple sage uplands and Nothsis Ahn would soon be in sight; rather it seemed that he would find something new, all-sufficient and soul-sustaining.

He rode up a bare slope of rock, a gradual mile in ascent, wavy and hummocky with ridges, and hills, canyons and holes, yet always bare yellow rock. Then he turned a great corner of wall and lost the backward view. To the fore was cedared flat, mile on mile, red-rocked and green-patched, stretching away to another wall. Nophaie rode at a trot now, and entered this flat belt, to come at length to a deep canyon. It yawned below him, half a mile in depth, with ragged slopes too precipitous for any but an Indian trail. Nophaie walked, leading the horse. The descent into the dry hot canyon, under the ragged cliffs, and through the maze of great blocks of red rock, down into the region of colored clay and dusty wash, was attended by a mounting joy. The old physical urge, the instinct of muscle achievement, the fighting of unknown forces by endurances, revived in Nophaie. Climbing the opposite side was travail. From the rim another flat stretched out endlessly toward the mountain wall, now vivid in colors of red, yellow and violet.

Nophaie arrived at its base in the gray of twilight, and made dry camp in a clump of cedars. He was getting away from the Indian reservation now. Little risk of meeting Indians from here on! Nophaie felt strange relief, that was almost shame. Was he running away from his race in more ways than one? Twenty-four hours and twice as many miles had removed him immeasurably from familiar scenes, from bound emotions. It began to be easier for him to hold long to the watching, listening, feeling, smelling perception that engendered happiness. If he could only abandon himself to that wholly! The night was cold, the wind mourned in the cedars, the coyotes howled.

Next morning Nophaie climbed the barefaced mountain wall that seemed insurmountable. It resembled a barrier of human passion. Spent, wet, and burning, he fell on the rim, and panted. Ten days ago he had been abandoned by his tribe as a dead man! But his white friends had ministered unto him. His white sweetheart had prayed for his life. She had not confessed that; no one had told him, but he knew. He was alive. He was a man.

Nophaie labored to his feet and mounted the horse.

Something ineffably sweet and precious went fleeting over him. He could not grasp it.

For miles he rode through cedar and sage upland. At noon the tremendous chasm of Nopah yawned in sight. It was wide and very deep, and marked by talus of many hues—clays of lilac, heliotrope, and mauve. There was no vegetation, only a barren abyss of erosion and decay. It opened into a colored gulf where all was dim, hazy, vast. Gazing down Nophaie experienced a thrill of exultation. He would cross this canyon where few Nopahs had ever set foot.

The ordeal consumed the rest of that day. Nophaie lost himself in absorption of declivity and descent, of sliding slope of weathered rock and dusty wash, of the heat of cliff and glare of red, of vivid green cottonwoods and shining surging stream, of sheer looming colossal wall, and of the crawl upwards like a lizard.

His reward was the rolling purple-saged, green-cedared plateau crowned by noble Nothsis Ahn. Crags of yellow, black belts of spruce, gleams of white snow—thus the Mountain of Light returned to Nophaie. It was the same. Only he had changed. How could wars of selfish men affect Nothsis Ahn? What was the trouble of Nophaie? As he gazed upward it flashed across him that there was really no trouble. But this idea seemed the calm, the strength, the soul of the mountain.

The sun was far down in the west. Nophaie chose an open patch of sage, backed by cedars, and here he made camp, with Nothsis Ahn looking down upon him.

Two days later Nophaie had crossed the uplands, traveled down under the north slope of the great mountain, down and down into the canyons.

It was summer down there. Hot, fragrant air moved lazily in gentle winds. Green trees and grass and flowers and silver scale bordered the narrow, red-walled lanes. Indian paintbrush added its vermillion and magenta to the colorful scene. Down and down Nophaie rode, under the gleaming walls, through sunlight and shade,

along and across the murmuring, rock-strewn brooks,
beside banks of amber moss and white lilies, and
through thickets of green oak and cottonwood, down at
last into the well-remembered and beloved place where
he had lived so long in loneliness and solitude—his
Canyon of Silent Walls.

Nophaie rested there that night and the next day. In
this deep canyon where water and grass were abundant
Nophaie's horse profited by the stay. As for Nophaie,
he strove valiantly to make the idle hours those of an
Indian contented with natural things. Still he felt the
swelling in him of a great wave of emotion. Something
was about to burst within him, like the breaking of a
dam. Yet he knew that with every moment he grew
farther away from any passion similar to that of Ba ho
zohnie. A power, of the working of which he was
conscious, seemed to be gradually taking possession of
his soul.

Starting on his pilgrimage again at sunset Nophaie
rode all night, down Naza Boco, the canyon in the far
depths of which hid the great Nopah god.

That ride seemed a vigil. Daylight would have
robbed it of some strange spiritual essence. The shadows under the mounting walls now showed black and
again silver. The star-fired stream of blue sky above
narrowed between the black rims, farther and higher as
he rode down and down into the silent bowels of the
rock-ribbed earth. Every hour augmented the sense of
something grand, all-sufficing, final, that awaited him
at the end of his pilgrimage.

Dawn came with an almost imperceptible change
from black to gray. Daylight followed slowly, reluctantly. It showed Nophaie the stupendously lofty walls of
Naza Boco. Sunrise heralded its state by the red-gold
crown on the rims. Gradually that gold crept down.

Nophaie rode round a rugged corner of wall to be
halted by a shock.

Naza! The stone bridge—god of the Nopahs arched
magnificently before him, gold against the deep blue

sky. He gazed spellbound for a long time, then rode on. At first it had seemed unreal. But grand as Naza towered there it was only a red-stained, black-streaked, notched and cracked, seamed and scarred masterpiece of nature. Wind and rain, sand and water were the gods that had sculptured Naza. But for Nophaie the fact that his education enabled him to understand the working of these elements did not mitigate in his sight their infinite power.

He rode under the bridge, something that a Nopah had never done before him. The great walls did not crumble; the stream of blue sky did not darken; Nothsis Ahn, showing his black and white crown far above the notch of the canyon, did not thunder at Nophaie for what would have been sacrilege for a Nopah. Nothing happened. The place was beautiful, lonely, silent, dry, and fragrant, strangely grand.

Leisurely Nophaie unsaddled and unpacked in the shade of a cedar. Already the canyon was hot. The crystal amber water of the stream invited relief from thirst and heat.

Nophaie spent the long, austere day watching the bridge from different angles, waiting for what was to happen to him.

Then came the slow setting of the sun, a strange thing here in the depths of the canyon. Nophaie watched the marvelous changing of colors, from the rainbow hues of the arch to the gold of the ramparts and the rosy glow on the snowy summit of Nothsis Ahn. Twilight lingered longer than in any other place Nophaie remembered. It was an hour full of beauty, and of a significance of something evermore about to be.

Darkness fell. The low murmur of the stream seemed to emphasize the lonesomeness. At long intervals owls mourned their melancholy refrain. Naza stood up dark and triumphant, silhouetted against the sky, crowned with silver stars. Nophaie saw the Dipper turned upside down. By night the bridge gained something spectral, and mysterious. Night augmented its grandeur.

Nophaie did not sleep. He never closed his eyes. Every moment hastened what he now divined to be an illumination of his mind.

Toward dawn a faint green light shone on the walls facing the south. The moon was rising. After a while the gleam grew stronger. Soon the shadow of the bridge curved on the opposite wall, and under the arch shone a dim moonlight, weird and beautiful.

After twenty-four hours of vigil under this shrine Nophaie prayed. With all the passion of his extremity he recalled the prayers of the Nopahs, and spoke them aloud, standing erect, with face uplifted in the moonlight. His impulse had been mystic and uncontrollable. It came from the past, the dim memories of his childhood. It was the last dying flash of Indian mysticism and superstition. The honesty and yearning of it had no parallel in all the complex appeals of the past. But it left him cold. Despair chained his soul. Then that strangely loosened its icy clutch. He was free. He realized it.

Time ceased for Nophaie. Earth and life seemed to stand still. Would there ever be another dawn? How locked he was in the rock confines of the earth! At last he found a seat against a huge fragment of cliff and from there he gazed with renewed eyes. What was the secret of Naza? The name was only Indian, handed down from those remote progenitors of the Nopahs who came from the north. Was there any secret? The spirit abiding in that magnificent bridge was an investiture from the soul of man. The Indian mind was still struggling far back along the dim trails of the progress of civilization. Blank wall of black on one side, wall of moonlit marble on the other, gleaming pale, sheered to the wan blue, star-fretted sky; and across the opaque space arched the spectral rock rainbow, magnified in its night shadows.

Nophaie saw it now as if blindness had fallen from his eyes—saw it in all its nakedness and strength, its appalling beauty, its terrific strangeness. But it had become a thing, physical, inanimate, static. It needed the tremendous sheer of walls to uphold that massive arch. Beauty upheld by stark stone! Sublimity carved by the chisels of wind and water! Elemental toil of ages! A monument to the spirit of nature! But it could not endure.

Naza! The Nopah God! Bridge of sandstone! It was there. How grand the walls it joined! Those walls had been cut by the flowing of water, by the blowing of wind. Thousands of millions of tons of sand had eroded away—to leave Naza arched so magnificently there, as if imperishable. But it was not imperishable. It was doomed. It must fall or wear away. All that exceeding beauty of line and color, that vastness of bulk must in time pass away in tiny grains of sand, flowing down the murmuring stream.

Then to Nophaie came the secret of its great spell.

Not all beauty or grandeur or mystery or immensity! These were only a part of its enchantment. For Nophaie it spelled freedom. Its isolation and loneliness and solitude meant for him the uttermost peace. There dawned upon Nophaie the glory of nature. Just so long as he could stay there he would be free, all-satisfied. Even sorrow was sweet. Memory of his white sweetheart was exalting.

The world of man, race against race, the world of men and women, of strife and greed, of hate and lust, of injustice and sordidness, the materialism of the Great War and its horrible aftermath, the rush and fever and ferocity of the modern day with its jazz and license and drink and blindness—with its Paganism, these were not here in the grand shadow of Naza. No sharp wolfish faces of men limned against this silence! No beautiful painted faces of women! No picture of the Indian tribes, driven from the green pastures and running water of their forefathers, herded into the waste places of the earth! The white man had not yet made Naza an object of his destructiveness. Nothing of the diseased in mind and body, the distorted images of mankind, the incomprehensible stupidity, the stony indifference to nature and beauty and ideals and good —nothing of these here in this moon-blanched canyon.

For the period of its endurance Naza would stand there, under its gleaming silent walls, with its rainbow hues and purple shadows at sunset, its golden glows and rosy veils at sunrise. The solemn days would pass and the dreamful nights. Peace and silence would reign. Loveliness would vie with austerity.

As the sun cleared away the shadows of night so the spell of Naza clarified Nophaie's mind of Indian superstition, of doubt and morbid fear. The tragic fate of the vanishing American, as he had nursed it to his sore heart, ceased to exist.

For Nophaie the still sweet air of that canyon was charged. In this deserted, haunted hall of the earth, peace, faith, resurging life all came simply to him. The intimation of immortality—the imminence of God! That strife of soul, so long a struggle between the Indian superstitions of his youth and the white teachings forced upon him, ended forever in his realization of the Universal God of Indian and white man, and his acceptance of Christianity.

Chapter 23

THREE DAYS LATER NOPHAIE CLIMBED OUT OF
the canyons under Nothsis Ahn to take the well-
trodden trails across the uplands.

Vigor of body and tranquility of mind made this
return trip something he wanted to prolong. But food
for himself and grain for the horse were almost gone.

His thoughts were profound and grave, pleasant and
reminiscent, according to the alternating states of consciousness. Traces of exalted emotion returned at intervals. Such happiness as he had experienced he had
never dreamed possible for mortal man. Wonder and
awe and regret mingled in the contemplation of his
salvation. Why could it not have come sooner? What
agony he might have been spared! He understood now
the failure of missionaries to make Christians of Indians.

As he had chosen the broad trails for his return, he
was surprised not to meet any of his tribe. He saw
bands of mustangs on the rolling sage flats, but not one
horseman. Towards noon Nophaie began to regard this
fact as strange. He passed many hogans without the
familiar column of blue smoke, the barking shepherd
dog, the color and movement of Indian life. At last he
rode off the trail to peer into a hogan. It had been
inhabited yesterday. Sticks of firewood, arranged like
the spokes of a wheel and burned at the hub end,
attested to a cooking fire that had been started, but not
used. A hurried departure had evidently been made by
the Indians from this hogan. Nophaie grew concerned
as to its cause. While he had ridden into the canyons, to
seek, to strive, to search and find, his people had been

actuated by the same old motives that had governed them for centuries. Then he remembered Ba ho zohnie.

Nophaie put the big horse to a swinging lope, and the fragrant, green and purple miles of upland country swept by. Toward midafternoon he descended into the shadow head of a canyon and here encountered an Indian shepherd lad with his flock of sheep. Farther down the canyon there was water. Nophaie questioned the lad as to the whereabouts of the Indians in that section. A reluctant response confirmed his fears—all the grown Nopahs had ridden in a hurry off to the east. The boy spoke bewilderingly of fires. He had been left alone with the sheep. Sharper queries from Nophaie seemed to frighten him.

Nophaie continued his journey, convinced now that the Indians were hastening to some point eastward for a reason which seemed ominous, but was not clear. When the lad spoke of fires he must have meant signal fires, because the gesture that accompanied his words suggested fires built on high places. Such had been the custom of Nopahs in years gone by. Nophaie had never seen signal fires, even in his boyhood. They had been a call to the different clans in wartime, when a common enemy threatened the whole clan. Nophaie, during his campaign to enlist Indians as soldiers for the World War, had endeavored to build these signal fires to excite his people and counteract Blucher's German propaganda, but the work had been too great for him alone.

Eastward! That was almost his direct route back to Kaidab. But Nophaie remembered that the most frequented trails here ran to the head of Noki Canyon and then turned to the south. Such a course would bring Indians out into the main pass about halfway between Kaidab and Mesa.

Nophaie had been traveling leisurely, loath to put behind him the wild solitude of the red-walled canyons and the sweet affinity that seemed to breathe upon him from the purple-sage uplands. But now he felt that he must make haste. By constant travel, putting the horse to its limit, he might reach Mesa in twenty-four hours. He was not sure, however, that he wanted to go to Mesa. It depended on developments. For the present his conclusion was that it would be wise to rest awhile at the water hole, feed the horse, and eat the last of his stock of food.

Twilight of that day found Nophaie approaching the end of the vast escarpment which constituted the higher country. In reality that was a fifty-mile bench leading down from Nothsis Ahn. Dropping off sheer two thousand feet this wall towered above the great valley below. Nophaie could look over the whole northern part of the Indian country. Southward, however, his view was shut off; and this direction led to the stronghold of the Nopahs.

Nophaie dismounted on the rim and composed himself there to wait for night. He watched the twilight creep out from the dark walls and up from the gray desert, to shadow and grow black and envelope the monuments and buttes and mesas. At an hour less intense Nophaie would have lingered merely to see and feel the sublimity of time and place. But his piercing gaze strained now through the opaque gloom on a level with the rim, or down into the black gulf. One by one stars appeared in the velvet blue sky.

Then far to the north a pinpoint of light shone. It was so high that Nophaie imagined it to be another star. But it was red, not white, and it grew perceptibly.

"Signal fire!" exclaimed Nophaie, aloud. "It's high up, across the valley."

Following that, here and there in the ebony void suddenly shone tiny lights, strangely growing and brightening. Some were low down on the desert floor, others higher, and a few on a level with the lofty eminence where Nophaie stood. More fires appeared, and it was significant that their number increased toward the west. Straight across from Nophaie's position, as he faced the south, the largest light appeared on a promontory. It was burning on a section of the upland escarpment, now separated from the main wall. Fuel was abundant up there. Whole cedar trees were being fed to that fire. The distance across that black abyss was only a few miles; and presently Nophaie could see dark forms moving around the red flames. They seemed like pygmies in furious action. A stream of golden sparks flowed straight upward. Soon the promontory showed wild and weird under the tremendous flare, and clouds of white smoke rolled away into the darkness.

"Withers must have been right," muttered Nophaie, mounting his horse. "It means an uprising against the whites. But where? *Mesa!* All the fights, murders, burned trading posts, uprisings have been at or near Mesa."

Nophaie, pondering, brooding over the sinister possibilities, slowly untied the pack from behind his saddle. He threw it aside under a clump of cedars. That meant decision. He was going to ride hard and fast. Whereupon he abruptly turned off the trail that led down into the valley toward Kaidab and cut across the sage to the south. He did not hurry the horse over the soft and bushy ground but after several miles when he dropped down into another trail he urged him into a fast lope. This was a broad, long-used trail winding away from the great wall, and it crossed a few shallow canyons, and descended gradually from the high country. Withers's horse showed his mettle now. Tireless and strong, sensing his rider's intensity of spirit, he settled into the long, smooth Indian lope that ate up the miles as if by magic. Nophaie walked him over the bad places, but these were few.

The night was cool, windless, starry, with pale silvery radiance on sage and cedar. Nophaie's keen faculties all went into riding the horse so as to make fast time yet save him. Long before midnight Nophaie rode off the uplands into the ridgy, rough canyoned country that led down to the pass.

Over the blank rise of ground ahead shone a yellow

flare, lighting up the sky. As he rode on this flare grew
in brightness and dimensions. Nophaie strove to restrain his impatience, to check his sense of catastrophe.
Shallow valley, miles long, separated him from the rise
of ground that hid the fires. They must have been built
along the pass. Nophaie rode on and on, climbed out of
the valley and up a thickly cedared slope, at last to
burst out of darkness into light.

Stunned at the spectacle he reined in his horse and
stared. Far below ran the pass, in the shadow of a great
black mesa that towered high and stretched as far north
and south as Nophaie could see.

Huge blazing fires burned along the rim of the mesa,
one on every prominent point. In the still night
Nophaie plainly heard the crackling roar of flames. At
the head of the pass the spectacle was grand. It held
Nophaie spellbound. It took him back to the war in
France where he had seen towns destroyed by fire. The
cold sweat broke out over his prickly skin. A strong
shuddering emotion roused in him—the drumbeats of
passion. The horse pranced and snorted, and was
difficult to hold. Nophaie laid a quieting hand on the
quivering flank, on the wet neck.

The signal fires fascinated Nophaie. He imagined he
heard the long scream, the dull boom of bursting shells.
War! Fire meant war. If not war between human beings
then war of the elements! It was the most terrible of all
destructive forces. Far as Nophaie could see fires
blazed from high places.

At the head of the wide pass the whole face of the
rock wall was notched into isolated peaks like the teeth
of a colossal saw. Upon every peak burned a signal fire
of amazing proportions. These peaks were naturally
red, but the fires gave them a deeper, more sinister
hue. Straight columns of sparks soared up with the
bellying smoke. A vast, gloomy pall, ruddy red, obscured the sky. The rough pass, with its magnificent
south wall, and the upflung rocky country opposite,
seemed a terrific defile leading down into a sulfurous

hell. Night magnified the grandeur and terror of that spectacle.

Nophaie plunged on down the trail, no longer sparing the horse. If he had been irresistibly drawn by the first sight of those fires he was now driven. The horse needed no urging; rather he had to be restrained at the breaks in that mile-long slope down to the pass.

Nophaie headed south on the road; behind him flared the ruddy glow at the head of the pass; above him two thousand feet on the rim the signal fires were dying out. No Indians were in sight. They had gone.

Suddenly, Nophaie remembered Presbrey's trading post, some miles west of the mouth of the pass. There he would surely get some information. Presbrey was a young man who had established a small post since the war. He had been kind to the Indians and they liked him. No Indian had ever been turned away hungry from that post.

Nophaie let the horse run to the end of the pass. Here was a gradual rise of wooded ground that obstructed view to the south. When Nophaie had surmounted this he was relieved to see the long line of signal fires on the mesa flickering and fading in the distance.

But as Nophaie swept the horizon he was dismayed to see a red glow over the ridge in the direction of Presbrey's trading post.

With passionate imprecation Nophaie wheeled the horse and goaded him down the slope into the sandy wash that would afford a shortcut to Presbrey's road. It was hard going. The big horse ploughed through the sand, out of the wash to hard ground. Then like the wind he sped on into the smooth gravelly road. Trees and banks flashed behind Nophaie, blurring in his sight. But the ringed spot of fire, the leaping flames, grew brighter in his sight. Soon he saw a string of moving black figures running between him and the circle of fire. Their action seemed in accord with the leaping flames. Nophaie thought of Presbrey's kind wife, and the

curly-haired little girl who always had a bright smile for
an Indian. The situation looked bad, but that was no
proof violence would be done Presbrey and his family.
Nophaie did not despair, but to the passion which had
augmented in him there was added a terrible zeal to
save white people imperilled, and the maddened Indians from vengeful and useless crime.

Swiftly the horse bore him down upon the burning
post. Soon Nophaie discerned things clearly. Presbrey's
little house was falling into blazing ruin. The corrals
and sheds were burning, and the trading post, a large
crude structure of wood, was on fire. It stood against a
bluff that reflected the red light. Nophaie saw against
this bright background a straggling circle of Indians,
perhaps numbering two hundred or more. Some were
running to and fro, round and round, in a frenzy
Nophaie had never before observed in Nopahs. A half
circle of Indians faced the burning post, and their intent
postures struck dread to Nophaie's heart. Above the
thundering hoofs of his horse he now caught the shrill,
wild yells of angered Indians. They had let loose. The
old war spirit of the Nopahs was in the ascendant.

Nophaie rode right upon that ragged black circle,
hauling his horse to a plunging halt, scattering the
Indians like frightened sheep.

He leaped off gun in hand. Dark gleam of faces
turned upon him. The shrill concerted yell broke
changed, became intermittent.

"Nophaie! Nophaie!" piercingly called an Indian.

Hesitating, Nophaie surveyed the scene. Directly
before him, a few rods from the post, stood an automobile, smoking heavily; it was burning. Then Nophaie
espied the trader Presbrey standing over to the left, in
the bright glare. His wife clung to him, and in his arms
he held his baby girl. Nophaie caught the glint of
shining curls. He leaped and ran across the intervening
space.

"Presbrey, tell me—"

"Hello, Nophaie. My God, I'm glad you came,"

interrupted the trader. His face was white and beaded
with sweat. Mrs. Presbrey was evidently unable to
stand without support. She cried out incoherently. The
little girl recognized Nophaie.

"Have you been hurt?" queried Nophaie shortly.

"No. They just drove us out. They didn't mean us
any harm."

"Why this fire? What're the Indians up to?" demanded Nophaie.

"Reckon it's the biggest uprisin' the reservation ever
seen," shouted Presbrey. "Ba ho zohnie is back of it.
He shore roused the Nopahs. An' I hear the Nokis are
worse. Five thousand Indians have passed here in two
days."

"Mesa!" flashed Nophaie.

"You're shore talkin' now," returned the trader, as
swiftly, "but listen to me. This bunch has trapped
Blucher, Morgan an' Glendon in the post, an' they're
goin' to burn them to death."

Nophaie's passionate excitement sustained a violent
shock. He gazed back at the dark post, with its vacant,
eyelike windows. The far side was burning freely.
Flames leaped above the roof; smoke rolled out from
under the eaves.

"*That missionary!* And Blucher, Glendon—in
there?" shouted Nophaie, hoarsely, bending to Presbrey's face.

"Shore as you're born. Here's how it happened.
They'd been over to Black Canyon for two days, an'
they came round the mesa, never stoppin' at Kaidab. It
was after dark. Wal, they got here late, out of gas. They
woke me, an' said they wanted gas an' grub. My wife
got out of bed to cook for them. Glendon was half
drunk, Morgan was surly, an' Blucher was sort of gay.
Reckon he'd seen a bottle too. Anyway, he was kiddin'
Morgan about steamrollin' some other poor devil of a
missionary. Wal, while they was eatin' I seen an Indian
peep in the winder. It was Shoie, that spellbinder
Nopah who had his tongue cut out in the war, you

know. I was scared, but I didn't let on. It wasn't my
mix. Pretty soon we heard Indians yellin' like hell. It
scared Morgan, but not Blucher or Glendon. All the
same they run out with Morgan. I hadn't put the gas in
their car. Then they locked themselves in the post. The
Indians surrounded the house an' set fire to it. They
shore was bad. But they let me out with the wife an'
kid. Next they burned Blucher's car. After that they
run around yellin' like mad. My house burned up, an'
from the way them Indians yelled you knew they
thought the three men had burned up, too. But the
damn fools shot from the post, cripplin' some Indians.
Reckon that was Glendon. Then Shoie set fire to the
post from the bluff. I saw him with a bale of blazin' hay.
He dropped it. Another Indian run in along that other
side to fire it. . . . An' now I reckon our steamrollin'
missionary, an' our pro-German agent an' their
shootin' hired hand will get what's been comin' to them
for years."

"But, oh, Bill, they shouldn't be burned alive," cried
Mrs. Presbrey, in horror.

Nophaie wheeled away toward the pressing circle of
Indians, now beginning to close in again. As he passed
a wagon he espied an axe leaning against a wheel.
Snatching it up he rushed with tremendous strides at
the center rank of the circle of Indians. He yelled with
all his lung power.

Shoie appeared as the keystone of that circle. His
face was hideous. He did not fear Nophaie. Instead, he
opened his deformed, tongueless mouth and gasped,
like a choked snake, in Nophaie's face. His defiance
was ghastly. Nophaie wasted no time on that poor
wretch, but struck him down. Then like a tiger he broke
the circle, beat the Indians back, dominated them with
his fierce passion and utter fearlessness.

Shoie lay in the center of that cleared space, his dark
visage upturned to the brightening blaze.

Nophaie bounded to the door of the post, and
dropping his gun he swung the axe. His powerful blows

shook the building. Crash! The door burst off its hinges and fell inward.

The Indians had become silent.

"Morgan! Blucher! Come out! It's Nophaie!" called Nophaie piercingly.

There was no reply. The low, crackling roar of the flames ominously broke the silence. Nophaie peered into the trading post. The light from behind him sent a flare through the gloom.

"It's Nophaie! Come out with me. I'll save you!" shouted Nophaie, with the ring of mastery in his voice. And he stepped into the big, barnlike room.

He heard rustling sounds, then shuffling feet. He smelled smoke. Tiny flames licked through apertures in the slanting roof. Two forms rose from behind a counter. The light fell upon the distorted faces of the missionary and the agent.

"It's a trick," shouted Blucher huskily. "Glendon, shoot him!"

Morgan's hair rose like the bristling mane of a terrified beast. His pale eyes shone with green fire.

"Kill that Indian atheist!" he yelled, foaming at the mouth.

Nophaie restrained his passion. "I'm here to save your lives," he called coldly. "If you hurry I can do it."

Glendon rose from behind the counter. A gun glinted darkly. Then followed a red flash and booming report. Nophaie felt the staggering impact of a bullet, then a hot agony tearing through his breast. The force knocked him backward, out of the door, down upon the porch floor. From this position he saw the three men dash out of the door. Two of them leaped over him. The third halted to kick him as he lay prostrate. Nophaie's darkening sight recorded pale face, pale eyes.

"Hurry . . . this way . . . along the cliff," whispered the foremost hoarsely.

Their forms vanished. Their thudding footsteps ceased. Nophaie endeavored to sit up. He still held to

the axe. Dropping that he placed his hand to his breast.
It came away wet with hot blood. Then Presbrey was
kneeling to support him.

"For God's sake! Nophaie—they shot you!" burst
out the trader brokenly.

Sensation ceased for Nophaie, except that strange
darkening of his sight.

Chapter 24

AT KAIDAB TRADING POST MARIAN WATCHED the desert horizon with troubled eyes.

Nophaie had been absent for over two weeks. And developments of the last few days and nights had violently disrupted the even tenor of the Withers's household. One night signal fires had suddenly blazed up on all the lofty points around Kaidab. Next day bands of Indians rode by, silent and grim, scarcely halting at the trading post. This latter fact was unprecedented. Then Withers's Indian riders left without a word. Even Mrs. Withers could not extract from any Indian what it was all about. But the trader said he did not need to be told.

"There'll be hell to pay at Mesa," he said, with fire in his eye. "Reckon I haven't seen the Indians like this since they killed my brother, eighteen years ago."

In the afternoon he drove away in his car.

That night more fires burned. Marian went with Mrs. Withers and others of the post to see the wonderful spectacle of signal fires on Echo Peaks. To Marian it seemed that the heavens were aflame. She, like Mrs. Withers, was silent, not joining in the loud acclaim and awe of their companions. The trader's wife had lived her life among the Indians, and her face was an augury of calamity.

Next day a thousand Nopahs and more trooped by the post. Then with the advent of darkness the magnificent panorama of fires was repeated. By midnight they burned out.

Marian lay sleepless in her dark little room. Some time late the hum of a motorcar thrilled her. Withers

331

was returning, and the fact of his return seemed propitious. But the automobile hummed on by the post, at a high rate of speed. That dismayed Marian. It had never happened before. Kaidab was a stopping place for every car, at any hour. Somehow this incident portended evil. Thereafter Marian slept fitfully and was harassed by fearful dreams.

Next morning she was on the verge of despair. Catastrophe had befallen Nophaie or he would have returned long ago. She connected his lengthy absence with this uprising of the Nopahs. Nevertheless she scanned the desert horizon to the north, praying that she might see Nophaie ride into sight.

Her attention, however, was attracted to the other direction. The droning of another motor car roused Marian to eagerness. She ran from the porch to the gate. Dust clouds were traveling swiftly along the road toward the post. Then they disappeared. Marian watched the point where the road turned over the ridge. Soon an open car shot into sight. She thought she recognized it. The driver appeared to neglect risk for the car or himself. Marian ran outside into the wide open space before the trading post.

In a moment more she was confronted by a dust-begrimed Withers.

"Howdy, Marian," he greeted her cheerfully. "Where's everybody? I shore drove some. But bad news travels fast on the desert, an' I wanted to beat it here."

"Bad . . . news?" faltered Marian.

"Wal, it would have been bad, if it'd got here before me," he said, taking her arm. "Come on in an' find my wife."

"Nophaie!" whispered Marian.

"Now see here, lass, you're white as a sheet. An' shakin' too, you poor kid. Wal, it has been pretty tough. . . . Nophaie's all right. He'll be here in a couple of hours. They're fetchin' him in Presbrey's car.

He was shot, but reckon it doesn't amount to much.
You can't kill that Indian."

"Shot!" gasped Marian, clutching Withers in terror.

"Marian, I'm a blunt man, I know," plaintively
replied Withers. "But haven't you sense enough to
see I'd lie or not talk at all if Nophaie was hurt serious? Come, there's the wife. An' she looks scared,
too."

While Withers half led and half carried her into the
living room Marian fought desperately to ward off the
sick faint blackness that threatened to overcome her.
Withers lowered her into a chair, and then stood erect
to wipe his dusty face.

"Wal, wife, you're most as pale round the gills as
Marian," he began, in cheerful banter. Then, having
cleaned his face he heaved a great breath of relief and
flopped into a chair. "Listen, Ba ho zohnie's uprisin'
flivvered worse than we'd have dared to hope for.
Strange! Reckon it's the strangest thing in all my desert
experience. . . . When I got to Mesa there was a mob
of five thousand Nopahs an' Nokis, hangin' around,
pow-wowin', waitin' for Blucher an' Morgan. Luckily
they'd gone away—to fire some poor devil off the
reservation, I heard. The Indians thought they'd run
away to Washington, to get the soldiers. They cooled
off. Then old Indians harangued them on the foolish-
ness of this uprisin' business. Ba ho zohnie was hustled
away to save him from arrest. So far so good!"

Withers paused to catch his breath, perhaps to
choose words less calculated to startle the staring
women.

"Late last night news come that Presbrey's post had
been burned," the trader went on. "I didn't believe it,
because Presbrey stands well with the Indians. But it
worried me, so I got up an' drove back to Presbrey's. I
reached there at sunup. Shore enough both his house
an' store had been burned to the ground. There were
no Indians around that I could see. But when I got out

of my car I found Presbrey an' his wife in a shed, workin' over Nophaie, who had been shot."

"Nophaie! What had he to do with Ba ho zohnie's uprising?" exclaimed Mrs. Withers, incredulously.

"Wal, Nophaie was the main reason Ba ho zohnie's uprisin' flivvered. Because it came damn near doin' for Morgan, Blucher an' Glendon—all by accident! Nophaie saved their lives. They'd have been burned alive."

"Good Heavens! And they shot him for it?"

"Precisely. But for an Indian like Nophaie the hurt is nothin'. Keep still now an' let me get this off my chest. . . . Presbrey told me Indians in droves rode past his post for three days. Yesterday they petered out. An' late last night Blucher an' Morgan came in with Glendon drivin' the car. They passed here before that, after dark, of course."

"I heard the car. I thought it was you returning. It was late," spoke up Marian.

"Wal, they wanted gas an' grub. While they were eatin' Presbrey saw our dumb friend Shoie peepin' in at the window. No wonder Presbrey had a jar! But the others didn't see. Not long after that a mob of howlin' Indians rode down. Morgan turned livid, Presbrey said. Glendon was half drunk an' Blucher had been drinkin'. They ran and locked themselves in the store. First the Indians set fire to Presbrey's house. But Presbrey got out safe with his family. The Indians burned Blucher's car. When the house fell in they howled like devils, satisfied they'd roasted the three men. Someone, Glendon probably, began to shoot from the store, an' that gave the snap away. Wal, Shoie promptly set fire to the store. Not long after that Nophaie rode down on them. He got the facts from Presbrey. Then with an axe an' a gun he made for that bunch of Indians. Presbrey said Nophaie was simply terrible. He knocked Shoie out an' drove the Indians back. Then he busted open the door of the post an' called for the men to come out, an' he'd save them. They didn't come, so Nophaie went in.

Then one of them shot him. Nophaie fell out on the porch. Glendon an' Blucher ran out, followed by Morgan. Presbrey swore he saw Morgan kick Nophaie as he lay there. . . . Wal, the three men got away, an' Presbrey went to Nophaie's assistance."

Neither Mrs. Withers nor Marian could speak on the moment. Withers gazed from his wife to the girl, and then hastened to conclude.

"Don't look like that. I found Nophaie shot through the shoulder, high up. Missed the lung! He's weak from loss of blood. But that's all. He'll be here presently an' you can see for yourself. Cheer up, now, it could have been a lot worse."

Mute and stifled, racked by a convulsion rising in her breast, Marian fled to her room, and locked the door, and pulled down the shades. She wanted it dark. She longed to hide herself from even her own sight.

Then in the gloom of the little adobe-walled room she succumbed to the tigress fury of a woman, once in her life reverting to primitive instincts. "Oh, damn those rotten men! I could kill them—with my bare hands!" she said, panting, and that outburst culminated in a terrible rage. No man could have felt or borne the storm of passion that swayed Marian. She had not known such black depths existed in her. But the motive was love. She was worse than a mother bereft of her child. Her mood was to destroy. But for collapse swiftly following she might have done herself physical violence.

When her mind cleared she found herself lying on the bed spent and disheveled. Slowly she realized what havoc had been wrought in her by passion. She was amazed at this hitherto unknown self, but she made no apologies or suffered no regrets. In a revulsion of feeling that ensured she crept off the bed to her knees, and thanked God for Nophaie's life and for his deliverance from doubt. For she divined that Nophaie's great deed had been dominated by the spirit of Christ.

Nophaie had always been a man, and one prompted to swift, heroic, generous acts, but this saving of the Mesa triumvirate from the vengeance of Gekin Yashi's race, from a horrible death by fire, could mean only that Nophaie's pilgrimage to Naza had saved his soul.

And the white girl prayed humbly and earnestly to be made to understand the nobility of this red man, to be worthy to follow him and serve him, and be granted to the uttermost a woman's love and fidelity.

A knock on the door interrupted her devotions.

"Marian, come," called Mrs. Withers. "Nophaie is here."

Leaping to her feet Marian stood a moment, trembling and absorbed.

It took a few moments to smooth out hair and attire, and erase somewhat the havoc of emotion from her face. Then she opened the door and stepped into the long hall. By the time she had traversed it and passed through the living room to the door she was outwardly composed.

Through the green cottonwoods Marian espied a car in front of the gate, with an excited crowd around it. Mrs. Withers stood holding the gate open. Marian halted outside the door. She saw moccasined feet and long limbs encased in yellow corduroy slowly slipping down out of the car. Then she saw a silver-ornamented belt, and a garnet velveteen shirt. She recognized them. They were moving. And her heart seemed to swell to bursting. Next Nophaie's dark face and bare black head emerged from the car. Withers and another man helped him out. He stood erect, supported on each side. He was walking, through the gate, up the path.

Marian's devouring gaze caught a glimpse of a white blood-stained bandage inside the neck of Nophaie's open shirt. She shuddered, and scarcely could withdraw her eyes. His step was free, his tall lithe form, so instinct with grace and strength, seemed the same as always. Then she saw his face distinctly. There shone upon it a kind of dark radiance. He smiled at her. And suddenly all the icy terror and numb agony within Marian vanished in a joyous certainty. She ran to meet him to halt the little procession, to embrace him before all. Then she fell back to look up into his face.

"Nophaie!" she said tremulously.

"Benow di cleash, all is well," he replied.

"Oh, you say that," rejoined Marian, as she slipped into Withers's place beside him, "but you'll have to show me. . . . There—let me help you in."

"Aw," burst Withers heartily, "he's not hurt much. I'll bet he could walk alone."

They got him into the living room and let him gently down on the couch. Marian lingered over the task of propping his head upon pillows, tinglingly aware of his piercing eyes upon her face.

"Wife," Withers was saying, "reckon we'll leave him right there for today. Presbrey, has that hole in his shoulder been properly dressed?"

"We did our best, but we had no medicines," returned the trader. "I'd advise a thorough job right now."

Withers sent his wife and the servants running for the necessary things, then he looked down at Nophaie.

"How do you feel?"

"Fine, just at this particular minute," replied Nophaie, and he smiled up at Marian, who was sitting on the couch beside him, holding his hand.

"Ahuh! Wal, you ought to," said Withers gruffly. "Did you spit any blood?"

"No. The bullet missed my lung."

"Honest Injun?" queried the trader, relaxing.

"Honest Nophaie," was the enigmatic reply.

"Wal, I'm darned glad. That worried me a little. . . . Presbrey, don't forget your wife an' kid out in the car. They'll be hungry. You, too. Clear out of here now, everybody."

"*I* shall not clear out," said Marian, calmly, as the trader returned from pushing the curious onlookers outside.

"Wal, I didn't mean you," replied Withers. "Reckon you're good medicine. You stay there till I come back."

Then Marian leaned over Nophaie and kissed him in a way that betokened all that had come to her during the long waiting days and these last fateful hours.

"Nophaie, you have come back to me," she asserted softly.

"If you will have it so," he replied, a dark mystic adoration in his gaze.

Marian assisted the skillful Withers in the dressing of Nophaie's wound. She managed somehow, though her fingers shook. That ugly red hole in the splendid bronze breast, going clear through to the broad back, struck terror to her heart. Yet she could not but see that it was nothing to Nophaie.

The cheery trader talked while he worked. "Marian, I've reckoned at times when I was in trouble or hurt that it'd be good to be an Indian."

"Why not *all* the time, then?" murmured Marian.

"Wal, by golly, there's somethin' to that," he agreed, with a laugh.

"Benow di cleash," said Nophaie, with his dark eyes absorbing her, "I've had many hurts, and some I got in the war were bad. But none were ever like that hurt I received at Cape May—when I met you."

"At Cape May!" exclaimed Marian, mystified. Then she divined his meaning and the scarlet blood burned from neck to face. She laid a hand on his cheek. "Oh! but *that*, too, will be cured now."

"Say, you folks talk in riddles," interposed Withers. "Reckon, though, I savvy. . . . Nophaie, this is a good job. The bullet hole was clean, just under your collar-bone. No sign of inflammation. It'll heal in a jiffy. Lie still an' try to sleep."

"Did you find your horse?" asked Nophaie.

"Presbrey put him in pasture."

"I hope I didn't kill Shoie."

"Wal, we reckon not, but if you did it'd be just as well. Shoie is a bad hombre."

"Give me cold water to drink."

Marian brought him water and held up his head while he allayed a feverish thirst. And she pressed his head to her breast. Then she darkened the room and left him.

Several times when she softly peeped in upon Nophaie that day she found him asleep. And next day he slept most of the time. Withers assured Marian that Nophaie's wound had closed without infection and that his condition was most favorable. Then on the morning of the third day Marian's fear, like a croaking raven, spread its black wings and disappeared. Nophaie got up despite the remonstrations of Withers and her own appeals; and he went out to walk around the yard of the post. Upon his return he said he was hungry. That remark appeared to give the final satisfaction to Withers.

"Wal, Marian, reckon you've a swell chance to be a grass widow, I don't think," he remarked facetiously. "When a Nopah's goin' to die he won't eat."

In the afternoon when Marian went into the living room Nophaie was there alone, and he arose to put his free arm around her.

"You have not asked what happened to me on my pilgrimage," he said.

"I've been waiting for you to tell me."

"Something very simple and beautiful."

"Yes?" she whispered, as she leaned to him.

"I spent a whole day at Naza," he replied solemnly. "It was an ordeal. I will never understand what I went through. But in the end it came to me naturally that there is only one God . . . for my race, for yours, for all peoples."

"Oh, Nophaie! You have become a—Christian?" she queried, breathlessly, encircling his neck with her arms.

"Yes, for it is through Christianity that one gets the

clearest conception of God. But He belongs not to race or creed, but to all humanity."

"I prayed for it. Oh, I believed," cried Marian, overcome by the strangeness and beauty of this revelation.

"It changed me into another being. It opened my eyes where they had been blind. My hate died. I see clearly now. I will help my people in the best ways that I can devise. I think my agony is over. . . . And as for you—"

"Well, for me?" she asked, as he hesitated.

"Can I persuade you to go back east?"

"Why?"

"That's hard to explain. I seem forced to say this. As if it wasn't natural! But—my desert is hard. You were born to comfort, to culture, to the things civilization has developed. To friends, relatives, home."

"Pooh!" murmured Marian, her face tilted up to his. "My home is here—on your breast."

She felt the shock that vibrated through him. That was the answer of his heart. It filled her with bliss.

"You will not give me up?" he went on unsteadily.

"No!"

"But marriage . . . for you . . . with me—"

She interrupted his pondering speech. "Marriage! That is for you to say. I can't *make* you marry me. But I can tell you, that if I were your wife I'd be the happiest and most blessed woman in this world."

"Marian! You talk—wildly," he said huskily. He was holding her tight now, bending over her so that she could no longer see his face. "Don't you know the world? If we ever had a child—a little Nophaie—people would call him a half-breed."

"Who? What people?" demanded Marian passionately. "You mean the white people who have damned the Indian? The civilization that sends men like Blucher and Morgan to *improve* Indians? So they would call our child a half-breed. Let them! And I would fling in their faces that I thanked God he *was* half Indian, that his red blood might be proof against the white blood he must inherit from me. For I am white. I belong to this greedy, pagan, merciless world, and though I am a Christian, though I hate with all my soul its sordid materialism, I may have in me much of its evil."

She silenced him. She felt the pound of his heart against her cheek. For Marian the moment was one of profound emotion—too deep to understand, yet something forever to recall as an infinite happiness.

Tramp of many hooves outside, and then the murmur of voices, and footsteps on the walk broke the thrall of the moment. Marian slipped out of Nophaie's arms. Not then was his face an inscrutable bronze mask!

The door opened to admit Withers.

"Mob of Indians out there," he announced. "On the way home, an' pretty quiet I'm darned glad to say. Ba ho zohnie has fled into the canyons. Shoie is with them, crazier than ever. He has a lump on his head as big as your fist. An' he's ravin' about throwin' his spell on you, Nophaie. You'll die in torture. Your body will go into a cedar tree an' be eaten by worms of fire."

"Poor Shoie," said Nophaie. "I'm glad I didn't kill him."

"Wal, you stay indoors till he's gone with the rest of them," replied Withers dryly. "Reckon they'll not hang here long. Fact is they're worried over the burnin' of Presbrey's post. But I must say Presbrey shows no hard feelin's. He told them he'd rebuild. Wal, wal, it shore could have been worse."

Some hours later Marian stood in the doorway with Nophaie watching the Indians ride away into the sunset.

It was a magnificent, far-flung sunset, the whole west flaming with intense golden-red that spread and paled far into the north.

Against this glorious background the Indians were riding away, in dense groups, in long, straggling lines, in small parties, down to couples. It was an austere and sad pageant. The broken Indians and the weary mustangs passed slowly out upon the desert. Shoie, the tongueless, was the last to depart. It appeared that he turned with gleaming visage and gesture of denunciation. Far to the fore the dark forms, silhouetted against the pure gold of the horizon, began to vanish, as if indeed they had ridden into that beautiful, prophetic sky.

"It is . . . symbolic, Marian," said Nophaie brokenly. "They are vanishing—vanishing. My Nopahs! Only a question of swiftly flying time! And I too—Nophaie, the warrior! In the end I shall be absorbed by you—by your love—by your children. . . . It is well!"

At last only one Indian was left on the darkening horizon—the solitary Shoie—bent in his saddle, a melancholy figure, unreal and strange against that dying sunset—moving on, diminishing, fading, vanishing—vanishing.